To Bill Fawcett:

A Friend in Need

A
SEPARATE
STAR

A Science Fiction Tribute
to
Rudyard Kipling

CREATED BY
DAVID DRAKE &
SANDRA MIESEL

A SEPARATE STAR: A TRIBUTE TO RUDYARD KIPLING

This is a work of fiction. All the characters and events
portrayed in this book are fictional, and any resemblance
to real people or incidents is purely coincidental.

Copyright © 1989 by David Drake and Sandra Miesel

A Baen Books Original

Baen Publishing Enterprises
260 Fifth Avenue
New York, N.Y. 10001

First printing, May 1989

ISBN: 0-671-69832-X

Cover art by Steve Hickman

Printed in the United States of America

Distributed by
SIMON & SCHUSTER
1230 Avenue of the Americas
New York, N.Y. 10020

ACKNOWLEDGMENTS

" 'Beyond the loom of the last lone star . . .' "
by Poul Anderson. Copyright Poul Anderson, 1988.

"Introduction"
by Poul Anderson. Copyright Poul Anderson, 1988.

"No Truce With Kings"
by Poul Anderson. Copyright Mercury Press, Inc., 1963.
Reprinted by permission of the author.

"Introduction"
by Gene Wolfe. Copyright Gene Wolfe, 1987.

"Continuing Westward"
by Gene Wolfe. Copyright Gene Wolfe, 1973.
Reprinted by permission of the author and the author's agent,
Virginia Kidd.

"Soldiers' Stories"
by David Drake. Copyright David Drake, 1988.

"Under the Hammer"
by David Drake. Copyright UPD Publishing Corp., 1974.
Reprinted by permission of the author.

"Introduction"
by Joe Haldeman. Copyright Joe Haldeman, 1988.

"Saul's Death"
by Joe Haldeman. Copyright Joe Haldeman, 1982.
Reprinted by permission of the author.

"The Art of Things as They Are"
by Gordon R. Dickson and Sandra Miesel. Copyright Gordon
R. Dickson and Sandra Miesel, 1988.

"Carry Me Home"
by Gordon R. Dickson. Copyright Quinn Publishing Co, Inc.,
1954 and Gordon R. Dickson, 1982.
Reprinted by permission of the author.

CONTENTS

" 'Beyond the loom of the last lone star . . .' "

Poul Anderson

"The little bespectacled journalist to whose pipe, whether we will or no, we must all dance." So did another literary idol of mine, a Dane named Johannes V. Jensen, describe Rudyard Kipling. It sums up the truth as well as anything that anybody has said on the subject.

For half a century after his death, through every upheaval in the world and every eddy of fashion, Kipling has endured. If at times he seemed in eclipse, it was merely among intellectuals who never liked him and wished he would go away. Real people went right on reading him, and passed their love on to their children. They still do. You can buy his collected works in a uniform edition—expensive, but you can't make a better investment—except for most of the poems, and they are available in a book of their own. Kipling bids fair to go on as long as our civilization does. He may well outlive it, as Homer did his.

Devotion is especially strong among enthusiasts of science fiction and fantasy. This is only in part because he was a master of those fields, too. He is for everyone who responds to vividness, word magic, sheer storytelling. Most readers go on to discover the subtleties and profundities. Also, much of the verse is ideal for reciting or singing; it is poetry of the old and truly kind. To "kipple" and to "filk" are frequent joys at the gatherings of such as we. Not just oldsters partake; the young are right there in the party.

Thus his influence pervades modern science fiction and fantasy writing. The book on hand is a celebration of that.

1

Were space not limited, it could have included stories by many more authors. Each who is represented tells what Kipling has meant to her or him. (An exception is the late Richard McKenna, for whom Gordon Dickson speaks. Death does not break a fellowship like ours.) In addition, I have been asked to give a general introduction.

That is a perilous honor. My colleagues explain so well what this undertaking is about. I must try to cover the territory as a whole, without intruding too much on them. Commentators rather better known have gone over the ground before me. Of those I have read, to me T. S. Eliot makes the most sense. I'll do my best to avoid repeating him or others and offer you, instead, a personal view. Quite likely you'll find points of disagreement. That is as it should be. The subject is too big and various for any single mind to grasp in its entirety—even, I suspect, Kipling's own mind, for genius has deeper wellsprings than does awareness.

We needn't go into his life, apart from a few reminders to place it within his times. He was born in Bombay, India, at the end of 1865; went to school in England; returned to India in 1882 as a newspaperman; came easterly around the world, back to England, in 1889; traveled widely; married an American woman in 1892 and spent several years in the States; settled again in England in 1896; received the Nobel Prize for literature in 1907; died in 1936. The joys and sorrows that he knew are in the biographies. Suffice it here that through both experience and insight, he understood reality, and through his gifts he still opens it to our gaze.

Nevertheless I cannot resist sharing with you an impression of the man himself, as seen through adoring youthful eyes. When he was in Stockholm to claim his Nobel, Johannes V. Jensen interviewed him and soon afterward wrote about the encounter. An excerpt—

"You don't really know where in his face it comes from, but his features laugh, in a strangely loving and grim way, a whisker-smile that only mirrors the sunshine in the world; and as he comes there so noiselessly on his claws, so altogether undangerous, while at the same time you cannot help noticing how his head is shaped around violent instincts—Kipling's head is not large but singularly full, as if the Lord God had distended it to the utmost while blowing the breath of life into him—when all these features gather before the imagination, it suddenly strikes through that of course this is Bagheera! The black panther, the affectionate beast of prey in *The Jungle Book* is, more than any other incarnation, Kipling himself. The coal-black brows, the small dark and hairy hands, the massive jaw with cleft chin, everything, yes, indeed, *Bagheera*."

Numerous remarks have been less complimentary. To this day Kipling is frequently regarded as an imperialist, an apologist for Victoria's British Empire who had some skill at composing jingly ballads. Even so generally perceptive a critic as George Orwell could not quite rid himself of that notion. How false it is.

True, Kipling stood for patriotism, which has since become unfashionable. This meant finding good in the Empire; and it did have its night side, as Orwell witnessed and documented unforgettably. (Now that it is gone, is the world any safer or happier?) However, ideology put such blinkers on him that his essay never mentions the far larger body of work irrelevant to politics. My mother had a freer spirit than that. An old-time liberal, she too had detested Western domination of the earth; but when she lay dying, on the last day she was conscious I read "The Brushwood Boy" aloud to her, and its tale of young love delighted her as much as ever in her girlhood. That sort of thing is what Kipling really means.

Besides, charges of chauvinism and racism are witless. He saw the dangers and cruelties of the world all too clearly. He felt that nothing stands between them and us but the rule of law—can the twentieth century call him wrong?—and that in his era its chief upholders happened to be Britain and, to a degree, the United States. This was not because their people were mostly white. (Orwell admits that "the lesser breeds without the Law" does not refer to dusky savages but to the Germans, who knew it and were taking themselves outside it.) Kipling could show despicable Westerners and admirable Easterners; he often satirized the English unmercifully. After reading, say, "Without Benefit of Clergy" and "The Story of Muhammad Din," only willful perversity can maintain that he lacked sympathy for "natives" or denied their humanity.

Nor did he imagine dominion could last forever. To give a single example, "The Bridge-Builders" raises the ancient, awesome power of the land, over which men flit like dreams. He hoped the Empire and its sisters would survive long enough to lay a firm foundation for those who came after. Their failure embittered his last years and menaces ours.

His sense for the uncertainties, ironies, and ambiguities of human affairs is evident in dozens of works. Among them is "As Easy As ABC," included in this volume because it is a wonderful science fiction yarn, showing the same eye for detail that would later distinguish the work of Robert Heinlein. Norbert Wiener opined that it depicts "rather a fascist" future, but that's more nonsense. What Kipling foresaw was technology driving the evolution of the managerial society; what he also pointed out was that democracy, too, has its inherent flaws and risks.

Granted, he was not infallible. Intensely interested in how things work, he sought to get them right. As a rule he succeeded. Sometimes, being mortal, he slipped. Thus we come upon dwarfish Picts, Roman galley slaves, and even, astonishingly, a ship's engineer who talks of speed in knots per hour. But the nits to pick are small and few. They never keep you from being *there*.

I need say no more about the novels and short stories. They speak for themselves. Join me over drinks one evening and we'll kipple, revel in the naming of our special favorites and declaim passages from them. The poetry, though, is so often misunderstood that two or three observations may be in order.

If I bring up Orwell again, it is not to belabor a man whose memory I respect, but because he is worthy of rebuttal rather than shrugging off. He called Kipling a "good bad poet" and went on: "But what is the peculiarity of a good bad poem? It records in memorable form—for verse is a mnemonic device, among other things—some emotion which very nearly every human being can share." The implication seems to be that this is, if not contemptible, much less meaningful than something more esoteric.

A. E. Housman did not take that mandarin attitude. He defined poetry, as opposed to mere verse, operationally, saying that he would recite lines to himself in the morning while shaving, and if they made the hair stand up they were poetry.

This quality is rare and precious. Doubtless it can occur in a highly cerebral context. (I find it here and there in Eliot, Pound, and a few more of that school. Are they oblique enough?) However, to deny that it can in works more accessible to people, which after all are in the large majority, is equivalent to stating that Mozart did not write music but John Cage did.

Since *Rudyard Kipling's Verse, Definitive Edition* runs to 834 pages plus supplemental material, inevitably there is a lot of what is simply that, verse. It gives great pleasure by striking imagery and pulsing rhythm, exciting story, humor gusty or sly, evocation of scenes and feelings. Some is didactic and, by strength of language, teaches more effectively than ever Pope did. For example, "The Gods of the Copybook Headings" explains most of the world's history in nine stanzas. All is full of life.

But some—really, an unfairly big percentage—goes beyond this. It touches the innermost soul and the outermost stars; it makes the hair stand up. People differ, so which of the pieces are true poetry may vary from person to person, though I expect we'd find a considerable measure of agreement. For me "The Song of the Red War-Boat" is one, partly because of the elements crashing through it but mainly because of what it says about being a man. In contrast, I have learned not to read aloud "The Gift of the Sea" or "The Return of the Children;" men aren't supposed to shed tears in public. To name the rest would be to tell you at length about myself, and it is Rudyard Kipling who interests us. I do suggest that he can help you understand yourself better than you did before you read him.

This essay has mentioned just a few of the readily, or almost readily, comprehensible works. In his later years Kipling as a writer, like Beethoven as a composer, went into realms entirely his own, where no fellow maker has quite been able to follow. Readers and listeners can, though they will never know how far they got and will ever afterward be haunted. Yet what strange treasures they bring back.

Here we seek to honor him to whom we owe so much.

We can but hope he would be pleased. He repeatedly declined a knighthood, and gave his reasons, I think, in "The Last Rhyme of True Thomas." It ends:

> *"I ha' harpit ye up to the Throne o' God,*
> * "I ha' harpit your midmost soul in three.*
> *"I ha' harpit ye down to the Hinges o' Hell,*
> *   "And—ye—would—make—a Knight o' me!"*

Introduction

Poul Anderson

Rudyard Kipling came rather gradually into my life, but perhaps all the more fully for that. As a child I was enchanted by *Just So Stories* and *The Jungle Book*. Presently other tales, poems, and travel reports took hold of me and have never let go. At first it was the storytelling and color that dazzled. Later I appreciated and helplessly envied the sheer writing, the magic of words that are the only right ones—which nobody else could have discovered. Later yet, as the years brought a little knowledge of the real world, I began to find the layer upon layer of meaning behind those words. I'm still doing that, and won't live long enough to finish.

Of course this has influenced my own works. His are a part of me, like the works of a few fellow creators in various fields. These are not necessarily parts that I understand well, let alone use as they deserve. Doubtless I have often been unaware that they were expressing themselves, however awkwardly. Sometimes, though, I have known what was going on.

In the case of Kipling, this could be slight—for instance, a quotation—or it could be the idea from which a plot grew or an insight of his which I tried to convey in my own fashion. I would scarcely have written *The Broken Sword* had I never read "Cold Iron." Whatever significance is in *The Enemy Stars* is more powerfully in the lines cited at its end. "The Master Key" is a deliberate pastiche. "Full Pack (Hokas Wild)," with Gordon R. Dickson, is an affectionate burlesque. *The Game of Empire* is an *hommage*, to use a current buzz word; with the first and last sentences, especially, I hoped to call forth a few smiles. As for *The King of Ys*, it was my collaborator Karen Anderson who insisted we start on the Wall with Parnesius of *Puck of Pook's Hill*, but she met no resistance from me.

Offhand, Kipling's presence seems less marked in "No Truce With Kings." He had helped instill in me a love of freedom and a sympathy for the professional soldier. The title is from a poem of his. Is that all?

Well, let's take a look at the poem. It's called "The Old Issue" and was published in 1899 with the subtitle "Outbreak of the Boer War." Ostensibly it's pure propaganda, relating how the Kruger government had oppressed English settlers in South Africa until their liberation became necessary. Surely the author believed he was serving his people by explaining the justice of their cause.

Yet he was both too intelligent and too wise to be a mere jingo. He also wrote several tributes to the courage of the Boers and the humanness they shared with the English, as well as to their General Joubert upon that man's death during the war. In "The Old Issue" he quickly went beyond the particular to the universal. Only listen:

> *All we have of freedom, all we use or know—*
> *This our fathers bought for us long and long ago.*
> *Ancient Right unnoticed as the breath we draw—*
> *Leave to live by no man's leave, underneath the Law—*
> *Lance and torch and tumult, steel and grey-goose wing,*
> *Wrenched it, inch and ell and all, slowly from the King.*

This is not a constitutional monarch. This is the absolute master.

> *Cruel in the shadow, crafty in the sun,*
> *Far beyond his borders shall his teachings run.*
> *Sloven, sullen, savage, secret, uncontrolled,*
> *Laying on a new land evil of the old—*
> *Long-forgotten bondage, dwarfing heart and brain—*
> *All our fathers died to loose he shall bind again.*

But read the whole piece for yourself, if you haven't already. Then look at the world around you. Here, once more, the Kipling part of me made me try to say what he long before had said much better.

No Truce With Kings

POUL ANDERSON

"Song, Charlie! Give's a song!"

"Yay, Charlie!"

The whole mess was drunk, and the junior officers at the far end of the table were only somewhat noisier than their seniors near the colonel. Rugs and hangings could not much muffle the racket, shouts, stamping boots, thump of fists on oak and clash of cups raised aloft, that rang from wall to stony wall. High up among shadows that hid the rafters they hung from, the regimental banners stirred in a draft, as if to join the chaos. Below, the light of bracketed lanterns and bellowing fireplace winked on trophies and weapons.

Autumn comes early on Echo Summit, and it was storming outside, wind-hoot past the watchtowers and rain-rush in the courtyards, an undertone that walked through the buildings and down all corridors, as if the story were true that the unit's dead came out of the cemetery each September Nineteenth night and tried to join the celebration but had forgotten how. No one let it bother him, here or in the enlisted barracks, except maybe the hex major. The Third Division, the Catamounts, was known as the most riotous gang in the Army of the Pacific States of America, and of its regiments the Rolling Stones who held Fort Nakamura were the wildest.

"Go on, boy! Lead off. You've got the closest thing to a voice in the whole goddamn Sierra," Colonel Mackenzie called. He loosened the collar of his black dress tunic and

10

lounged back, legs asprawl, pipe in one hand and beaker of whisky in the other: a thickset man with blue wrinkle-meshed eyes in a battered face, his cropped hair turned gray but his mustache still arrogantly red.

"Charlie is my darlin', my darlin', my darlin'," sang Captain Hulse. He stopped as the noise abated a little. Young Lieutenant Amadeo got up, grinned, and launched into one they well knew.

"I am a Catamountain, I guard a border pass.
And every time I venture out, the cold will freeze m—"

"Colonel, sir. Begging your pardon."

Mackenzie twisted around and looked into the face of Sergeant Irwin. The man's expression shocked him. "Yes?"

"I am a bloody hero, a decorated vet:
The Order of the Purple Shaft, with pineapple clusters
yet!"

"Message just come in, sir. Major Speyer asks to see you right away."

Speyer, who didn't like being drunk, had volunteered for duty tonight; otherwise men drew lots for it on a holiday. Remembering that last word from San Francisco, Mackenzie grew chill.

The mess bawled forth the chorus, not noticing when the colonel knocked out his pipe and rose.

"The guns go boom! Hey, tiddley boom!
The rockets vroom, the arrows zoom.
From slug to slug is damn small room.
Get me out of here and back to the good old womb!
(Hey, doodle dee day!)"

All right-thinking Catamounts maintained that they could operate better with the booze sloshing up to their eardrums than any other outfit cold sober. Mackenzie ignored the tingle in his veins; forgot it. He walked a straight line to the door, automatically taking his sidearm off the rack as he passed by. The song pursued him into the hall.

"For maggots in the rations, we hardly ever lack.
You bite into a sandwich and the sandwich bites right
*   back.*
The coffee is the finest grade of Sacramento mud.
The ketchup's good in combat, though, for simulating
*   blood.*

(Cho-orus)!
*   The drums go bump! Ah-tumpty-tump!*
*   The bugles make like Gabri'l's trump—"*

Lanterns were far apart in the passage. Portraits of former commanders watched the colonel and the sergeant from eyes that were hidden in grotesque darknesses. Footfalls clattered too loudly here.

*   "I've got an arrow in my rump.*
Right about and rearward, heroes, on the jump!
*   (Hey, doodle dee day!)"*

Mackenzie went between a pair of fieldpieces flanking a stairway—they had been captured at Rock Springs during the Wyoming War, a generation ago—and upward. There was more distance between places in this keep than his legs liked at their present age. But it was old, had been added to decade by decade; and it needed to be massive, chiseled and mortared from Sierra granite, for it guarded a key to the nation. More than one army had broken against its revetments, before the Nevada marches were pacified, and more young men than Mackenzie wished to think about had gone from this base to die among angry strangers.

But she's never been attacked from the west. God, or whatever you are, you can spare her that, can't you?

The command office was lonesome at this hour. The room where Sergeant Irwin had his desk lay so silent: no clerks pushing pens, no messengers going in or out, no wives making a splash of color with their dresses as they waited to see the colonel about some problem down in the Village. When he opened the door to the inner room, though, Mackenzie heard the wind shriek around the angle of the wall. Rain slashed at the black windowpane and ran down in streams which the lanterns turned molten.

"Here the colonel is, sir," Irwin said in an uneven voice. He gulped and closed the door behind Mackenzie.

Speyer stood by the commander's desk. It was a beat-up old object with little upon it: an inkwell, a letter basket, an interphone, a photograph of Nora, faded in these dozen years since her death. The major was a tall and gaunt man, hook-nosed, going bald on top. His uniform always looked unpressed, somehow. But he had the sharpest brain in the Cats, Mackenzie thought; and Christ, how could any man read as many books as Phil did! Officially he was the adjutant, in practice the chief adviser.

"Well?" Mackenzie said. The alcohol did not seem to numb him, rather make him too acutely aware of things: how the lanterns smelled hot (when would they get a big enough generator to run electric lights?), and the floor was hard under his feet, and a crack went through the plaster of the north wall, and the stove wasn't driving out much of the chill. He forced bravado, stuck thumbs in belt and rocked back on his heels. "Well, Phil, what's wrong now?"

"Wire from Frisco," Speyer said. He had been folding and unfolding a piece of paper, which he handed over.

"Huh? Why not a radio call?"

"Telegram's less likely to be intercepted. This one's in code, at that. Irwin decoded it for me."

"What the hell kind of nonsense is this?"

"Have a look, Jimbo, and you'll find out. It's for you, anyway. Direct from GHQ."

Mackenzie focused on Irwin's scrawl. The usual formalities of an order; then:

You are hereby notified that the Pacific States Senate has passed a bill of impeachment against Owen Brodsky, formerly Judge of the Pacific States of America, and deprived him of office. As of 2000 hours this date, former Vice Humphrey Fallon is Judge of the PSA in accordance with the Law of Succession. The existence of dissident elements constituting a public danger has made it necessary for Judge Fallon to put the entire nation under martial law, effective at 2100 hours this date. You are therefore issued the following instructions:

1. The above intelligence is to be held strictly confidential until an official proclamation is made. No person

who has received knowledge in the course of transmitting this message shall divulge same to any other person whatsoever. Violators of this section and anyone thereby receiving information shall be placed immediately in solitary confinement to await court-martial.

2. You will sequestrate all arms and ammunition except for ten percent of available stock, and keep same under heavy guard.

3. You will keep all men in the Fort Nakamura area until you are relieved. Your relief is Colonel Simon Hollis, who will start from San Francisco tomorrow morning with one battalion. They are expected to arrive at Fort Nakamura in five days, at which time you will surrender your command to him. Colonel Hollis will designate those officers and enlisted men who are to be replaced by members of his battalion, which will be integrated into the regiment. You will lead the men replaced back to San Francisco and report to Brigadier General Mendoza at New Fort Baker. To avoid provocations, these men will be disarmed except for officers' sidearms.

4. For your private information, Captain Thomas Danielis has been appointed senior aide to Colonel Hollis.

5. You are again reminded that the Pacific States of America are under martial law because of a national emergency. Complete loyalty to the legal government is required. Any mutinous talk must be severely punished. Anyone giving aid or comfort to the Brodsky faction is guilty of treason and will be dealt with accordingly.

Gerald O'Donnell, Gen. APSA, CINC

Thunder went off in the mountains like artillery. It was a while before Mackenzie stirred, and then merely to lay the paper on his desk. He could only summon feeling slowly, up into a hollowness that filled his skin.

"They dared," Speyer said without tone. "They really did."

"Huh?" Mackenzie swiveled eyes around to the major's face. Speyer didn't meet that stare. He was concentrating his own gaze on his hands, which were now rolling a cigarette. But the words jerked from him, harsh and quick:

"I can guess what happened. The warhawks have been hollering for impeachment ever since Brodsky compromised the border dispute with West Canada. And Fallon, yeah, he's got ambitions of his own. But his partisans are a minority and he knows it. Electing him Vice helped soothe the warhawks some, but he'd never make Judge the regular way, because Brodsky isn't going to die of old age before Fallon does, and anyhow more than fifty percent of the Senate are sober, satisfied bossmen who don't agree that the PSA has a divine mandate to reunify the continent. I don't see how an impeachment could get through an honestly convened Senate. More likely they'd vote out Fallon."

"But a Senate had been called," Mackenzie said. The words sounded to him like someone else talking. "The newscasts told us."

"Sure. Called for yesterday 'to debate ratification of the treaty with West Canada.' But the bossmen are scattered up and down the country, each at his own Station. They have to *get* to San Francisco. A couple of arranged delays— hell, if a bridge just happened to be blown on the Boise railroad, a round dozen of Brodsky's staunchest supporters wouldn't arrive on time—so the Senate has a quorum, all right, but every one of Fallon's supporters are there, and so many of the rest are missing that the warhawks have a clear majority. Then they meet on a holiday, when no cityman is paying attention. Presto, impeachment and a new Judge!" Speyer finished his cigarette and stuck it between his lips while he fumbled for a match. A muscle twitched in his jaw.

"You sure?" Mackenzie mumbled. He thought dimly that this moment was like one time he'd visited Puget City and been invited for a sail on the Guardian's yacht, and a fog had closed in. Everything was cold and blind, with nothing you could catch in your hands.

"Of course I'm not sure!" Speyer snarled. "Nobody will be sure till it's too late." The matchbox shook in his grasp.

"They, uh, they got a new Cinc, too, I noticed."

"Uh-huh. They'd want to replace everybody they can't trust, as fast as possible, and De Barros was a Brodsky appointee." The match flared with a hellish *scrit*. Speyer inhaled till his cheeks collapsed. "You and me included, naturally. The regiment reduced to minimum armament so that nobody will get ideas about resistance when the new colonel arrives. You'll note he's coming with a battalion at his heels just the same, just in case. Otherwise he could take a plane and be here tomorrow."

"Why not a train?" Mackenzie caught a whiff of smoke and felt for his pipe. The bowl was hot in his tunic pocket.

"Probably all rolling stock has to head north. Get troops among the bossmen there to forestall a revolt. The valleys are safe enough, peaceful ranchers and Esper colonies. None of them'll pot-shot Fallonite soldiers marching to garrison Echo and Donner outposts." A dreadful scorn weighted Speyer's words.

"What are we going to do?"

"I assume Fallon's take-over followed legal forms; that there was a quorum," Speyer said. "Nobody will ever agree whether it was really Constitutional. . . . I've been reading this damned message over and over since Irwin decoded it. There's a lot between the lines. I think Brodsky's at large, for instance. If he were under arrest this would've said as much, and there'd have been less worry about rebellion. Maybe some of his household troops smuggled him away in time. He'll be hunted like a jackrabbit, of course."

Mackenzie took out his pipe but forgot he had done so. "Tom's coming with our replacements," he said thinly.

"Yeah. Your son-in-law. That was a smart touch, wasn't it? A kind of hostage for your good behavior, but also a backhand promise that you and yours won't suffer if you report in as ordered. Tom's a good kid. He'll stand by his own."

"This is his regiment, too," Mackenzie said. He squared his shoulders. "He wanted to fight West Canada, sure. Young and . . . and a lot of Pacificans did get killed in the Idaho Panhandle during the skirmishes. Women and kids among 'em."

"Well," Speyer said, "you're the colonel, Jimbo. What should we do?"

"Oh, Jesus, I don't know. I'm nothing but a soldier." The pipestem broke in Mackenzie's fingers. "But we're not some bossman's personal militia here. We swore to support the Constitution."

"I can't see where Brodsky's yielding some of our claims in Idaho is grounds for impeachment. I think he was right."

"Well—"

"A *coup d'état* by any other name would stink as bad. You may not be much of a student of current events, Jimbo, but you know as well as I do what Fallon's Judgeship will mean. War with West Canada is almost the least of it. Fallon also stands for a strong central government. He'll find ways to grind down the old bossman families. A lot of their heads and scions will die in the front lines; that stunt goes back to David and Uriah. Others will be accused of collusion with the Brodsky people—not altogether falsely—and impoverished by fines. Esper communities will get nice big land grants, so their economic competition can bankrupt still other estates. Later wars will keep bossmen away for years at a time, unable to supervise their own affairs, which will therefore go to the devil. And thus we march toward the glorious goal of Reunification."

"If Esper Central favors him, what can we do? I've heard enough about psi blasts. I can't ask my men to face them."

"You could ask your men to face the Hellbomb itself, Jimbo, and they would. A Mackenzie has commanded the Rolling Stones for over fifty years."

"Yes. I thought Tom, someday—"

"We've watched this brewing for a long time. Remember the talk we had about it last week?"

"Uh-huh."

"I might also remind you that the Constitution was written explicitly 'to confirm the separate regions in their ancient liberties.' "

"Let me alone!" Mackenzie shouted. "I don't know what's right or wrong, I tell you! Let me alone!"

Speyer fell silent, watching him through a screen of foul smoke. Mackenzie walked back and forth a while, boots slamming the floor like drumbeats. Finally he threw the broken pipe across the room so it shattered.

"Okay." He must ram each word past the tension in his throat. "Irwin's a good man who can keep his lip buttoned. Send him out to cut the telegraph line a few miles downhill. Make it look as if the storm did it. The wire breaks often enough, heaven knows. Officially, then, we never got GHQ's message. That gives us a few days to contact Sierra Command HQ. I won't go against General Cruikshank . . . but I'm pretty sure which way he'll go if he sees a chance. Tomorrow we prepare for action. It'll be no trick to throw back Hollis' battalion, and they'll need a while to bring some real strength against us. Before then the first snow should be along, and we'll be shut off for the winter. Only we can use skis and snowshoes, ourselves, to keep in touch with the other units and organize something. By spring—we'll see what happens."

"Thanks, Jimbo." The wind almost drowned Speyer's words.

"I'd . . . I'd better go tell Laura."

"Yeah." Speyer squeezed Mackenzie's shoulder. There were tears in the major's eyes.

Mackenzie went out with parade-ground steps, ignoring Irwin: down the hall, down a stairway at its other end, past guarded doors where he returned salutes without really noticing, and so to his own quarters in the south wing.

His daughter had gone to sleep already. He took a lantern off its hook in his bleak little parlor, and entered her room. She had come back here while her husband was in San Francisco.

For a moment Mackenzie couldn't quite remember why he had sent Tom there. He passed a hand over his stubbly scalp, as if to squeeze something out . . . oh, yes, ostensibly to arrange for a new issue of uniforms; actually to get the boy out of the way until the political crisis had blown over. Tom was too honest for his own good, an admirer of Fallon and the Esper movement. His outspokenness had led to friction with his brother officers. They were mostly of bossman stock or from well-to-do protectee families. The existing social order had been good to them. But Tom Danielis began as a fisher lad in a poverty-stricken village on the Mendocino coast. In spare moments he'd learned the three R's from a local Esper; once literate, he joined the Army and earned a commission by sheer guts and brains. He had never forgotten that the Espers helped the poor and that Fallon promised to help the Espers. . . .

Then, too, battle, glory, Reunification, Federal Democracy, those were heady dreams when you were young.

Laura's room was little changed since she left it to get married last year. And she had only been seventeen then. Objects survived which had belonged to a small person with pigtails and starched frocks—a teddy bear loved to shapelessness, a doll house her father had built, her mother's picture drawn by a corporal who stopped a bullet at Salt Lake. Oh, God, how much she had come to look like her mother.

Dark hair streamed over a pillow turned gold by the light. Mackenzie shook her as gently as he was able. She awoke instantly, and he saw the terror within her.

"Dad! Anything about Tom?"

"He's okay." Mackenzie set the lantern on the floor and himself on the edge of the bed. Her fingers were cold where they caught at his hand.

"He isn't," she said. "I know you too well."

"He's not been hurt yet. I hope he won't be."

Mackenzie braced himself. Because she was a soldier's daughter, he told her the truth in a few words; but he was not strong enough to look at her while he did. When he had finished, he sat dully listening to the rain.

"You're going to revolt," she whispered.

"I'm going to consult with SCHQ and follow my commanding officer's orders," Mackenzie said.

"You know what they'll be . . . once he knows you'll back him."

Mackenzie shrugged. His head had begun to ache. Hangover started already? He'd need a good deal more booze before he could sleep tonight. No, no time for sleep—yes, there would be. Tomorrow would do to assemble the regiment in the courtyard and address them from the breech of Black Hepzibah, as a Mackenzie of the Rolling Stones always addressed his men, and—. He found himself ludicrously recalling a day when he and Nora and this girl here had gone rowing on Lake Tahoe. The water was the color of Nora's eyes, green and blue and with sunlight shimmering across the surface, but so clear you could see the rocks on the bottom; and Laura's own little bottom had stuck straight in the air as she trailed her hands astern.

She sat thinking for a space before saying flatly: "I

suppose you can't be talked out of it." He shook his head. "Well, can I leave tomorrow early, then?"

"Yes. I'll get you a coach."

"T-t-to hell with that. I'm better in the saddle than you are."

"Okay. A couple of men to escort you, though." Mackenzie drew a long breath. "Maybe you can persuade Tom—"

"No. I can't. Please don't ask me to, Dad."

He gave her the last gift he could: "I wouldn't want you to stay. That'd be shirking your own duty. Tell Tom I still think he's the right man for you. Goodnight, duck." It came out too fast, but he dared not delay. When she began to cry he must unfold her arms from his neck and depart the room.

"But I had not expected so much killing!"

"Nor I . . . at this stage of things. There will be more yet, I am afraid, before the immediate purpose is achieved."

"You told me—"

"I told you our hopes, Mwyr. You know as well as I that the Great Science is only exact on the broadest scale of history. Individual events are subject to statistical fluctuation."

"That is an easy way, is it not, to describe sentient beings dying in the mud?"

"You are new here. Theory is one thing, adjustment to practical necessities is another. Do you think it does not hurt me to see that happen which I myself have helped plan?"

"Oh, I know, I know. Which makes it no easier to live with my guilt."

"To live with your responsibilities, you mean."

"Your phrase."

"No, this is not semantic trickery. The distinction is real. You have read reports and seen films, but I was here with the first expedition. And here I have been for more than two centuries. Their agony is no abstraction to me."

"But it was different when we first discovered them. The aftermath of their nuclear wars was still so horribly

present. That was when they needed us—the poor starveling anarchs—and we, we did nothing but observe."

"Now you are hysterical. Could we come in blindly, ignorant of every last fact about them, and expect to be anything but one more disruptive element? An element whose effects we ourselves would not have been able to predict. That would have been criminal indeed, like a surgeon who started to operate as soon as he met the patient, without so much as taking a case history. We had to let them go their own way while we studied in secret. You have no idea how desperately hard we worked to gain information and understanding. That work goes on. It was only seventy years ago that we felt enough assurance to introduce the first new factor into this one selected society. As we continue to learn more, the plan will be adjusted. It may take us a thousand years to complete our mission."

"But meanwhile they have pulled themselves back out of the wreckage. They are finding their own answers to their problems. What right have we to—"

"I begin to wonder, Mwyr, what right you have to claim even the title of apprentice psychodynamician. Consider what their 'answers' actually amount to. Most of the planet is still in a state of barbarism. This continent has come farthest toward recovery, because of having the widest distribution of technical skills and equipment before the destruction. But what social structure has evolved? A jumble of quarrelsome successor states. A feudalism where the balance of political, military, and economic power lies with a landed aristocracy, of all archaic things. A score of languages and subcultures developing along their own incompatible lines. A blind technology worship inherited from the ancestral society that, unchecked, will lead them in the end back to a machine civilization as demoniac as the one that tore itself apart three centuries ago. Are you distressed that a few hundred men have been killed because our agents promoted a revolution which did not come off quite so smoothly as we hoped? Well, you have the word of the Great Science itself that, without our guidance, the totaled misery of this race through the

*next five thousand years would outweigh by three or-
ders of magnitude whatever pain we are forced to inflict."*

*"—Yes. Of course. I realize I am being emotional. It
is difficult not to be at first, I suppose."*

*"You should be thankful that your initial exposure to
the hard necessities of the plan was so mild. There is
worse to come."*

"So I have been told."

*"In abstract terms. But consider the reality. A gov-
ernment ambitious to restore the old nature will act
aggressively, thus embroiling itself in prolonged wars
with powerful neighbors. Both directly and indirectly,
through the operation of economic factors they are too
naïve to control, the aristocrats and freeholders will be
eroded away by those wars. Anomic democracy will
replace their system, first dominated by a corrupt capi-
talism and later by sheer force of whoever holds the
central government. But there will be no place for the
vast displaced proletariat, the one-time landowners and
the foreigners incorporated by conquest. They will offer
fertile soil to any demagogue. The empire will undergo
endless upheaval, civil strife, despotism, decay, and
outside invasion. Oh, we will have much to answer for
before we are done!"*

*"Do you think . . . when we see the final result . . .
will the blood wash off us?"*

"No. We pay the heaviest price of all."

Spring in the high Sierra is cold, wet, snowbanks melting away from forest floor and giant rocks, rivers in spate
until their canyons clang, a breeze ruffling puddles in the
road. The first green breath across the aspen seems infinitely tender against pine and spruce, which bloom into a
brilliant sky. A raven swoops low, gruk, gruk, look out for
that damn hawk! But then you cross timber line and the
world becomes tumbled blue-gray immensity, with the
sun ablaze on what snows remain and the wind sounding
hollow in your ears.

Captain Thomas Danielis, Field Artillery, Loyalist Army
of the Pacific States, turned his horse aside. He was a dark
young man, slender and snub-nosed. Behind him a squad
slipped and cursed, dripping mud from feet to helmets,

trying to get a gun carrier unstuck. Its alcohol motor was too feeble to do more than spin the wheels. The infantry squelched on past, stoop-shouldered, worn down by altitude and a wet bivouac and pounds of mire on each boot. Their line snaked from around a prowlike crag, up the twisted road and over the ridge ahead. A gust brought the smell of sweat to Danielis.

But they were good joes, he thought. Dirty, dogged, they did their profane best. His own company, at least, was going to get hot food tonight, if he had to cook the quartermaster sergeant.

The horse's hoofs banged on a block of ancient concrete jutting from the muck. If this had been the old days . . . but wishes weren't bullets. Beyond this part of the range lay lands mostly desert, claimed by the Saints, who were no longer a menace but with whom there was scant commerce. So the mountain highways had never been considered worth repaving, and the railroad ended at Hangtown. Therefore the expeditionary force to the Tahoe area must slog through unpeopled forests and icy uplands, God help the poor bastards.

God help them in Nakamura, too, Danielis thought. His mouth drew taut, he slapped his hands together and spurred the horse with needless violence. Sparks shot from iron shoes as the beast clattered off the road toward the highest point of the ridge. The man's saber banged his leg.

Reining in, he unlimbered his field glasses. From here he could look across a jumbled sweep of mountainscape, where cloud shadows sailed over cliffs and boulders, down into the gloom of a canyon and across to the other side. A few tufts of grass thrust out beneath him, mummy brown, and a marmot wakened early from winter sleep whistled somewhere in the stone confusion. He still couldn't see the castle. Nor had he expected to, as yet. He knew this country . . . how well he did!

There might be a glimpse of hostile activity, though. It had been eerie to march this far with no sign of the enemy, of anyone else whatsoever; to send out patrols in search of rebel units that could not be found; to ride with shoulder muscles tense against the sniper's arrow that never came. Old Jimbo Mackenzie was not one to sit passive behind walls, and the Rolling Stones had not been given their nickname in jest.

If Jimbo is alive. How do I know he is? That buzzard yonder may be the very one which hacked out his eyes.

Danielis bit his lip and made himself look steadily through the glasses. Don't think about Mackenzie, how he outroared and outdrank and outlaughed you and you never minded, how he sat knotting his brows over the chessboard where you could mop him up ten times out of ten and *he* never cared, how proud and happy he stood at the wedding. . . . Nor think about Laura, who tried to keep you from knowing how often she wept at night, who now bore a grandchild beneath her heart and woke alone in the San Francisco house from the evil dreams of pregnancy. Every one of those dogfaces plodding toward the castle which has killed every army ever sent against it—every one of them has somebody at home and hell rejoices at how many have somebody on the rebel side. Better look for hostile spoor and let it go at that.

Wait! Danielis stiffened. A rider— He focused. *One of our own.* Fallon's army added a blue band to the uniform. *Returning scout.* A tingle went along his spine. He decided to hear the report firsthand. But the fellow was still a mile off, perforce riding slowly over the hugger-mugger terrain. There was no hurry about intercepting him. Danielis continued to survey the land.

A reconnaissance plane appeared, an ungainly dragonfly with sunlight flashing off a propeller head. Its drone rumbled among rock walls, where echoes threw the noise back and forth. Doubtless an auxiliary to the scouts, employing two-way radio communication. Later the plane would work as a spotter for artillery. There was no use making a bomber of it; Fort Nakamura was proof against anything that today's puny aircraft could drop, and might well shoot the thing down.

A shoe scraped behind Danielis. Horse and man whirled as one. His pistol jumped into his hand.

It lowered. "Oh. Excuse me, Philosopher."

The man in the blue robe nodded. A smile softened his stern face. He must be around sixty years old, hair white and skin lined, but he walked these heights like a wild goat. The Yang and Yin symbol burned gold on his breast.

"You're needlessly on edge, son," he said. A trace of Texas accent stretched out his words. The Espers obeyed the laws wherever they lived, but acknowledged no country their own: nothing less than mankind, perhaps ultimately all life through the space-time universe. Nevertheless, the Pacific States had gained enormously in prestige and influence when the Order's unenterable Central was established in San Francisco at the time when the city was being rebuilt in earnest. There had been no objection—on the contrary—to the Grand Seeker's desire that Philosopher Woodworth accompany the expedition as an observer. Not even from the chaplains; the churches had finally gotten it straight that the Esper teachings were neutral with respect to religion.

Danielis managed a grin. "Can you blame me?"

"No blame. But advice. Your attitude isn't useful. Does nothin' but wear you out. You've been fightin' a battle for weeks before it began."

Danielis remembered the apostle who had visited his home in San Francisco—by invitation, in the hope that Laura might learn some peace. His simile had been still homelier: "You only need to wash one dish at a time." The memory brought a smart to Danielis' eyes, so that he said roughly:

"I might relax if you'd use your powers to tell me what's waiting for us."

"I'm no adept, son. Too much in the material world, I'm afraid. Somebody's got to do the practical work of the Order, and someday I'll get the chance to retire and explore the frontier inside me. But you need to start early, and stick to it a lifetime, to develop your full powers." Woodworth looked across the peaks, seemed almost to merge himself with their loneliness.

Danielis hesitated to break into that meditation. He wondered what practical purpose the Philosopher was serving on this trip. To bring back a report, more accurate than untrained senses and undisciplined emotions could prepare? Yes, that must be it. The Espers might yet decide to take a hand in this war. However reluctantly, Central had allowed the awesome psi powers to be released now and again, when the Order was seriously threatened; and Judge Fallon was a better friend to them than

Brodsky or the earlier Senate of Bossmen and House of People's Deputies had been.

The horse stamped and blew out its breath in a snort. Woodworth glanced back at the rider. "If you ask me, though," he said, "I don't reckon you'll find much doin' around here. I was in the Rangers myself, back home, before I saw the Way. This country feels empty."

"If we could know!" Danielis exploded. "They've had the whole winter to do what they liked in the mountains, while the snow kept us out. What scouts we could get in reported a beehive—as late as two weeks ago. What have they planned?"

Woodworth made no reply.

It flooded from Danielis, he couldn't stop, he had to cover the recollection of Laura bidding him good-by on his second expedition against her father, six months after the first one came home in bloody fragments:

"If we had the resources! A few wretched little railroads and motor cars; a handful of aircraft; most of our supply trains drawn by mules—what kind of mobility does that give us? And what really drives me crazy . . . we know how to make what they had in the old days. We've got the books, the information. More, maybe, than the ancestors. I've watched the electrosmith at Fort Nakamura turn out transistor units with enough bandwidth to carry television, no bigger than my fist. I've seen the scientific journals, the research labs, biology, chemistry, astronomy, mathematics. And all useless!"

"Not so," Woodworth answered mildly. "Like my own Order, the community of scholarship's becomin' supranational. Printin' presses, radiophones, telescribes—"

"I say useless. Useless to stop men killing each other because there's no authority strong enough to make them behave. Useless to take a farmer's hands off a horse-drawn plow and put them on the wheel of a tractor. We've got the knowledge, but we can't apply it."

"You do apply it, son, where too much power and industrial plant isn't required. Remember, the world's a lot poorer in natural resources than it was before the Hellbombs. I've seen the Black Lands myself, where the firestorm passed over the Texas oilfields." Woodworth's serenity cracked a little. He turned his eyes back to the peaks.

"There's oil elsewhere," Danielis insisted. "And coal, iron, uranium, everything we need. But the world hasn't got the organization to get at it. Not in any quantity. So we fill the Central Valley with crops that'll yield alcohol, to keep a few motors turning; and we import a dribble of other stuff along an unbelievably inefficient chain of middlemen; and most of it's eaten by the armies." He jerked his head toward that part of the sky which the handmade airplane had crossed. "That's one reason we've got to have Reunification. So we can rebuild."

"And the other?" Woodworth asked softly.

"Democracy—universal suffrage—" Danielis swallowed. "And so fathers and sons won't have to fight each other again."

"Those are better reasons," Woodworth said. "Good enough for the Espers to support. But as for that machinery you want—" He shook his head. "No, you're wrong there. That's no way for men to live."

"Maybe not," Danielis said. "Though my own father wouldn't have been crippled by overwork if he'd had some machines to help him. . . . Oh, I don't know. First things first. Let's get this war over with and argue later." He remembered the scout, now gone from view. "Pardon me, Philosopher, I've got an errand."

The Esper raised his hand in token of peace. Danielis cantered off.

Splashing along the roadside, he saw the man he wanted, halted by Major Jacobsen. The latter, who must have sent him out, sat mounted near the infantry line. The scout was a Klamath Indian, stocky in buckskins, a bow on his shoulder. Arrows were favored over guns by many of the men from the northern districts: cheaper than bullets, no noise, less range but as much firepower as a bolt-action rifle. In the bad old days before the Pacific States had formed their union, archers along forest trails had saved many a town from conquest; they still helped keep that union loose.

"Ah, Captain Danielis," Jacobsen hailed. "You're just in time. Lieutenant Smith was about to report what his detachment found out."

"And the plane," said Smith imperturbably. "What the

pilot told us he's seen from the air gave us the guts to go there and check for ourselves."

"Well?"

"Nobody around."

"What?"

"Fort's been evacuated. So's the settlement. Not a soul."

"But—but—" Jacobsen collected himself. "Go on."

"We studied the signs as best's we could. Looks like noncombatants left some time ago. By sledge and ski, I'd guess, maybe north to some strong point. I suppose the men shifted their own stuff at the same time, gradual-like, what they couldn't carry with 'em at the last. Because the regiment and its support units, even field artillery, pulled out just three-four days ago. Ground's all tore up. They headed downslope, sort of west by northwest, far's we could tell from what we saw."

Jacobsen choked. "Where are they bound?"

A flaw of wind struck Danielis in the face and ruffled the horses' manes. At his back he heard the slow plop and squish of boots, groan of wheels, chuff of motors, rattle of wood and metal, yells and whipcracks of muleskinners. But it seemed very remote. A map grew before him, blotting out the world.

The Loyalist Army had had savage fighting the whole winter, from the Trinity Alps to Puget Sound—for Brodsky had managed to reach Mount Rainier, whose lord had furnished broadcasting facilities, and Rainier was too well fortified to take at once. The bossmen and the autonomous tribes rose in arms, persuaded that a usurper threatened their damned little local privileges. Their protectees fought beside them, if only because no rustic had been taught any higher loyalty than to his patron. West Canada, fearful of what Fallon might do when he got the chance, lent the rebels aid that was scarcely even clandestine.

Nonetheless, the national army was stronger: more matériel, better organization, above everything an ideal of the future. Cinc O'Donnell had outlined a strategy—concentrate the loyal forces at a few points, overwhelm resistance, restore order and establish bases in the region, then proceed to the next place—which worked. The government now controlled the entire coast, with naval units to keep an eye on the Canadians in Vancouver and guard the important Hawaii trade routes; the northern half of Washington almost to the Idaho line; the Columbia Valley; central California as far north as Redding. The remaining rebellious Stations and towns were isolated from each other in mountains, forests, deserts. Bossdom after bossdom fell as the loyalists pressed on, defeating the enemy in detail, cutting him off from supplies and hope. The only real worry had been Cruikshank's Sierra Command, an army in its own right rather than a levy of yokels and citymen, big and tough and expertly led. This expedition against Fort Nakamura was only a small part of what had looked like a difficult campaign.

But now the Rolling Stones had pulled out. Offered no fight whatsoever. Which meant that their brother Catamounts must also have evacuated. You don't give up one anchor of a line you intend to hold. So?

"Down into the valleys," Danielis said; and there sounded in his ears, crazily, the voice of Laura as she used to sing. *Down in the valley, valley so low.*

"Judas!" the major exclaimed. Even the Indian grunted as if he had taken a belly blow. "No, they couldn't. We'd have known."

Hang your head over, hear the wind blow. It hooted across cold rocks.

"There are plenty of forest trails," Danielis said. "Infantry and cavalry could use them, if they're accustomed to such country. And the Cats are. Vehicles, wagons, big guns, that's slower and harder. But they only need to outflank us, then they can get back onto Forty and Fifty—and cut us to pieces if we attempt pursuit. I'm afraid they've got us boxed."

"The eastern slope—" said Jacobsen helplessly.

"What for? Want to occupy a lot of sagebrush? No, we're trapped here till they deploy in the flatlands." Danielis closed a hand on his saddlehorn so that the knuckles went bloodless. "I miss my guess if this isn't Colonel Mackenzie's idea. It's his style, for sure."

"But then they're between us and Frisco! With damn near our whole strength in the north—"

Between me and Laura, Danielis thought.

He said aloud: "I suggest, Major, we get hold of the C.O. at once. And then we better get on the radio." From some well he drew the power to raise his head. The wind lashed his eyes. "This needn't be a disaster. They'll be easier to beat out in the open, actually, once we come to grips."

Roses love sunshine, violets love dew,
Angels in heaven know I love you.

The rains which fill the winter of the California lowlands were about ended. Northward along a highway whose pavement clopped under hoofs, Mackenzie rode through a tremendous greenness. Eucalyptus and live oak, flanking the road, exploded with new leaves. Beyond them on either side stretched a checkerboard of fields and vineyards, intricately hued, until the distant hills on the right and the higher, nearer ones on the left made walls. The freeholder houses that had been scattered across the land a ways back were no longer to be seen. This end of the Napa Valley belonged to the Esper community at St. Helena. Clouds banked like white mountains over the western ridge. The breeze bore to Mackenzie a smell of growth and turned earth.

Behind him it rumbled with men. The Rolling Stones were on the move. The regiment proper kept to the highway, three thousand boots slamming down at once with an earthquake noise, and so did the guns and wagons. There was no immediate danger of attack. But the cavalrymen attached to the force must needs spread out. The sun flashed off their helmets and lance heads.

Mackenzie's attention was directed forward. Amber walls and red tile roofs could be seen among plum trees that were a surf of pink and white blossoms. The community was big, several thousand people. The muscles tightened in his abdomen. "Think we can trust them?" he asked, not for the first time. "We've only got a radio agreement to a parley."

Speyer, riding beside him, nodded. "I expect they'll be honest. Particularly with our boys right outside. Espers believe in non-violence anyway."

"Yeah, but if it did come to fighting—I know there aren't very many adepts so far. The Order hasn't been around long enough for that. But when you get this many Espers together, there's bound to be a few who've gotten somewhere with their damned psionics. I don't want my men blasted, or lifted in the air and dropped, or any such nasty things."

Speyer threw him a sidelong glance. "Are you scared of them, Jimbo?" he murmured.

"Hell, no!" Mackenzie wondered if he was a liar or not. "But I don't like 'em."

"They do a lot of good. Among the poor, especially."

"Sure, sure. Though any decent bossman looks after his own protectees, and we've got things like churches and hospices as well. I don't see where just being charitable— and they can afford it, with the profits they make on their holdings—I don't see where that gives any right to raise the orphans and pauper kids they take in, the way they do: so's to make the poor tikes unfit for life anywhere outside."

"The object of that, as you well know, is to orient them toward the so-called interior frontier. Which American civilization as a whole is not much interested in. Frankly, quite apart from the remarkable powers some Espers have developed, I often envy them."

"You, Phil?" Mackenzie goggled at his friend.

The lines drew deep in Speyer's face. "This winter I've helped shoot a lot of my fellow countrymen," he said low. "My mother and wife and kids are crowded with the rest of the Village in the Mount Lassen fort, and when we said good-by we knew it was quite possibly permanent. And in the past I've helped shoot a lot of other men who never did me any personal harm." He sighed. "I've often wondered what it's like to know peace, inside as well as outside."

Mackenzie sent Laura and Tom out of his head.

"Of course," Speyer went on, "the fundamental reason you—and I, for that matter—distrust the Espers is that they do represent something alien to us. Something that may eventually choke out the whole concept of life that we grew up with. You know, a couple weeks back in Sacramento I dropped in at the University research lab to see what was going on. Incredible! The ordinary soldier would swear it was witchwork. It was certainly more weird than . . . than simply reading minds or moving objects by thinking at them. But to you or me it's a shiny new marvel. We'll wallow in it.

"Now why's that? Because the lab is scientific. Those men work with chemicals, electronics, subviral particles. That fits into the educated American's world-view. But the mystic unity of creation . . . no, not our cup of tea. The only way we can hope to achieve Oneness is to renounce everything we've ever believed in. At your age or mine, Jimbo, a man is seldom ready to tear down his whole life and start from scratch."

"Maybe so." Mackenzie lost interest. The settlement was quite near now.

He turned around to Captain Hulse, riding a few paces behind. "Here we go," he said. "Give my compliments to Lieutenant Colonel Yamaguchi and tell him he's in charge till we get back. If anything seems suspicious, he's to act at his own discretion."

"Yes, sir." Hulse saluted and wheeled smartly about. There had been no practical need for Mackenzie to repeat what had long been agreed on; but he knew the value of ritual. He clicked his big sorrel gelding into a trot. At his back he heard bugles sound orders and sergeants howl at their platoons.

Speyer kept pace. Mackenzie had insisted on bringing an extra man to the discussion. His own wits were probably no match for a high-level Esper, but Phil's might be.

Not that there's any question of diplomacy or whatever. I hope. To ease himself, he concentrated on what was real and present—hoofbeats, the rise and fall of the saddle beneath him, the horse's muscles rippling between his thighs, the creak and jingle of his saber belt, the clean odor of the animal—and suddenly remembered this was the sort of trick the Espers recommended.

None of their communities was walled, as most towns and every bossman's Station was. The officers turned off the highway and went down a street between colonnaded buildings. Side streets ran off in both directions. The settlement covered no great area, though, being composed of groups that lived together, sodalities or superfamilies or whatever you wanted to call them. Some hostility toward the Order and a great many dirty jokes stemmed from that practice. But Speyer, who should know, said there was no more sexual swapping around than in the outside world. The idea was simply to get away from possessiveness, thee versus me, and to raise children as part of a whole rather than an insular clan.

The kids were out, staring round-eyed from the porticoes, hundreds of them. They looked healthy and, underneath a natural fear of the invaders, happy enough. But pretty solemn, Mackenzie thought; and all in the same blue garb. Adults stood among them, expressionless. Everybody had come in from the fields as the regiment neared. The silence was like barricades. Mackenzie felt sweat begin to trickle down his ribs. When he emerged on the central square, he let out his breath in a near gasp.

A fountain, the basin carved into a lotus, tinkled in the middle of the plaza. Flowering trees stood around it. The square was defined on three sides by massive buildings that must be for storage. On the fourth side rose a smaller templelike structure with a graceful cupola, obviously headquarters and meeting house. On its lowest step were ranked half a dozen blue-robed men, five of them husky youths. The sixth was middle-aged, the Yang and Yin on his breast. His features, ordinary in themselves, held an implacable calm.

Mackenzie and Speyer drew rein. The colonel flipped a soft salute. "Philosopher Gaines? I'm Mackenzie, here's Major Speyer." He swore at himself for being so awkward about it and wondered what to do with his hands. The young fellows he understood, more or less; they watched him with badly concealed hostility. But he had some trouble meeting Gaines' eyes.

The settlement leader inclined his head. "Welcome, gentlemen. Won't you come in?"

Mackenzie dismounted, hitched his horse to a post and removed his helmet. His worn reddish-brown uniform felt shabbier yet in these surroundings. "Thanks. Uh, I'll have to make this quick."

"To be sure. Follow me, please."

Stiff-backed, the young men trailed their elders, through an entry chamber and down a short hall. Speyer looked around at the mosaics. "Why, this is lovely," he murmured.

"Thank you," said Gaines. "Here's my office." He opened a door of superbly grained walnut and gestured the visitors through. When he closed it behind himself, the acolytes waited outside.

The room was austere, whitewashed walls enclosing little more than a desk, a shelf of books, and some backless chairs. A window opened on a garden. Gaines sat down. Mackenzie and Speyer followed suit, uncomfortable on this furniture.

"We'd better get right to business," the colonel blurted.

Gaines said nothing. At last Mackenzie must plow ahead:

"Here's the situation. Our force is to occupy Calistoga, with detachments on either side of the hills. That way we'll control both the Napa Valley and the Valley of the Moon . . . from the northern ends, at least. The best place to station our eastern wing is here. We plan to establish a fortified camp in the field yonder. I'm sorry about the damage to your crops, but you'll be compensated once the proper government has been restored. And food, medicine— you understand this army has to requisition such items, but we won't let anybody suffer undue hardship and we'll give receipts. Uh, as a precaution we'll need to quarter a few men in this community, to sort of keep an eye on things. They'll interfere as little as possible. Okay?"

"The charter of the Order guarantees exemption from military requirements," Gaines answered evenly. "In fact, no armed man is supposed to cross the boundary of any land held by an Esper settlement. I cannot be a party to a violation of the law, Colonel."

"If you want to split legal hairs, Philosopher," Speyer said, "then I'll remind you that both Fallon and Judge Brodsky have declared martial law. Ordinary rules are suspended."

Gaines smiled. "Since only one government can be legitimate," he said, "the proclamations of the other are necessarily null and void. To a disinterested observer, it would appear that Judge Fallon's title is the stronger, especially when his side controls a large continuous area rather than some scattered bossdoms."

"Not any more, it doesn't," Mackenzie snapped.

Speyer gestured him back. "Perhaps you haven't followed the developments of the last few weeks, Philosopher," he said. "Allow me to recapitulate. The Sierra Command stole a march on the Fallonites and came down out of the mountains. There was almost nothing left in the middle part of California to oppose us, so we took over rapidly. By occupying Sacramento, we control river and rail traffic. Our bases extend south below Bakersfield, with Yosemite and King's Canyon not far away to provide sites for extremely strong positions. When we've consolidated this northern end of our gains, the Fallonite forces around Redding will be trapped between us and the powerful bossmen who still hold out in the Trinity, Shasta, and Lassen regions. The very fact of our being here has forced the enemy to evacuate the Columbia Valley, so that San Francisco may be defended. It's an open question which side today has the last word in the larger territory."

"What about the army that went into the Sierra against you?" Gaines inquired shrewdly. "Have you contained them?"

Mackenzie scowled. "No. That's no secret. They got out through the Mother Lode country and went around us. They're down in Los Angeles and San Diego now."

"A formidable host. Do you expect to stand them off indefinitely?"

"We're going to make a hell of a good try," Mackenzie said. "Where we are, we've got the advantage of interior communications. And most of the freeholders are glad to slip us word about whatever they observe. We can concentrate at any point the enemy starts to attack."

"Pity that this rich land must also be torn apart by war."

"Yeah. Isn't it?"

"Our strategic objective is obvious enough," Speyer said. "We have cut enemy communications across the middle, except by sea, which is not very satisfactory for troops operating far inland. We deny him access to a good part of his food and manufactured supplies, and most especially to the bulk of his fuel alcohol. The backbone of our own side is the bossdoms, which are almost self-contained economic and social units. Before long they'll be in better shape than the rootless army they face. I think Judge Brodsky will be back in San Francisco before fall."

"If your plans succeed," Gaines said.

"That's our worry." Mackenzie leaned forward, one fist doubled on his knee. "Okay, Philosopher. I know you'd rather see Fallon come out on top, but I expect you've got more sense than to sign up in a lost cause. Will you cooperate with us?"

"The Order takes no part in political affairs, Colonel, except when its own existence is endangered."

"Oh, pipe down. By 'cooperate' I don't mean anything but keeping out from under our feet."

"I am afraid that would still count as cooperation. We cannot have military establishments on our lands."

Mackenzie stared at Gaines' face, which had set into granite lines, and wondered if he had heard aright. "Are you ordering us off?" a stranger asked with his voice.

"Yes," the Philosopher said.

"With our artillery zeroed in on your town?"

"Would you really shell women and children, Colonel?" *O Nora—* "We don't need to. Our men can walk right in."

"Against psi blasts? I beg you not to have those poor boys destroyed." Gaines paused, then: "I might also point out that by losing your regiment you imperil your whole cause. You are free to march around our holdings and proceed to Calistoga."

Leaving a Fallonite nest at my back, spang across my communications southward. The teeth grated together in Mackenzie's mouth.

Gaines rose. "The discussion is at an end, gentlemen," he said. "You have one hour to get off our lands."

Mackenzie and Speyer stood up, too. "We're not done yet," the major said. Sweat studded his forehead and the long nose. "I want to make some further explanations."

Gaines crossed the room and opened the door. "Show these gentlemen out," he said to the five acolytes.

"No, by God!" Mackenzie shouted. He clapped a hand to his sidearm.

"Inform the adepts," Gaines said.

One of the young men turned. Mackenzie heard the slap-slap of his sandals, running down the hall. Gaines nodded. "I think you had better go," he said.

Speyer grew rigid. His eyes shut. They flew open and he breathed, *"Inform* the adepts?"

Mackenzie saw the stiffness break in Gaines' countenance. There was no time for more than a second's bewilderment. His body acted for him. The gun clanked from his holster simultaneously with Speyer's.

"Get that messenger, Jimbo," the major rapped. "I'll keep these birds covered."

As he plunged forward, Mackenzie found himself worrying about the regimental honor. Was it right to open hostilities when you had come on a parley? But Gaines had cut the talk off himself—

"Stop him!" Gaines yelled.

The four remaining acolytes sprang into motion. Two of them barred the doorway, the other two moved in on either side. "Hold it or I'll shoot!" Speyer cried, and was ignored.

Mackenzie couldn't bring himself to fire on unarmed men. He gave the youngster before him the pistol barrel in his teeth. Bloody-faced, the Esper lurched back. Mackenzie stiff-armed the one coming in from the left. The third tried to fill the doorway. Mackenzie put a foot behind his ankles and pushed. As he went down, Mackenzie kicked him in the temple, hard enough to stun, and jumped over him.

The fourth was on his back. Mackenzie writhed about to face the man. Those arms that hugged him, pinioning his gun, were bear strong. Mackenzie put the butt of his free left hand under the fellow's nose, and pushed. The acolyte must let go. Mackenzie gave him a knee in the stomach, whirled, and ran.

There was not much further commotion behind him. Phil must have them under control. Mackenzie pelted along the hall, into the entry chamber. Where had that goddamn runner gone? He looked out the open entrance, onto the square. Sunlight hurt his eyes. His breath came in painful gulps, there was a stitch in his side, yeah, he was getting old.

Blue robes fluttered from a street. Mackenzie recognized the messenger. The youth pointed at this building. A gabble of his words drifted faintly through Mackenzie's pulse. There were seven or eight men with him—older men, nothing to mark their clothes . . . but Mackenzie knew a high-ranking officer when he saw one. The acolyte was dismissed. Those whom he had summoned crossed the square with long strides.

Terror knotted Mackenzie's bowels. He put it down. A Catamount didn't stampede, even from somebody who could turn him inside out with a look. He could do nothing about the wretchedness that followed, though. *If they clobber me, so much the better. I won't lie awake nights wondering how Laura is.*

The adepts were almost to the steps. Mackenzie trod forth. He swept his revolver in an arc. "Halt!" His voice sounded tiny in the stillness that brooded over the town.

They jarred to a stop and stood there in a group. He saw them enforce a catlike relaxation, and their faces became blank visors. None spoke. Finally Mackenzie was unable to keep silent.

"This place is hereby occupied under the laws of war," he said. "Go back to your quarters."

"What have you done with our leader?" asked a tall man. His voice was even but deeply resonant.

"Read my mind and find out," Mackenzie gibed. *No, you're being childish.* "He's okay, long's he keeps his nose clean. You too. Beat it."

"We do not wish to pervert psionics to violence," said the tall man. "Please do not force us."

"Your chief sent for you before we'd done anything," Mackenzie retorted. "Looks like violence was what he had in mind. On your way."

The Espers exchanged glances. The tall man nodded. His companions walked slowly off. "I would like to see Philosopher Gaines," the tall man said.

"You will pretty soon."

"Am I to understand that he is being held a prisoner?"

"Understand what you like." The other Espers were rounding the corner of the building. "I don't want to shoot. Go on back before I have to."

"An impasse of sorts," the tall man said. "Neither of us wishes to injure one whom he considers defenseless. Allow me to conduct you off these grounds."

Mackenzie wet his lips. Weather had chapped them rough. "If you can put a hex on me, go ahead," he challenged. "Otherwise scram."

"Well, I shall not hinder you from rejoining your men. It seems the easiest way of getting you to leave. But I most solemnly warn that any armed force which tries to enter will be annihilated."

Guess I had better go get the boys, at that. Phil can't mount guard on those guys forever.

The tall man went over to the hitching post. "Which of these horses is yours?" he asked blandly.

Almighty eager to get rid of me, isn't he—Holy hellfire! There must be a rear door!

Mackenzie spun on his heel. The Esper shouted. Mackenzie dashed back through the entry chamber. His boots threw echoes at him. No, not to the left, there's only the office that way. Right . . . around this corner—

A long hall stretched before him. A stairway curved from the middle. The other Espers were already on it.

"Halt!" Mackenzie called. "Stop or I'll shoot!"

The two men in the lead sped onward. The rest turned and headed down again, toward him.

He fired with care, to disable rather than kill. The hall reverberated with the explosions. One after another they dropped, a bullet in leg or hip or shoulder. With such small targets, Mackenzie missed some shots. As the tall man, the last of them, closed in from behind, the hammer clicked on an empty chamber.

Mackenzie drew his saber and gave him the flat of it alongside the head. The Esper lurched. Mackenzie got past and bounded up the stair. It wound like something in a nightmare. He thought his heart was going to go to pieces.

At the end, an iron door opened on a landing. One man was fumbling with the lock. The other blue-robe attacked.

Mackenzie stuck his sword between the Esper's legs. As his opponent stumbled, the colonel threw a left hook to the jaw. The man sagged against the wall. Mackenzie grabbed the robe of the other and hurled him to the floor. "Get out," he rattled.

They pulled themselves together and glared at him. He thrust air with his blade. "From now on I aim to kill," he said.

"Get help, Dave," said the one who had been opening the door. "I'll watch him." The other went unevenly down the stairs. The first man stood out of saber reach. "Do you want to be destroyed?" he asked.

Mackenzie turned the knob at his back, but the door

was still locked. "I don't think you can do it," he said. "Not without what's here."

The Esper struggled for self-control. They waited through minutes that stretched. Then a noise began below. The Esper pointed. "We have nothing but agricultural implements," he said, "but you have only that blade. Will you surrender?"

Mackenzie spat on the floor. The Esper went on down.

Presently the attackers came into view. There might be a hundred, judging from the hubbub behind them, but because of the curve Mackenzie could see no more than ten or fifteen—burly fieldhands, their robes tucked high and sharp tools aloft. The landing was too wide for defense. He advanced to the stairway, where they could only come at him two at a time.

A couple of sawtoothed hay knives led the assault. Mackenzie parried one blow and chopped. His edge went into meat and struck bone. Blood ran out, impossibly red, even in the dim light here. The man fell to all fours with a shriek. Mackenzie dodged a cut from the companion. Metal clashed on metal. The weapons locked. Mackenzie's arm was forced back. He looked into a broad suntanned face. The side of his hand smote the young man's larynx. The Esper fell against the one behind and they went down together. It took a while to clear the tangle and resume action.

A pitchfork thrust for the colonel's belly. He managed to grab it with his left hand, divert the tines, and chop at the fingers on the shaft. A scythe gashed his right side. He saw his own blood but wasn't aware of pain. A flesh wound, no more. He swept his saber back and forth. The forefront retreated from its whistling menace. *But God, my knees are like rubber, I can't hold out another five minutes.*

A bugle sounded. There was a spatter of gunfire. The mob on the staircase congealed. Someone screamed.

Hoofs banged across the ground floor. A voice rasped: "Hold everything, there! Drop those weapons and come on down. First man tries anything gets shot."

Mackenzie leaned on his saber and fought for air. He hardly noticed the Espers melt away.

When he felt a little better, he went to one of the small

windows and looked out. Horsemen were in the plaza. Not yet in sight, but nearing, he heard infantry.

Speyer arrived, followed by a sergeant of engineers and several privates. The major hurried to Mackenzie. "You okay, Jimbo? You been hurt!"

"A scratch," Mackenzie said. He was getting back his strength, though no sense of victory accompanied it, only the knowledge of aloneness. The injury began to sting. "Not worth a fuss. Look."

"Yes, I suppose you'll live. Okay, men, get that door open."

The engineers took forth their tools and assailed the lock with a vigor that must spring half from fear. "How'd you guys show up so soon?" Mackenzie asked.

"I thought there'd be trouble," Speyer said, "so when I heard shots I jumped through the window and ran around to my horse. That was just before those clodhoppers attacked you; I saw them gathering as I rode out. Our cavalry got in almost at once, of course, and the dogfaces weren't far behind."

"Any resistance?"

"No, not after we fired a few rounds in the air." Speyer glanced outside. "We're in full possession now."

Mackenzie regarded the door. "Well," he said, "I feel better about our having pulled guns on them in the office. Looks like their adepts really depend on plain old weapons, huh? And Esper communities aren't supposed to have arms. Their charters say so. . . . That was a damn good guess of yours, Phil. How'd you do it?"

"I sort of wondered why the chief had to send a runner to fetch guys that claim to be telepaths. There we go!"

The lock jingled apart. The sergeant opened the door. Mackenzie and Speyer went into the great room under the dome.

They walked around for a long time, wordless, among shapes of metal and less identifiable substances. Nothing was familiar. Mackenzie paused at last before a helix which projected from a transparent cube. Formless darknesses swirled within the box, sparked as if with tiny stars.

"I figured maybe the Espers had found a cache of old-time stuff, from just before the Hellbombs," he said in a muffled voice. "Ultra-secret weapons that never got a chance to be used. But this doesn't look like it. Think so?"

"No," Speyer said. "It doesn't look to me as if these things were made by human beings at all."

"But do you not understand? They occupied a settlement! That proves to the world that Espers are not invulnerable. And to complete the catastrophe, they seized its arsenal."

"Have no fears about that. No untrained person can activate those instruments. The circuits are locked except in the presence of certain encephalic rhythms which result from conditioning. That same conditioning makes it impossible for the so-called adepts to reveal any of their knowledge to the uninitiated, no matter what may be done to them."

"Yes, I know that much. But it is not what I had in mind. What frightens me is the fact that the revelation will spread. Everyone will know the Esper adepts do not plumb unknown depths of the psyche after all, but merely have access to an advanced physical science. Not only will this lift rebel spirits, but worse, it will cause many, perhaps most of the Order's members to break away in disillusionment."

"Not at once. News travels slowly under present conditions. Also, Mwyr, you underestimate the ability of the human mind to ignore data which conflict with cherished beliefs."

"But—"

"Well, let us assume the worst. Let us suppose that faith is lost and the Order disintegrates. That will be a serious setback to the plan, but not a fatal one. Psionics was merely one bit of folklore we found potent enough to serve as the motivator of a new orientation toward life. There are others, for example the widespread belief in magic among the less educated classes. We can begin again on a different basis, if we must. The exact form of the creed is not important. It is only scaffolding for the real structure: a communal, anti-materialistic social group, to which more and more people will turn for sheer lack of anything else, as the coming empire breaks up. In the *end, the new culture can and will discard whatever superstitions gave it the initial impetus.*"

"*A hundred-year setback, at least.*"

"*True. It would be much more difficult to introduce a radical alien element now, when the autochthonous society has developed strong institutions of its own, than it was in the past. I merely wish to reassure you that the task is not impossible. I do not actually propose to let matters go that far. The Espers can be salvaged.*"

"*How?*"

"*We must intervene directly.*"

"*Has that been computed as being unavoidable?*"

"*Yes. The matrix yields an unambiguous answer. I do not like it any better than you. But direct action occurs oftener than we tell neophytes in the schools. The most elegant procedure would of course be to establish such initial conditions in a society that its evolution along desired lines becomes automatic. Furthermore, that would let us close our minds to the distressing fact of our own blood guilt. Unfortunately, the Great Science does not extend down to the details of day-to-day practicality.*

"*In the present instance, we shall help to smash the reactionaries. The government will then proceed so harshly against its conquered opponents that many of those who accept the story about what was found at St. Helena will not live to spread the tale. The rest . . . well, they will be discredited by their own defeat. Admittedly, the story will linger for lifetimes, whispered here and there. But what of that? Those who believe in the Way will, as a rule, simply be strengthened in their faith, by the very process of denying such ugly rumors. As more and more persons, common citizens as well as Espers, reject materialism, the legend will seem more and more fantastic. It will seem obvious that certain ancients invented the tale to account for a fact that they in their ignorance were unable to comprehend.*"

"*I see. . . .*"

"*You are not happy here, are you, Mwyr?*"

"*I cannot quite say. Everything is so distorted.*"

"*Be glad you were not sent to one of the really alien planets.*"

"*I might almost prefer that. There would be a hostile*

environment to think about. One could forget how far it is to home."

"Three years' travel."

"You say that so glibly. As if three shipboard years were not equal to fifty in cosmic time. As if we could expect a relief vessel daily, not once in a century. And . . . as if the region that our ships have explored amounts to one chip out of this one galaxy!"

"That region will grow until someday it engulfs the galaxy."

"Yes, yes, yes. I know. Why do you think I chose to become a psychodynamician? Why am I here, learning how to meddle with the destiny of a world where I do not belong? 'To create the union of sentient beings, each member species a step toward life's mastery of the universe.' Brave slogan! But in practice, it seems, only a chosen few races are to be allowed the freedom of that universe."

"Not so, Mwyr. Consider these ones with whom we are, as you say, meddling. Consider what use they made of nuclear energy when they had it. At the rate they are going, they will have it again within a century or two. Not long after that they will be building spaceships. Even granted that time lag attenuates the effects of interstellar contact, those effects are cumulative. So do you wish such a band of carnivores turned loose on the galaxy?

"No, let them become inwardly civilized first; then we shall see if they can be trusted. If not, they will at least be happy on their own planet, in a mode of life designed for them by the Great Science. Remember, they have an immemorial aspiration toward peace on earth; but that is something they will never achieve by themselves. I do not pretend to be a very good person, Mwyr. Yet this work that we are doing makes me feel not altogether useless in the cosmos."

Promotion was fast that year, casualties being so high. Captain Thomas Danielis was raised to major for his conspicuous part in putting down the revolt of the Los Angeles citymen. Soon after occurred the Battle of Maricopa, when the loyalists failed bloodily to break the stranglehold of the Sierran rebels on the San Joaquin Valley, and he was brevetted lieutenant colonel. The army was ordered northward and moved warily under the coast ranges, half expecting attack from the east. But the Brodskyites seemed too busy consolidating their latest gains. The trouble came from guerrillas and the hedgehog resistance of bossman Stations. After one particularly stiff clash, they stopped near Pinnacles for a breather.

Danielis made his way through camp, where tents stood in tight rows between the guns and men lay about dozing, talking, gambling, staring at the blank blue sky. The air was hot, pungent with cookfire smoke, horses, mules, dung, sweat, boot oil; the green of the hills that lifted around the site was dulling toward summer brown. He was idle until time for the conference the general had called, but restlessness drove him. *By now I'm a father,* he thought, *and I've never seen my kid.*

At that, I'm lucky, he reminded himself. *I've got my life and limbs.* He remembered Jacobsen dying in his arms at Maricopa. You wouldn't have thought the human body could hold so much blood. Though maybe one was no longer human, when the pain was so great that one could do nothing but shriek until the darkness came.

And I used to think war was glamorous. Hunger, thirst, exhaustion, terror, mutilation, death, and forever the sameness, boredom grinding you down to an ox. . . . I've had it. I'm going into business after the war. Economic integration, as the bossman system breaks up, yes, there'll be a lot of ways for a man to get ahead, but decently, without a weapon in his hand— Danielis realized he was repeating thoughts that were months old. What the hell else was there to think about, though?

The large tent where prisoners were interrogated lay near his path. A couple of privates were conducting a man inside. The fellow was blond, burly, and sullen. He wore a sergeant's stripes, but otherwise his only item of uniform was the badge of Warden Echevarry, bossman in this part of the coastal mountains. A lumberjack in peacetime, Danielis guessed from the look of him; a soldier in a private army whenever the interests of Echevarry were threatened; captured in yesterday's engagement.

On impulse, Danielis followed. He got into the tent as

Captain Lambert, chubby behind a portable desk, finished the preliminaries, and blinked in the sudden gloom.

"Oh." The intelligence officer started to rise. "Yes, sir?"

"At ease," Danielis said. "Just thought I'd listen in."

"Well, I'll try to put on a good show for you." Lambert reseated himself and looked at the prisoner, who stood with hunched shoulders and widespread legs between his guards. "Now, sergeant, we'd like to know a few things."

"I don't have to say nothing except name, rank, and home town," the man growled. "You got those."

"Um-m-m, that's questionable. You aren't a foreign soldier, you're in rebellion against the government of your own country."

"The hell I am! I'm an Echevarry man."

"So what?"

"So my Judge is whoever Echevarry says. He says Brodsky. That makes you the rebel."

"The law's been changed."

"Your mucking Fallon got no right to change any laws. Especially part of the Constitution. I'm no hillrunner, Captain. I went to school some. And every year our Warden reads his people the Constitution."

"Times have changed since it was drawn," Lambert said. His tone sharpened. "But I'm not going to argue with you. How many riflemen and how many archers in your company?"

Silence.

"We can make things a lot easier for you," Lambert said. "I'm not asking you to do anything treasonable. All I want is to confirm some information I've already got."

The man shook his head angrily.

Lambert gestured. One of the privates stepped behind the captive, took his arm, and twisted a little.

"Echevarry wouldn't do that to me," he said through white lips.

"Of course not," Lambert said. "You're his man."

"Think I wanna be just a number on some list in Frisco? Damn right I'm my bossman's man!"

Lambert gestured again. The private twisted harder.

"Hold on, there," Danielis barked. "Stop that!"

The private let go, looking surprised. The prisoner drew a sobbing breath.

"I'm amazed at you, Captain Lambert," Danielis said. He felt his own face reddening. "If this has been your usual practice, there's going to be a court-martial."

"No, sir," Lambert said in a small voice. "Honest. Only . . . they don't talk. Hardly any of them. What'm I supposed to do?"

"Follow the rules of war."

"With rebels?"

"Take that man away," Danielis ordered. The privates made haste to do so.

"Sorry, sir," Lambert muttered. "I guess . . . I guess I've lost too many buddies. I hate to lose more, simply for lack of information."

"Me too." A compassion rose in Danielis. He sat down on the table edge and began to roll a cigarette. "But you see, we aren't in a regular war. And so, by a curious paradox, we have to follow the conventions more carefully than ever before."

"I don't quite understand, sir."

Danielis finished the cigarette and gave it to Lambert: olive branch or something. He started another for himself. "The rebels aren't rebels by their own lights," he said. "They're being loyal to a tradition that we're trying to curb, eventually to destroy. Let's face it, the average bossman is a fairly good leader. He may be descended from some thug who grabbed power by strong-arm methods during the chaos, but by now his family's integrated itself with the region he rules. He knows it, and its people, inside out. He's there in the flesh, a symbol of the community and its achievements, its folkways and essential independence. If you're in trouble, you don't have to work through some impersonal bureaucracy, you go direct to your bossman. His duties are as clearly defined as your own, and a good deal more demanding, to balance his privileges. He leads you in battle and in the ceremonies that give color and meaning to life. Your fathers and his have worked and played together for two or three hundred years. The land is alive with the memories of them. You and he *belong*.

"Well, that has to be swept away, so we can go on to a higher level. But we won't reach that level by alienating everyone. We're not a conquering army; we're more like the Householder Guard putting down a riot in some city. The opposition is part and parcel of our own society."

Lambert struck a match for him. He inhaled and finished: "On a practical plane, I might also remind you, Captain, that the federal armed forces, Fallonite and Brodskyite together, are none too large. Little more than a cadre, in fact. We're a bunch of younger sons, countrymen who failed, poor citymen, adventurers, people who look to their regiment for that sense of wholeness they've grown up to expect and can't find in civilian life."

"You're too deep for me, sir, I'm afraid," Lambert said.

"Never mind," Danielis sighed. "Just bear in mind, there are a good many more fighting men outside the opposing armies than in. If the bossmen could establish a unified command, that'd be the end of the Fallon government. Luckily, there's too much provincial pride and too much geography between them for this to happen—unless we outrage them beyond endurance. What we want the ordinary freeholder, and even the ordinary bossman, to think, is: 'Well, those Fallonites aren't such bad guys, and if I keep on the right side of them I don't stand to lose much, and should even be able to gain something at the expense of those who fight them to a finish.' You see?"

"Y-yes. I guess so."

"You're a smart fellow, Lambert. You don't have to beat information out of prisoners. Trick it out."

"I'll try, sir."

"Good." Danielis glanced at the watch that had been given him as per tradition, together with a sidearm, when he was first commissioned. (Such items were much too expensive for the common man. They had not been so in the age of mass production; and perhaps in the coming age—) "I have to go. See you around."

He left the tent feeling somewhat more cheerful than before. *No doubt I am a natural-born preacher,* he admitted, *and I never could quite join in the horseplay at mess, and a lot of jokes go completely by me; but if I can get even a few ideas across where they count, that's pleasure enough.* A strain of music came to him, some men and a banjo under a tree, and he found himself whistling along. It was good that this much morale remained, after Maricopa and a northward march whose purpose had not been divulged to anybody.

The conference tent was big enough to be called a pavilion. Two sentries stood at the entrance. Danielis was nearly the last to arrive, and found himself at the end of the table, opposite Brigadier General Perez. Smoke hazed the air and there was a muted buzz of conversation, but faces were taut.

When the blue-robed figure with a Yang and Yin on the breast entered, silence fell like a curtain. Danielis was astonished to recognize Philosopher Woodworth. He'd last seen the man in Los Angeles, and assumed he would stay at the Esper center there. Must have come here by special conveyance, under special orders. . . .

Perez introduced him. Both remained standing, under the eyes of the officers. "I have some important news for you, gentlemen," Perez said most quietly. "You may consider it an honor to be here. It means that in my judgment you can be trusted, first, to keep absolute silence about what you are going to hear, and second, to execute a vital operation of extreme difficulty." Danielis was made shockingly aware that several men were not present whose rank indicated they should be.

"I repeat," Perez said, "any breach of secrecy and the whole plan is ruined. In that case, the war will drag on for months or years. You know how bad our position is. You also know it will grow still worse as our stocks of those supplies the enemy now denies us are consumed. We could even be beaten. I'm not defeatist to say that, only realistic. We could lose the war.

"On the other hand, if this new scheme pans out, we may break the enemy's back this very month."

He paused to let that sink in before continuing:

"The plan was worked out by GHQ in conjunction with Esper Central in San Francisco some weeks ago. It's the reason we are headed north—" He let the gasp subside that ran through the stifling air. "Yes, you know that the Esper Order is neutral in political disputes. But you also know that it defends itself when attacked. And you probably know that an attack was made on it by the rebels. They seized the Napa Valley settlement and have been spreading malicious rumors about the Order since then. Would you like to comment on that, Philosopher Woodworth?"

The man in blue nodded and said coolly: "We've our own ways of findin' out things—intelligence service, you might say—so I can give y'all a report of the facts. St. Helena was assaulted at a time when most of its adepts were away, helpin' a new community get started out in Montana." *How did they travel so fast?* Danielis wondered. *Teleport, or what?* "I don't know, myself, if the enemy knew about that or were just lucky. Anyhow, when the two or three adepts that were left came and warned them off, fightin' broke out and the adepts were killed before they could act." He smiled. "We don't claim to be immortal, except the way every livin' thing is immortal. Nor infallible, either. So now St. Helena's occupied. We don't figure to take any immediate steps about that, because a lot of people in the community might get hurt.

"As for the yarns the enemy command's been handin' out, well, I reckon I'd do the same, if I had a chance like that. Everybody knows an adept can do things that nobody else can. Troops that realize they've done wrong to the Order are goin' to be scared of supernatural revenge. You're educated men here, and know there's nothin' supernatural involved, just a way to use the powers latent in most of us. You also know the Order doesn't believe in revenge. But the ordinary foot soldier doesn't think your way. His officers have got to restore his spirit somehow. So they fake some equipment and tell him that's what the adepts were really usin'—an advanced technology, sure, but only a set of machines that can be put out of action if you're brave, same as any other machine. That's what happened.

"Still, it is a threat to the Order; and we can't let an attack on our people go unpunished, either. So Esper Central has decided to help out your side. The sooner this war's over, the better for everybody."

A sigh gusted around the table, and a few exultant oaths. The hair stirred on Danielis' neck. Perez lifted a hand.

"Not too fast, please," the general said. "The adepts are not going to go around blasting your opponents for you. It was one hell of a tough decision for them to do as much as they agreed to. I, uh, understand that the, uh, personal development of every Esper will be set back many years by this much violence. They're making a big sacrifice.

"By their charter, they can use psionics to defend an establishment against attack. Okay . . . an assault on San Francisco will be construed as one on Central, their world headquarters."

The realization of what was to come was blinding to Danielis. He scarcely heard Perez' carefully dry continuation:

"Let's review the strategic picture. By now the enemy holds more than half of California, all of Oregon and Idaho, and a good deal of Washington. We, this army, we're using the last land access to San Francisco that we've got. The enemy hasn't tried to pinch that off yet, because the troops we pulled out of the north—those that aren't in the field at present—make a strong city garrison that'd sally out. He's collecting too much profit elsewhere to accept the cost.

"Nor can he invest the city with any hope of success. We still hold Puget Sound and the southern California ports. Our ships bring in ample food and munitions. His own sea power is much inferior to ours: chiefly schooners donated by coastal bossmen, operating out of Portland. He might overwhelm an occasional convoy, but he hasn't tried that so far because it isn't worth his trouble; there would be others, more heavily escorted. And of course he can't enter the Bay, with artillery and rocket emplacements on both sides of the Golden Gate. No, about all he can do is maintain some water communication with Hawaii and Alaska.

"Nevertheless, his ultimate object is San Francisco. It has to be—the seat of government and industry, the heart of the nation.

"Well, then, here's the plan. Our army is to engage the Sierra Command and its militia auxiliaries again, striking out of San Jose. That's a perfectly logical maneuver. Successful, it would cut his California forces in two. We know, in fact, that he is already concentrating men in anticipation of precisely such an attempt.

"We aren't going to succeed. We'll give him a good stiff battle and be thrown back. That's the hardest part: to feign a serious defeat, even convincing our own troops, and still maintain good order. We'll have a lot of details to thresh out about that.

"We'll retreat northward, up the Peninsula toward Frisco. The enemy is bound to pursue. It will look like a God-given chance to destroy us and get to the city walls.

"When he is well into the Peninsula, with the ocean on his left and the Bay on his right, we will outflank him and attack from the rear. The Esper adepts will be there to help. Suddenly he'll be caught, between us and the capital's land defenses. What the adepts don't wipe out, we will. Nothing will remain of the Sierra Command but a few garrisons. The rest of the war will be a mopping-up operation.

"It's a brilliant piece of strategy. Like all such, it's damn difficult to execute. Are you prepared to do the job?"

Danielis didn't raise his voice with the others. He was thinking too hard of Laura.

Northward and to the right there was some fighting. Cannon spoke occasionally, or a drumfire of rifles; smoke lay thin over the grass and the wind-gnarled live oaks which covered those hills. But down along the seacoast was only surf, blowing air, a hiss of sand across the dunes.

Mackenzie rode on the beach, where the footing was easiest and the view widest. Most of his regiment were inland. But that was a wilderness: rough ground, woods, the snags of ancient homes, making travel slow and hard. Once this area had been densely peopled, but the firestorm after the Hellbomb scrubbed it clean and today's reduced population could not make a go on such infertile soil. There didn't even seem to be any foemen near this left wing of the army.

The Rolling Stones had certainly not been given it for that reason. They could have borne the brunt at the center as well as those outfits which actually were there, driving the enemy back toward San Francisco. They had been bloodied often enough in this war, when they operated out of Calistoga to help expel the Fallonites from northern California. So thoroughly had that job been done that now only a skeleton force need remain in charge. Nearly the whole Sierra Command had gathered at Modesto, met the northward-moving opposition army that struck at them out of San Jose, and sent it in a shooting retreat. Another day or so, and the white city should appear before their eyes.

And there the enemy will be sure to make a stand, Mackenzie thought, *with the garrison to reinforce him. And his positions will have to be shelled; maybe we'll have to take the place street by street. Laura, kid, will you be alive at the end?*

Of course, maybe it won't happen that way. Maybe my scheme'll work and we'll win easy— What a horrible word "maybe" *is!* He slapped his hands together with a pistol sound.

Speyer threw him a glance. The major's people were safe; he'd even been able to visit them at Mount Lassen, after the northern campaign was over. "Rough," he said.

"Rough on everybody," Mackenzie said with a thick anger. "This is a filthy war."

Speyer shrugged. "No different from most, except that this time Pacificans are on the receiving as well as the giving end."

"You know damn well I never liked the business, anyplace."

"What man in his right mind does?"

"When I want a sermon I'll ask for one."

"Sorry," said Speyer, and meant it.

"I'm sorry, too," said Mackenzie, instantly contrite. "Nerves on edge. Damnation! I could almost wish for some action."

"Wouldn't be surprised if we got some. This whole affair smells wrong to me."

Mackenzie looked around him. On the right the horizon was bounded by hills, beyond which the low but massive San Bruno range lifted. Here and there he spied one of his own squads, afoot or ahorse. Overhead sputtered a plane. But there was plenty of concealment for a redoubt. Hell could erupt at any minute . . . though necessarily a small hell, quickly reduced by howitzer or bayonet, casualties light. (Huh! Every one of those light casualties was a man dead, with women and children to weep for him, or a man staring at the fragment of his arm, or a man with eyes and face gone in a burst of shot, and what kind of unsoldierly thoughts were these?)

Seeking comfort, Mackenzie glanced left. The ocean

rolled greenish-gray, glittering far out, rising and breaking in a roar of white combers closer to land. He smelled salt and kelp. A few gulls mewed above dazzling sands. There was no sail or smoke-puff—only emptiness. The convoys from Puget Sound to San Francisco and the lean swift ships of the coastal bossmen were miles beyond the curve of the world.

Which was as it should be. Maybe things were working out okay on the high waters. One could only try, and hope. And . . . it had been his suggestion, James Mackenzie speaking at the conference General Cruikshank held between the battles of Mariposa and San Jose; the same James Mackenzie who had first proposed that the Sierra Command come down out of the mountains, and who had exposed the gigantic fraud of Esperdom, and succeeded in playing down for his men the fact that behind the fraud lay a mystery one hardly dared think about. He would endure in the chronicles, that colonel, they would sing ballads about him for half a thousand years.

Only it didn't feel that way. James Mackenzie knew he was not much more than average bright under the best of conditions, now dull-minded with weariness and terrified of his daughter's fate. For himself he was haunted by the fear of certain crippling wounds. Often he had to drink himself to sleep. He was shaved, because an officer must maintain appearances, but realized very well that if he hadn't had an orderly to do the job for him he would be as shaggy as any buck private. His uniform was faded and threadbare, his body stank and itched, his mouth yearned for tobacco but there had been some trouble in the commissariat and they were lucky to eat. His achievements amounted to patchwork jobs carried out in utter confusion, or to slogging like this and wishing only for an end to the whole mess. One day, win or lose, his body would give out on him—he could feel the machinery wearing to pieces, arthritic twinges, shortness of breath, dozing off in the middle of things—and the termination of himself would be as undignified and lonely as that of every other human slob. Hero? What an all-time laugh!

He yanked his mind back to the immediate situation. Behind him a core of the regiment accompanied the artillery along the beach, a thousand men with motorized gun carriages, caissons, mule-drawn wagons, a few trucks, one precious armored car. They were a dun mass topped with helmets, in loose formation, rifles or bows to hand. The sand deadened their footfalls, so that only the surf and the wind could be heard. But whenever the wind sank, Mackenzie caught the tune of the hex corps: a dozen leathery older men, mostly Indians, carrying the wands of power and whistling together the Song Against Witches. He took no stock in magic himself, yet when that sound came to him the skin crawled along his backbone.

Everything's in good order, he insisted. *We're doing fine.*

Then: *But Phil's right. This is a screwball business. The enemy should have fought through to a southward line of retreat, nor let themselves be boxed.*

Captain Hulse galloped close. Sand spurted when he checked his horse. "Patrol report, sir."

"Well?" Mackenzie realized he had almost shouted. "Go ahead."

"Considerable activity observed about five miles northeast. Looks like a troop headed our way."

Mackenzie stiffened. "Haven't you anything more definite than that?"

"Not so far, with the ground so broken."

"Get some aerial reconnaissance there, for Pete's sake!"

"Yes, sir. I'll throw out more scouts, too."

"Carry on here, Phil." Mackenzie headed toward the radio truck. He carried a minicom in his saddlebag, of course, but San Francisco had been continuously jamming on all bands and you needed a powerful set to punch a signal even a few miles. Patrols must communicate by messenger.

He noticed that the firing inland had slacked off. There were decent roads in the interior Peninsula a ways further north, where some resettlement had taken place. The enemy, still in possession of that area, could use them to effect rapid movements.

If they withdrew their center and hit our flanks, where we're weakest—

A voice from field HQ, barely audible through the squeals and buzzes, took his report and gave back what had been seen elsewhere. Large maneuvers right and left, yes, it did seem as if the Fallonites were going to try a break-through. Could be a feint, though. The main body of the Sierrans must remain where it was until the situation became clearer. The Rolling Stones must hold out a while on their own.

"Will do." Mackenzie returned to the head of his columns. Speyer nodded grimly at the word.

"Better get prepared, hadn't we?"

"Uh-huh." Mackenzie lost himself in a welter of commands, as officer after officer rode to him. The outlying sections were to be pulled in. The beach was to be defended, with the high ground immediately above.

Men scurried, horses neighed, guns trundled about. The scout plane returned, flying low enough to get a transmission through: yes, definitely an attack on the way; hard to tell how big a force, through the damned tree cover and down in the damned arroyos, but it might well be at brigade strength.

Mackenzie established himself on a hilltop with his staff and runners. A line of artillery stretched beneath him, across the strand. Cavalry waited behind them, lances agleam, an infantry company for support. Otherwise the foot soldiers had faded into the landscape. The sea boomed its own cannonade, and gulls began to gather as if they knew there would be meat before long.

"Think we can hold them?" Speyer asked.

"Sure," Mackenzie said. "If they come down the beach, we'll enfilade them, as well as shooting up their front. If they come higher, well, that's a textbook example of defensible terrain. 'Course, if another troop punches through the lines further inland, we'll be cut off, but that isn't our worry right now."

"They must hope to get around our army and attack our rear."

"Guess so. Not too smart of them, though. We can approach Frisco just as easily fighting backwards as forwards."

"Unless the city garrison makes a sally."

"Even then. Total numerical strengths are about equal, and we've got more ammo and alky. Also a lot of bossman militia for auxiliaries, who're used to disorganized warfare in hilly ground."

"If we do whip them—" Speyer shut his lips together.

"Go on," Mackenzie said.

"Nothing."

"The hell it is. You were about to remind me of the next step: how do we take the city without too high a cost to both sides? Well, I happen to know we've got a hole card to play there, which might help."

Speyer turned pitying eyes away from Mackenzie. Silence fell on the hilltop.

It was an unconscionably long time before the enemy came in view, first a few outriders far down the dunes, then the body of him, pouring from the ridges and gullies and woods. Reports flickered about Mackenzie—a powerful force, nearly twice as big as ours, but with little artillery; by now badly short of fuel, they must depend far more than we on animals to move their equipment. They were evidently going to charge, accept losses in order to get sabers and bayonets among the Rolling Stones' cannon. Mackenzie issued his directions accordingly.

The hostiles formed up, a mile or so distant. Through his field glasses Mackenzie recognized them, red sashes of the Madera Horse, green and gold pennon of the Dagos, fluttering in the iodine wind. He'd campaigned with both outfits in the past. It was treacherous to remember that Ives favored a blunt wedge formation and use the fact against him. . . . One enemy armored car and some fieldpieces, light horsedrawn ones, gleamed wickedly in the sunlight.

Bugles blew shrill. The Fallonite cavalry laid lance in rest and started trotting. They gathered speed as they went, a canter, a gallop, until the earth trembled with them. Then their infantry got going, flanked by its guns. The car rolled along between the first and second line of foot. Oddly, it had no rocket launcher on top or repeater barrels thrust from the fire slits. Those were good troops, Mackenzie thought, advancing in close order with that ripple down the ranks which bespoke veterans. He hated what must happen.

His defense waited immobile on the sand. Fire crackled from the hillsides, where mortar squads and riflemen crouched. A rider toppled, a dogface clutched his belly and went to his knees, their companions behind moved forward to close the lines again. Mackenzie looked to his howitzers. Men stood tensed at sights and lanyards. Let the foe get well in range— There! Yamaguchi, mounted just rearward of the gunners, drew his saber and flashed the blade downward. Cannon bellowed. Fire spurted through smoke, sand gouted up, shrapnel sleeted over the charging force. At once the gun crews fell into the rhythm of reloading, relaying, refiring, the steady three rounds per minute which conserved barrels and broke armies. Horses screamed in their own tangled red guts. But not many had been hit. The Madera cavalry continued in full gallop. Their lead was so close now that Mackenzie's glasses picked out a face, red, freckled, a ranch boy turned trooper, his mouth stretched out of shape as he yelled.

The archers behind the defending cannon let go. Arrows whistled skyward, flight after flight, curved past the gulls and down again. Flame and smoke ran ragged in the wiry hill grass, out of the ragged-leaved live oak copses. Men pitched to the sand, many still hideously astir, like insects that had been stepped on. The fieldpieces on the enemy left flank halted, swiveled about, and spat return fire. Futile . . . but God, their officer had courage! Mackenzie saw the advancing lines waver. An attack by his own horse and foot, down the beach, ought to crumple them. "Get ready to move," he said into his minicom. He saw his men poise. The cannon belched anew.

The oncoming armored car slowed to a halt. Something within it chattered, loud enough to hear through the explosions.

A blue-white sheet ran over the nearest hill. Mackenzie shut half-blinded eyes. When he opened them again, he saw a grass fire through the crazy patterns of after-image. A Rolling Stone burst from cover, howling, his clothes ablaze. The man hit the sand and rolled over. That part of the beach lifted in one monster wave, crested twenty feet high, and smashed across the hill. The burning soldier vanished in the avalanche that buried his comrades.

"Psi blast!" someone screamed, thin and horrible, through chaos and ground-shudder. "The Espers—"

Unbelievably, a bugle sounded and the Sierran cavalry lunged forward. Past their own guns, on against the scattering opposition . . . and horses and riders rose into the air, tumbled in a giant's invisible whirligig, crashed bone-breakingly to earth again. The second rank of lancers broke. Mounts reared, pawed the air, wheeled and fled in every direction.

A terrible deep hum filled the sky. Mackenzie saw the world as if through a haze, as if his brain were being dashed back and forth between the walls of his skull. Another glare ran across the hills, higher this time, burning men alive.

"They'll wipe us out," Speyer called, a dim voice that rose and fell on the air tides. "They'll re-form as we stampede—"

"No!" Mackenzie shouted. "The adepts must be in that car. Come on!"

Most of his horse had recoiled on their own artillery, one squealing, trampling wreck. The infantry stood rigid, but about to bolt. A glance thrown to his right showed Mackenzie how the enemy themselves were in confusion, this had been a terrifying surprise to them too, but as soon as they got over the shock they'd advance and there'd be nothing left to stop them. . . . It was as if another man spurred his mount. The animal fought, foam-flecked with panic. He slugged its head around, brutally, and dug in spurs. They rushed down the hill toward the guns.

He needed all his strength to halt the gelding before the cannon mouths. A man slumped dead by his piece, though there was no mark on him. Mackenzie jumped to the ground. His steed bolted.

He hadn't time to worry about that. Where was help? "Come here!" His yell was lost in the riot. But suddenly another man was beside him, Speyer, snatching up a shell and slamming it into the breach. Mackenzie squinted through the telescope, took a bearing by guess and feel. He could see the Esper car where it squatted among dead and hurt. At this distance it looked too small to have blackened acres.

Speyer helped him lay the howitzer. He jerked the lanyard. The gun roared and sprang. The shell burst a few yards short of target, sand spurted and metal fragments whined.

Speyer had the next one loaded. Mackenzie aimed and fired. Overshot this time, but not by much. The car rocked.

Concussion might have hurt the Espers inside; at least, the psi blasts had stopped. But it was necessary to strike before the foe got organized again.

He ran toward his own regimental car. The door gaped, the crew had fled. He threw himself into the driver's seat. Speyer clanged the door shut and stuck his face in the hood of the rocket-launcher periscope. Mackenzie raced the machine forward. The banner on its rooftop snapped in the wind.

Speyer aimed the launcher and pressed the firing button. The missile burned across intervening yards and exploded. The other car lurched on its wheels. A hole opened in its side.

If the boys will only rally and advance— Well, if they don't, I'm done for anyway. Mackenzie squealed to a stop, flung open the door and leaped out. Curled, blackened metal framed his entry. He wriggled through, into murk and stenches.

Two Espers lay there. The driver was dead, a chunk of steel through his breast. The other one, the adept, whimpered among his unhuman instruments. His face was hidden by blood. Mackenzie pitched the corpse on its side and pulled off the robe. He snatched a curving tube of metal and tumbled back out.

Speyer was still in the undamaged car, firing repeaters at those hostiles who ventured near. Mackenzie jumped onto the ladder of the disabled machine, climbed to its roof and stood erect. He waved the blue robe in one hand and the weapon he did not understand in the other. "Come on, you sons!" he shouted, tiny against the sea wind. "We've knocked 'em out for you! Want your breakfast in bed, too?"

One bullet buzzed past his ear. Nothing else. Most of the enemy, horse and foot, stayed frozen. In that immense stillness he could not tell if he heard surf or the blood in his own veins.

Then a bugle called. The hex corps whistled triumphantly; their tomtoms thuttered. A ragged line of his infantry began to move toward him. More followed. The cavalry joined them, man by man and unit by unit, on their flanks. Soldiers ran down the smoking hillsides.

Mackenzie sprang to sand again and into his car. "Let's get back," he told Speyer. "We got a battle to finish."

"Shut up!" Tom Danielis said.

Philosopher Woodworth stared at him. Fog swirled and dripped in the forest, hiding the land and the brigade, gray nothingness through which came a muffled noise of men and horses and wheels, an isolated and infinitely weary sound. The air was cold, and clothing hung heavy on the skin.

"Sir," protested Major Lescarbault. The eyes were wide and shocked in his gaunted face.

"I dare tell a ranking Esper to stop quacking about a subject of which he's totally ignorant?" Danielis answered. "Well, it's past time that somebody did."

Woodworth recovered his poise. "All I said, son, was that we should consolidate our adepts and strike the Brodskyite center," he reproved. "What's wrong with that?"

Danielis clenched his fists. "Nothing," he said, "except it invites a worse disaster than you've brought on us yet."

"A setback or two," Lescarbault argued. "They did rout us on the west, but we turned their flank here by the Bay."

"With the net result that their main body pivoted, attacked, and split us in half," Danielis snapped. "The Espers have been scant use since then . . . now the rebels know they need vehicles to transport their weapons, and can be killed. Artillery zeroes in on their positions, or bands of woodsmen hit and run, leaving them dead, or the enemy simply goes around any spot where they're known to be. We haven't got enough adepts!"

"That's why I proposed gettin' them in one group, too big to withstand," Woodworth said.

"And too cumbersome to be of any value," Danielis replied. He felt more than a little sickened, knowing how the Order had cheated him his whole life; yes, he thought, that was the real bitterness, not the fact that the adepts had failed to defeat the rebels—by failing, essentially, to break their spirit—but the fact that the adepts were only someone else's cat's paws and every gentle, earnest soul in every Esper community was only someone's dupe.

Wildly he wanted to return to Laura—there'd been no

chance thus far to see her—Laura and the kid, the last honest reality this fog-world had left him. He mastered himself and went on more evenly:

"The adepts, what few of them survive, will of course be helpful in defending San Francisco. An army free to move around in the field can deal with them, one way or another, but your . . . your weapons can repel an assault on the city walls. So that's where I'm going to take them."

Probably the best he could do. There was no word from the northern half of the loyalist army. Doubtless they'd withdrawn to the capital, suffering heavy losses en route. Radio jamming continued, hampering friendly and hostile communications alike. He had to take action, either retreat southward or fight his way through to the city. The latter course seemed wisest. He didn't believe that Laura had much to do with his choice.

"I'm no adept myself," Woodworth said. "I can't call them mind to mind."

"You mean you can't use their equivalent of radio," Danielis said brutally. "Well, you've got an adept in attendance. Have him pass the word."

Woodworth flinched. "I hope," he said, "I hope you understand this came as a surprise to me, too."

"Oh, yes, certainly, Philosopher," Lescarbault said unbidden.

Woodworth swallowed. "I still hold with the Way and the Order," he said harshly. "There's nothin' else I can do. Is there? The Grand Seeker has promised a full explanation when this is over." He shook his head. "Okay, son, I'll do what I can."

A certain compassion touched Danielis as the blue robe disappeared into the fog. He rapped his orders the more severely.

Slowly his command got going. He was with the Second Brigade; the rest were strewn over the Peninsula in the fragments into which the rebels had knocked them. He hoped the equally scattered adepts, joining him on his march through the San Bruno range, would guide some of those units to him. But most, wandering demoralized, were sure to surrender to the first rebels they came upon.

He rode near the front, on a muddy road that snaked over the highlands. His helmet was a monstrous weight.

The horse stumbled beneath him, exhausted by—how many days?—of march, countermarch, battle, skirmish, thin rations or none, heat and cold and fear, in an empty land. Poor beast, he'd see that it got proper treatment when they reached the city. That all those poor beasts behind him did, after trudging and fighting and trudging again until their eyes were filmed with fatigue.

There'll be chance enough for rest in San Francisco. We're impregnable there, walls and cannon and the Esper machines to landward, the sea that feeds us at our backs. We can recover our strength, regroup our forces, bring fresh troops down from Washington and up from the south by water. The war isn't decided yet . . . God help us . . .

I wonder if it will ever be.

And then, will Jimbo Mackenzie come to see us, sit by the fire and swap yarns about what we did? Or talk about something else, anything else? If not, that's too high a price for victory.

Maybe not too high a price for what we've learned, though. Strangers on this planet . . . what else could have forged those weapons? The adepts will talk if I myself have to torture them till they do. But Danielis remembered tales muttered in the fisher huts of his boyhood, after dark, when ghosts walked in old men's minds. Before the holocaust there had been legends about the stars, and the legends lived on. He didn't know if he would be able to look again at the night sky without a shiver.

This damned fog—

Hoofs thudded. Danielis half drew his sidearm. But the rider was a scout of his own, who raised a drenched sleeve in salute. "Colonel, an enemy force about ten miles ahead by road. Big."

So we'll have to fight now. "Do they seem aware of us?"

"No, sir. They're proceeding east along the ridge there."

"Probably figure to occupy the Candlestick Park ruins," Danielis murmured. His body was too tired for excitement. "Good stronghold, that. Very well, Corporal." He turned to Lescarbault and issued instructions.

The brigade formed itself in the formlessness. Patrols went out. Information began to flow back, and Danielis sketched a plan that ought to work. He didn't want to try for a decisive engagement, only brush the enemy aside and discourage them from pursuit. His men must be spared, as many as possible, for the city defense and the eventual counteroffensive.

Lescarbault came back. "Sir! The radio jamming's ended!"

"What?" Danielis blinked, not quite comprehending.

"Yes, sir. I've been using a minicom—" Lescarbault lifted the wrist on which his tiny transceiver was strapped— "for very short-range work, passing the battalion commanders their orders. The interference stopped a couple of minutes ago. Clear as daylight."

Danielis pulled the wrist toward his own mouth. "Hello, hello, radio wagon, this is the C.O. You read me?"

"Yes, sir," said the voice.

"They turned off the jammer in the city for a reason. Get me the open military band."

"Yes, sir." Pause, while men mumbled and water runneled unseen in the arroyos. A wraith smoked past Danielis' eyes. Drops coursed off his helmet and down his collar. The horse's mane hung sodden.

Like the scream of an insect:

"—here at once! Every unit in the field, get to San Francisco at once! We're under attack by sea!"

Danielis let go Lescarbault's arm. He stared into emptiness while the voice wailed on and forever on.

"—bombarding Potrero Point. Decks jammed with troops. They must figure to make a landing there—"

Danielis' mind raced ahead of the words. It was as if Esp were no lie, as if he scanned the beloved city himself and felt her wounds in his own flesh. There was no fog around the Gate, of course, or so detailed a description could not have been given. Well, probably some streamers of it rolled in under the rusted remnants of the bridge, themselves like snowbanks against blue-green water and brilliant sky. But most of the Bay stood open to the sun. On the opposite shore lifted the Eastbay hills, green with gardens and agleam with villas; and Marin shouldered heavenward across the strait, looking to the roofs and walls and heights that were San Francisco. The convoy had gone between the coast defenses that could have smashed it, an unusually large convoy and not on time: but still the familiar big-bellied hulls, white sails, occasional fuming

stacks, that kept the city fed. There had been an explanation about trouble with commerce raiders; and the fleet
was passed on into the Bay, where San Francisco had no
walls. Then the gun covers were taken off and the holds
vomited armed men.

*Yes, they did seize a convoy, those piratical schooners.
Used radio jamming of their own; together with ours, that
choked off any cry of warning. They threw our supplies
overboard and embarked the bossman militia. Some spy or
traitor gave them the recognition signals. Now the capital
lies open to them, her garrison stripped, hardly an adept
left in Esper Central, the Sierrans thrusting against her
southern gates, and Laura without me.*

"We're coming!" Danielis yelled. His brigade groaned
into speed behind him. They struck with a desperate
ferocity that carried them deep into enemy positions and
then stranded them in separated groups. It became knife
and saber in the fog. But Danielis, because he led the
charge, had already taken a grenade on his breast.

East and south, in the harbor district and at the wreck
of the Peninsula wall, there was still some fighting. As he
rode higher, Mackenzie saw how those parts were dimmed
by smoke, which the wind scattered to show rubble that
had been houses. The sound of firing drifted to him. But
otherwise the city shone untouched, roofs and white walls
in a web of streets, church spires raking the sky like masts,
Federal House on Nob Hill and the Watchtower on Telegraph Hill as he remembered them from childhood visits.
The Bay glittered insolently beautiful.

But he had no time for admiring the view, nor for
wondering where Laura huddled. The attack on Twin
Peaks must be swift, for surely Esper Central would defend itself.

On the avenue climbing the opposite side of those great
humps, Speyer led half the Rolling Stones. (Yamaguchi lay
dead on a pockmarked beach.) Mackenzie himself was
taking this side. Horses clopped along Portola, between
blankly shuttered mansions; guns trundled and creaked,
boots knocked on pavement, moccasins slithered, weapons
rattled, men breathed heavily and the hex corps whistled
against unknown demons. But silence overwhelmed the

noise, echoes trapped it and let it die. Mackenzie recollected nightmares when he fled down a corridor which had no end. *Even if they don't cut loose at us,* he thought bleakly, *we've got to seize their place before our nerve gives out.*

Twin Peaks Boulevard turned off Portola and wound steeply to the right. The houses ended; wild grasses alone covered the quasi-sacred hills, up to the tops where stood the buildings forbidden to all but adepts. Those two soaring, iridescent, fountainlike skyscrapers had been raised by night, within a matter of weeks. Something like a moan stirred at Mackenzie's back.

"Bugler, sound the advance. On the double!"

A child's jeering, the notes lifted and were lost. Sweat stung Mackenzie's eyes. If he failed and was killed, that didn't matter too much . . . after everything which had happened . . . but the regiment, the regiment—

Flame shot across the street, the color of hell. There went a hiss and a roar. The pavement lay trenched, molten, smoking and reeking. Mackenzie wrestled his horse to a standstill. *A warning only. But if they had enough adepts to handle us, would they bother trying to scare us off?* "Artillery, open fire!"

The field guns bellowed together, not only howitzers but motorized 75s taken along from Alemany Gate's emplacements. Shells went overhead with a locomotive sound. They burst on the walls above and the racket thundered back down the wind.

Mackenzie tensed himself for an Esper blast, but none came. Had they knocked out the final defensive post in their own first barrage? Smoke cleared from the heights and he saw that the colors which played in the tower were dead and that wounds gaped across loveliness, showing unbelievably thin framework. It was like seeing the bones of a woman murdered by his hand.

Quick, though! He issued a string of commands and led the horse and foot on. The battery stayed where it was, firing and firing with hysterical fury. The dry brown grass started to burn, as red-hot fragments scattered across the slope. Through mushroom bursts, Mackenzie saw the building crumble. Whole sheets of facing broke and fell to earth. The skeleton vibrated, took a direct hit and sang in metal agony, slumped and twisted apart.

What was that which stood within?

There were no separate rooms, no floors, nothing but girders, enigmatic machines, here and there a globe still aglow like a minor sun. The structure had enclosed something nearly as tall as itself, a finned and shining column, almost like a rocket shell but impossibly huge and fair.

Their spaceship, Mackenzie thought in the clamor. *Yes, of course, the ancients had begun making spaceships, and we always figured we would again someday. This, though—!*

The archers lifted a tribal screech. The riflemen and cavalry took it up, crazy, jubilant, the howl of a beast of prey. By Satan, we've whipped the stars themselves! As they burst onto the hillcrest, the shelling stopped, and their yells overrode the wind. Smoke was acrid as blood smell in their nostrils.

A few dead blue-robes could be seen in the debris. Some half-dozen survivors milled toward the ship. A bowman let fly. His arrow glanced off the landing gear but brought the Espers to a halt. Troopers poured over the shards to capture them.

Mackenzie reined in. Something that was not human lay crushed near a machine. Its blood was deep violet color. *When the people have seen this, that's the end of the Order.* He felt no triumph. At St. Helena he had come to appreciate how fundamentally good the believers were.

But this was no moment for regret, or for wondering how harsh the future would be with man taken entirely off the leash. The building on the other peak was still intact. He had to consolidate his position here, then help Phil if need be.

However, the minicom said, "Come on and join me, Jimbo. The fracas is over," before he had completed his task. As he rode alone toward Speyer's place, he saw a Pacific States flag flutter up the mast on that skyscraper's top.

Guards stood awed and nervous at the portal. Mackenzie dismounted and walked inside. The entry chamber was a soaring, shimmering fantasy of colors and arches, through which men moved troll-like. A corporal led him down a hall. Evidently this building had been used for quarters,

offices, storage, and less understandable purposes. . . .
There was a room whose door had been blown down with
dynamite. The fluid abstract murals were stilled, scarred,
and sooted. Four ragged troopers pointed guns at the two
beings whom Speyer was questioning.

One slumped at something that might answer to a desk.
The avian face was buried in seven-fingered hands and the
rudimentary wings quivered with sobs. *Are they able to
cry, then?* Mackenzie thought, astonished, and had a sudden wish to take the being in his arms and offer what
comfort he was able.

The other one stood erect in a robe of woven metal.
Great topaz eyes met Speyer's from a seven-foot height,
and the voice turned accented English into music.

"—a G-type star some fifty light-hears hence. It is barely
visible to the naked eye, though not in this hemisphere."

The major's fleshless, bristly countenance jutted forward
as if to peck. "When do you expect reinforcements?"

"There will be no other ship for almost a century, and it
will only bring personnel. We are isolated by space and
time; few can come to work here, to seek to build a bridge
of minds across that gulf—"

"Yeah," Speyer nodded prosaically. "The light-speed
limit. I thought so. If you're telling the truth."

The being shuddered. "Nothing is left for us but to
speak truth, and pray that you will understand and help.
Revenge, conquest, any form of mass violence is impossible when so much space and time lies between. Our labor
has been done in the mind and heart. It is not too late,
even now. The most crucial facts can still be kept hidden—
oh, listen to me, for the sake of your unborn!"

Speyer nodded to Mackenzie. "Everything okay?" he
said. "We got us a full bag here. About twenty left alive,
this fellow's the bossman. Seems like they're the only ones
on Earth."

"We guessed there couldn't be many," the colonel said.
His tone and his feelings were alike ashen. "When we
talked it over, you and me, and tried to figure what our
clues meant. They'd have to be few, or they'd've operated
more openly."

"Listen, listen," the being pleaded. "We came in love.
Our dream was to lead you—to make you lead yourselves—

toward peace, fulfillment. . . . Oh, yes, we would also gain, gain yet another race with whom we could someday converse as brothers. But there are many races in the universe. It was chiefly for your own tortured sakes that we wished to guide your future."

"That controlled history notion isn't original with you," Speyer grunted. "We've invented it for ourselves now and then on Earth. The last time it led to the Hellbombs. No, thanks!"

"But we *know!* The Great Science predicts with absolute certainty—"

"Predicted this?" Speyer waved a hand at the blackened room.

"There are fluctuations. We are too few to control so many savages in every detail. But do you not wish an end to war, to all your ancient sufferings? I offer you that for your help today."

"You succeeded in starting a pretty nasty war yourselves," Speyer said.

The being twisted its fingers together. "That was an error. The plan remains, the only way to lead your people toward peace. I, who have traveled between suns, will get down before your boots and beg you—"

"Stay put!" Speyer flung back. "If you'd come openly, like honest folk, you'd have found some to listen to you. Maybe enough, even. But no, your do-gooding had to be subtle and crafty. You knew what was right for us. We weren't entitled to any say in the matter. God in heaven, I've never heard anything so arrogant!"

The being lifted its head. "Do you tell children the whole truth?"

"As much as they're ready for."

"Your child-culture is not ready to hear these truths."

"Who qualified you to call us children—besides yourselves?"

"How do you know you are adult?"

"By trying adult jobs and finding out if I can handle them. Sure, we make some ghastly blunders, we humans. But they're our own. And we learn from them. You're the ones who won't learn, you and that damned psychological science you were bragging about, that wants to fit every living mind into the one frame it can understand.

"You wanted to re-establish the centralized state, didn't you? Did you ever stop to think that maybe feudalism is what suits man? Some one place to call our own, and belong to, and be part of; a community with traditions and honor; a chance for the individual to make decisions that count; a bulwark for liberty against the central overlords, who'll always want more and more power; a thousand different ways to live. We've always built supercountries, here on Earth, and we've always knocked them apart again. I think maybe the whole idea is wrong. And maybe this time we'll try something better. Why not a world of little states, too well rooted to dissolve in a nation, too small to do much harm—slowly rising above petty jealousies and spite, but keeping their identities—a thousand separate approaches to our problems. Maybe then we can solve a few of them . . . for ourselves!"

"You will never do so," the being said. "You will be torn in pieces all over again."

"That's what you think. I think otherwise. But whichever is right—and I bet this is too big a universe for either of us to predict—we'll have made a free choice on Earth. I'd rather be dead than domesticated.

"The people are going to learn about you as soon as Judge Brodsky's been reinstated. No, sooner. The regiment will hear today, the city tomorrow, just to make sure no one gets ideas about suppressing the truth again. By the time your next spaceship comes, we'll be ready for it: in our own way, whatever that is."

The being drew a fold of robe about its head. Speyer turned to Mackenzie. His face was wet. "Anything . . . you want to say . . . Jimbo?"

"No," Mackenzie mumbled. "Can't think of anything. Let's get our command organized here. I don't expect we'll have to fight any more, though. It seems to be about ended down there."

"Sure." Speyer drew an uneven breath. "The enemy troops elsewhere are bound to capitulate. They've got nothing left to fight for. We can start patching up pretty soon."

There was a house with a patio whose wall was covered by roses. The street outside had not yet come back to life, so that silence dwelt here under the yellow sunset. A maidservant showed Mackenzie through the back door and departed. He walked toward Laura, who sat on a bench beneath a willow. She watched him approach but did not rise. One hand rested on a cradle.

He stopped and knew not what to say. How thin she was!

Presently she told him, so low he could scarcely hear: "Tom's dead."

"Oh, no." Darkness came and went before his eyes.

"I learned the day before yesterday, when a few of his men straggled home. He was killed in the San Bruno."

Mackenzie did not dare join her, but his legs would not upbear him. He sat down on the flagstones and saw curious patterns in their arrangement. There was nothing else to look at.

Her voice ran on above him, toneless: "Was it worth it? Not only Tom, but so many others, killed for a point of politics?"

"More than that was at stake," he said.

"Yes, I heard on the radio. I still can't understand how it was worth it. I've tried very hard, but I can't."

He had no strength left to defend himself. "Maybe you're right, duck. I wouldn't know."

"I'm not sorry for myself," she said. "I still have Jimmy. But Tom was cheated out of so much."

He realized all at once that there was a baby, and he ought to take his grandchild to him and think thoughts about life going on into the future. But he was too empty.

"Tom wanted him named after you," she said.

Did you, Laura? he wondered. Aloud: "What are you going to do now?"

"I'll find something."

He made himself glance at her. The sunset burned on the willow leaves above and on her face, which was now turned toward the infant he could not see. "Come back to Nakamura," he said.

"No. Anywhere else."

"You always loved the mountains," he groped. "We—"

"No." She met his eyes. "It isn't you, Dad. Never you. But Jimmy is not going to grow up a soldier." She hesitated. "I'm sure some of the Espers will keep going, on a new basis, but with the same goals. I think we should join them. He ought to believe in something different from what killed his father, and work for it to become real. Don't you agree?"

Mackenzie climbed to his feet against Earth's hard pull. "I don't know," he said. "Never was a thinker. . . . Can I see him?"

"Oh, Dad—"

He went over and looked down at the small sleeping form. "If you marry again," he said, "and have a daughter, would you call her for her mother?" He saw Laura's head bend downward and her hands clench. Quickly he said, "I'll go now. I'd like to visit you some more, tomorrow or sometime, if you'll have me."

Then she came to his arms and wept. He stroked her hair and murmured, as he had done when she was a child. "You do want to return to the mountains, don't you? They're your country, too, your people, where you belong."

"Y-you'll never know how much I want to."

"Then why not?" he cried.

His daughter straightened herself. "I can't," she said. "Your war is ended. Mine has just begun."

Because he had trained that will, he could only say, "I hope you win it."

"Perhaps in a thousand years—" She could not continue.

Night had fallen when he left her. Power was still out in the city, so the street lamps were dark and the stars stood forth above all roofs. The squad that waited to accompany their colonel to barracks looked wolfish by lantern light. They saluted him and rode at his back, rifles ready for trouble; but there was only the iron sound of horseshoes.

Introduction

Gene Wolfe

The would-be writer of short fiction can profit from reading the stories of almost any author, I believe. But there are two that he *must* read: Poe and Kipling. It was my good luck to encounter them both while still quite young; I attended Edgar Allen Poe Elementary School, where we tots were encouraged to read stories and poems of soul-wrenching morbidity. And my mother read me—again and again in response to my repeated demands—the *Just So Stories*. By the time that I was old enough for "The Murders in the Rue Morgue" (and I was old enough while still very small), I was also old enough for *The Jungle Book*. Their effect on a boy named Wolfe may easily be imagined. By the time I left Poe for junior high, I knew that Kipling was a social pariah; but it was too late by then, and anyway so was I.

I'm reading and rereading Kipling still, and I'm delighted to say that there are still a few of his tales that I have never read. One of the ten thousand things I learned from him was the timelessness of the East and the paranoia it can evoke in those from the West. Some thirty years after I learned it, it struck me that for a long while a man shot forward in time in the East might fail to understand what had happened to him. The result, "Continuing Westward," is given here.

Continuing Westward

GENE WOLFE

Continuing westward until nearly sundown we came to a village of stone huts. Earlier it had been very hot, even with the wind from the airscrew in our faces. The upper wing had provided a certain amount of shade for me, but Sanderson, my observer, had nothing but his leather flying helmet between his head and the sun, and I believe that by the time we halted he was near delirium. Every few miles he would lean forward, tap me on the shoulder, and ask, "Suppose the landing gear goes, too, eh? What then? What shall we do then?" and I would try to shout something reassuring over my shoulder as we jolted along, or swear at him.

Both the upper and lower wings had broken about midway on the left. The ends of them and what remained of the bamboo struts and silk trailed on the ground, the focal point of the long plume of dust we raised. I was afraid the dust might be seen by Turkish horse and wanted to get out and cut the wreckage away; but Sanderson argued against it, saying that when we halted it might be possible to effect some repairs. Every few miles one or the other of us would get out and try to tie it up onto the good sections, but it always worked loose again. By the time we reached the village there wasn't much left but rags and wires.

The sound of our engine had frightened the people away. We stopped in front of the largest of the huts and I drew my Webley and went up and down the village street looking into doors while Sanderson covered me with the swivel-mounted Lewis gun, but no one was there. A hundred yards off, camels tethered in the scrub watched us with haughty eyes while we found the village well and drank from big, unglazed jars. It was wonderful and we slopped it, letting the water run down our faces and soak our tunics. Then we sat on the coping and smoked until the people, in timorous twos and threes, began to come back.

The children came first, dirty, very unappealing children with sad silent faces and thin or bow-bellied bodies; the smaller children naked, the larger in garments like short nightshirts, grey with perspiration and dust.

Then the women. They wore black camel's-hair gowns that reached their ankles, yashmaks, and black head shawls. Between shawl and veil their eyes looked huge and very dark, but I noticed that many were blind, or blind in one eye. They didn't touch us as the children had, or try to talk to us. They pulled the children back, whispering; and when they spoke among themselves, standing in small groups twenty yards away and gesticulating with flashing brown arms, the sound was precisely that of sparrows quarreling in the street, heard from a window several stories high.

The men came last, all of them bearded, wearing grey or white or blue-dyed robes. They had daggers in their sashes, and although they never touched them we kept our hands on our revolvers. These men said nothing to us or to each other or the women, but stood around us in a half circle watching and, I thought, waiting. Only the children seemed really interested by our aircraft, and they were too much in awe to do more than stroke the hot cowling with the tips of their fingers. It came to me then that the scene was Old Testament biblical, and I suppose it was; people like this not changing much.

Eventually a man older than the rest came forward and began to talk to us. His beard was almost white, and he had a deep, solemn voice like an ambassador on a state occasion. I looked at Sanderson, who claims to parley-voo wog, but he was as out of it as I. We waited until the old boy had finished, then pointed to our mouths and rubbed our bellies to show that we wanted something to eat.

It was mutton stewed in rice when we got it, everything flavored strongly with saffron and herbs. Not a dish that would have appealed under normal circumstances, but these were far from that, and for a time I dug in as heartily as Sanderson, sitting crosslegged and dipping the stuff up with my fingers.

The chief and two of his men sat across from us, trying to pretend that this was a normal social dinner. More of the men had tried to crowd in at the beginning, but Sanderson and I had discouraged that, cocking our revolvers and shouting at them until all but these had left. It had resulted, as they say, in a strained atmosphere; but there had been no help for it. At close quarters in the hut we couldn't have managed more than the three of them if they had decided to rush us with their knives.

When we had eaten all we could, a sweet was brought out, a sticky pink paste neither of us wanted. Then strong unsweetened coffee in brass cups, and the chief's daughter.

Or perhaps his granddaughter or the daughter of one of the other men. We had no way of really knowing; at any rate a young girl in linen trousers and vest, with her fingers and toes hennaed red-pink and her eyes heavily outlined by some black cosmetic. Her hair was braided and coiled high on her head, bound and twined with copper wire and little black discs like coins, and she wore more tinkling junk, hundreds of glass things like jelly beans, around her neck and wrists and on her fingers. She danced for us, jingling and swaying, while an older woman played the flute.

In cafés I'd seen that sort of thing done so often, and often so much better, that it was absurd that it should affect me as it did. Perhaps I can make it clear: think of a chap who's learned to swim, and done it often, in tiled natatoriums, seeing the sort of pool a clear brook makes under a willow. Better: a dog raised on butcher's meat feels his jaws snap the first time on his own rabbit. I glanced at Sanderson and saw that, stuffed as he was with rice and mutton (the man has eaten like a pig ever since I've known him and is a joke in our mess), he felt the same way. Once she bent backward and put her head in my lap the way they do, which gave me a really good look at her; she was a choice piece right enough, but there was one thing I must say gave me a bit of a turn. The little black thingummies I'd thought were coins were really electric dohickies of some sort, though you could see the wires had been twisted together and nothing worked anymore. Even the glass jelly beans had wires in them. I suppose these wogs must have stolen radios or some such from the Turks and torn them up to make jewelry. Then she laid her head in Sanderson's lap, and looking at him I knew he'd go along.

They had pitched a tent for us near the plane, and after we had taken her out there the two of us discussed in a friendly way what was to be done. In the end we matched out for her. Sanderson won and I lay down with my Webley in my hand to watch the door of the tent.

In a way I was glad to be second—happy, you know, for a bit of a rest first. It had been bloody early in the morning when we'd landed to dynamite the Turkish power line, and I kept recalling how the whole great thing had flashed up in our faces while we were still setting the charge. It seemed such a devil of a long time ago, and after that taxiing across the desert dragging the smashed wings while mirages flitted about—a good half million years of that, if the time inside one's head means anything . . .

Mustn't sleep, though. Sit up. Now her.

She had taken off her veil when we had brought her in. I kept remembering that, knowing that no act however rash or lewd performed by an Englishwoman could have quite the same meaning that that did for her. She had reached up with a kind of last-gasp panache and unfastened one side of it like a man before a firing squad throwing aside his blindfold—a girl of perhaps fifteen with a high-bridged nose and high cheekbones.

I had thought then that she would merely submit unless (or until) something broke through that hawk-face reserve. Sitting there listening to her with Sanderson, I knew I had been wrong. They were whispering endearments though neither could understand the other, and there was a sensuous sound to the jingle of the glass beans and little disks that made it easy to imagine her hands stroking an accompaniment to words she scarcely breathed. It seemed incredible that Sanderson had not removed the rubbish when he undressed her but he had not. After a time I felt

I could distinguish the locations from which those tiny chimings came: the fingers and wrists, the ankles, the belt over the hips loudest of all.

It reached a crescendo, a steady ringing urgent as a cry for help, and over it I could hear Sanderson's harsh breathing. Then it was over and I waited for her to come to me, but she did not.

Just as I was about to call out or go over and take hold of her they began again. I couldn't make out what Sanderson was saying—something about loving forever—but I could hear his voice and hers, and I heard the ringing begin again. Outside, the moon rose and sent cold white light through the door.

They were longer this time; and the pause, too, was longer; but at last they began the third. I tried to stare through the blackness in the tent, but I could see nothing except when a wire or one of the glass beans flashed in the inky shadow. Then there was the insistent jingling again, louder and louder. At last Sanderson gave a sort of gasp, and I heard a rustle as he rolled away from her.

Half a minute and the jingling began again as she stood up; her feet made soft noises on the matting walking over to where I lay. She spoke, and although I could not understand the words the meaning was clear enough: "Now you." I holstered my revolver and pulled her down to me. She came willingly enough, sinking to a sitting posture and then, gradually it seemed to me, though I could not see her, lying at full length.

I ran my hands over her. In the half minute between Sanderson's gasp and the present I had come to understand what had happened; the only question that remained was the hiding place of her weapon. I stroked her, pretending to make love to her. Under the arms—no. Strapped to the calf—no. She hissed with pleasure, a soft exhalation.

Then it came to me. There is almost no place where a man will not put his hands when he takes a woman; but there is one, and thus this girl had been able to kill Sanderson after lying with him half the night.

A man will touch a woman's legs and arms everywhere, caress her body, kiss her lips and eyes and cheeks and ears. But he will not, if she is elaborately coifed, put his hands in her hair. And if he attempts to, she may stop him without arousing his suspicions.

She cried out, then bit my hand, as I tore away the disk-threaded wires, but I found it—a knife not much larger than a penknife yet big enough to open the jugular. I knew what I was going to do.

I threw the knife aside and used the wires to tie her, first stuffing my handkerchief in her mouth as a gag. Then with my revolver in my hand I stepped out into the village street, looking around in the moonlight. I could see no one, but I knew they were there, watching and waiting for her signal. They would be too late.

Back in the tent I picked her up in my arms, drew a deep breath, then burst out sprinting for the aircraft. Even with her arms and legs bound she fought as best she could, but I stuffed her into Sanderson's place. They would be after us in moments, but I squandered a few seconds on the compass, striking a lucifer to look at it though it was hopelessly dotty as usual, having crawled thirty degrees at least away from the north star. The engine coughed, then caught, as I spun the airscrew; and before the aircraft could build up speed I had jumped onto the wing and vaulted into the cockpit. The roar of the exhaust shook the little village now. We rolled forward faster and faster and I felt the tail come up.

I knew she couldn't understand me, but I turned back to the girl shouting, "We'll do it! We'll find something tomorrow, bamboo or something, and repair the wing! We'll get back!"

Sanderson was running after us in his underclothes, so I had been wrong, but I didn't care. I had her and the aircraft, racing across the desert while meteors miles ahead shot upward into the sky. "We'll do it," I called back. "We'll fly!" Her eyes said she understood.

Soldiers' Stories

David Drake

I became a Kipling fan at age thirteen.

Which is not to say that I hadn't been introduced to him earlier. I grew up in a house with a lot of books in it. (I don't say ". . . a house full of books . . ." because my own house is now, as John Kessel once put it, "decorated in Early Literary.") Still, my parents had (and read) a lot of books, and one of them was *The Jungle Book*.

I read and re-read *The Jungle Book* . . . but then, I read and re-read *Bob, Son of Battle, Black Beauty*, and goodness knows what all else, courtesy of the children's rooms of public libraries and various school collections. The Mowgli stories and "The White Seal" were okay; "Rikki-Tikki-Tavi" was great; and I didn't understand "Her Majesty's Servants," though I certainly didn't forget it the way I did "Toomai of the Elephants."

Thereafter, I read a few of the *Just So Stories*, but they didn't make any particular impression. "How the Rhinoceros Got Its Skin" was in a school text. I'm quite sure if I went back over the story, I'd learn that I'd been misinformed as badly on the subject of Parsees as I was regarding the behavior of cobras and mongooses. I could have very easily passed into adulthood without a proper appreciation of, and grounding in, the work of Kipling.

I got my card to the adult section of the public library when I became thirteen, and began to devour SF. I can't claim any more discrimination than I'd shown earlier with animal stories. If it was marked SF, I read it. And I mostly liked it, even *Hawk of the Spaceways* by "Anthony Gilmore."

Still, some writers were better than others, and Poul Anderson stood high on my list. When a new Anderson, *The Enemy Stars*, appeared, I read it at once.

And there at the end was a stanza of poetry: "We have fed our sea for a thousand years. . . ."

At once to Bartlett's *Familiar Quotations* to find the source; and then to the poetry shelves, to find Rudyard Kipling. That first fragment had struck a chord; and oh, my, what chords and crescendoes some of the other verse struck.

I'm not fit to judge Kipling as a poet; but I do not recognize a better storyteller in English, and it was as a storyteller in verse that I grew to love him.

In general, Kipling's most effective verse is really a sketch of the narrator. He put in verse the attitudes of a lot of people—workmen and matelots and most particularly common soldiers—who couldn't themselves speak in a socially-acceptable idiom.

There weren't any kings or generals where I grew up, but there were men who worked in factories, men who farmed; and men—often the same men—who'd sweated their way through the jungles of New Guinea with a rifle and a pack heavier than even they could believe, now that it was over. Kipling had known the sort of people *I* knew; and when they spoke through his words, they described themselves much better than an outsider could have done— had an outsider cared.

Kipling's taken a lot of flak, in his own day and later for his glorification of war. Without getting into the question of what Kipling's own beliefs on the subject were, the attitudes portrayed in his verse are those of the men to whom he talked. These men served in the professional army of the largest empire in history. They'd seen action in countless brushfire wars, all across the world.

If they hadn't liked their work, they'd have done something else. When they described themselves, they became very human; as of course they were, and as their brothers are, the men with whom *I* served.

That's disturbing to people who haven't been there themselves, and who really don't want to believe that a normal human being could do things so matter-of-factly brutal. "Loot," for instance: a veteran grousing not about battle but about burial detail afterwards—and explaining how to rob and torture civilians as well. And "Snarleyow."

Snarleyow is a gun horse who's wounded in action, and then driven over by the very crew who'd trained and cared for him. And after that happens. . . .

I read "Snarleyow" and thought I understood the poem. Then I went to 'Nam; and came back.

And not long after I came back, I wrote "Under the Hammer."

Under the Hammer

DAVID DRAKE

"Think you're going to like killing, boy?" asked the old man on double crutches.

Rob Jenne turned from the streams of moving cargo to his unnoticed companion in the shade of the starship's hull. His own eyes were pale gray, suited like his dead-white skin to Burlage, whose ruddy sun could raise a blush but not a tan. When they adjusted, they took in the clerical collar which completed the other's costume. The smooth, black synthetic contrasted oddly with the coveralls and shirt of local weave. At that, the Curwinite's outfit was a cut above Rob's own, the same worksuit of Burlage sisal that he had worn as a quarryhand at home. Uniform issue would come soon.

At least, he hoped and prayed it would.

When the youth looked away after an embarrassed grin, the priest chuckled. "Another damned old fool, hey, boy? There were a few in your family, weren't there . . . the ones who'd quote the Book of the Way saying not to kill—and here you go off for a hired murderer. Right?" He laughed again, seeing he had the younger man's attention. "But that by itself wouldn't be so hard to take—you were leaving your family anyway, weren't you, nobody really believes they'll keep close to their people after five years, ten years of star hopping. But your mates, though, the team you worked with . . . how did you explain to them why you were leaving a good job to go on contract? 'Via!' " the priest mimicked, his tones so close to those of Barney

Larsen, the gang boss, that Rob started in surprise, " 'you get your coppy ass shot off, lad, and it'll serve you right for being a fool!' "

"How do you know I signed for a mercenary?" Jenne asked, clenching his great, callused hands on the handle of his carry-all. It was everything he owned in the universe in which he no longer had a home. "And how'd you know about my Aunt Gudrun?"

"Haven't I seen a thousand of you?" the priest blazed back, his eyes like sparks glinting from the drill shaft as the sledge drove it deeper into the rock. "You're young and strong and bright enough to pass Alois Hammer's tests—you be proud of that, boy, few enough are fit for Hammer's Slammers. There you were, a man grown who'd read all the cop about mercenaries, believed most of it . . . more'n ever you did the Book of the Way, anyhow. Sure, I know. So you got some off-planet factor to send your papers in for you, for you, for the sake of the bounty he'll get from the colonel if you make the grade—"

The priest caught Rob's blink of surprise. He chuckled again, a cruel, unpriestly sound, and said, "He told you it was for friendship? One a these days you'll learn what friendship counts, when you get an order that means the death of a friend—and you carry it out."

Rob stared at the priest in repulsion, the grizzled chin resting on interlaced fingers and the crutches under either armpit supporting most of his weight. "It's my life," the recruit said with sulky defiance. "Soon as they pick me up here, you can go back to living your own. 'Less you'd be willing to do that right now?"

"They'll come soon enough, boy," the older man said in a milder voice. "Sure, you've been ridden by everybody you know . . . now that you're alone, here's a stranger riding you, too. I don't mean it like I sound . . . wasn't born to the work, I guess. There's priests—and maybe the better ones—who'd say that signing on with mercenaries means so long a spiral down that maybe your soul won't come out of it in another life or another hundred. But I don't see it like that.

"Life's a forge, boy, and the purest metal comes from the hottest fire. When you've been under the hammer a few times, you'll find you've been beaten down to the real, no lies, no excuses. There'll be a time, then, when you got to look over the product . . . and if you don't like what you see, well, maybe there's time for change, too."

The priest turned his head to scan the half of the horizon not blocked by the bellied-down bulk of the starship. Ant columns of stevedores manhandled cargo from the ship's rollerway into horse and oxdrawn wagons in the foreground: like most frontier worlds, Burlage included, self-powered machinery was rare in the backcountry. Beyond the men and draft animals stretched the fields, studded frequently by orange-golden clumps of native vegetation.

"Nobody knows how little his life's worth till he's put it on the line a couple times," the old man said. "For nothing. Look at it here on Curwin—the seaboard taxed these uplands into revolt, then had to spend what they'd robbed and more to hire an armored regiment. So boys like you from—Scania? Felsen?—"

"Burlage, sir."

"Sure, a quarryman, should have known from your shoulders. You come in to shoot farmers for a gang of coastal moneymen you don't know and wouldn't like if you did." The priest paused, less for effect than to heave in a quick, angry breath that threatened his shirt buttons. "And maybe you'll die, too; if the Slammers were immortal, they wouldn't need recruits. But some that die will die like saints, boy, die martyrs of the Way, for no reason, for no reason . . .

"Your ride's here, boy."

The suddenly emotionless words surprised Rob as much as a scream in a silent prayer would have. Hissing like a gun-studded dragon, a gray-metal combat car slid onto the landing field from the west. Light dust puffed from beneath it: although the flatbed trailer behind was supported on standard wheels, the armored vehicle itself hovered a hand's-breadth above the surface at all points. A dozen powerful fans on the underside of the car kept it floating on an invisible bubble of air, despite the weight of the fusion power unit and the iridium-ceramic armor. Rob had seen combat cars on the entertainment cube occasionally, but those skittering miniatures gave no hint of the awesome power that emanated in reality from the machines. This one was seven meters long and three wide at the base, the armored sides curving up like a turtle's back to the open fighting compartment in the rear.

From the hatch in front of the powerplant stuck the driver's head, a blank-mirrored ball in a helmet with full face shield down. Road dust drifted away from the man in a barely-visible haze, cleaned from the helmet's optics by a static charge. Faceless and terrible to the unfamiliar Burlager, the driver guided toward the starship a machine that appeared no more inhuman than did the man himself.

"Undercrewed," the priest murmured. "Two men on the back deck aren't enough for a car running single."

The older man's jargon was unfamiliar but Rob could follow his gist by looking at the vehicle. The two men standing above the waist-high armor of the rear compartment were clearly fewer than had been contemplated when the combat car was designed. Its visible armament comprised a heavy powergun forward to fire over the head of the driver, and similar weapons, also swivel-mounted, on either side to command the flanks and rear of the vehicle. But with only two men in the compartment there was a dangerous gap in the circle of fire the car could lay down if ambushed. Another vehicle for escort would have eased the danger, but this one was alone save for the trailer it pulled.

Though as the combat car drew closer, Rob began to wonder if the two soldiers present couldn't handle anything that occurred. Both were in full battle dress, wearing helmets and laminated back and breast armor over their khaki. Their faceplates were clipped open. The one at the forward gun, his eyes as deep-sunken and deadly as the three revolving barrels of his weapon, was in his forties and further aged by the dust sweated into black grime in the creases of his face. His head rotated in tiny jerks, taking in every nuance of the sullen crowd parting for his war-car. The other soldier was huge by comparison with the first and lounged across the back in feigned leisure: feigned, because either hand was within its breadth of a powergun's trigger, and his limbs were as controlled as spring steel.

With careless expertise, the driver backed his trailer up to the conveyor line. A delicate hand with the fans allowed him to angle them slightly, drifting the rear of the combat car to edge the trailer in the opposite direction. The larger soldier contemptuously thumbed a waiting horse and wagon out of its slot. The teamster's curse brought only a grin and a big hand rested on a powergun's receiver, less a threat than a promise. The combat car eased into the space.

"Wait for an old man," the priest said as Rob lifted his carry-all, "and I'll go with you." Glad even for that company, the recruit smiled nervously, fitting his stride to the other's surprisingly nimble swing-and-pause, swing-and-pause.

The driver dialed back minusculy on the power and allowed the big vehicle to settle to the ground without a skip or a tremor. One hand slid back the face shield to a high, narrow nose and eyes that alertly focused on the two men approaching. "The Lord and his martyrs!" the driver cried in amazement. "It's Blacky himself come in with our newbie!"

Both soldiers on the back deck slewed their eyes around at the cry. The smaller one took one glance, then leaped the two meters to the ground to clasp Rob's companion. "Hey!" he shouted, oblivious to the recruit shifting his weight uncertainly. "Via, it's good to see you! But what're you doing on Curwin?"

"I came back here afterwards," the older man answered with a smile. "Born here, I must've told you . . . though we didn't talk a lot. I'm a priest now, see?"

"And I'm a flirt like the load we're supposed to pick up," the driver said, dismounting with more care than his companion. Abreast of the first soldier, he too took in the round collar and halted gapemouthed. "Lord, I'll be a coppy rag if you ain't," he breathed. "Whoever heard of a blower chief taking the Way?"

"Shut up, Jake," the first soldier said without rancor. He stepped back from the priest to take a better look, then seemed to notice Rob. "Umm," he said, "you the recruit from Burlage?"

"Yessir. M-my name's Rob Jenne, sir."

"Not 'sir,' there's enough sirs around already," the veteran said. "I'm Chero, except if there's lots of brass around, then make it Sergeant-Commander Worzer. Look, take your gear back to the trailer and give Leon a hand with the load.

"Hey, Blacky," he continued with concern, ignoring Rob again, "what's wrong with your legs? We got the best there was."

"Oh, they're fine," Rob heard the old man reply, "but they need a weekly tuning. Out here we don't have the computers, you know; so I get the astrogation boys to sync me up on the ships' hardware whenever one docks in— just waiting for a chance now. But in six months the servos are far enough out of line that I have to shut off the power till the next ship arrives. You'd be surprised how well I get around on these pegs, though. . . ."

Leon, the huge third crew member, had loosed the top catches of his body armor for ventilation. From the look of it, the laminated casing should have been a size larger; but Rob wasn't sure anything larger was made. The gunner's skin where exposed was the dense black of a basalt outcropping. "They'll be a big crate to go on, so just set your gear down till we get it loaded," he said. Then he grinned at Rob, teeth square and slightly yellow against his face. "Think you can take me?"

That was a challenge the recruit could understand, the first he could meet fairly since boarding the starship with a one-way ticket to a planet he had never heard of. He took in the waiting veteran quickly but carefully, proud of his own rock-hardened muscles but certain the other man had been raised just as hard. "I give you best," the blond said. "Unless you feel you got to prove it?"

The grin broadened and a great black hand reached out to clasp Rob's. "Naw," the soldier said, "just like to clear the air at the start. Some of the big ones; Lord, testy ain't the word. All they can think about's what they want to prove with me . . . so they don't watch their side of the car, and then there's trouble for everybody."

"Hammer's Regiment?" called an unfamiliar voice. Both men looked up. Down the conveyor rode a blue-tunicked ship's man in front of what first appeared to be a huge crate. At second glance Rob saw that it was a cage of light alloy holding four . . . "Dear Lord!" the recruit gasped.

"Roger, Hammer's," Leon agreed, handing the crewman a plastic chit while the latter cut power to the rollers to halt the cage. The chit slipped into the computer linkage on the crewman's left wrist, lighting a green indicator when it proved itself a genuine bill of lading.

There were four female humanoids in the cage—stark naked except for a dusting of fine blue scales. Rob blinked. One of the near-women stood with a smile—Lord, she had no teeth!—and rubbed her groin deliberately against one of the vertical bars.

"First quality Genefran flirts," Leon chuckled. "Ain't human, boy, but the next best thing."

"Better," threw in Jake, who had swung himself into the fighting compartment as soon as the cage arrived. "I tell you, kid, you never had it till you had a flirt. Surgically modified and psychologically prepared. Rowf!"

"N-not human?" Rob stumbled, unable to take his eyes off the cage, "you mean like *monkeys?*"

Leon's grin lit his face again, and the driver cackled, "Well, don't know about monkeys, but they're a whole lot like sheep."

"You take the left side and we'll get this aboard," Leon directed. The trailer's bed was half a meter below the rollerway so that the cage, though heavy and awkward, could be slid without much lifting.

Rob gripped the bars numbly, turning his face down from the tittering beside him. "Amazing what they can do with implants and a wig," Jake was going on, "though a course there's a lot of cutting to do first, but those ain't the differences you see, if you follow. The scales, now—they have a way—"

"Lift!" Leon ordered, and Rob straightened at the knees. They took two steps backward with the cage wobbling above them as the girls—the flirts!—squealed and hopped about. "Down!" and cage clashed on trailer as the two big men moved in unison.

Rob stepped back, his mouth working in distaste, unaware of the black soldier's new look of respect. Quarry work left a man used to awkward weights. "This is foul," the recruit marveled. "Are those really going back with us for, for . . ."

"Rest'n relaxation," Leon agreed, snapping tiedowns around the bars.

"But how . . ." Rob began, looking again at the cage. When the red-wigged flirt fondled her left breast upward, he could see the implant scars pale against the blue. The scales were more thinly spread where the skin had been stretched in molding it. "I'll *never* touch something like that. Look, maybe Burlage is pretty backward about . . . things, about sex, I don't know. But I don't see how anybody could . . . I mean—"

"Via, wait till you been here as long as we have," Jake gibed. He clenched his right hand and pumped it suggestively. "Field expedients, that's all."

"On this kinda contract," Leon explained, stepping around to get at the remaining tiedowns, "you can't trust the local girls. Least not in the field, like we are. The colonel likes to keep us patrol sections pretty much self-contained."

"Yeah," Jake broke in—would his cracked tenor never cease? "Why, some of these whores, they take a razor blade, see—in a cork you know?—and, well, never mind." He laughed, seeing Rob's face.

"Jake," Sergeant Worzer called, "shut up and hop in."

The driver slipped instantly into his hatch. Disgusting as Rob found the little man, he recognized his ability. Jake moved with lethal certainty and a speed that belied the weight of his body armor.

"Ready to lift, Chero?" he asked.

The priest was levering himself toward the starship again. Worzer watched him go for a moment, shook his head. "Just run us out to the edge of the field," he directed. "I got a few things to show our recruit before we head back; nobody rides in my car without knowing how to work the guns." With a sigh he hopped into the fighting compartment. Leon motioned Rob in front of him. Gingerly, the recruit stepped onto the trailer hitch, gripped the armored rim with both hands, lifted himself aboard. Leon followed. The trailer bonged as he pushed off from it, and his bulk cramped the littered compartment as soon as he grunted over the side.

"Put this on," Worzer ordered, handing Rob a dusty, bulbous helmet like the others wore. "Brought a battle suit for you, too," he said, kicking the jointed armor leaning against the back of the compartment, "but it'd no more fit you than it would Leon there."

The black laughed. "Gonna be tight back here till the kid or me gets zapped."

"Move 'er out," Worzer ordered. The words came through unsuspected earphones in Rob's helmet, although the sergeant had simply spoken, without visibly activating a pick up.

The car vibrated as the fans revved, then lifted with scarcely a jerk. From behind came the squeals and chirrups of the flirts as the trailer rocked over the irregularities in the field.

Worzer looked hard at the starship's open crew portal as they hissed past it. "Funny what folks go an' do," he said to no one in particular. "Via, wonder what I'll be in another ten years."

"Pet food, likely," joked the driver, taking part in the conversation although physically separated from the other crewmen.

"Shut up, Jake," repeated the blower captain. "And you can hold it up here, we're out far enough."

The combat car obediently settled on the edge of the stabilized area. The port itself had capacity for two ships at a time; the region it served did not. Though with the high cost of animal transport many manufactures could be starhopped to Curwin's back country more cheaply than they could be carried from the planet's own more urbanized areas, the only available exchange was raw agricultural produce—again limited to the immediate locality by the archaic transport. Its fans purring below audibility, the armored vehicle rested on an empty area of no significance to the region—unless the central government should choose to land another regiment of mercenaries on it.

"Look," the sergeant said, his deep-set eyes catching Rob's, "we'll pass you on to the firebase when we take the other three flirts in next week. They got a training section there. We got six cars in this patrol, that's not enough margin to fool with training a newbie. But neither's it enough to keep somebody useless underfoot for a week, so we'll give you some basics. Not so you can wise-ass when you get to training section, just so you don't get somebody killed if it drops in the pot. Clear?"

"Yessir." Rob broke his eyes away, then realized how

foolish he must look staring at his own clasped hands. He looked back at Worzer.

"Just so it's understood," the sergeant said with a nod. "Leon, show him how the gun works."

The big black rotated his weapon so that the muzzles faced forward and the right side was toward Rob and the interior of the car. The mechanism itself was encased in dull-enameled steel ornamented with knobs and levers of unguessable intent. The barrels were stubby iridium cylinders with smooth, 2 cm. bores. Leon touched one of the buttons, then threw a lever back. The plate to which the barrels were attached rotated 120 degrees around their common axis, and a thick disk of plastic popped out into the gunner's hand.

"When the bottom barrel's ready to fire, the next one clockwise is loading one a these"—Leon held up the 2 cm. disk—"and the other barrel, the one that's just fired, blows out the empty."

"There's a liquid nitrogen ejector," Worzer put in. "Cools the bore same time it kicks out the empty."

"She feeds up through the mount," the big soldier went on, his index finger tracing the path of the energized disks from the closed hopper bulging in the sidewall, through the ball joint, and into the weapon's receiver. "If you try to fire and she don't, check this." The columnar finger indicated but did not move the stud it had first pressed on the side of the gun. "That's the safety. She still doesn't fire, pull this"—he clacked the lever, rotating the barrel cluster another one-third turn and catching the loaded round that flew out. "Maybe there was a dud round. She still don't go, just get down outa the way. We start telling you about second-order malfunctions and you won't remember where the trigger is."

"Ah, where is the trigger?" Rob asked diffidently.

Jake's laughter rang through the earphones and Worzer himself smiled for the first time. The sergeant reached out and rotated the gun. "See the grips?" he asked, pointing to the double handles at the back of the receiver. Rob nodded.

"OK," Worzer continued, "you hold it there"—he demonstrated—"and to fire, you just press your thumbs against the trigger plate between 'em. Let up and it quits. Simple."

"You can clear this field as quick as you can spin this little honey," Leon said, patting the gun with affection. "The hicks out there"—his arm swept the woods and cultivated fields promiscuously—"got some rifles, they hunted before the trouble started, but no powerguns to mention. About all they do since we moved in is maybe pop a shot or two off, and hide in their holes."

"They've got some underground stockpiles," Worzer said, amplifying Leon's words, "explosives, maybe some factories to make rifle ammo. But the colonel set up a recce net—spy satellites, you know—as part a the contract. Any funny movement day or night, a signal goes down to whoever's patrolling there. A couple calls and we check out the area with ground sensors . . . anything funny then—vibration, hollows showing up on the echo sounder, magnetics—anything!—and bam! we call in the artillery."

"Won't take much of a jog on the way back," Leon suggested, "and we can check out that report from last night."

"Via, that was just a couple dogs," Jake objected.

"OK, so we prove it was a couple dogs," rumbled the gunner. "Or maybe the hicks got smart and they're shielding their infra-red now. Been too damn long since anything popped in this sector."

"Thing to remember, kid," Worzer summed up, "is never get buzzed at this job. Stay cool, you're fine. This car's got more firepower'n everything hostile in fifty klicks. One call to the firebase brings in our arty, anything from smoke shells to a nuke. The rest of our section can be here in twenty minutes, or a tank platoon from the firebase in two hours. Just stay cool."

Turning forward, the sergeant said, "OK, take her home. Jake. We'll try that movement report on the way."

The combat car shuddered off the ground, the flirts shrieking. Rob eyed them, blushed, and turned back to his powergun, feeling conspicuous. He took the grips, liking the deliberate way the weapon swung. The safety button was glowing green, but he suddenly realized that he didn't know the color code. Green for safe? Or green for ready? He extended his index finger to the switch.

"Whoa, careful, kid!" Leon warned. "You cut fifty civvies in half your first day and the colonel won't like it one bit."

Sheepishly, Rob drew back his finger. His ears burned, mercifully hidden beneath the helmet.

They slid over the dusty road in a flat, white cloud at about forty kph. It seemed shockingly fast to the recruit, but he realized that the car could probably move much faster were it not for the live cargo behind. Even as it was, the trailer bounced dangerously from side to side.

The road led through a gullied scattering of grain plots, generally fenced with withes rather than imported metal. Houses were relatively uncommon. Apparently each farmer plowed several separate locations rather than trying to work the rugged or less productive areas. Occasionally they passed a rough-garbed local at work. The scowls thrown up at the smoothly-running war-car were hostile, but there was nothing more overt.

"OK," Jake warned, "here's where it gets interesting. Sure you still want this half-assed check while we got the trailer hitched?"

"It won't be far," Worzer answered. "Go ahead." He turned to Rob, touching the recruit's shoulder and pointing to the lighted map panel beside the forward gun. "Look, Jenne," he said, keeping one eye on the countryside as Jake took the car off the road in a sweeping turn, "if you need to call in a location to the firebase, here's the trick. The red dot"—it was in the center of the display and remained there although the map itself seemed to be flowing kitty-corner across the screen as the combat car moved—"that's us. The black dot"—the veteran thumbed a small wheel beside the display and the map, red dot and all, shifted to the right on the panel, leaving a black dot in the center—"that's your pointer. The computer feeds out the grid coordinates here"—his finger touched the window above the map display. Six digits, changing as the map moved under the centered black dot, winked brightly. "You just put the black dot on a bunker site, say, and read off the figures to Fire Central. The arty'll do all the rest."

"Ah," Rob murmured, "ah . . . Sergeant, how do you get the little dot off that and onto a bunker like you said?"

There was a moment's silence. "You know how to read a map, don't you, kid?" Worzer finally asked.

"What's that, sir?"

The earphones boomed and cackled with raucous laughter. "Oh my coppy ass!" the sergeant snarled. He snapped the little wheel back, re-centering the red dot. "Lord, I don't know how the training cadre takes it!"

Rob hid his flaming embarrassment by staring over his gunsights. He didn't really know how to use them, either. He didn't know why he'd left Conner's Stoneworks, where he was the cleanest, fastest driller on the whole coppy crew. His powerful hands squeezed at the grips as if they were the driver's throat through which bubbles of laughter still burst.

"Shut up, Jake," the sergeant finally ordered. "Most of us had to learn something new when we joined. Remember how the ol' man found you your first day, pissing up against the barracks?"

Jake quieted.

They had skirted a fence of cane palings, brushing it once without serious effect. Russet grass flanking the fence flattened under the combat car's downdraft, then sprang up unharmed as the vehicle moved past. Jake seemed to be following a farm track leading from the field to a rambling, substantially-constructed building on the near hilltop. Instead of running with the ground's rise, however, the car cut through brush and down a half-meter bank into a broad-based arroyo. The bushes were too stiff to lie down under the fans. They crunched and howled in the blades, making the car buck, and ricocheted wildly from under the skirts. The bottom of the arroyo was sand, clean-swept by recent run-off. It boiled fiercely as the car first shoomped into it, then ignored the fans entirely. Somehow Jake had managed not to overturn the trailer, although its cargo had been screaming with fear for several minutes.

"Hold up," Worzer ordered suddenly as he swung his weapon toward the left-hand bank. The wash was about thirty meters wide at that point, sides sheer and a meter high. Rob glanced forward to see that a small screen to

Worzer's left on the bulkhead, previously dark, was now crossed by three vari-colored lines. The red one was bouncing frantically.

"They got an entrance, sure 'nough," Leon said. He aimed his powergun at the same point, then snapped his face shield down. "Watch it, kid," he said. The black's right hand fumbled in a metal can welded to the blower's side. Most of the paint had chipped from the stencilled legend: GRENADES. What appeared to be a lazy overarm toss snapped a knobby ball the size of a child's fist straight and hard against the bank.

Dirt and rock fragments shotgunned in all directions. The gully side burst in a globe of black streaked with garnet fire, followed by a shock wave that was a physical blow.

"Watch your side, kid!" somebody shouted through the din, but Rob's bulging eyes were focused on the collapsing bank, the empty triangle of black gaping suddenly through the dust—the two ravening whiplashes of directed lightning ripping into it to blast and scatter.

The barrel clusters of the two veterans' powerguns spun whining, kicking gray, eroded disks out of their mechanisms in nervous arcs. The bolts they shot were blue-green flashes barely visible until they struck a target and exploded it with transferred energy. The very rocks burst in droplets of glassy slag splashing high in the air and even back into the war-car to pop against the metal.

Leon's gun paused as his fingers hooked another grenade. "Hold it!" he warned. The sergeant, too, came off the trigger, and the bomb arrowed into the now-vitrified gap in the tunnel mouth. Dirt and glass shards blew straight back at the bang. A stretch of ground sagged for twenty meters beyond the gully wall, closing the tunnel the first explosion had opened.

Then there was silence. Even the flirts, huddled in a terrified heap on the floor of their cage, were soundless.

Glowing orange specks vibrated on Rob's retinas; the cyan bolts had been more intense than he had realized. "Via," he said in awe, "how do they dare . . . ?"

"Bullet kills you just as dead," Worzer grunted. "Jake, think you can climb that wall?"

"Sure. She'll buck a mite in the loose stuff." The gully

side was a gentle declivity, now, where the grenades had blown it in. "Wanna unhitch the trailer first?"

"Negative, nobody gets off the blower till we cleaned this up."

"Umm, don't want to let somebody else in on the fun, maybe?" the driver queried. If he was tense, his voice did not indicate it. Rob's palms were sweaty. His glands had understood before his mind had that his companions were considering smashing up, unaided, a guerrilla stronghold.

"Cop," Leon objected determinedly. "We found it, didn't we?"

"Let's go," Worzer ordered. "Kid, watch your side. They sure got another entrance, maybe a couple."

The car nosed gently toward the subsided bank, wallowed briefly as the driver fed more power to the forward fans to lift the bow. With a surge and a roar, the big vehicle climbed. Its fans caught a few pebbles and whanged them around inside the plenum chamber like a rattle of sudden gunfire. At half speed, the car glided toward another fenced grainplot, leaving behind it a rising pall of dust.

"Straight as a plumb line," Worzer commented, his eyes flicking his sensor screen. "Bastards'll be waiting for us."

Rob glanced at him—a mistake. The slam-spang! of shot and ricochet were nearly simultaneous. The recruit whirled back, bawling in surprise. The rifle pit had opened within five meters of him, and only the haste of the dark-featured guerrilla had saved Rob from his first shot. Rob pivoted his powergun like a hammer, both thumbs mashing down the trigger. Nothing happened. The guerrilla ducked anyway, the black circle of his foxhole shaped into a thick crescent by the lid lying askew.

Safety, *safety!* Rob's mind screamed and he punched the button fat-fingered. The rifleman raised his head just in time to meet the hose of fire that darted from the recruit's gun. The guerrilla's head exploded. His brains, flash-cooked by the first shot, changed instantly from a colloid to a blast of steam that scattered itself over a three-meter circle. The smoldering fragments of the rifle followed the torso as it slid downward.

The combat car roared into the field of waist-high grain, ripping down twenty meters of woven fencing to make its passage. Rob, vaguely aware of other shots and cries forward, vomited onto the floor of the compartment. A colossal explosion nearby slewed the car sideways. As Rob raised his eyes, he noticed three more swarthy riflemen darting through the grain from the right rear of the vehicle.

"Here!" he cried. He swiveled his weapon blindly, his hips colliding with Worzer in the cramped space. A rifle bullet cracked past his helmet. He screamed something again but his own fire was too high, blue-green droplets against the clear sky, and the guerrillas had grabbed the bars while the flirts jumped and blatted.

The rifles were slamming but the flirts were in the way of Rob's gun. "Down! Down!" he shouted uselessly, and the red-haired flirt pitched across the cage with one synthetic breast torn away by the bullet she had leaped in front of. Leon cursed and slumped against Rob's feet, and then it was Chero Worzer shouting, "Hard left, Jake," and leaning across the fallen gunner to rotate his weapon. The combat car tilted left as the bow came around, pinching the trailer against the left rear of the vehicle—in the path of Worzer's powergun. The cage's light alloy bloomed in superheated fireballs as the cyan bolts ripped through it. Both tires exploded together, and there was a red mist of blood in the air. The one guerrilla who had ducked under the burst dropped his rifle and ran.

Worzer cut him in half as he took his third step.

The sergeant gave the wreckage only a glance, then knelt beside Leon. "Cop, he's gone," he said. The bullet had struck the big man in the neck between helmet and body armor, and there was almost a gallon of blood on the floor of the compartment.

"Leon?" Jake asked.

"Yeah. Lord, there musta been twenty kilos of explosive in that satchel charge. If he hadn't hit it in the air . . ." Worzer looked back at the wreck of the trailer, then at Rob. "Kid, can you unhitch that yourself?"

"You just *killed* them," Rob blurted. He was half blinded by tears and the after-image of the gunfire.

"Via, they did their best on us, didn't they?" the sergeant snarled. His face was tiger striped by dust and sweat.

"No, not them!" the boy cried. "Not them—the girls. You just—"

Worzer's iron fingers gripped Rob by the chin and turned the recruit remorselessly toward the carnage behind. The flirts had been torn apart by their own fluids, some pieces flung through gaps in the mangled cage. "Look at 'em, Jenne!" Worzer demanded. "They ain't human but if they was, if it was *Leon* back there, I'd a done it."

His finger uncurled from Rob's chin and slammed in a fist against the car's armor. "This ain't heroes, it ain't no coppy game you play when you want to! You do what you got to do, 'cause if you don't, some poor bastard gets killed later when he tries to.

"Now get down there and unhitch us."

"Yes, sir." Rob gripped the lip of the car for support.

Worzer's voice, more gently, came through the haze of tears: "And watch it, kid. Just because they're keeping their heads down don't mean they're all gone." Then, "Wait." Another pause while the sergeant unfastened the belt and holstered handgun from his waist and handed it to Rob. Leon wore a similar weapon, but Worzer did not touch the body. Rob wordlessly clipped the belt, loose for not being fitted over armor, and swung down from the combat car.

The hitch had a quick-release handle, but the torqueing it had received in the last seconds of battle had jammed it. Nervously aware that the sergeant's darting-eyed watchfulness was no pretense, that the shot-scythed grainfield could hide still another guerrilla, or a platoon of them, Rob smashed his boot heel against the catch. It held. Wishing for his driller's sledge, he kicked again.

"Sarge!" Jake shouted. Grain rustled on the other side of the combat car, and against the sky beyond the scarred armor loomed a parcel. Rob threw himself flat.

The explosion picked him up from the ground and bounced him twice, despite the shielding bulk of the combat car. Stumbling upright, Rob steadied himself on the armored side.

The metal felt odd. It no longer trembled with the ready power of the fans. The car was dead, lying at rest on the torn-up soil. With three quick strides, the recruit rounded the bow of the vehicle. He had no time to inspect the dished-in metal, because another swarthy guerrilla was approaching from the other side.

Seeing Rob, the ex-farmer shouted something and drew a long knife. Rob took a step back, remembered the pistol. He tugged at its unfamiliar grip and the weapon popped free into his hand. It seemed the most natural thing in the world to finger the safety, placed just as the tribarrel's had been, then trigger two shots into the face of the lunging guerrilla. The snarl of hatred blanked as the body tumbled face-down at Rob's feet. The knife had flown somewhere into the grain.

"Ebros?" a man called. Another lid had raised from the ground ten meters away. Rob fired at the hole, missed badly. He climbed the caved-in bow, clumsily one-handed, keeping the pistol raised. There was nothing but twisted metal where the driver had been. Sergeant Worzer was still semi-erect, clutched against his powergun by a length of structural tubing. It had curled around both his thighs, fluid under the stunning impact of the satchel charge. The map display was a pearly blank, though the window above it still read incongruously 614579 and the red line on the detector screen blipped in nervous solitude. Worzer's helmet was gone, having flayed a bloody track across his scalp as it sailed away. His lips moved, though, and when Rob put his face near the sergeant's he could hear, "The red . . . pull the red tab . . ."

Over the left breast of each set of armor were a blue and a red tab. Rob had assumed they were decorations of some sort. He shifted the sergeant gently. The tab was locked down by a cotter pin which he yanked out. Something hissed in the armor as he pulled the tab, and Sergeant Worzer murmured, "Oh Lord. Oh Lord." Then, "Now the stimulant, the blue tab."

After the second injection sped into his system, the sergeant opened his eyes. Rob was already trying to straighten the entrapping tube. "Forget it," Worzer ordered weakly. "It's inside, too . . . damn armor musta flexed. Oh Lord." He closed his eyes, opened them in time to see another head peak cautiously from the tunnel mouth. "Bastard!" he rasped, and faster than he spoke he triggered his powergun. Its motor whined spitefully though the burst went wide. The head disappeared.

"I want you to run back to the gully," the sergeant said, resting his eyes again. "You get there, you say 'Fire Central.' That cuts in the arty frequency automatic. Then you say, 'Bunker complex . . .'" Worzer looked down. "'Six-one-four, five-seven-nine.' Stay low and wait for a patrol."

"It won't bend!" Rob snarled in frustration as his fingers slid again from the blood-slick tubing.

"Jenne, get your ass out of here, *now*."

"Sergeant—"

"Lord curse your soul, get out or I'll call it in myself! Do I look like I wanna live?"

"Oh, Via . . ." Rob tried to reholster the pistol he had set on the bloody floor. It slipped back with a clang. He left it, gripping the sidewall again.

"Maybe tell Dad it was good to see him," Worzer whispered. "You lose touch in this business, Lord knows you do."

"Sir?"

"The priest . . . you met him. Sergeant-Major Worzer, he was. Oh Lord, *move it*—"

At the muffled scream, the recruit leaped from the smashed war-car and ran blindly back the way they had come. He did not know he had reached the gully until the ground flew out from under him and he pitched spread-eagled onto the sand. "Fire Central," he sobbed through strangled breaths. "Fire Central."

"Clear," a strange voice snapped crisply. "Data?"

"Wh-what?"

"Lord and martyrs," the voice blasted, "if you're screwing around on firing channels, you'll wish you never saw daylight!"

"S-six . . . oh Lord, yes, six-one—four, five-seven-nine," Rob sing-songed. He was staring at the smooth sand. "Bunkers, the sergeant says it's bunkers."

"Roger," the voice said, businesslike again. "Ranging in fifteen."

Could they really swing those mighty guns so swiftly, those snub-barrelled rocket howitzers whose firing looked so impressive on the entertainment cube?

"On the way," warned the voice.

The big tribarrel whined again from the combat car, the silent lash of its bolts answered this time by a crash of rifle shots. A flattened bullet burred through the air over where Rob lay. It was lost in the eerie, thunderous shriek from the northwest.

"Splash," the helmet said.

The ground bucked. From the grainplot spouted rock, smoke, and metal fragments into a black column fifty meters high.

"Are we on?" the voice demanded.

"Oh Lord," Rob prayed, beating his fists against the sand. "Oh Lord."

"Via, what is this?" the helmet wondered aloud. Then, "All guns, battery five."

And the earth began to ripple and gout under the hammer of the guns.

Introduction

Joe Haldeman

I was a Kipling enthusiast before I could read. I was
lucky enough to grow up in a territory (Alaska) that hadn't
yet been cursed with television, and every night after she
tucked us in, my mother would read to my brother and
me from books that were comprehensible to us but adult
enough to engage her interest as well. So we heard *Little
Women* and *Ivanhoe*, the Potts stories from the *Saturday
Evening Post*—and *The Jungle Book* and *Kim*. When the
Disney version of that tale came out I couldn't have been
more than nine or ten, but I remember being disap-
pointed because it wasn't as good as the book.

I wrote several booklets of poetry as a child, now fortu-
nately lost. (My first publication was a poem in the *Washington Post* at the age of nine. "Poetry" might be too
exalted a classification: it was doggerel occasionally aspir-
ing to verse. Kipling and Poe were my major influences, I
suppose; at least it was Kipling and Poe that I carried
around through those long static summers. I vaguely recall
that some of the verses were scary and some were heroic
tales, probably close to plagiarism.

Then puberty struck, and with it the predictable attack
of liberalism and suddenly Kipling embarrassed me. I
don't suppose I read him at all until late in college, when
(in *The Magazine of Fantasy and Science Fiction*) I ran
across his charmingly bleak poem "Tomlinson." I picked
up a couple of volumes of his stories and poems in used
book stores, and again found much to admire. I suspect

that the pieces I now appreciate most are ones I didn't care for, or didn't understand, when I was a child.

It's interesting that the editor of this volume approved "Saul's Death" as a Kipling-influenced work, because I honestly didn't synape one synapse about Kipling while I was writing it. The story is just a science fiction story that I thought had to be told as a poem; the form of it is a sort of wry hommage to Ezra Pound, not Kipling. It is interesting that the poem it refers to, "Sestina: Altaforte," is an exemplar of Pound at his politically most embarrassing—sanguinary, jingoistic, bombastic; the same sort of adjectives some might use to dismiss Kipling. Both men were more complex than that.

Saul's Death

JOE HALDEMAN

1.
I used to be a monk, but gave it over
Before books and prayer and studies cooled my blood,
And joined with Richard as a mercenary soldier.
(No Richard that you've heard of, just
A man who'd bought a title for his name.)
And it was in his service I met Saul.

The first day of my service I liked Saul;
His easy humor quickly won me over.
He confided Saul was not his name;
He'd taken up another name for blood.
(So had I—my fighting name was just
(A word we use at home for private soldier.)

I felt at home as mercenary soldier
I liked the company of men like Saul.
(Though most of Richard's men were just
(Fighting for the bounty when it's over.)
I loved the clash of weapons, splashing blood—
I lived the meager promise of my name.

Saul promised that he'd tell me his real name
When he was through with playing as a soldier.
(I said the same; we took an oath in blood.)
But I would never know him but as Saul;
He'd die before the long campaign was over,
Dying for a cause that was not just.

Only fools require a cause that's just,
Fools and children out to make a name.
Now I've had sixty years to think it over
(Sixty years of being no one's soldier).
Sixty years since broadsword opened Saul
And splashed my body with his precious blood.

But damn! we lived for bodies and for blood.
The reek of dead men rotting, it was just
A sweet perfume for those like me and Saul.
(My peaceful language doesn't have a name
(For lewd delight in going off to soldier.)
It hurts my heart sometimes to know it's over.

My heart was hard as stone when it was over;
When finally I'd had my fill of blood.
(And knew I was too old to be a soldier.)
Nothing left for me to do but just
Go back home and make myself a name
In ways of peace, forgetting war and Saul.

In ways of blood he made himself a name
(Though he was just a mercenary soldier)—
I loved Saul before it all was over.

2.
A mercenary soldier has no future;
Some say his way of life is hardly human.
And yet, we had our own small bloody world
(Part aches and sores and wrappings soaking blood,
(Partly fear and glory grown familiar)
Confined within a shiny fence of swords.

But how I learned to love to fence with swords!
Another world, my homely past and future—
Once steel and eye and wrist became familiar
With each other, then that steel was almost human
(With an altogether human taste for blood).
I felt that sword and I could take the world.

I felt that Saul and I could take the world:
Take the whole world hostage with our swords.
The bond we felt was stronger than mere blood
(Though I can see with hindsight in the future
(The bond we felt was something only human:
(A need for love when death becomes familiar).

We were wizards, and death was our familiar;
Our swords held all the magic in the world.
(Richard thought it almost wasn't human,
(The speed with which we parried others' swords,
(Forever end another's petty future.)
Never scratched, though always steeped in blood.

Ambushed in a tavern, splashing ankle-deep in blood;
Fighting back-to-back in ways familiar.
Saul slipped: lost his footing and our future.
Broad blade hammered down and sent him from this
    world.
In angry grief I killed that one, then all the other swords;
Then locked the doors and murdered every human.

No choice, but to murder every human.
No one in that tavern was a stranger to blood.
(To those who live with pikes and slashing swords,
(The inner parts of men become familiar.)
Saul's vitals looked like nothing in this world:
I had to kill them all to save my future.

Saul's vitals were not human, but familiar:
He never told me he was from another world;
I never told him I was from his future.

The Art of Things As They Are

Gordon R. Dickson and Sandra Miesel

"I've been reading Kipling so long, I can't even remember when I started," says Gordon Dickson. But he knows that he first loved *The Jungle Book* and the tales of soldiers in India. All those adventures on the Northwestern frontier spoke to his inborn fascination with mountains. "But what grabbed me from the beginning was Kipling's tremendous storytelling. He had a great instinct for the story-within-the-story."

Absorbing Kipling's technique helped Dickson develop his own "consciously-thematic" approach to fiction in which the story itself demonstrates its own meaning. For example, *The Jungle Book* dramatize the need for learning by showing the process in action: the human child Mowgli is taught by animals but must go back to being human once he's mastered his lessons.

Similarly, "Carry Me Home" argues about the need for belonging. The hero starts out as a mountain tribesman—a bit like those who took service with the British Raj—and is destined to return to his own people despite what happens to him and what he has achieved in the larger world outside. "His tragedy lies in being what he is, able to see his Promised Land, but unable to inhabit it. He can only win victories for other people because he's just a tool of the racial id."

This also connects to Kipling's obsession with "things as

they are." Kipling was perennially concerned about people and their duty: humans have to "be what they are and do what they must." This certainly is useful to the race, but damned hard on the individuals involved.

Carry Me Home

GORDON R. DICKSON

Partially, it was the youth of Jason Jonasse that made it difficult for him to understand his fellow man. But mainly, it was his background.

His family was of the military. From their native city on Kilbur Two, during the past two hundred years or so, had come a steady stream of Jonasses. Mostly, they died, in one way or another, while serving humanity on the Frontier of man's expanding spatial area. Those who did not, won through to advancement and posts of high honor. All, however, without exception, made the first step of transfer from the backwaters of military duty, earning their right to carry their officer's buttons to Class A Service in the Frontier Zone.

It was this transfer that Jason had just received and which was propped now on the toilet shelf beside the shaving mirror in his quarters, where he could feast his eyes on it during the process of trimming the straight black lines of his little mustache, with the aid of that self-same mirror. The mustache was an index of his character, so essentially Kilburnian, so uncompromisingly military, so uniquely Jonasse. It was the final seal upon his difference, the crown upon his height and the lean good looks of his breed, and the uniform of which tunic cape and boots were custom-tailored.

There was no one thing about him which did not set him off from the other officers of this small military garrison on Aster. For this small lost planet out in the Beltane

Quadrant was class C duty; and the other officers were Class C officers, as Jason had been, serving his apprenticeship in a sort of police duty, until the blessed arrival of the transfer, welcome as a pardon to a life sentence prisoner. Jason beamed at it, working the clippers carefully over the ends of the mustache, for his baggage was packed and ready for the next courier ship that came and the transfer was his passport to the future.

A buzzer rang through his room, and Jason jerked at the unexpected suddenness of the sound. For a split-second the clippers slipped, chopping a little, ragged v out of the top line of the mustache, a v unfortunately beyond the ability of any clipping to disguise and anything but time to mend. For a moment, Jason stared at its reflection in the mirror. Then he cursed, threw down the clippers and thumbed the switch of the intercom.

"Officer Five Jonasse here," he said.

"Headquarters, Chief Troopman Basker, sir," said the Speaker. "The Commandant would like you to report to his office right away, Officer."

"I'll be right there, Chief."

"Right, sir."

Scowling, Jason buttoned his tunic and clipped his cape about his shoulders. There was no good reason why the Commandant should want to see him, unless there had been some change in his orders directing the transfer. And if that . . .

Jason clamped down on the speculative section of his mind and left his quarters, hurrying across the drill-ground to the Headquarters Building.

Hot sunlight hit him a solid blow as he stepped out of the shade of his quarters. The Timudag, as the plains country of Aster's one large continent was known, broiled during the summer months under a cloudless sky. Jason strode across it and stepped gratefully into the air conditioned coolness of the Headquarters Building.

The Commandant was waiting for him in the outer office. Like Jason, a Kilburnian, but without the Jonasse family tradition of Service, he had won little recognition during his short term of Frontier Class A Service; and, having no prospects to speak of on retirement from that,

had fallen back on Class C duty, where the retirement age
was much higher. A thin, cold man, he did not particularly
like Jason though a scrupulous sense of fairness forced him
to admit that the younger Kilburnian was far and away the
most valuable of his men.

"You messaged for me, sir?" said Jason.

The Commandant took Jason's elbow and drew him
aside, out of earshot of the troopmen at work at clerical
tasks about the outer office. "Something has come up,
Jason."

Jason felt cold apprehension and hot resentment. But he
held it locked within him.

"The courier ship has just arrived," the Commandant
said. "It brought your replacement—and another man."

The Commandant looked out the window and back to
Jason again.

"The other man's an officer retired from Class A Service," he went on. "And he carries a request from the
General Commander of our Quadrant to give him every
assistance in returning home."

Jason looked at the Commandant in puzzlement. This
was nonsensical. If the man was from Aster, he was already home. If he was not from Aster, why had he come
to Aster, to this outlying station to obtain assistance?

"I don't understand," he said honestly.

"His home," explained the Commandant briefly, "is in
the Timumang."

At that, Jason began to understand.

North of the Timudag, on Aster's one large land mass,
lay the Timumang, the Mountains of the People. Boulder-
strewn upthrust of the continental geosyncline to the north,
it housed the degenerate descendants of an early abortive
attempt at colonization, four hundred years before the
coming of civilization proper to Aster. Wild and suspicious, these forgotten people had backslid to a clan-tribal
form of organization. They warred on each other, lived off
their inhospitable country in the course of nomadic wan-
derings, and shunned their latter-day cousins of the lowlands as if they had been plague-ridden.

The Timumang ignored the Timudag. Jason had not, in

his term of service guarding the Intersteller Message Station and the few raw little towns of the Timudag, been anywhere near the Mountains of the People. Nor, as far as he knew, had any of the other men at the station. But of course he had heard stories.

There were other worlds where the tragic accident of too-early colonization had taken place, and the settlers had backslid to savagery or near-savagery. They were the cobwebbed corners that the Central Headquarters on Earth, like a busy housewife, was always planning to do something about and never getting to. From them, every so often, would come the rare case of a degenerate who ran away or escaped from his own people to join the ranks of civilization. Sometimes such men rose to respectable positions. But the tendency of ordinary people was to feel some repugnance toward them—reminders as they were of the fact that the human race was not completely without exception shooting up the dizzy stairs toward the millenium.

"A degenerate!" Jason muttered.

"An ex-officer," corrected the Commandant coldly.

Jason felt his temper rising, but held it back. He returned to the crux of the matter.

"I interrupted you, sir," he said. "Pardon me."

"Well," said the Commandant. "He'll need an escort and an officer to command the escort."

"You don't mean me, sir?" said Jason, aghast. "My orders—"

"I've no choice," said the Commandant, irritably. "And the delay in your transfer needn't be fatal. I've got no one else I can trust with such a job. He won't take more than twenty men."

Jason stared, incredulous.

"You can't go into the Timumang with just twenty men," he said, at last.

The Commandant snorted.

"Come and talk to him, yourself," he said, turning and leading the way toward his private office. "And remember, the Commander General requests our assistance. There's no dodging this."

Bitterly, Jason followed him, the sour anger of the betrayed curdling in his stomach. Mere hours from shipping out, they had to send him off on a what sounded like a suicide mission. Not that Jason had any objections to dying, if the time and place were right—but to be possibly clubbed to death in what amounted to a backyard brawl!

The Commandant ushered him in and a man sitting in one of the easy chairs of the office rose to greet them. He was a curious figure, as tall as the two Kilburnians, but so broad of shoulder and long of arm that he seemed much shorter. In the dark skin of his face, set above flat, heavy cheekbones and beneath pronounced brows, his brown eyes looked out at them with the soft liquidity of an animal. There was something yielding and sad about him. No guts, thought Jason, harshly, out of the fury of his resentment. No backbone.

The Commandant was introducing the two men. Jason shook hands briefly.

"Mr. Potter, this is Officer Five Jason Jonasse," said the Commandant. "Jason, this is Mr. Kerl Potter, formerly an Officer Three."

"Honored to meet you," said the degenerate. His voice was husky and so deep that he almost seemed to croon the words.

"Pleasure is mine," replied Jason briefly and mechanically. "The Commandant tells me you think twenty men is a sufficient escort into the Timumang."

"Yes," replied Potter, nodding.

"Why, that isn't nearly enough strength," said Jason. "The average clan usually musters at least a hundred fighting men."

"I know," Kerl Potter smiled, a warm, but deprecating smile. "I grew up in the Timumang—or had the Commandant told you?"

He didn't have to, thought Jason, looking at the man with disgust and disfavor. Aloud he said, "Any single tribe would be more than a match for us."

"Please—" Kerl held up his hand. "Let me explain."

Jason nodded, curtly.

"I wish to get back to my own clan—the Potter Clan," said the dark man. "For that we must go in on foot and search, because the clans move constantly, and from the air—which would be the quickest way of going—there is no way to tell which tribe is which. They go to earth when they see a flyer."

"I'll admit that—" began Jason.

"So we must go in on foot," continued Potter, his deep voice like distant summer thunder in the office. "We must hunt for campsites until we find Potter sign at one. And then we must trail the clan until we catch up with it." He paused, looking at Jason and the Commandant to see if they understood.

"Now," he said, "that means we must go through much Timumang territory. If we are too large a group, the word will go ahead of us and all the clans will hide and we will never catch up with the Potters. If we are too few, the first tribe we meet with will destroy us. Therefore the solution is to have enough men to discourage attack, but not enough to frighten the clans into moving out of our way. When we have found the Potter Clan, you can drop me off and call for air transport to pick you and the men up and bring you back."

Kerl wound up the argument and smiled at Jason as if to soften the young man's opposition with good humor. Jason looked helplessly at the Commandant, who shrugged and looked out the window, washing his hands of the matter.

"Look, Mr. Potter," said Jason, turning back to the man and making an effort to be reasonable. "These men of ours are all Class C. They know something of police duty in the towns here, and maintaining order generally. What they know about expeditioning is nothing—"

"You can take your pick of the station, Jason," said the Commandant.

It was the culminating blow, the stab in the back. Turning to look at his superior office, Jason realized finally that he was not to be allowed to avoid this expedition, nor to alter the conditions of it. For some reason, some intricacy of inter-branch politicking, it had become necessary for the General Commander to oblige Kerl Potter and for the Commandant to oblige the General Commander. It struck him as symbolic. As the degenerates were a clog and hamper upon the progress of humanity, here was Kerl Potter, their representative, to be a clog and hamper upon the progress of Jason, representative of the out-seeking spirit of Man. His spirit bent under the blow, but pride held his body upright.

"Well, thank you, Commandant," said Kerl, turning to the commanding officer. "I'll look forward to leaving tomorrow then." He turned back to Jason. "Until then, sir."

"Until then," said Jason, and watched him leave. When the door had shut behind the broad back, he turned once more to the Commandant.

"This is unfortunate," said the Commandant, reading his eyes. "But into each life some rain must fall, eh?"

Damn him! thought Jason.

"Yes, sir," he replied woodenly.

Jason picked the twenty men for the expedition with the same lack of sympathy the Commandant had shown in the choice of Jason, himself. He was curt with the Quartermaster, harsh with Ordnance, and unfeeling toward Transportation. At the end of the day the expedition had been outfitted with brilliant organization and Jason returned to his quarters to write a letter to his family on Kilbur Two, explaining that his expected entrance into the realm of glory would be somewhat delayed.

". . . the duty (he wrote his father, after the usual family well-wishes) is hardly one that I would have wished for at this time. Aside from the fact that I am naturally eager to enter on my Class A assignment at the Frontier, I do not expect to find it pleasant to be cooped up, possibly for weeks, with such a man. Your instincts, I know, would cause you to advise me to treat him with respect for his former rank as an Officer Three. Ordinarily, such respect would be automatic on my part. However, this is no ordinary case. In the first place, he has obviously left the Service long before the earliest age of retirement, which argues a lack of courage, or at least of character. And in the second place, to meet the man is to realize there is nothing at all to respect about him. And finally (if any more were needed) the fact that he is turning his back on the competition of civilized life and running back to hide in the stagnant safety of the primitive. If there is one thing that revolts me, it is a lack of courage . . ."

And more in that vein. By the time Jason had filled a couple of micro-reels, he was more resigned, if not reconciled to his task. He got to bed and managed to get to sleep.

He awoke to the day's duty. The men were mustered on the drill field under the leadership of Chief Troopman Acy, a non-commissioned officer who had grown up in the foothills of the Timudag to the north, and whose knowledge of local conditions, slight as it was, might prove to be useful. Looking the detachment over, Jason had to admit that if any men from the station could do this job properly, these were the ones. All were fit professionals with more than one hitch to their credit and a few had even had some combat experience. Jason nodded and ordered Chief Troopman Acy to move them over to Transportation.

Kerl Potter was waiting for them when they arrived, his dark figure a still monument of patience in the clear morning sunlight. A transport was waiting for them, already loaded with two man cars and supplies. They embarked.

The transport flew them to a spot where the foothills gave way to the mountains. Here they landed and transferred all personnel and equipment to the two man cars. When all was ready, Jason signed off the transport and gave the order to mount, taking the lead car himself, with Kerl in the bucket seat beside him. The transparent tops of the cars were shut and the caravan led off up a steep and unmarked valley toward a pass into the mountains.

"Now," said Jason, turning to his passenger as they topped the pass. "Where to?"

Kerl turned brown eyes to him and away and pointed out and ahead to where a long canyon that lay like a knife slash through the mountains, its further end lost in distance.

"North," he said. "Straight north until we pick up sign."

Jason nodded and turned the car off in the direction of the canyon. Like obedient mechanical sheep, the cars behind swung through the turn, each in their proper order, and followed him.

It was about an hour's run to the beginning of the canyon. From there, the route they were following sloped down and the steep walls rose high and forbiddingly above them. Gazing at this barrenness and the apparent lack of life, with the exception of the stunted bushes clinging in the cracks of the boulders, Jason felt his stomach turn over at the thought of deliberately spending a lifetime, *by choice*, in such an environment. It would be worse than being dead. It would be hell without a purpose. How did these people live?

"Mainly off game," said Kerl beside him; and, turning with a jerk, Jason realized he had spoken his last thoughts aloud. "There's quite a bit of it. Wild mountain sheep and goats descended from stock the early settlers themselves brought in. Native species, too, of course, but they aren't edible. Only their furs are useful."

"I see," said Jason, stiffly.

"It's not a bad life when you're used to it," Kerl went on. "You'd be surprised, Jason—you don't mind me calling you Jason, do you? Seems foolish to be formal when we're cooped up like this—but if you like the mountains and like to hunt, it can come close to being ideal."

Jason had meant to keep his mouth shut; but this last statement was too much.

"Exactly," he said, bitterly, "and let the rest of the race take care of you."

Kerl looked at him in surprise.

"The Peoples of the Mountain don't ask help from others," he protested, mildly.

"How about the Frontier?" demanded Jason. "How about the Class A troops that protect the inner worlds like this from attack by some inimical life form?"

"What inimical life form?" countered Kerl. "We've never run across one intelligent enough to be a threat."

"That's no sign there isn't one," said Jason.

"Nonsense," said Kerl, but without heat. "The Class A troops have only one real function and that's to clean up planets we want to take over. You know that."

"I—" Jason realized he was getting into the sort of argument he had promised himself to avoid. He bit his tongue and closed his mouth. Two seconds more and he would be telling this man what he thought of degenerates in general.

"The mountaineers are a sturdy self-sufficient people," Kerl went on. "They even have a few virtues that are largely lacking in the outside world."

"Virtues!" said Jason.

His hard-held temper was about to snap when an interruption occurred that saved him from himself. From nowhere there was suddenly the sound of thin, crescendoing screams. Something slapped with sickening violence against the transparent cover of the car, leaving a small grey smudge; and half a second later came the sound of a distant report.

"What was that?" Jason snapped.

Kerl pointed away and up to the high rim of the canyon where a tiny plume of white smoke rose lazily in the still air.

"They're shooting at us," he said. "They use chemical firearms, you know, with solid missile projectiles. We've moved into the area of one of the clans."

Jason's hand shot toward the intercom button that would activate the speakers in all the cars behind him. Kerl caught his fingers before they could activate the mike.

"Let it go," he said. "That was just a warning to make sure we keep traveling. If they meant to attack they wouldn't give themselves away by shooting from a distance." He pointed at the smudge on the overhead transparency. "No harm to it. The plastic is missile proof."

Jason looked at him icily for a minute then continued to reach for the intercom. His fingers touched the button.

"All cars," he said, into the mike. "Keep your tops up. There'll be sporadic shooting at us from now on."

Kerl smiled a little sadly, and looked away, into the distance of the canyon, winding out of sight ahead.

For a week they searched, always headed north. They traveled by day, barracking at night, sentries posted, and sleepers locked in their individual cars. By night, the stars glittered, cold and frosty and distant, far above the jagged tops of the mountains; and every rattle and slither of falling stone made the sentries jerk nervously and grab their power rifles in sweat-dampened hands.

By day it was better only because of sunlight and company. The eleven cars jolted and rocked their way down one valley and up the next, moving in single file. From time to time they would run across the cold ashes and litter of an abandoned clan campsite and halt for a few minutes while Kerl prowled about it, sifting the ashes with his finger, sniffing like a huge black bear at any discarded equipment. Then they would rebark and be moving again. Every so often from the cliff tops above them would spurt a little puff of grey smoke and seconds later would come the report of a chemical energy missile firearm and the whack and scream of a solid slug as it bounced off the transparent cover of one of the cars. The shooting ground on the nerves, a constant reminder of the unseen, inimical, mountain dwellers waiting just out of sight and reach for something to happen to the detachment.

It was hard on the nerves of the men of the detachment. And it was hard on Jason, chafing at the bit to be free of this degrading duty, faced with the responsibility of holding untested troops to their work, and forced to live cheek by jowl with a man whom training and his own inclinations forced him to despise.

It was a situation with explosive potentials. And the first touch of violence brought these out into the open.

On their seventh day out and some nine hundred miles north and slightly west of the point at which they had entered the Timumang, they were proceeding down a long narrow valley. To the left, a small stream marked their road for them, clear water singing down the narrow, level throat of the valley. Beyond it, a series of slopes faded up and back to the skyline. To the right, the cliffs rose more steeply, sharp, pitching angles rubbled with boulder and sharp-cornered loose rock. Jason had been guiding the caravan of cars as usual, his hands on the controls, his mind a dozen light years off on the Frontier and the job he had yet to do there.

Abruptly he felt a hand on his arm.

Yanked abruptly back to the present and the Timumang, he turned with no great pleasure to see Kerl staring at him with a frown line deep-graven between the brown eyes.

"What is it?" said Jason.

"I've got a hunch," answered Kerl. His deep voice filled the interior of the little car with hollow sound. "I think we ought to turn back."

"Turn back?" echoed Jason.

"This valley," said Kerl. "I don't like it. I don't like the feel of it. We could go back and take another one."

Jason throttled down the speed of the car but kept it moving forward.

"Now let's get this straight," he said, impatiently. "You

don't think we ought to go any further down this valley. Why?"

"We may be attacked," answered Kerl. "We haven't been shot at for some hours now. That's a bad sign."

"Couldn't we be traveling through an area where there are no people?"

"Could be," admitted Kerl. "But I've got this hunch—"

Jason considered, keeping his face blank. On the one hand, the man beside him was supposed to know these mountains. On the other hand, the little knowledge he had so far gained of the mountaineers had given him a kind of contempt for them.

"Tell me," said Jason abruptly, "have you any definite reason for warning us out of this valley? Any—" he stressed the word slightly—"*real* evidence?"

"No," said Kerl.

"We'll go on," Jason said flatly.

The detachment proceeded without trouble. As they approached the far end of the valley, it became too narrow for two of the cars abreast. Abruptly, Kerl shot out an arm and skidded the car to a halt. Behind them the rest of the detachment slammed brakes to keep from piling up.

"What now?" demanded Jason, exasperated.

"I was right. Look—" Kerl pointed directly ahead to a low mound of stones that half-blocked the route. "A food cache. The tribe around here has been on a hunting sweep."

"What's that got to do with us?" demanded Jason. "We don't want their food."

"But they don't know that," said Kerl.

Jason looked at him; and the thought crossed his mind that the other man was pushing his point home out of sheer stubbornness. It bolstered his belief that there was a cowardly streak in Kerl.

"We'll go forward," he said. "If trouble comes, it'll be time enough to turn back."

"I don't—" said Kerl; and suddenly his face twisted in alarm. He thrust out with both hands, slamming home the throttle and activating the intercar communicator.

"Forward! Full speed!" he yelled. And Jason, slammed back in his seat by the acceleration, had just time to grab for the steering bar as the little car leaped forward.

As he shot past the cache, the reason for Kerl's actions became horribly apparent. High up the steep slope to the right the top of the cliff seemed to be bowing forward like the head of an old man and crumbling slowly and majestically into a thousand pieces. Distance lent it a gentle air as if the whole process was taking place in slow motion, but Jason realized suddenly with a sickening sense of shock that thousands of tons of rock were in that land-slide, tumbling down upon him and upon the detachment that was his responsibility. With no time for cursing fate or bawling orders, he hung grimly to the controls of the car and prayed that the men behind him had followed.

For an agonizingly long time it seemed that they would make it. And finally, when the dust and the rattle of smaller stones closed about them, it proved impossible to tell. At that moment a huge rock came springing out of nowhere at Jason's car, and he felt a terrific blow that flung him into darkness.

Late that night, after two dead troopers had been buried in the shattered frame of one of the cars, Kerl went hunting Jason.

He found the young officer standing off by himself, wrestling with his devils in the darkness. It is not easy at any time, but particularly the first, to have to face the fact that an arbitrary decision of yours has cost two men their lives. And this becomes worse when there is ground for self-blame in the reasons behind that decision. Rightly or wrongly, Jason believed, and would go on believing for the rest of his days, that his dislike of Kerl had killed two men. He was not particularly glad, therefore, when Kerl loomed up out of the darkness beside him.

"Well?" he said.

"The man are pretty well bedded down," replied Kerl. "I thought you'd like to know. They've got the last car fixed, so we can go on with nine of them tomorrow."

They stood in silence for a little while.

"I know how you're feeling," volunteered Kerl, finally.

"Do you?" said Jason, savagely.

"I did the same thing myself once," said Kerl. "Shortly after I was taken into Class A Service. I was on Kelmesh and I thought I'd save time by fording a river. It was shallow enough and the water was clear enough, but there was more current than I thought and I hadn't the foresight to rope the men together. I lost five troopers."

Jason said nothing

"You'd better come back inside the ring of cars," said Kerl.

Jason looked up at the cliff. And then, just at that moment, the moon crept into sight, bathing the whole long valley suddenly in silvery luster. And in that same split second, born almost it seemed of the light itself, came a long, keening, wavering cry, that quivered out alone over the valley for a minute and then was taken up by many voices in something half-song, half-wail.

Jason halted as if struck.

"What's that?" he said, staring at Kerl.

The dark man's face in the bright moonlight was etched and hollowed by mysterious shadows. He looked off at the hills.

"There was some shooting while you were unconscious," he answered. "One of the men evidently hit and killed the clan's head. That's the lament for a chieftain."

They turned in silence and went back to the cars. The voices followed, crying on their ears.

The men in the cars were somber and quiet as they broke camp the next morning. Once they were moving, their little car trundling up out of the valley to head into the next one, Kerl spoke to Jason.

"Things may start occurring to the men," he said.

"Things?" repeated Jason, sharply. "What things?"

"That if I was out of the way, they could start back to the lowlands."

Jason stared at him.

"What?" he said, half-unable or unwilling to believe he had heard right.

"Don't look so shocked," said Kerl. "It's a natural reaction."

"These troops are completely trustworthy!" Jason felt his face warming with anger.

Kerl shrugged and looked away, out front at the barren cliffs.

"It's something to think of," he said. "It's important to me to reach my destination."

Jason felt words coming to his lips. He tried to check them, but the pressure inside him was too great.

"More important than men's lives?"

Kerl turned to face him again. His features were unreadable.

"To me," he said, "yes."

For what seemed a very long moment they seemed to sit poised, staring at each other. Then Kerl said, very softly:

"You don't understand."

"No," said Jason

"Tell me," said Kerl. "What do you intend to do with your life?"

"I am a career officer," answered Jason stiffly.

"Serving humanity on the Frontier, eventually, no doubt?"

"Of course." Effort kept Jason's voice level. "I was ready to leave for the Frontier when you arrived."

"And I held up your transfer," said Kerl, thoughtfully.

Jason could think of no rejoinder to this that would not be explosive; and so said nothing.

"Each to his own," Kerl went on, after a pause. "I was a Frontier officer myself, as I said. On Kelmesh."

It was the one weak spot in the armor of Jason's resentment. This man was a former officer. To Jason the words implied the very opposite of all that the word degenerate implied. He felt his fury ebb with a rush leaving him floundering in uncertainty.

"I don't understand you," he said helplessly. "I don't understand you at all."

The new valley dipped abruptly before them and Jason found that all the attention of his eyes was required to guide the car.

"Let me tell you about myself," he heard Kerl say.

"I was a chief's son," said Kerl. "I am still, for that matter, for there is nothing that can take that away from you. If my father has died while I was gone I am chieftain; my people will offer their hands to me as if I had never been away. But I am also a deserter."

"Deserter," murmured Jason, finding the military ring of the word odd in context with the mountain people.

"Deserter," repeated Kerl, strangely, as if for him the word had some hidden, personal meaning. "I ran away. I wanted to go down to the lowlands. I wanted to go to civilization and become famous. Not that being famous in itself was important. It was what it stood for. I wanted to leave my mark on the race."

"So you ran away?"

"We were camped one day near the southern foothills. My father had refused permission for about the thousandth time. That night I went. Three days later I was wearing a uniform back at your station there. That was twenty years ago. I was fourteen years old."

Jason shot him a glance of shocked surprise.

"You were in the service for twenty years?" he asked.

Kerl shook his head.

"I put in three years and saved my money. Then I took off toward the Frontier as a civilian pioneer. I bounced from new planet to new planet, doing everything—mines, timber, weather, construction. It was a rough life, but I liked it. It was like home."

He means the Timumang, thought Jason, looking bewilderedly at the bleak mountains.

"Then one day I woke up. I was twenty-eight and I hadn't even started to do the things I wanted to do. I hadn't left my mark on the progress of civilization, but it had left its mark on me. Suddenly all the wishing dreams I'd had as a boy came back. I just had to build something permanent and lasting that would be my own."

He paused.

"I went to Kelmesh," he said. He turned his head to look at Jason. "You've heard of Kelmesh?"

Jason nodded.

"A good world," said Kerl, his voice thoughtful as if he was half-talking to himself. "A fine world. Sweet water and clean air and all the natural resources. Nothing but little harmless life forms as far as we could see. Everything was beautiful. I looked at Kelmesh and I told myself that here was where I would make my mark and finish my days. Someday Kelmesh would have schools where history was taught. And near the beginning of that history would be the name of Kerl Potter." He sighed, a thin husk of a sound.

"I went to work," he said. "People were pouring into Kelmesh in those first couple of years after the planet was cleared and opened up. I bought land. I bought into the new towns and started things—an ore processing plant here, a tool factory there. I backed prospecting expeditions, and news services and everything else that I had the time or finances for." He looked down at his big hands in his lap with something like satisfaction. "I got a lot done."

"I suppose you made money," said Jason, thoughtlessly.

"Oh, I made it, all right," said Kerl. "But I ploughed it back in, every cent of it, as fast as I got my hands on it. It was history I was really after. And I made it, too, until the hordes came."

"Locusts, weren't they?" asked Jason, his eyes on the ground as he guided the little car through a small scattered forest of huge boulders.

"No," said Kerl, "they just resembled them in their life habits. Like the seven year (is it seven years?) locust. Millions of eggs were buried as much as ten feet underground. Every forty years they worked their way to the surface as worms and came out as little, hopping creatures as big as a small frog. Then they grew. They swelled up to the size of a grown sheep and spread out by the millions all over Kelmesh and devoured everything."

His voice stopped on a flat note.

"Everything," he repeated.

Jason had the good sense to keep his mouth shut. After a little bit, Kerl went on again.

"The colonists ran," he said. "God, I didn't blame them. Homes, lands, the grass, the trees, everything up to and including the clothing they wore was meat for the hordes. But I hated them for it. I stood on the spaceport landing stage with a silicoid jumper over what was left of my clothing and a thermite gun in my hand and cursed the last ship out of sight."

"You didn't leave?" asked Jason, incredulously. "I thought everybody left."

"Not I," said Kerl. "And not some others. It took us about two weeks to find each other for we were scattered all over the planet. But at the end of that time there were sixty of us gathered together in what was left of Kelmesh's governing city hall. Sixty-odd lousy, dirty, hungry men, with just one thought in common: that the hordes might chew the planet to the bone this time around, but the next generation wasn't going to live to boast about it."

The fierce note on which Kerl ended rang through the little car. He stopped, as if abashed by it, and then went on in a mild voice.

"They live for five years, you know," he said, "and lay their eggs at six week intervals all during that time. They don't all lay at once, either. A bunch go off somewhere by themselves and bury themselves alive. The body of the parent is food for the grubs when they hatch."

Jason shivered.

"Well, our first plan was to take to the air and track down a group that was about to lay and incinerate it. The first few months we tried it. Then we woke up to the fact that the job was too big and started just tracking them down and marking the laying areas. When the hordes began to split up and the individuals began to spread all over the place, we finally yelled for help. By that time we were down to about eighteen men."

Jason glanced sideways at him in surprise. Kerl caught the look.

"Lack of food," he explained. "Long hours in the air. Men would go asleep at the controls and crash. On foot you couldn't count on lasting very long. A human being's organic, and anything organic suited their appetites.

"We messaged our story out of the nearest Message Relay Station. Three months later a spruce Frontier Cruiser dropped down on our spaceport. I was there to meet it with two other men. A neatly tailored little commandant came down the landing ramp and looked me over.

" 'Where is everybody?' he asked.

" 'Dead,' I said.

"He looked at me as if I was pulling some kind of joke on him.

" 'Well, come on inside,' he said. 'We'll fix you up with some food and clothes.'

" 'The hell with food and clothes,' I said. 'Give us thermite recharges for the guns.'

"He peered at me.

" 'You're out of your head, planter,' he said. And I took

a swing at him and woke up in the ship's hospital two days later.

"Well, they wanted to send us back to civilization, but none of the three of us would go. So we compromised all around by having us sign on as Frontier Special Troops. Then the war began.

"It wasn't what Sector Headquarters ten light years away had thought it would be. It wasn't even what I thought it would be. It was worse. The whole thing tied in with the evolution process of these critters. They had no natural enemies, so they weeded each other out on a survival of the fittest basis. Within a few months they came out of the ground—inside half a year at the latest— they'd cleaned up everything else worth eating. That meant the only source of food was—each other.

"Sounds good, doesn't it?" Kerl smiled briefly at Jason. "Sounds as if they were helping us along in our extermination program? But it turned out that this process had bred some intelligence into them and with that intelligence, the ability to learn—fast.

"They had no use for brains when the whole planet was one big dinner table. But when the numbers began to thin out—when they were down to the last few millions of them—intelligence began to show up.

"First, they took to cooperating. Each little group began to show signs of internal organization. Then the groups began to work together, and we woke up to the fact that the critters were fighting back; what had started out as a fumigating project had turned into a war."

Kerl broke off suddenly to stare intently out the transparent front of the car. The seconds lengthened into minutes, and finally Jason spoke.

"What is it?" he demanded.

"Potter sign, I think," said Kerl. "A campsite about five hundred yards ahead. Drive on up to the foot of that big rock and halt the detachment."

The sign was Potter sign. Kerl toured the area of the camp, like a hunting animal, running the cold ashes from the cooking fires through his fingers, and raking through the discarded litter around them. His investigation kept him occupied until noon, so the midday meal was eaten where they stood. They pushed on after lunch, covering another fifty miles before night brought them to a stop.

The going was slower now, for Kerl was forced to watch the ground and the rocky walls closely to make sure that they were staying on the Potter trail and not drifting off on the track of some other clan that might have crossed or paralleled the same route. Consequently, there was no further chance for conversation between him and Jason and it was not until that evening that Jason had an opportunity to draw him aside.

They sat down in their car and closed the top—that being the only meager means to privacy the situation afforded.

"How much farther before we catch up with them?" asked Jason.

"Not far," replied Kerl. His voice seemed to have grown old and weary since the morning. "Say thirty miles. We should catch up with them tomorrow afternoon."

"Good," said Jason.

They sat in silence for a little while, each occupied by his own thoughts. Finally Jason broke the pause.

"You were telling me about Kelmesh earlier today—"

"Oh—yes," said Kerl abruptly, like someone whose thoughts are suddenly recalled from a great distance. "I was. Well—right now I'm a little tired. If you don't mind—"

"Of course," replied Jason promptly. He threw back the lid of the car and stepped out. "Good night."

"Good night," said Kerl from the interior shadows of the car.

Jason did not feel like sleeping. He had always been a straightforward man, as honest with himself as nature permitted. He believed thoroughly in the solid universe that he knew. It contained space and the human race, whose manifest destiny it was to occupy space. Occasionally, among the teeming hordes of mankind emerged those who perceived this destiny. These went out and dedicated themselves to it. The rest lived and bred in happy ignorance. To them, no blame, but no glory.

But among the dedicated— By no possible stretch of the imagination could Jason imagine a man who saw the light, followed it, then turned his back on it, and went again to dwell in darkness. What flaw in the ideal of man's manifest destiny could prompt such an action? The thought was very disturbing to Jason. After all, this was the ideal he was probably going to get himself killed for—unless good luck and skill preserved him.

Jason could no longer write Kerl off as a man basically lacking in courage and the virtues that the Frontier demands. Jason had read and heard enough about Kelmesh to recognize that the other man was speaking the truth. Had Kerl's nerve finally broken under those conditions? Jason could not believe it. There was nothing broken about the big, dark man.

What then? Pacing the narrow circle of the camp, Jason looked up at the stars and did not know the answer.

But he would find out tomorrow, before Kerl parted company with them for good—he made himself that promise.

Morning came bright and sudden. A little of the sparse rain that fell upon these mountains had fallen during the night, and the rocks around them were dark and had a damp smell that began to fade quickly as a thirsty sun licked up the moisture through the dry air. Camp was struck, and the circle of cars took up the trail again in customary file.

For four hours, the going was the same as it had been the day before, the detachment crawling along slowly, with Kerl in the lead car tensely scrutinizing the ground for sign. They crossed out of the valley and into another that ran parallel for some twenty miles. Then at a point where the mountains split three ways, Kerl called a halt.

He got down from the lead car and began to examine the little open area where the four valleys came together. For some time he combed the area minutely, eyes bent on the rock at his feet; long arms dangling loosely from hunched shoulders, so that he looked almost more ape than human from a distance. Finally, he returned to the car where Jason waited.

"There," he said, pointing to the rightmost of the three new valleys as he climbed into the car. "And about thirty miles off. I know where they're headed, now."

Jason looked at him; then closed the open top of the car

and gave the order to move out over the intercom. They rolled ahead between the rocky walls that had been steadily about them since the beginning.

In his bucket seat in the car, Kerl leaned back and sighed, rubbing one big, square-fingered hand across his eyes.

"A strain, that tracking, I suppose," said Jason.

Kerl turned to look at him. He managed a tired grin.

"I'm out of practice," he replied. "Too much being done for me by gadgets has spoiled the senses."

His eyes had wandered off to look at the mountains. Now he brought them back again to Jason.

"You've done a good job for me," he said. "I'm grateful."

"My duty—" said Jason, with a little deprecating shrug. He half-turned to look at the other man.

"Can I ask you a question?" he said.

"Go ahead," Kerl told him.

The strict Kilburnian ethics of Jason's upbringing fought a momentary, short and silent battle with his curiosity and lost.

"Why are you going back?" he asked.

Jason could see the sharp barb of his question strike home. Kerl did not answer. And, as the seconds slipped past and were lost in silence, he began to think that he had, indeed, stepped beyond the bounds of all propriety and right. And, then, just as he was about to apologize, words did come from the other man.

"You asked me to tell you about the rest of what happened to me on Kelmesh," said Kerl.

"I—yes," replied Jason. "Yes, I did."

"I'll tell you now," said Kerl. "You've heard what it was like, no doubt."

"I had a cousin who came in on the tail end of it," said Jason. "I read some letters from him."

"A lot of men died," Kerl spoke softly, "more men than I could ever have imagined dying in one place at one time. That's why I earned rank so quickly. They discharged me as an Officer Two, but I was acting Commandant for the last six months."

"You know," Jason said. "I have trouble understanding how creatures like that, even with a little intelligence, could stand up to our war equipment so long, and cause such trouble."

Kerl chuckled a little bitterly. "Sector Headquarters had trouble understanding it, too. But then, they weren't on the planet."

Jason blinked at such open criticism of the Frontier's military leadership. Kerl went on:

"It was easy enough to understand when it was under your nose. There were two reasons. One was that we were not fighting a war, we were conducting an extermination project, in which all of those critters had to be killed off. The second was that we couldn't defend, we had to attack. Impose those conditions on men fighting in what amounted to a wasteland, and what did you have?

"You had small patrol action and nothing but small patrol action. There was so much ground to be covered and so many of the things to be killed. You called in your junior officers and lined them up in front of a map and drew out their routes for them. Then out they went to make their patrols on foot—on foot, mind you, because the critters buried themselves in the ground during the daytime and even in a two man car you'd drive right over them.

"They'd take off—" Kerl's eyes had grown bleak and distant, seeing again the bitter plains of his memories. "—extended in a skirmish line, looking for spots where the earth was loose. And when they found one, they'd dig it out and incinerate it, unless it woke up first and got away before the thermite charges could cripple it enough to make escape impossible.

"When night came the men would bivouak and dig in, with their guns charged and portable searchlights illuminating the ground all around them. And they'd try to sleep—but the night would be one long battle.

"Nothing kept the critters away. The searchlights even attracted them—but what could you do? The men needed light to shoot by, and some warning when they came. For they came at top speed. They must have been crazy mad with hunger, during this period when there was nothing for them to live on but each other and us. One would spot the light and come up quietly, then suddenly charge in as fast as it could. And they could move fast. The idea seemed to be to pick up a man and carry him off into the darkness.

"Sometimes, two or three would work together and we'd have them charging at once. The horrible thing was, there was a sort of instinct in them that made them try to continue eating even when they were dying. If they grabbed a man and couldn't make it out of the circle, they still tried to make a meal of him, even while being burned by the gun charges.

"Their notion of fighting was just to start eating their enemy. In fact, fighting and feeding was the same thing. In the beginning the losses from night attacks were fantastically high. But after a while we began to keep them down to a minimum. The men kept their lives, but they lost their nerve—"

This was so close to what Jason had been thinking about Kerl himself the night before, that the young officer started involuntarily. Kerl, however, went on without noticing.

"—and cracked. And the commonest form of cracking was to blow up some night when the patrol was dug in, to jump out of the hole you had dug and go running off into the darkness to hunt down the critters that were prowling out there. That waiting—" Kerl shuddered, "—it was bad. Sooner or later, the men would lose their self-possession and go to meet them halfway." He turned to look at Jason. "They estimate around a hundred thousand men were lost that way."

"A hundred thousand!" Even Jason's military-conditioned mind was shocked by the number. "But not all of them. Not—" his tone was almost accusing, —"not you."

"No, not me," said Kerl. He sighed. "I was the exception—the freak. It bothered me, but I lasted through five long years of it. I even kept other men from cracking up as long as they were with me. Nothing particular I did—just knowing I was around seemed to brace them."

Jason stared at him.

"But that was marvelous—wasnt' it?" he said. "I mean, they could study you and find out what was needed to keep other men from cracking up. You could turn yourself into Service Research and . . ." his voice faltered, died before a supposition so monstrous that it overwhelmed him. Finally he put it into words. "You aren't—that isn't what you're running away from?"

Kerl laughed.

"Nothing so melodramatic," he said. "Research didn't even wait for the business to finish on Kelmesh before pulling me back to Earth. They tested me and worked me over and scratched their heads and finally came up with an answer. In plain words, what was happening was that the civilized man of today was many times as susceptible to the emotional strains of war as his remote ancestor. It was a matter of environment—what the psychologists called having a 'wider mental horizon'."

"But what are they going to do about it?" asked Jason.

"There isn't too much they can do," said Kerl soberly. "There are two obvious solutions. One is to return to the environment of eighteenth-nineteenth century Earth, which is impossible. The other is to freeze the present environment long enough for the human race to mature up to it. Which is unpalatable and which people won't stand for."

"Of course not!" cried Jason. "Why, that'd be ridiculous! It—it'd be fantastic. To hold up our proper and necessary expansion for a little problem like that. The human race solves problems—it doesn't knuckle under to them."

A shadow passed across Kerl's face for an instant, saddening it.

"You're right," he said. "The race does."

"There must be some practical steps they can take," continued Jason. "Some conditioning process, or such."

Kerl shrugged.

"Some factors seem to help a little," he said. "You may have wondered why you've been held in Class C duty so long when it's usual to promote to Class A Frontier posts fairly quickly."

"They have been slow with me," frowned Jason.

"And with a lot of others in your class," said Kerl. "That's one of the little things that seems to help some—a longer tour of garrison work."

"Look here!" said Jason. "*I'm* not liable to crack up. My mental health is excellent."

"A fresh water fish," replied Kerl, "can be in fine shape. But put him in salt water and he sickens and dies."

"But this is all backward!" exploded Jason. "You're supposed to have come through on Kelmesh. To you that environment should have been much more of a shock than to a man like me—I take new and different worlds for granted. I grew up with an open mind. Why, if what you say is true, then these mountain people of yours—"

He broke off abruptly, a realization taking startling form in his mind. In the little silence that followed, Kerl's voice answered him.

"It *is* the opposite from what you might expect," he said. "Early in the beginnings of psychology, men began to notice that some primitive peoples were amazingly well adjusted. Not all primitive peoples, of course. The majority ran the scale from bad to worse. But a few stood out."

"But you can't scrap civilization!" cried Jason, desperately.

"I don't know," answered Kerl. "Can't you? I can't. You can't. No government or controlling power can—or wants to. Maybe we won't have to. But when Research dug into the matter they came up with some funny answers. For instance—the individual has a survival instinct. They've known that for a long time. Now they think the race has one, too."

"Of course," said Jason. "Survival of the fittest—"

"No," said Kerl. "Think of the race as a single individual with instincts. And one of the instincts is not to put all his eggs in one basket."

Jason merely looked puzzled. Again, that shadow crossed Kerl's face, shading his eyes with an obscure pain.

"Never at any time," Kerl said, "have all the people been all alike. Some were more one way than another. Geographical accident, they used to think—and of course it was, largely. But there's a real instinctive tendency for groups to be different, even as there is for the individual to be different—and for the same reason, survival. It wouldn't be good for them all to be alike. Then, some new thing that could wipe out one, could wipe out all."

"Do you mean to tell me," said Jason, spacing the words slowly, and, he thought, calmly, "that the trillions or quadrillions or whatever it is we have of people on all the civilized worlds, are an evolutionary dead end; that you and these mountaineers squatting on their rocks represent the future of the race?"

"No," Kerl shook his head, "not *the* future. A possible future. A remotely possible future. One of nature's extra strings to its bow. Imagine civilization breaking down. Would that make any difference to my people here? Not a bit. They're completely self-supporting. They don't need and don't want the rest of you. They might pull humanity back up out of the mud again."

Kerl's words died in the car. For what seemed a long while, Jason sat thinking. Finally, he turned to Kerl.

"But *you* think your people will make the future," he said. It was an accusation. "That's why you've come back."

Kerl's dark face was suddenly ravaged with sorrow.

"No," he said. "No. I came back for an entirely different reason."

Jason waited.

"Research turned me inside out," said Kerl, painfully. "When they were through with me, I knew myself—too well. I knew myself inside and out. And I realized—" his voice faltered, then picked up with a new strength—"that I was different. From the time when that difference came home to me, living in civilization became living among strangers. There was a barrier there I could not cross because it was inside me and now I knew it was there." He stopped.

"I had no choice," he said suddenly. "I had to go home."

He let out his breath and looked down at his hands, big and dark, folded in his lap.

"I—am sorry," said Jason, stiffly. "I beg your pardon."

"That's all right," said Kerl. "It's almost over now." He raised his eyes from his lap and looked out ahead. "You can stop anyplace along here. We don't want to drive up to the camp. We'll stop a bit short and let them find us."

"All right," said Jason. He switched on the intercom and gave the necessary orders.

The cars circled in the light of the afternoon sun, halted, men got out, and camp was made.

About an hour before twilight, the Potter clan put in its appearance. One moment, the valley was empty beyond the camp and then—it seemed, almost without transition—a small host of rough-clad figures had sprung into view, on the valley floor and down the rocky slopes some two hundred yards from the circle of cars. They stood silent, waiting. Two groups with centuries of apparent difference between them. Silent, they stood and watched. Jason went to get Kerl and found him sitting in their car, chin on hand, his eyes absent and thoughtful.

"Well, they're here," said Jason.

Kerl nodded.

"I know," he answered.

"They've come right out in the open," continued Jason. "Almost as if they knew you were with us."

"I imagine they do," said Kerl. "Other tribes will have seen me with you and passed the word along." He got heavily to his feet and stepped out of the car. Beyond the cars were the troopers. Followed by Jason, Kerl walked to an open space where a number of the men of the tribe stood waiting. Kerl turned and looked at the troopers.

"Goodby," he said. "Thanks."

The men murmured self-consciously. Kerl turned again and started off, stepping surely down the rugged path. Jason followed, without quite knowing why.

Where the rough going ceased and the valley began to broaden out, Kerl stopped again and turned to Jason as the younger man came up level with him. They were far enough from the troopers now so that low voices would not carry their words back.

"Goodby," said Kerl.

"Goodby," Jason replied. Kerl put out his hand and Jason took it. They shook briefly, but Kerl held on to Jason's hand for a minute before releasing it.

"Don't—" he began earnestly, but the words seemed to stick in his throat.

"Yes?" said Jason.

Kerl's face was twisted as if with a mighty inner effort.

"Don't be afraid of the future," he said, tightly. "Keep going. Keep looking. There's nothing so wonderful as that."

Jason stared at him.

"*You* say that?" He could not keep the incredulity out of his voice. He nodded toward the waiting mountaineers. "But you're going back!"

"Yes," whispered Kerl. "I told you. I have no choice."

Jason swallowed.

"Come back with us," he said. "I didn't know. But if it's

our future you want, not theirs, come back. You can if you want to."

"I can't."

"Why not?" cried Jason. "It's all a matter of what you want. I thought you wanted this."

"This?" echoed Kerl, looking bleakly about him at the mountains. "This?" His face worked.

"God, *no!*" he cried. "The only thing I ever wanted was Kelmesh!"

He turned, tearing himself away from Jason and facing towards the clansmen. Pebbles rattled and rolled under his uncaring feet as he lurched away.

Walking like a blind man, he went down the valley.

Of Kipling And Me

L. Sprague de Camp

When I was a child, my mother read to me Kipling's *Just So Stories* and *The Jungle Book*. 1 especially remember certain lines: "a man of infinite resource and sagacity"; "more-than-oriental splendour"; "the cat that walks by himself". They must have stuck in many other minds, too, thus becoming clichés. Incidents remain bright: Mowgli kicking stones into the bees' nests; eight-legged Quiquern howling on his ice hummock; Kaa the python knocking down a wall with his head (something no real snake could do).

In adolescence I was a Pleistocene buff, dreaming of what fun it would be to live back then and see mammoths. (Having watched wild elephants in Africa, I now know what a bore mammoth-watching would soon become.) Then I was struck by Kipling's poems, especially the prehistoric: "In the Neolithic age, savage warfare did I wage. . . ." and "Once, on a glittering ice field, ages and ages ago. . . ."

Now, as a very senior citizen, I am interested in Kipling as a celebrant of one of history's most consequential movements: European conquest of the world. Having the gun, the compass, and the ocean-going ship when nobody else had that combination, Europeans set out around 1500 to impose their rule and creeds on the rest of the world. By 1900 they ruled nearly all of it save East Asia. The mainspring of this conquest was technological. Other tries at world conquest, such as the Macedonian, the Arab, or the Napoleonic, based on mere generalship or religious fervor, were much less successful.

During this expansion, Europeans ("white men") moved into any place they liked and told the dwellers, who thought they owned it, to get lost. When "natives" objected too vigorously, the whites mowed them down by superior fire power. When the natives had spears, Europeans had muskets; when the natives got muskets, the whites had machine guns.

In the Americas, Australia, and Oceania the natives were so obliging as to die off in vast numbers from smallpox, measles, yellow fever, etc., to which they lacked resistance. And Asians and Africans, having long been exposed to these ills, survived the conquest. Being more numerous than the white settlers, they eventually recovered their lands, save in a few places like South Africa and Russian Central Asia.

With the usual human tendency to blame the victim, Europeans justified their conquests. They said the natives of the Americas, Australia, Oceania, Central Asia, and black Africa were stupid barbarians who needed firm European rule to "civilize and Christianize" them, as William McKinley said in ballyhooing American conquest of the Philippines, 1899–1902. They could not say that of most Asians, since during the European Dark Ages the Indians and Chinese had been much more civilized than they. So they called the Asians morally inferior villains. Hence the "yellow peril" scare of the early twentieth century and the popularity of the Fu-Manchurian theme in fiction.

Kipling epitomizes this vast movement, declaiming: "Take up the white man's burden. . . ." (I have read that he wrote that poem as a warning to the Americans against the responsibilities they were taking on by their conquest of the Philippines, 1899–1902.)

Although in many ways a typical English gentleman of his time, Kipling was too intelligent and took too long a view to take all this rationalization at face value. While he did not much like the Indians among whom he had lived, and while he never went so far as Talbot Mundy (who has an English hero call for the British to quit India), Kipling does drop hints that the conquered will not submit forever: "And then we shall dance on your graves!" He did not love to see the European retreat from Asia and Africa, but I doubt if it would have greatly surprised him.

Ghost Ships

L. Sprague de Camp

The ghosts of ships were gathered at a harbor in the sky;
I saw a swarm of vessels, great and small, from years of
 yore,
From proas, junks, and triremes to the liners looming high.
The warships formed a snobbish club, their feats to glorify,
And boasted of their battles in the lengthy log of war.
A graceful, clinkered galley, with a dragon at her prow,
Proclaimed: "I hight Great Serpent, and by Christus and
 by Thor,
"I was the finest ship King Olaf made the main to plow.
"I bore him to his hero's battle-death at Svold; but now
"This coward's tool, the gun, has spoiled the noble game of
 war."

Then spake the three-deck Victory, with spiritsails at her
 head:
"You're but an overgrown canoe, despite your length of
 oar.
"I was the boast of Britain's fleet, when scuppers ran with
 red.
"Aboard me, at Trafalgar, deathly wounded, Nelson bled;
"But now these damned steam engines take the glory out
 of war."

The hulking paddle-frigate Mississippi then began:
"The twain of you are out of date; but I, ten years before
"I perished on a river bar, did open up Japan

"(Which some would say was rash) as Perry's flagship; but
  this plan
"Of iron-plating ships has drained the honor out of war."
A burly British battleship, the Warspite, spoke at last:
"I've waged two wars, the like of which was never known
  before.
"At Jutland and at Matapan, the foeman felt my blast;
"But heavy guns are silent now, their days of thunder
  past.
"These beastly, bloody aeroplanes have ruined naval war."
A huge, lopsided carrier, the Enterprise, professed:
"I own my life was not so long as yours but swear my
  score
"Of battles fought, from Midway to Nippon, is still the
  best.
"But though my sisters scour the sea, they sail with little
  zest;
"These villainous atomic bombs have spoiled the art of
  war."

An old Phoenician bireme eyed a nuclear submarine
And spake as follows to the ships in accents harsh and
  hoar:
"The next big fray our makers fight may end the earthly
  scene.
"If any live, they'll fight from bark canoes in broils marine;
"So take your sentimental leave of human naval war!"

What Kipling Meant to Richard McKenna

Gordon R. Dickson

"Take out all these pages on the moonlight," Chekov once wrote to a younger and far less famous writer than himself, on a manuscript sent him by the younger writer for criticism. *"Give me instead simply the reflection of it on a piece of broken bottle."*

It is necessary for writers to have an eye or an ear beyond the ordinary, to pick just the minimum of words that will give the sharpest and most memorable picture of what the writer is painting. Some have eye or ear so far beyond the ordinary that they seem over the horizon and out of sight of the rest of us. Shakespeare had both, but besides him there are few so gifted.

Kipling's eye, above all, was remarkable. He has influenced generations of writers in the art of storytelling, including some who would deny any such influence, but show it anyway, having acquired it from writers who acquired it from other writers, who in turn acquired it from Kipling.

The happy are those among storytellers who can enjoy Kipling and acknowledge that influence. Among them was Mac—Richard McKenna. He had an eye like Kipling's; and he—and I—were two of a group who "kippled" when they forgathered. To "kipple" is to take turns capping each other in quotations by memory from Kipling's many works of prose and poetry; particularly his poetry. We indulged in this whenever and wherever events brought us together, whether it might be at the Milford Science Fiction

Conferences (published writers of science fiction only) or at Science Fiction Conventions (writers and readers both).

You must imagine what it was like at these get-togethers. Mac had spent a working lifetime at sea; and the mark of the sea was on him. He was a little under six feet, built like a battleship, with bushy eyebrows and a surprising, contrasting gentleness toward all things. I was lanky, in my twenties and thirties, mountainbred, and about as far removed from the sea as possible. But we were at one over Kipling; and our sessions lasted late into the night, talking about the man and quoting his lines to each other.

We were pleasuring ourselves with words that could have been said, for their maximum effect and absolute economy, in no other way—*"Thus and no otherwise . . ."*—to quote Kipling himself. At the same time we were unconsciously sharpening our own writing skills by reference to a Master of our art.

As Mac, himself, has come to be recognized as a Master in his own right.

As his writing shows.

The Night of Hoggy Darn

RICHARD MCKENNA

Red-haired Flinter Cole sipped his black coffee and looked around the chrome and white tile galley of Space Freighter *Gorbals*, in which he was riding down the last joint of a dogleg journey to the hermit planet of New Cornwall.

"Nothing's been published about the planet for the last five hundred years," he said in a nervous, jerky voice. "You people on *Gorbals* at least *see* the place, and I understand you're the only ship that does."

"That's right, twice every standard year," said the cook. He was a placid, squinting man, pink in his crisp whites. "But like I said, no girls, no drinks, nothing down there but hard looks and a punch in the nose for being curious. We mostly stay aboard, up in orbit. Them New Cornish are the biggest, meanest men I ever did see, Doc."

"I'm not a real doctor yet," Cole said, glancing down at the scholar grays he was wearing. "If I don't do a good job on New Cornwall I may never be. This is my Ph.D trial field assignment. I should be *stuffing* myself with data on the ecosystem so I can ask the right questions when I get there. But there's nothing!"

"What's a pee aitch dee?"

"That's being a doctor. I'm an ecologist—that means I deal with everything alive, and the way it all works in with climate and geography. I can use *any* kind of data. I have only six months until *Gorbals* comes again to make my survey and report. If I fumble away my doctorate, and I'm

146

twenty-three already. . . ." Cole knitted shaggy red eyebrows in worry.

"Well hell, Doc, I can tell you things like, it's got four moons and only one whopper of a continent and it's low grav, and the forest there you won't believe even when you see it—"

"I need to know about *stompers*. Bidgrass Company wants Belconti U. to save them from extinction, but they didn't say what the threat is. They sent travel directions, a visa and passage scrip for just one man. And I only had two days for packing and library research, before I had to jump to Tristan in order to catch this ship. I've been running in the dark ever since. You'd think the Bidgrass people didn't really care."

"Price of stomper egg what it is, I doubt that," the cook said, scratching his fat jaw. "But for a fact, they're shipping less these days. Must be some kind of trouble. I never saw a stomper, but they say they're big birds that live in the forest."

"You see? The few old journal articles I did find, said they were flightless bird-homologs that lived on the plains and preyed on the great herds of something called darv cattle."

"Nothing but forest and sea for thousands of miles around Bidgrass Station, Doc. Stompers are pure hell on big long legs, they say."

"There again! *I* read they were harmless to man."

"Tell you what, you talk to Daley. He's cargo officer and has to go down with each tender trip. He'll maybe know something can help you."

The cook turned away to inspect his ovens. Cole put down his cup and clamped a freckled hand over his chin, thinking. He thought about stomper eggs, New Cornwall's sole export and apparently, for five hundred years, its one link with the other planets of Carina sector. Their reputedly indescribable flavor had endeared them to gourmets on a hundred planets. They were symbols of conspicuous consumption for the ostentatious wealthy. No wonder most of the literature under the New Cornwall reference had turned out to be cookbooks.

Orphaned and impecunious, a self-made scholar, Cole had never tasted stomper egg.

The cook slammed an oven door on the fresh bread smell.

"Just thought, Doc. I keep a can or two of stomper egg, squeeze it from cargo for when I got a passenger to feed. How'd you like a mess for chow tonight?"

"Why not?" Cole said, grinning suddenly. "Anything may be data for an ecologist especially if it's good to eat."

The stomper egg came to the officers' mess table as a heaped platter of bite-sized golden spheres, deep-fried in bittra oil. Their delicate, porous texture hardly required chewing. Their flavor was like—cinnamon? Peppery sandalwood? Yes, yes, and yet unique. . . .

Cole realized in confusion that he had eaten half the platterful and the other six men had not had any. He groped for a lost feeling—was it that he and the others formed a connected biomass and that he could eat for all of them? Ridiculous!

"I'm a pig," he laughed weakly. "Here, Mr. Daley, have some."

Daley, a gingery, spry little man, said "By me" and slid the platter along. It rounded the table and returned to Cole untouched.

"Fall to, Doc," Daley said, grinning.

Cole was already reaching . . . lying in his stateroom and he *was* the bunk cradling a taut, messianic body flaming with imageless dreams. He dreamed himself asleep and slept himself into shamed wakefulness needing coffee.

It was ship-night. Cole walked through dimmed lights to the galley and carried his cup of hot black coffee to main control, where he found Daley on watch, lounging against the gray enamel computer.

"I feel like a fool," Cole said.

"You're a martyr to science, Doc. Which reminds me, Cookie told me you got questions about Bidgrass Station."

"Well, yes, about stompers. What's wiping them out, what's their habitat and life pattern, oh anything."

"I learned quick not to ask about stompers. I gather they're twenty feet high or so and they're penned up behind a stockade. I never saw one."

"Well, dammit! I read they couldn't be domesticated."

"They're not. Bidgrass Station is in a clearing the New

Cornish cut from sea to sea across a narrow neck of land. On the west is this stockade and beyond it is Lundy Peninsula, a good half-million square miles of the damnedest forest ever grew on any planet. That's where the stompers are."

"How thickly settled is this Lundy Peninsula?"

"Not a soul there, Doc. The settlement is around Car Truro on the east coast, twelve thousand miles east of Bidgrass. I never been there, but you can see from the air it isn't much."

"How big a city is Bidgrass? Does it have a university?"

Daley smiled again and shook his head. "They got fields and pastures, but it's more like a military camp than a town. I see barracks for the workers and egg hunters, hangars and shops, a big egg-processing plant and warehouses around the landing field. I never get away from the field, but I'd guess four, five thousand people at Bidgrass."

Cole sighed and put down his cup on the log desk.

"What is it they import, one half so precious as the stuff they sell?"

Daley chuckled and rocked on his toes. "Drugs, chemicals, machinery parts, hundreds of tons of Warburton energy capsules. Pistols, blasters, cases of flame charge, tanks of fire mist—you'd think they had a war on."

"That's no help. I'll make up for lost time when I get there. I'll beat their ears off with questions."

Daley's gnomish face grew serious. "Watch what you ask and who you ask, Doc. They're suspicious as hell and they hate strangers."

"They need my help. Besides, I'll deal only with scientists."

"Bidgrass isn't much like a campus. I don't know, Doc, something's wrong on that planet and I'm always glad to lift out."

"Why didn't you and the others eat any of that stomper egg?" Cole asked abruptly.

"Because the people at Bidgrass turn sick and want to slug you if you mention eating it. That's reason enough for me."

Well, that was data, too, Cole thought, heading back to his stateroom.

Two days later Daley piloted the cargo tender down in a three-lap braking spiral around New Cornwall. Cole sat beside him in the cramped control room, eyes fixed on the view panel. Once he had the bright and barren moon Cairdween at upper left, above a vastly curving sweep of sun-glinting ocean, and he caught his breath in wonder.

"I know the feeling, Doc," Daley said softly. "Like being a giant and jumping from world to world."

Clouds obscured much of the sprawling, multi-lobed single continent. The sharpening of outline and hint of regularity Cole remembered noting on Tristan and his own planet of Belconti, the mark of man, was absent here. Yet New Cornwall, as a human settlement, was two hundred years older than Belconti.

The forests stretched across the south and west, broken by uplands and rain shadows, as the old books said. He saw between cloud patches the glint of lakes and the crumpled leaf drainage pattern of the great northeastern plain but, oddly, the plain was darker in color than the pinkish-yellow forest. He mentioned it to Daley.

"It's flowers and vines and moss makes it that color," the little man said, busy with controls. "Whole world in that forest top—snakes, birds, jumping things big as horses. Doc, them trees are *big*."

"Of course! I read about the epiphytal biota. And low gravity always conduces to gigantism."

"There's Lundy," Daley grunted, pointing.

It looked like a grinning ovoid monster-head straining into the western ocean at the end of a threadlike neck. Across the neck Bidgrass Station slashed between parallel lines of forest edge like a collar. Cole watched it again on the landing approach, noting the half-mile of clearing between the great wall and the forest edge, the buildings and fields rectilinear in ordered clumps east of the wall, and then the light aberration of the tender's life field blotted it out.

"Likely I won't see you till next trip," Daley said, taking leave. "Good luck, Doc."

Cole shuffled down the personnel ramp, grateful for the weight of his two bags in the absurdly light gravity. Trucks and cargo lifts were coming across the white field from the silvery warehouses along its edge. Men also, shaggy-haired big men in loose blue garments, walking oddly without the stride and drive of leg muscles. Their faces were uniformly grim and blank to Cole, standing there uncertainly. Then a ground car pulled up and a tall old man in the same rough clothing got out and walked directly toward him. He had white hair, bushy white eyebrows over deepset gray eyes, and a commanding beak of a nose.

"Who might you be?" he demanded.

"I'm Flinter Cole, from Belconti University. Someone here is expecting me."

The old man squinted in thought and bit his lower lip. Finally he said, "The biologist, hey? Didn't expect you until next *Gorbals*. Didn't think you could make the connections for this one."

"It left me no time at all to study up in. But when species extinction is the issue, time is important. And I'm an ecologist."

"Well," the old man said. "Well. I'm Garth Bidgrass."

He shook Cole's hand, a powerful grip quickly released.

"Hawkins there in the car will take you to the manor house and get you settled. I'll phone ahead. I'll be tied up checking cargo for a day or two, I expect. You just rest up awhile."

He spoke to the driver in what sounded like Old English, then moved rapidly across the field toward the warehouses in the same strange walk as the other men. As far as Cole could see, he did not bend his knees at all.

Hawkins, also old but frail and stooped, took Cole's bags to the car. When the ecologist tried to follow him he almost fell headlong, then managed a stiff-legged shuffle. Momentarily he longed for the Earth-normal gravity of Belconti and the ship.

They drove past unfenced fields green with vegetable and cereal crops, and fenced pastures holding beef and dairy cattle of the old Earth breeds. It was a typical human ecosystem. Then they passed a group of field workers, and surprise jolted the ecologist. They were huge—eight or nine feet tall, both men and women, all with long hair and some of them naked. They did not look up.

Cole looked at Hawkins. The old man glared at him from red-rimmed eyes and chattered something in archaic English. He speeded up, losing the giants behind a hedge, and the manor house with the palisade behind it loomed ahead.

The great fence dwarfed the house. Single baulks of grassy brown timber ten feet on a side soared two hundred feet into the air, intricately braced and stayed. High above, a flyer drifted as if on sentry duty. Half a mile beyond, dwarfing the fence in its turn, arose the thousand-foot black escarpment of the forest edge.

The manor house huddled in a walled garden with armed guards at the gate. It was two-storied and sprawling, with a flat-roofed watch tower at the southeast corner, and made of the same glassy brown timber. Hawkins stopped the car by the pillared veranda where a lumpy, gray, nondescript woman waited. Cole got out, awkwardly careful in the light gravity.

The woman would not meet his glance. "I'm Flada Vignoli, Mr. Bidgrass's niece and housekeeper," she said in a dead voice. "I'll show you your rooms." She turned away before Cole could respond.

"Let me carry the bags, I need to," he said to Hawkins, laughing uncertainly. The old man hoisted his skinny shoulders and spat.

The rooms were on the second floor, comfortable but archaic in style. The gray woman told him that Hawkins would bring his meals, that Garth Bidgrass would see him in a few days to make plans, and that Mr. Bidgrass thought he should not go about unescorted until he knew more about local conditions.

Cole nodded. "I'll want to confer with your leading biologists, Mrs. Vignoli, as soon as I can. For today, can you get me a copy of your most recent biotic survey?"

"Ain't any biologists, ain't any surveys," she said, standing in the half-closed door.

"Well, any recent book about stompers or your general zoölogy. It's important that I start at once."

The face under the scraggly gray hair went blanker still. "You'll have to talk to Mr. Bidgrass." She closed the door.

Cole unpacked, bathed, dressed again, and explored his three rooms. Like a museum, he thought. He looked out his west windows at the palisade and forest edge. Then he decided to go downstairs, and found his door was locked.

The shock was more fear than indignation, he realized,

wondering at himself. He paced his sitting room, thinking about his scholarly status and the wealth and power of Belconti, until he had the indignation flaming. Then a knock came at the door and it opened to reveal old Hawkins with a wheeled food tray.

"What do you mean, locking me in?" Cole asked hotly.

He pushed past the food tray into the hall. Hawkins danced and made shooing motions with his hands, chattering shrilly in the vernacular. Cole walked to the railing around the stairwell and looked down. At the foot of the stair a giant figure, man or woman he could not say, sat and busied itself with something in its lap.

Cole went back into his room. The food was boiled beef, potatoes, and beets, plain but plentiful, plus bread and coffee. He ate heartily and looked out his windows again to see night coming on. Finally he tried the door and it was not locked. He shrugged, pushed the food tray into the hall and closed the door again. Then he shot the inside bolt.

In bed, he finally dropped off into a restless, disturbed sleep.

Emboldened by morning and a hearty tray breakfast, Cole explored. He was in a two-floor wing, and the doors into the main house were locked. Through them he heard voices and domestic clatter. Unlocked across the second-floor hall was another suite of rooms like his own. Downstairs was still another suite and along the south side a library. The door into the garden was locked.

My kingdom, Cole thought wryly. Prisoner of state!

He explored the library. Tristanian books, historical romances for the most part, none less than three hundred years old. No periodicals, nothing of New Cornwall publication. He drifted from window to window looking out at the formal garden of flower beds, hedges, and white sand paths. Then he saw the girl.

She knelt in a sleeveless gray dress trimming a hedge. Her tanned and rounded arms had dimpled elbows, he noted. She turned suddenly and he saw, framed by reddish-brown curls, her oval face with small nose and firm chin. The face was unsuitably grave and the eyes wide.

She was not staring at his window, Cole decided after a

qualm, but listening. Then she rose, picked up her basket of trimmings and glided around the corner of the house. Before he could pursue her plump vision to another window, a man appeared.

He looked taller than Cole and was built massively as a stone. Straight black hair fell to his shoulders, cut square across his forehead and bound by a white fillet. Under the black bar of eyebrow the heavy face held itself in grim, unsmiling lines. He moved with that odd, unstriding New Cornish walk that suggested tremendous power held in leash.

Cole crossed the hall and watched the blue-clad form enter a door in the wing opposite. The girl was nowhere. Again Cole felt a twinge of fear, and boiled up anger to mask it.

Inside looking out, he thought. Peeping like an ecologist in a bird blind!

When Hawkins brought lunch Cole raged at him and demanded to see Garth Bidgrass. The old man chattered incomprehensibly and danced like a fighting cock. Thwarted, the ecologist ate moodily and went down to the library. The garden was empty and he decided on impulse to open a window. A way of retreat, but from what and to where, he wondered as he worked at the fastenings. Just as he got it free, a woman stooped through the library door. She was at least seven feet tall.

Cole stood erect and held his breath. Not looking at him, the woman dropped to her knees and began dusting the natural wood half-panelling that encircled the room between bookcases. She had long blonde hair and a mild, vacant face; she wore a shapeless blue dress.

"Hello," Cole said.

She paid no attention.

"Hello!" he said more sharply. "Do you speak Galactic English?"

She looked at him out of empty blue eyes and went back to her work. He went past her gingerly and up to his room. There he wrote a note to Garth Bidgrass, paced and fanned his indignation, tore up the note and wrote a stronger one. When Hawkins brought his dinner, Cole beat down his chattering objections and stuffed the note into the old man's coat pocket.

"See that Bidgrass gets it at once! Do you hear, at once!" he shouted.

After nightfall, nervous and wakeful, Cole looked out on the garden by the pale light of two moons. He saw the girl, wearing the same dress, come out of the opposite wing, and decided on impulse to intercept her.

As he climbed through the library window he said to himself, "Anything may be data to an ecologist, especially if it's pretty to look at."

He met her full face at the house corner and her hands flew up, fending. She turned and he said, "Please don't run away from me. I want to talk to you."

She turned back with eyes wide and troubled, in what nature had meant to be a merry, careless face.

"Do you know who I am?" he asked.

She nodded. "Uncle Garth says I'm not to talk to you." It was a little girl's voice, tremulous.

"Why? What am I, some kind of monster?"

"N-no. You're an outworlder, from a great, wealthy planet."

"Belconti is a very ordinary planet. What's your name?"

"I'm Pia—Pia Vignoli." The voice took on more assurance, but the plump body stayed poised for flight.

"Well, I'm Flinter Cole, and I have a job to do on this planet. It's *terribly* important that I get started. Will you help me?"

"How can I, Mr. Cole? I'm nobody. I don't know anything." She moved away, and he followed, awkwardly.

"Girls know all sorts of things that would interest an ecologist," he protested. "Tell me all you know about stompers."

"Oh *no!* I mustn't talk about stompers."

"Well talk about nothing then, like girls do," he said impatiently. "What's the name of that moon?" He pointed overhead.

Tension left her and she smiled a little. "Morwenna," she said. "That one just setting into Lundy Forest is Annis. You can tell Annis by her bluish shadows that are never the same."

"Good girl! How about the other two, the ones that aren't up?"

"One's Cairdween and the other, the red one—oh, I daren't talk about moons either."

"Not even *moons?* Really, Miss Vignoli—"

"Let's not talk at all. I'll show you how to walk, you do look so funny all spraddled and scraping your feet. I was born off-planet and I had to learn it myself."

She showed him the light downflex of the foot that threw the body more forward than up, and he learned to wait out the strange micropause before his weight settled on the other foot. With a little practice he got it, walking up and down the moonlit path beside her in an effortless toe dance. Then he learned to turn corners and to jump.

"Pia," he said once. "Pia. I like the sound, but it doesn't suit this rough planet."

"I was born on Tristan," she murmured. "Please don't ask—"

"I won't. But no reason why I can't talk. May I call you Pia?"

He described Belconti and the university, and his doctorate, at stake in this field assignment. Suddenly she stopped short and pointed to where a red moon lifted above the dark cliff of the eastern forest.

"It's late," she said. "There comes Hoggy Darn. Good night, Mr. Cole."

She danced away faster than he could follow. He crawled back through his window in the reddish moonlight.

Next afternoon Cole faced Garth Bidgrass in the library. The old man sat with folded arms, craggy face impassive. Cole, standing, leaned his weight on his hands and thrust his sharp face across the table. His freckles stood out against his angry pallor, and sunlight from the end window blazed in his red hair.

"Let me sum up," he said, thin-lipped. "For obscure reasons I must be essentially a prisoner. All right. You have no education here, no biologists of any kind. All right. Now here is what they expect of me on Belconti: to rough out the planetary ecosystem, set up a functional profile series for the stomper and its interacting species, make energy flow charts and outline the problem. If my report is incorrect or incomplete, Belconti won't send the right task group of specialists. Then you spend your money for nothing and I lose my doctorate. I must have skilled helpers, a clerical staff, *masses* of data!"

"You've said all that before," Bidgrass said calmly. "I told you, I can provide none of that."

"Then it's hopeless! Why did you ever send for an ecologist?"

"I sent for help. Belconti sent the ecologist."

"Help me to *help* you, then. You must try to understand, Mr. Bidgrass, science can't operate in a vacuum. I can't work up a total planetary biology. I must *start* with that data."

"Do what you can for us," Bidgrass said. "They won't blame you on Belconti when they know and we won't blame you here if it doesn't help."

Cole sat down, shaking his head. "But Belconti won't count it as a field job, not in ecology. You *will* not understand my position. Let me put it this way: suppose someone gave you a hatchet and told you, only one man, to cut down Lundy Forest?"

"I could start," the old man said. His eyes blazed and he smiled grimly. "I'd leave my mark on one tree."

Cole felt suddenly foolish and humbled.

"All right," he said. "I'll do what I can. What do you think is wiping out the stompers?"

"I know what. A parasite bird that lays its eggs on stomper eggs. Its young hatch first and eat the big egg. The people call them piskies."

"I'll need to work out its life cycle, look for weak points and natural enemies. Who knows a lot about these piskies?"

"I know as much as anybody, and I've never seen a grown one. We believe they stay in the deep forest. But there are always three to each stomper egg and they're vicious. Go for a man's eyes or jugular. Egg hunters kill dozens every day."

"I'll want dozens, alive if possible, and a lab. Can you do that much?"

"Yes. You can use Dr. Rudall's lab at the hospital." Bidgrass stood up and looked at his watch. "The egg harvest should start coming in soon down at the plant and there may be a dead pisky. Come along and see."

As Hawkins guided the car past a group of the giant

field workers, Cole felt Bidgrass' eyes on him. He turned, and the old man said slowly, "Stick to piskies, Mr. Cole. We'll all be happier."

"Anything may be data to an ecologist, especially if he overlooks it," Cole murmured stubbornly.

Hawkins cackled something about "Hoggy Darn itha hoose" and speeded up.

In the cavernous, machinery-lined plant Cole met the manager. He was the same powerful, long-haired man Cole had seen in the garden. "Morgan," Bidgrass introduced him with the one name, adding, "He doesn't use Galactic English."

Morgan bent his head slightly, unsmiling, ignoring Cole's offered hand. His wide-set eyes were so lustrously black that they seemed to have no pupils, and under the hostile stare Cole flushed angrily. They walked through the plant, Morgan talking to Bidgrass in the vernacular. His voice was deep and resonant, organ-like.

Bidgrass explained to Cole how stomper egg was vac-frozen under biostat and sealed in plastic for export. He pointed out a piece of shell, half an inch thick and highly translucent. From its radius of curvature Cole realized that stomper eggs were much larger than he had pictured them. Then someone shouted and Bidgrass said a flyer was coming in. They went out on the loading dock.

The flyer alongside carried six men forward of the cargo space and had four heavy blasters mounted almost like a warcraft. As the dock crew unloaded two eggs onto dollies, other flyers were skittering in, further along the dock. Bidgrass pointed out to Cole on one huge four by three-foot egg the bases of broken parasite eggs cemented to its shell. Through a hole made by piskies, the ecologist noted that the substance of the large egg was a stiff gel. Morgan flashed a strong pocket lamp on the shell and growled something.

"There may be a pisky hiding inside," Bidgrass said. "You are lucky, Mr. Cole."

Morgan stepped inside and returned almost at once wearing goggles and heavy gloves, and carrying a small power saw. He used the light again, traced an eight-inch square with his finger, and sawed it out. The others, all but Cole, stood back. Morgan pulled away the piece and something black flew up, incredibly swift, with a shrill, keening sound.

Cole looked after it and Morgan struck him heavily in the face, knocking him to hands and knees. Feet stamped and scraped around him and Cole saw his own blood dripping on the dock. He stood up dazed and angry.

"Morgan saved your eye," Bidgrass told him, "but the pisky took a nasty gouge at your cheekbone. I'll have Hawkins drive you to the hospital—you wanted to meet Dr. Rudall anyway."

Cole examined the crushed pisky on the way to the hospital. Big as his fist, with a tripartite beak, it was no true bird. The wings were flaps of black skin that still wrinkled and folded flexibly with residual life. It had nine toes on each foot and seemed covered with fine scales.

Dr. Rudall treated Cole's cheek in a surprisingly large and well appointed dressing room. He was a gray, defeated-looking man and told Cole in an apologetic voice that he had taken medical training on Planet Tristan many years ago . . . out of touch now. His small lab looked hopelessly archaic, but he promised to biostat the dead pisky until Cole could get back to it.

Hawkins was not with the ground car. Cole drove back to the plant without him. He wanted another look at the mode of adhesion of pisky egg on stomper egg. He drove to the further end of the plant and mounted the dock from outside, to freeze in surprise. Twenty feet away, the dock crew was unloading a giant.

He was naked, strapped limply to a plank, and his face was bloody. Half his reddish hair and beard was singed away. Then a hand hit Cole's shoulder and spun him around. It was Morgan.

"Clear out of here, you!" the big man said in fluent, if plain, Galactic English. "Don't you ever come here without Garth Bidgrass brings you!" He seemed hardly to move his lips, but the voice rumbled like thunder.

"Well," thought Cole, driving back after Hawkins, "datums are data, if they bite off your head."

"For your own safety, Mr. Cole, you must not again leave the company of either Hawkins or Dr. Rudall when you are away from the house," Bidgrass told Cole the next morning. "The people have strange beliefs that would seem sheer nonsense to you, but their impulsive acts, if you provoke them, will be unpleasantly real."

"If I knew their beliefs I might know how to behave."

"It is your very presence that is provoking. If you were made of salt you would have to stay out of the rain. Here you are an outworlder and you must stay within certain limits. It's like that."

"All right," Cole said glumly.

He worked all day at the hospital dissecting the pisky, but found no parasites. He noted interesting points of anatomy. The three-part beak of silicified horn was razor sharp and designed to exert a double shearing stress. The eye was triune and of fixed focus; the three eyeballs lay in a narrow isosceles triangle pattern, base down, behind a common triangular conjunctiva with incurved sides and narrow base. The wings were elastic and stiffened with a fan of nine multi-jointed bones that probably gave them grasping and manipulating power in the living organism. None of it suggested the limit factor he sought.

Dr. Rudall helped him make cultures in a sterile broth derived from the pisky's own tissues. In the evening a worker from the plant brought eleven dead piskies and Cole put them in biostat. He rode home with Hawkins to his solitary dinner feeling he had made a start.

Day followed day. Cole remained isolated in his wing, coming and going through his back door into the garden. He became used to the mute giant domestics who swept and cleaned. Now and then he exchanged a few words with the sad Mrs. Vignoli, Pia's mother, he learned, or with old Bidgrass, in chance meetings. He watched Pia through his windows sometimes and knew she fled when he came out. There was something incongruous in the timid wariness with which her plump figure and should-be-merry face confronted the world.

Once he caught her and held her wrist. "Why do you run away from me, Pia?"

She pulled away gently. "I'll get you in trouble, Mr. Cole. They don't trust me either. My father was a Tristanian."

"Who are *they*?"

"Just they. Morgan, all of them."

"If we're both outworld, we should stick together. I'm the loneliest man on this planet, Pia."

"I know the feeling," she said, looking down

He patted her curls. "Let's be friends then, and you help me. Where do these giant people come from?"

Her head jerked up angrily. "That has nothing to do with your work! I'm inworld, too, Mr. Cole. My mother is of the old stock."

Cole let her go in silence.

He began working evenings in the lab, losing himself in work. Few of the blue-clad men and women he encountered would look at him, but he sensed their hostile glances on the back of his neck. He felt islanded in a sea of dull hatred. Only Dr. Rudall was vaguely friendly.

Cole found no parasites in hundreds of dissected piskies, but his cultures were frequently contaminated by a fungus that formed dark red, globular fruiting bodies. When he turned to cytology he found that what he had supposed to be an incredibly complex autonomic nervous system was instead a fungal mycelium, so fine as to be visible only in phase contrast. He experimented with staining techniques and verified it in a dozen specimens, then danced the surprised Dr. Rudall around the lab.

"I've done it! One man against a planet!" he chortled. "We'll culture it, then work up mutant strains of increasing virulence—oh for a Belconti geno-mycologist now!"

"It's not pathogenic, I'm afraid," Dr. Rudall said. "I . . . ah . . . read once, that idea was tried centuries ago . . . all the native fauna have fungal symbiotes . . . protect them against all known pathogenic microbiota . . . should have mentioned it, I suppose. . . ."

"*Yes*, you should have told me! My God, there go half the weapons of applied ecology over the moon . . . my time wasted . . . *why* didn't you tell me?" The ecologist's sharp face flushed red as his hair with frustrated anger.

"You didn't ask . . . hardly know what ecology means . . . didn't realize it was important . . ." the old doctor stammered.

"*Everything* is important to an ecologist, especially what people won't tell him!" Cole stormed.

He tried to stamp out of the lab, and progressed in a ludicrous bouncing that enraged him even more. He shouted for Hawkins and went home early.

In his rooms he brooded on his wrongs for an hour, then went downstairs and thundered on the locked door into the main house, shouting Garth Bidgrass' name. The sounds beyond hushed. Then Garth Bidgrass opened the door, looking stern and angry.

"Come into the library, Mr. Cole," he said. "Try to control yourself."

In the library Cole poured out his story while Bidgrass, standing with right elbow resting atop a bookcase, listened gravely.

"You must understand," Cole finished, "to save the stompers we must cut down the piskies. Crudely put, the most common method is to find a disease or a parasite that affects them, and breed more potent strains of it. But that won't work on piskies, and I could have and should have known that to begin with."

"Then you must give up?"

"*No!* Something must prey on them or their eggs in their native habitat, a macrobiotic limit factor I can use. I must learn the adult pisky's diet; if its range is narrow enough that can be made a limit factor."

The old man frowned. "How would you learn all this?"

"Field study. I want at least twenty intelligent men and a permanent camp somewhere in Lundy Forest."

Bidgrass folded his arms and shook his head. "Can't spare the men. And it's too dangerous—stompers would attack you day and night. I've had over two hundred egg hunters killed this year, and they're trained men in teams."

"Let me go out with a team then, use my own two eyes."

"Men wouldn't have you. I told you, they're superstitious about outworlders."

"Then it's failure! Your money and my doctorate go down the drain."

"You're wrong, you'll get your doctorate another place," the old man said. "You've tried hard, and I'll tell Belconti that." His voice was placating, but Cole thought he saw a wary glint in the hard gray eyes.

Cole shrugged. "I suppose I'll settle in and wait for *Gorbals*. But I've had pleasanter vacations."

He turned his back and scanned the shelves ostentatiously for a book. Bidgrass left the room quietly.

It was a boring evening. Pia was not in the garden. Cole looked at the barrier and the incredible cliff of Lundy Forest. He would like to get into that forest, just once. Hundred and fifty days before *Gorbals . . . why* had they ever sent for him? They seemed to be conspiring to cheat him of his doctorate. They had, too. . . . Finally he slept.

He woke to a distant siren wail and doors slamming and feet scraping in the main house. Dressing in haste, he noted a red glow in the sky to southward and heard a booming noise. In the hall outside his room he met Pia, face white and eyes enormous.

"Stomper attack!" she cried. "Come quickly, you must hide in the basement with us!"

He followed her into the main house and downstairs to where Mrs. Vignoli was herding a crowd of the giant domestics down a doored staircase. The giant women were tossing their heads nervously. Several were naked and one was tearing off her dress. Cole drew back.

"I'm an ecologist, I want to see," he said. "Stompers are data."

He pushed her gently toward the women and walked out on the front veranda. From southward came an incredibly rich and powerful chord of organ music, booming and swelling, impossibly sustained. Old Hawkins danced in the driveway in grotesque pointed leaps, shrieking "Hoosa maida! Hoosa maida!" Overhead the moons Cairdween, Morwenna and Annis of the blue shadows were arranged in a perfect isosceles triangle, narrow base parallel to the horizon. It stirred something in Cole, but the swelling music unhinged his thought. With a twinge of panic he turned, to find Pia at his elbow.

"They're after me, after us," she cried against the music.

"I must see. You go find shelter, Pia."

"With you I feel less alone now," she said. "One can't really hide, anyway. Come to the watch tower and you'll see."

He followed her through the house and up two flights to the roof of the tower on the southeast corner. As they stepped into the night air, the great organ sound enwrapped them, and Cole saw the southern sky ablaze, with flyers swooping and black motes hurtling through the glare.

Interwoven pencils of ion-flame flickered in the verging darkness and the ripping sound of heavy blasters came faintly through the music.

A hundred-yard section of the barrier was down in flames, and the great, bobbing, leggy shapes of stompers came bounding through it while others glided down from the top. Flyers swarmed like angry bees around the top of the break, firing mounted blasters and tearing away great masses of wood. The powerful chord of music swelled unendurably in volume and exultant richness until Cole cried out and shook the girl.

"It plucks at my backbone and I can't think! Pia, Pia, what *is* that music?"

"It's the stompers singing," she shouted back.

He shook his head. Bidgrass Station seethed, lights everywhere, roads crowded with trucks. Around the base of the breakthrough a defense perimeter flared with the blue-violet of blasters and the angry red of flame guns. As Cole watched it was overrun and darkened in place after place, only to reform further out as reserves came into action. Expanding jerkily, pushed this way and that, the flaming periphery looked like a fire-membrane stressed past endurance by some savage contained thing. With a surge of emotion Cole realized it was men down there, with their guns and their puny muscles and their fragile lives against two-legged, boat-shaped monsters twenty feet high.

"Sheer power of biomass," he thought. "Even their shot-down bodies are missiles, to crush and break." A sudden eddy in the flaming defense line brought it to within half a mile of the house. Cole could see men die against the glare, in the great music.

The girl pressed close to him and whimpered, "Oh, start the fire mist! Morwenna pity them!" Cole put his arm tightly around her.

A truck convoy pulled up by the manor house and soldiers were everywhere, moving quickly and surely. A group hauled a squat, vertical cylinder on wheels crashing through the ornamental shrubbery. Violet glowing metal vaning wound about it in a double helix.

"It's a Corbin powercaster," Pia shouted into Cole's ear. "It broadcasts power to the portable blasters so the men don't need to carry pack charges or lose time changing them."

Cole looked at the soldiers. The same big men he saw every day, the same closed and hostile faces, but now a wild and savage joy shone in them. This was their human meaning to themselves, their justification. The red boundary roared down on them, they would be dying in a few minutes, but they were braced and fiercely ready.

The music swelled impossibly loud and Cole knew that he too was going to die with them, despised outworlder that he was. He hugged the girl fiercely and tried to kiss her.

"Let me in your world, Pia!" he cried.

She pulled away. "Look! The fire mist! Oh thank you, good Morwenna!"

He saw it, a rose pink paled by nearer flame, washing lazily against the black cliff edge of Lundy Forest. It grew, boiling up over the barrier in places, spilling through the gap, and the great, agonizing chord of music muted and dwindled. The flame-perimeter began shrinking and still the fire mist grew, staining the night sky north and south beyond eye-reach. The song became a mournful wailing and the soldiers in the garden moved forward for the mopping up.

"Pia, I've got to go down there. I've got to see a stomper close up."

She was trembling and crying with reaction. "I think they'll be too busy to mind," she said. "But don't go too far in . . . Flinter."

He ran down the stairs and through the unguarded gate toward the fought-over area. Wounded men were being helped or carried past him, but no one noticed him. He found a stomper, blaster-torn but not yet dead, and stopped to watch the four-foot tripart beak snap feebly and the dark wings writhe and clutch. The paired vertical eyelid folds rolled apart laterally to reveal three eyes under a single triangular conjunctiva, lambent in the flame-shot darkness. Soldiers passed unheeding while Cole stood and wondered. Then a hand jerked violently at his arm. It was Morgan.

Morgan wordlessly marched him off to a knot of men nearer the mopping up line and pushed him before Garth

Bidgrass. Sweat dripped from flaring eyebrows down the grim old face, and over a blistered right cheek. A heavy blaster hung from the old man's body harness.

"Well, Mr. Cole, is this data?" he asked dourly. "Have you come out to save stompers?"

"I wish I could have saved men, Mr. Bidgrass. I wanted to help," Cole said.

"Another like this and you may have to," Bidgrass said, less sharply. "It was close work, lad."

"I can help Dr. Rudall. You must have many wounded."

"Good, good," the old man said approvingly. "The men will take that kindly and so will I."

"One favor," Cole said. "Will you have your men save half a dozen living stompers for me? I have another idea."

"Well, I don't know," Bidgrass said. "The men won't like it . . . but a few days, maybe . . . yes, I'll save you some."

"Thank you, sir." Cole turned away, catching a thick scowl from Morgan. Overhead the three moons were strung in a ragged line across the sky, and Hoggy Darn was rising.

Cole worked around the clock at the hospital, sterilizing instruments and helping Dr. Rudall with dressings. He was surprised to see other doctors, many nurses and numerous biofield projectors as modern as any on Belconti. Some of the wounded were women. All of them, wounded and unwounded, seemed in a shared mood of exaltation. He caught glimpses of Pia working, too. She seemed less poised for flight, tired but happy, and she smiled at him.

After three days Cole saw his stompers in a stone-floored pen at the slaughter house. Earth breed cattle lowed in adjacent pens. Four stompers still lived, their bodies blaster torn and their legs crudely hamstrung so they could not stand. They lay with heads together and the sun glinted on the blue-black, iridescent scales covering the domed heads and long necks.

Three shock-headed butchers stood by, assigned to help him. Their distaste for Cole and the job was so evident that he hurried through the gross dissection of the two dead stompers at one end of the same pen. After an hour he thought to ask, as best he could, whether the living stompers were being given food and water. When one man understood, black hatred crossed his face and he spat on Cole's shoe. The ecologist flushed, then shrugged and got on with the job.

It brought him jarring surprises culminating in a tentative conclusion late on the second day. Then the situation began to fall apart. Working alone for the moment, Cole opened the stomach of the second stomper and found in it half-digested parts of a human body. Skull and humerus size told him it was one of the giants.

First pulling a flap of mesentery over the stomach incision, Cole went into the office and phoned Dr. Rudall to come at once. Coming out, he heard angry shots and saw two of his helpers running to join the third, who stood pointing into the carcass. Then all three seized axes, ran across the pen and began hacking at the necks of the living stompers.

The great creatures boomed and writhed, clacking their beaks and half rising on their wings, unable to defend themselves. The butchers howled curses, and the stompers broke into a mournful wailing harmonized with flesh-creeping subsonics. Cole shouted and pleaded, finally wrested an axe from one and mounted guard over the last living stomper. He stood embattled, facing a growing crowd of butchers from the plant, when Dr. Rudall arrived.

"Dr. Rudall, explain to these maniacs why I must keep this stomper alive!" he cried angrily.

"I'm sorry, Mr. Cole, they will kill it in spite of you."

"But Garth Bidgrass ordered—"

"In spite of him. There are factors you don't understand, Mr. Cole. You are yourself in great danger." The old doctor's hands trembled.

Cole thought rapidly. "All right, will they wait a day? I want tissue explants for a reason I'll explain later. If you'll help me work up the nutrient tonight—"

"Our pisky nutrient will work. We can take your samples within the hour. Let me call the hospital."

He spoke rapidly to the glowering butchers in the vernacular, then hurried into the building. An hour later the stomper was dead, and Hawkins drove Cole and the doctor back to their lab with the explants.

"I've almost got it," Cole said happily. "Several weeks

and two more bits of information and I'll tell you. In spite of all odds, one man against a planet—this will found my professional reputation back on Belconti."

Once again Cole faced Garth Bidgrass across the round table in the library. This time he felt vastly different.

"The piskies are really baby stompers," he said, watching the craggy old face for its reaction. It did not change.

"I suspected it when I saw how the smaller eggs fused with the large egg, with continuous laminae," Cole went on. "There was the morphological resemblance, too. But when I dissected two mature stompers I found immature eggs. Even before entry into the oviduct what you call pisky eggs are filamented to the main body of cytoplasm."

Disappointingly, Bidgrass did not marvel. He squinted and cocked his head. Finally he said, "Do you mean the piskies lay their eggs internally in the stompers?"

"Impossible! I made a karyotype analysis of pisky and stomper tissue and they are *identical*, I tell you. My working hypothesis for now is that pisky eggs are fertilized polar bodies. It's not unknown. But that the main body should be sterile and serve as an external food source— that's new, I'm sure. That will get my name in the journals all through Carina sector."

He could not help smiling happily. Bidgrass bit his lower lip and stared keenly, not speaking. Cole became nettled.

"I hope you see the logic," he said. "What threatens your stompers is harvest pressure from your own egg hunters. Stop it for a few decades, or set aside breeding areas, and you can have a whole planetful again."

The old man scowled and stood up. "We'll not stop," he said gruffly. "There are still plenty of stompers. Remember last month." He walked to the end window and back, then sat down again still looking grim.

"Don't be too sure," Cole objected. "I haven't finished my report. I made a Harvey analysis on the tissues of one stomper. It involves culturing clones, measuring growth rates and zones of migration and working out a complex set of ratios—I won't go into details. But when I fitted my figures into Harvey's formula it indicated *unmistakably* that the stompers have a critical biomass."

"What does that mean?"

"Think of a species as one great animal that never dies, of which each individual is only a part. Can you do that?"

"Yes!" the old man exploded, sitting bolt upright.

"Well, the weight of a cross-section of the greater animal at any moment in time is its biomass. Many species have a point or value of critical biomass such that, if it falls below that point, the greater animal dies. The species loses its will to live, decays, drifts into extinction in spite of all efforts to save it. The stomper is such a species, no doubt whatever. Do you see how the slaughter a month ago may *already* have extinguished them as a species?"

Bidgrass nodded, smiling grimly. His eyes held a curious light.

"Tell me, Mr. Cole, your Harvey formula—do *human beings* have a critical biomass?"

"Yes, biologically," Cole said, surprised. "But in our case a varying part of the greater animal is carried in our culture, our symbol system, and is not directly dependent on biomass. A mathematical anthropologist could tell you more than I can."

Bidgrass placed his hands palm down on the table and leaned back in sudden resolution.

"Mr. Cole, you force me to tell you something I had been minded to hold back. I already know a good part of what you have just told me. I *wish* to exterminate the stompers and I will do so. But I meant for you to go back to Belconti thinking it was the piskies."

Cole propped his chin on folded hands and raised his eyebrows. "I half suspected that. But I fooled you, didn't I?"

"Yes, and I admire you for it. Now let me tell you more. Stomper egg brings a very high price and I have kept it higher by storing large reserves. When it is known the stomper is extinct, the rarity value of my reserve will be enormous. It will mean an end of this harsh life for me and for my grandniece after me."

Cole's lip curled, and red mounted in the old man's face as he talked, but he went on doggedly.

"I want the pisky theory and the news of stomper extinction to be released through Belconti University. The news will spread faster and be more readily believed and I will avoid a certain moral stigma—"

"And now I've crossed you up!"

"You can still do it. I can ease your conscience with a settlement of—say—five thousand solars a year for life."

Cole leaped up and leaned across the table.

"No!" he snapped. "Old man, you don't know how ecologists feel about the greed-murder of species. What I *will* do is work through Belconti on your government at Car Truro, warn it that you are about to destroy an important planetary resource."

Bidgrass stood up, too, scowling darkly red.

"Not so fast, young fellow. I have copies of your early notes in which you call the piskies the critical limit factor in stomper extinction. Almost three hundred people were killed in that stomper attack, and you could easily have been one of them. If you had, I would naturally have reported it via the next *Gorbals* to Belconti and sent along your notes to date—do you follow me?"

"Yes. A threat."

"A counter-threat. Think it over for a few days, Mr. Cole."

Cole sat glumly in his room waiting for his dinner and wondering if it would be poisoned. When old Hawkins tapped, he pulled open the door, only to find Pia instead with a service for two. She was rosy and smiling in a low-cut, off-shoulder brown dress he had not seen before.

"May I eat dinner with you tonight, Flinter?" she asked.

"Please do," he said, startled. "Am I people now, or something?"

"Uncle Garth says now that you know—" She broke off, blushing still more.

"I don't like what I know," he said somberly, "but it's not you, Pia. Here, let me."

He pulled the cart into the room and helped her set the things on his table. Pia *was* lovely, he decided, wanting to caress the smooth roundness of her shoulders and dimpled arms. When she sat across the small table from him he could not help responding to the swell of her round breasts barely below the neckline. But her manner seemed forced and she looked more frightened than ever.

"You look like a little rabbit that knows it's strayed too far from the woods, Pia. What *are* you always afraid of?"

Her smile faded. "Not because I'm too far from the woods," she said. "What's a rabbit? But let's not talk about fear."

They talked of food and weather through a more than usually elaborate dinner. There was a bottle of Tristanian *kresch* to follow it. Cole splashed the blue wine into the two crystal goblets, gave her one and held up his own.

"Here's to the richest little girl on Tristan someday," he said, half mockingly.

Tears sprang to her eyes. "I don't want to be rich. I just want a home away from New Cornwall, just anywhere. I was born on Tristan. Oh, Flinter, what you must think—" She began crying in earnest.

He patted her shoulder. "Forgive me for a fool, Pia. Tell me about Tristan. I had only one day there, waiting for *Gorbals'* tender."

She spoke of her childhood on Tristan, and the tension eased in both. Finally she proposed a picnic for the next day, the two of them to take a sports flyer into the forest top. He agreed with pleasure and squeezed her hand in saying good night.

She squeezed back a little. But she still looked frightened.

Next day Pia wore a brief yellow playsuit, and Cole could not keep his eyes off her. When he was loading the picnic hamper into the small flyer before the main hangar, she suddenly pressed close to him. He followed her wide-eyed gaze over his right shoulder and saw Morgan bulking darkly ten feet away.

"Hello there, Mr. Morgan," Cole said into the impassive face under the black bar of eyebrow.

Morgan rumbled in vernacular and walked on. His lips did not move.

"You're afraid of Morgan," Cole said when he had the flyer aloft and heading east.

"He's a bard. He has a power," she said. "Today, let's forget him."

Cole looked back at the bulk of Lundy Peninsula, swelling lost into blue-green distance from the narrow isthmus. The straight slash of Bidgrass Station from sea to sea looked puny beside the mighty forest towering on either side. Then Pia had his arm and wanted him to land.

He grounded on a pinkish-green mass of lichen several acres in area. Pia assured him it would support the flyer, reminding him of the planet's low gravity.

The resilient surface gave off a fragrance as they walked about on it. In a sea all around their island, branches of the great forest trees thrust up, leafy and flowering and bedecked with a profusion of epiphytal plants in many shapes and colors. Bright-hued true birds darted from shadow into sunlight and back again, twittering and crying.

"It's beautiful," he said. And so was Pia, he thought, watching her on tiptoe reaching to a great white flower. The attractive firmness of her skin, the roundness and dimpling, *ripeness*, that was the word he wanted. And her eyes.

"Pia, you're not frightened any more!"

It was true. The long-lashed brown eyes were merry as nature meant them to be.

"It's peaceful and safe," she said. "When I come to the forest top I never want to go back to Bidgrass Station."

"Too bad we must, and let's pretend we don't," he said, pointing to a cluster of red-gold fruits. "Are those good to eat?"

"Too good. That's the trouble with New Cornwall."

"What do you mean?"

"Race you back to the flyer," she cried, and danced away, bare limbs twinkling in the sunlight. He floundered after.

The lunch was good and she had brought along the rest of the bottle of *kresch*. They sipped it seated beside the flyer while she tried to teach him New Cornish folk songs. Her small, clear singing blended with that of the birds around them.

"I catch parts of it," he said. "As an undergraduate a few years ago I studied the pre-space poets. I can read Old English, but it is strange to my ear."

"I could teach you."

"I love one wry-witted ancient named Robert Graves. How does it go: *If strange things happen where she is*—no, I can't recall it now."

"I could write the songs out for you."

"The beauty is in you and your voice. Just sing."

She sang, something about a king with light streaming

from his hair, coming naked out of the forest to bring love into his kingdom. Small white clouds drifted in the blue sky, and blue Annis slept just above the rustling branches that guarded the secret of their island. He listened and watched her.

She was softly rounded as the clouds, and her clustered brown curls made an island of the vivid face expressing the song she sang so bird-like and naturally. She was vital, compact, self closed, perfect—like one of the great flowers nodding in the breeze along the island shore—and his heart yearned across to her.

"Pia," he said, breaking into the song, "do you really want to get away from New Cornwall?"

She nodded, eyes suddenly wide, lips still parted.

"Come with me to Belconti then. Right now. We'll cross to Car Truro and wait there for *Gorbals*."

The light dimmed in her face. "Why Car Truro?"

"Pia, it's hard to tell you. I'm afraid of your great-uncle . . . I want to contact the planetary government."

"It's no good at Car Truro, Flinter. Can't you just come back to Bidgrass Station and . . . and . . . do what Uncle Garth wants?"

He could barely hear the last. The fear was back in her eyes.

"Do you know what he wants?"

"Yes." The brown curls drooped.

Cole stood up. "So *that's* the reason—well, I'll not do it, do you hear? Garth Bidgrass is an evil, greedy old man and maybe it runs in the blood."

She jumped up, eyes more angry now than fearful. "He is not! He's trying to save you! He's good and noble and . . . and *great!* If you only knew the truth—Morwenna forgive me!" She clapped her hand to her mouth.

"*Tell* me the truth then, since I'm still being made a Belconti fool of. What *is* the truth?"

"I've said too much. Now I'll have to tell Uncle Garth—" She began crying.

"Tell him what? That I know he's a liar? That you failed as a—" He could not quite say the word.

"It's true I was supposed to make you love me and I tried and I can't because . . . because . . ." she ended in incoherent sobbing.

Cole stroked her hair and comforted her. "I've been hasty again," he apologized. "I'm still running in the dark, and that makes for stumbles. Let's go back, and I'll talk to your great-uncle again."

In the morning Garth Bidgrass, looking tired and stern, invited Cole to breakfast with the family. Cole had never been in the large, wood-panelled room overlooking the south garden through broad windows. Pia was subdued, Mrs. Vignoli strangely cheerful. The meal, served by a giant maid, was the customary plain porridge and fried meat.

The women left when the maid cleared the table. Bidgrass poured more coffee, then leaned back and looked across at Cole.

"Mr. Cole, I did you a wrong in having you sent here. I kept you in the dark for your own protection. Can you believe that?"

"I can believe that you believe it."

"You came too soon. You were too curious, too smart. I have had to compound that wrong with others to Pia and my own good name."

Cole smiled. "I know I'm curious. But why can't I know—"

"You can, lad. You've nosed through to it and I'll tell you if you insist. But it will endanger you even more and I wish you would forego it."

Cole shook his head. "I'm an ecologist. If I have the big picture, maybe I can help."

"I thought you'd say that. Well, history first, and settle yourself because it *is* a big picture and not a pretty one. This planet was settled directly from Earth in the year 145 After Space, almost eight hundred years ago. It seemed ideal—native protein was actually superior to Earth protein in human metabolism. Easy climate, geophysically stable, no diseases—but planetology was not much of a science in those days.

"The colony won political independence in 202 A.S. It had a thriving trade in luxury foods, mostly stomper egg concentrates—freight was dear then. Settlements radiated out from Car Truro across the plains. Food was to be had for the taking in the mild climate and it was a kind of paradise. *Paradise!*"

The old man's voice rang hard on the last word and Cole stiffened. Bidgrass went on.

"Early in the third century our social scientists began to worry about the unnatural way the culture graded from the complexity of Car Truro to a simple pattern of mud huts and food gathering along the frontiers. Children of successive generations were taller than their parents and much less willing or able to use symbols. By the time a minority decided the trend should be reversed, the majority of the people could not be roused to see a danger."

"Earth life is normally resistant to low-grav gigantism," Cole said. "I wonder—"

"It was all the native foods they ate, but mainly stomper egg. There are more powerful and quicker-acting substances in the forest fungi, but then the population was all in the eastern grasslands, where the stompers ranged."

"I read they were a plains animal."

"Yes, and harmless, too, except for their eggs. Well, the minority set up a dictatorship and began cultivating Earth plants and animals. They passed laws limiting the mechanical simplicity of households and regulating diets. They took children from subnormal parents and educated and fed them in camps. But the normals were too few and the trend continued.

"Shortly after mid-century the population reached the edge of the southern forest, and there many were completely wild. They drifted along the forest edge naked, without tools or fire or language or even family groupings. Their average stature was nearly eight feet. The normals knew they were losing. Can you imagine how they *felt*, lad?"

Cole relaxed a little. "Ah . . . yes, I can . . . I imagine the fight was inside them, too."

Bidgrass nodded. "Yes, they were all tainted. But they fought. They asked Earth for help and learned that Earth regarded them as tyrants oppressing a simple, natural folk. The economy broke down and more had to be imported. The only way to pay was in stomper egg exports. In spite of that, in about the year 300, they decided to restrict the stompers to the western part of the grasslands, thousands of miles beyond the human range.

"The egg hunters began killing piskies and grown stompers. They killed off the great, stupid herds of darv cattle on which the stompers fed. The stompers that survived became wary and hostile, good at hiding and fierce to attack. But killing off the eastern darv herds broke them and in a generation they vanished from the eastern plains. Things seemed to improve and they thought the tide was turned. Then, in the year 374, came what our bards now call the Black Learning."

"Bards," Cole said. He drained his coffee cup.

"Morgan could sing you this history to shiver the flesh on your bones," the old man said, pouring more coffee. "What I am telling you is nowhere written down, but it is engraved in thousands of hearts. Well, to go on.

"We knew some of the stompers had gone into the southern forest—you see, they had to incubate their eggs in direct sunlight and we kept finding them along the forest edge. But we had assumed they were eating the snakes and slugs and fungi native to the forest floor. Now we learned that a large population of wild humans had grown up unknown to us in the deep forest—and the stompers were eating them.

"You have seen our forests from a distance, lad. Do you realize how impossible it is to patrol them? We hadn't the men, money, or machines for it. We appealed, and learned we would get no help from any planet in Carina sector except for pay. But the egg market fell off and our income with it. Ships did come, however, small ones in stealth, to ground along the forest edge and capture the young women of the wild people."

Cole struck the table. "How rotten . . . !" His voice failed.

Bidgrass nodded. "We call that the Lesser Shame. The young women were without personality or language, yet tractable and responsive to affection. They were flawless in health and physique, and eight feet tall. They could be sold for fantastic prices on loosely organized frontier planets and yes, even to Earth, as we learned. Something dark in a man responds to that combination. You feel it as I speak—no, don't protest, I know. We had long had that trouble among our own people."

"Did my own people of Belconti—" Again Cole's voice failed. He brushed back his red hair angrily.

"Belconti was new then, still a colony. Well, that was the *help* we got. We hadn't the power to fight stompers, let alone slave raiders. But the Galactic Patrol was just getting organized and the sector admiral agreed to keep a ship in orbit blockading us. We broke off all contact except with Tristan, and the Patrol let only one freight line come through to handle our off-planet trade. It was then we began to hate the other planets. We call it the Turning Away.

"Now we are forgotten, almost a myth. The Patrol ship has been gone since two hundred years ago. But we remember."

"I wish I'd known this," Cole said. "Mr. Bidgrass, things are greatly changed in Carina sector—"

Bidgrass held up his hand. "I know, lad. That's why you're here, and I'll come to it. But let me go on. Early in the fifth century we decided to exterminate the stompers altogether and in two decades killed off all the darv cattle. But the stompers went into the forests in the south and west and from there came out to raid the plains. Not to kill, but to carry off normal and semi-wild people into the forest for breeding stock. A stomper's wing is more flexible than a hand. One of them can carry half a dozen men and women and run a thousand miles in a day. Some fungi in the forest can dull a man in an hour and take his mind in a week. Few who were carried in ever came out again.

"This went on, lad, for *centuries*. From our fortified towns and hunting camps we ranged along the forest edge like wolves. The stompers *must* lay their eggs in direct sunlight. That forced them out where we could get at them, into clearings and uplands and along the forest edge. We killed all we could.

"We found rhythms in their life pattern keyed to our four moons. When the three lady moons form a tall triangle, the stompers group in the open to mill and dance and sing. About every three months this happens over several days and in old times it was the peak raid season. It was also our chance to kill. The people call the configuration the House of the Maidens."

Cole nodded vigorously. "I remember that. Strange how lunar periodicity is bionative in every planet having a moon."

"It saved us here, praise Morwenna, but once almost destroyed us. There is a longer, sixty-two year cycle called the Nights of Hoggy Darn. Then the red moon passes through the House of the Maidens and the stompers go completely berserk. The first one after the war was joined fully, in 434, caught us unprepared and cost us more than three-fourths of our normal population in the week that we remember as the Great Taking. We were thrown back into Car Truro for decades and the stompers came back on the plains. They snatched people from the streets of Car Truro itself. That we call the Dark Time."

The old man's craggy face shadowed with sorrow and he sighed, leaning back. Cole opened his mouth but Bidgrass leaned forward again, new, fierce energy in his voice.

"We rallied and came back. We fought from the air and killed them in large numbers when we caught them in the open on Maiden nights. We drove them back off the plains and harried them along the forest edges and in the upland clearings where they came to lay eggs. We gathered all the eggs we could find. They defended their eggs and caused us steady losses. But we fought.

"We built our strategy on the Maidens and in time we drove the enemy out of the southern forest and into the west. Then we crowded him into Lundy Peninsula, made it a sanctuary for a hundred years to draw him in. When I was your age we fought out the last Nights of Hoggy Darn a few miles east of here. Ten years later we finished Bidgrass Station and the barrier and the continent was free of stompers."

Cole shifted his chair to get the sun off his neck. "I hardly know what to say," he began, but Bidgrass raised his hand.

"I've more to tell you, that you must know. By the late seventh century things were normal around Car Truro as regards regression. We began a pilot program of reclamation. The egg hunters captured wild people along the forest edge, still do. But some are beyond saving, and those they kill. We have to pen them like animals at first, but they can be trained to work in the fields, and for a long time now we have had few machines except what we need for war. Their children, on an Earth diet, come back toward normal in size and intelligence. The fourth and fifth generations are normal enough to join in the war. But war has always come first and we have never been able to spare many normals for reclamation work.

"Even so, ex-wilds make up more than half our normal population now. That's about forty thousand; there are nearly a hundred thousand on the reclamation ladder, mostly around Car Truro. The ex-wilds have a queer, poetic strain, and mainly through them we've developed a sort of religion along the way. It helps the subnormals who are so powerfully drawn to run back to the forests. It's a strange mixture of poetry and prophecy, but it's breath of life to the ex-wilds. I guess I pretty well believe it myself and even you believe some of it."

Cole looked his question, hitching his chair nearer the table.

"Yes, your notion of the greater animal, critical biomass, that you spoke of. We speak of Grandfather Stomper and we are trying to kill him. He is trying to enslave Grandfather Man. The whole purpose and meaning of human life, to an ex-wild, is to kill Grandfather Stomper and then to reclaim Grandfather Man from the forest. You would have to hear Morgan sing it to appreciate how deeply they feel that, lad."

"I feel it, a little. I understand Morgan now, I think. He's an ex-wild, isn't he?"

"Yes, and our master bard. In some ways he has more power than I."

Cole got up. "Mind if I pull a curtain? That sun is hot."

"No, go ahead. Our coffee is cold," the old man said, rising, too. "I'll ask for a fresh pot."

Seated again in the shaded room, Bidgrass resumed, "There's not much more. After the barrier was up it seemed as if Grandfather Stomper knew his time was running out. Don't laugh now. Individual stompers don't have intelligence, symbol-using, that is, as far as we know. But they changed from plains to forest. They learned to practise a gruesome kind of animal husbandry—oh, I could tell you things. *Something* had to figure it out."

"I'm not laughing," Cole said. "You're talking sound ecology. Go on."

"Well, they began laying eggs right along the barrier and didn't try to defend them. We picked up hundreds, even thousands, every day. The people said Grandfather Stomper was trying to make peace, to pay rent on Lundy Forest. And maybe he was.

"But we spat in his face. We gathered his tribute and still took all the eggs we could find in the inland clearings. We killed every stomper we saw. Then, for the first time I think, Grandfather Stomper knew it was war to the death. He began to fight as never before. Where once a stomper would carry a captured egg hunter a hundred miles into the forest and turn him loose, now it killed out of hand. They began making mass attacks on the station and they didn't come to capture, they came to kill. So it has gone for forty years now."

The old man's voice changed, less fierce, more solemn. He sat up straight.

"Lundy Forest is near eight hundred thousand square miles. No one knows how many millions of wild humans are in it or how many scores of thousands of stompers. But this I knew long before you came to tell me about critical biomass: Grandfather Stomper is very near to death. He ruled this planet for a million years and he fought me for near a thousand, but his time is come.

"Don't laugh, lad, at what I am about to say now. Mass belief, blind faith over centuries of people like our ex-wilds and semi-wilds, can do strange things. To them and even to myself I *represent* Grandfather Man, and from them a power comes into me that is more than myself. I know in a *direct* way that in the Nights of Hoggy Darn to come I will at long last kill Grandfather Stomper and the war will be won. That time is only eight weeks away."

"Then I'll still be here. Grand—Mr. Bidgrass, I want to fight with you."

"You may and welcome, lad. Must, even, to redeem yourself. Because, for what you know now, your life is forfeit if the ex-wilds suspect."

"Why so? Are you not *proud*—" Cole half stood and Bidgrass waved him down.

"Consider, lad. For centuries across the inhabited planets people of wealth and influence have been eating stomper egg, serving it at state banquets. But now *you* know it is human flesh at one remove. How will they feel toward us when they learn that?"

"How should they feel? Man has to be consumed at some trophic level. His substance is as much in the biogeochemical cycles as that of a pig or a chicken. I suppose we *do* feel he should cap the end of a food chain and not short-cycle through himself, but I'm damned if I'm horrified—"

"Any non-ecologist would be. You know that."

The giant maid came in with a pot of coffee and clean cups. Bidgrass poured and both men sipped in silence. Then Bidgrass said slowly, "Do you know what the people here call outworlders? Cannibals! For centuries we have had the feeling that we have been selling our own flesh to the outworlds in exchange for the weapons to free Grandfather Man."

He stood up, towering over Cole, and his voice deepened. "It has left bone-deep marks: of guilt, for making the outworlders unknowing cannibals; of hatred, because we feel the outworlds left us no choice. And shame, lad, deep, deep shame, more than a man can bear, to have been degraded to food animals here in our forests and across the opulent tables of the other planets. Morgan is only second-generation normal—his father was killed beside me, last Hoggy Darn. If Morgan knew you had learned our secret he would kill you out of hand. I could not stop him. Do you understand now why we didn't want you until next *Gorbals?* Do you see into the hell you have been skating over?"

Cole nodded and rubbed his chin. "Yes, I do. But I don't despise Morgan, I think I love him. On Belconti, Grandfather Man is mainly concerned to titillate his own appetites, but here, well . . . how do I feel it? . . . I think what you have just told me makes me more proud to be a man than I have ever been before. I will carry through the deception of Belconti University with all my heart. Can't Morgan understand that?"

"Yes, and kill you anyway. Because you *know*. You will not lightly be forgiven that."

Cole shook his head helplessly. "Well *dammit* then—"

"Now, now, there's a way out," Bidgrass said, sitting down again. "The prophecies all foretell a change of heart after Grandfather Stomper dies. They speak of joy, love, good feeling. Morgan did agree to your coming here—he wants to hide the past as much as I do and he could see the value of my plan. In the time of good feeling I hope he will accept you."

"I hope so, too," Cole said. "Morgan is a strange man. Why is Pia so afraid of him?"

"I'll tell you that, lad—maybe it will help you to appreciate your own danger. Some few of us are educated on Tristan. Twenty-three years ago my younger brother took my niece Flada there. She ran away and married a Tristanian named Ralph Vignoli. My brother persuaded them to come back and live at our installation there, and Ralph swore to keep secret the little he knew.

"The ex-wilds of New Cornwall kept wanting Ralph to come here so they could be sure of the secret. He kept refusing and finally they sent an emissary to kill him. My brother was killed protecting him. I stepped in then with a compromise, persuaded Ralph to come here for the sake of his wife and daughter. Pia was seven at the time.

"Ralph was a good man and fought well in battles, but two years later Morgan and some others came to the house in my absence and took him away. They took him to a clearing in Lundy Forest, where the stompers come to lay eggs, stripped off his clothing and left him. That was so the stompers would not take him for an egg hunter and kill him outright, but would carry him into the forest like they do with strayed wild stock. Morgan said the command came to him in a dream.

"I think Pia feels she is partly responsible for Ralph's death. I think she sometimes fears Morgan will dream about her, her Tristanian blood. . . ."

"Poor Pia," Cole said softly. "These *years* of grief and fear. . . ."

"They'll be ended come Hoggy Darn again, Morwenna grant. Don't you grieve her with your death, too, lad. Stay close to the house, in the house."

Bidgrass rose and gulped the last of his coffee standing.

"I must go, I'm late," he said, more cheerfully than Cole had ever heard his voice. "I have a conference with General Arscoate, our military leader, whom you'll meet soon."

He went out. Cole went out, too, thoughts wrestling with feelings, looking for Pia.

In the days that followed Cole took his meals with the family except when there were guests not in Bidgrass' confidence. The doors into the main house remained unlocked and he saw much of Pia, but she seemed unexpectedly elusive and remote. Cole, busy with his report to Belconti University, had little time to wonder about it.

He faked statistics wholesale and cited dozens of nonexistent New Cornish authorities. To his real data indicating critical biomass he added imaginary values for the parameters of climate, range, longevity, fertility period, and Ruhan indices to get an estimated figure. Then he faked field census reports going back fifty years, and drew a curve dipping below critical ten years before his arrival. He made the latest field census show new biomass forty-two percent below critical and juggled figures to make the curve extrapolate to zero in twelve more years.

It pained him in his heart to leave out the curious inverse reproduction data. But it was a masterpiece of deception that should put the seal on his doctorate, and because it reported the extinction of a planetary dominant, he knew it would make the journals and the general news all through the sector.

The night he finished it, working late in the library, Pia brought him milk and cookies and sat with him as he explained what he had done.

"It's right," he defended himself to her against his scholar's conscience. "Humans on New Cornwall are a threatened species, too. The secret must be hidden forever."

"Yes," she agreed soberly. "I think if all the sector knew, the ex-wilds would literally die of shame and rage. Being wild is not so bad, but—that other!" She shuddered under her gray dress.

"Pia, sometimes I feel you're still avoiding me. Surely now it's all right and genuine between us."

She smiled sadly. "I'll bring you trouble, with Morgan. Father came to New Cornwall because of me."

"But I didn't. I've been thinking I may *stay*, partly because of you. You've been afraid so long it's habitual."

"Strangely, Flinter, I don't feel it as fear any more. It's like bowing with sadness, my strength to run is gone. My old dreams—Morgan coming for me—I have them every night now."

"Morgan! Always Morgan!"

She shook her head and smiled faintly. "He has a dark, poetic power. He is what he is, just like the stompers. I feel . . . not hate, not even fear . . . a kind of *dread*."

He stroked the back of her hand and she pulled it away.

"An old song runs through my head," she went on. "A prophecy that Grandfather Stomper cannot be killed while outworld blood pumps through any heart on the planet. I feel like my own enemy, like . . . like your enemy. You should not have come until next *Gorbals*. Flinter, *stay away from me!*"

He talked soothingly, to little avail. When they parted he said heartily, "Forget those silly prophecies, Pia. I'll look out for you."

Privately, he wondered how.

Cole sat beside Pia and across the food-laden table from General Arscoate, a large pink-faced man in middle life.

"It's an old and proven strategy, Mr. Cole," the general explained. "When Hoggy Darn starts we will harass the enemy from the air in all but one of the fourteen sizable open spaces in Lundy Forest. That one is Emrys Upland, the largest. They will concentrate in Emrys, more each night, until the climactic night of peak frenzy. Then we come down with all the men and women we can muster and we kill. We may go on killing stragglers for years after, but Grandfather Stomper will die on that night."

"Why not kill from the air?"

"More firepower on the ground. I can only lift ninety-four flyers all told. But I will shuttle twenty thousand fighting men into Emrys in an hour or two on the big night."

"So quickly? How can you?" Cole laid down his fork.

"They will be waiting in the forest top all around the periphery, in places where we are already building weapons dumps. In the first days of harrying, we will stage in the fighters."

"Morgan will visit each group in the forest top and sing our history," Bidgrass said from the head of the table. "On the evening of the climactic night, as Hoggy Darn rises, they will take a sacramental meal of stomper egg. At no other time is it eaten on this planet."

Mrs. Vignoli looked down. "Garth!" Arscoate said.

"The lad must know, must take it with us," Bidgrass said. "Lad, the real reason for not killing from the air is that the people *need* to kill personally, with their feet on the ground. So our poetry has always described that last, great fight. I must *personally* kill Grandfather Stomper."

Cole toyed with his knife. "But he is only a metaphor, a totem image—"

"The people believe in an actual individual who is the stomper counterpart of Garth here," the general broke in. "You know, Mr. Cole, the stompers we kill ordinarily are all females. The males are smaller, with a white crest, and they keep to the deep forest except on Hoggy Darn nights. Maybe the frenzy then has something to do with mating—no one knows. But Garth will kill the largest male he can find. The people, and I expect Garth and I as well, are going to believe that he has killed Grandfather Stomper in person."

The general sipped water and looked sternly over his glass at Cole. Cole glanced at Pia, who seemed lost in a dream of her own, not there to them.

"I see. A symbol," he agreed.

"Not the less real," Arscoate said tartly. "Symbols both mean and are. Garth here is a symbol too and that is why, old as he is, he must be in the thick of it. He is like the ancient battle flags of romantic prespace history. People before now have actually *seen* Grandfather Stomper. I am *not* a superstitious backworlder, Mr. Cole, but—"

Cole raised a placatory hand. "I know you are not, general. Forgive me if I seemed to suggest it."

"Let's have wine," Bidgrass said, pushing back his chair. "We'll take it in the parlor and Pia can sing for us."

When General Arscoate said good-night he told Cole not to worry, that he would have reliable guards at the manor gate during Garth Bidgrass' absence in Car Truro.

"I meant to tell you and Pia in the morning, lad," Bidgrass said. "Arscoate and I must go to Car Truro. There's heartburning there over who gets to fight and who must stay behind. It will be only two days."

Cole felt uneasy all day. He spent most of it writing the covering letter for his report and phrasing his resignation from the university field staff. He wrote personal letters to his uncle and a few friends. After dinner he finally signed the official letters and took the completed report to Bidgrass' desk. Then he went to bed and slept soundly.

Pia wakened him with frantic shaking.

"Dress quickly, Flinter. The guard at the gate was just changed and it's not time."

She darted out to the hall window while he struggled with clothing, then back again.

"*Quickly,* darling! Morgan's crossing the garden, with men. Follow me."

She led him through the kitchen and out a pantry window, then stooping along the base of a hedge to where a flowering tree overshadowed the garden wall.

"I planned this, out of sight of guard posts, when I was a little girl," she whispered. "I always knew—over, Flinter, quickly!"

Outside was rough ground, a road, a wide field of cabbages and then the barrier. Veiled Annis rode high and bluish in the clear sky. They crossed the field in soaring leaps, and shouts pursued them. The girl ran north a hundred yards behind the shadowy buttresses and squeezed through a narrow crack between two huge timber baulks. Cole barely made it, skinning his shoulders.

"I found this too when I was a little girl," Pia whispered. "I had to enlarge it when my hips grew, but only just enough. Morwenna grant they're all too big!"

"Morgan is, for sure," Cole said, rubbing his shoulder. "Pia, I *hate* to run."

"We must still run. My old plan was to reach here unseen, but now they know and they'll come over the wall in flyers. We'll have to hide in the thick brush near the forest edge until Uncle Garth returns."

She pulled a basket out of the shadows.

"Food," she said. "I brought it last night."

He carried the basket and they raced across the half-mile belt to concealment among high shrubbery and enormous mounds of fungi. Flyers with floodlights came low along the wall and others quartered the clearing. Cole and Pia stole nearer to the forest edge, into its shadow. They did not sleep.

Once he asked, "How about stompers?"

"They're a chance," she whispered. "Morgan's *sure*."

With daylight they saw four flyers patrolling instead of the usual one. At their backs colossal blackish-gray, deeply rugose tree trunks eighty feet in diameter rose up and up without a branch for many hundreds of feet. Then branches jutted out enormously and the colorful cascade of forest-top epiphytes came down the side and hung over their heads a thousand feet above.

Pia opened the food basket and they ate, seated on a bank. She wore her brown dress, her finest, he had learned, and she had new red shoes. She was quiet, as if tranced.

Cole remembered the picnic on the forest top, the secret island of beauty and innocence, and his heart stirred. He saw that the food basket was the same one. He did not tell her his thoughts.

They talked of trivial things or were silent for long periods. He held her hand. Once she roused herself to say, "Tomorrow, about this time, Uncle Garth will come looking for us." Shortly after, she gasped and caught his arm, pointing.

He peered, finally made a gestalt of broken outlines through the shrubbery. It was a stomper, swinging its head nervously.

"It smells us," she whispered. "Oh, Flinter, forgive me, darling. Take off your clothes, *quickly!*"

She undressed rapidly and hid her clothes. Cole undressed, too, fear prickling his skin, remembering what Bidgrass had told him. The stomper moved nearer in a crackle of brush and stopped again.

Man and girl knelt trembling under a fan of red-orange fungus. The girl broke off a piece and motioned the man to do the same.

"When it comes, pretend to eat," she breathed, almost inaudibly. "Don't look up and don't say a word. Morwenna be with us now."

The stomper's shadow fell across them. The man's skin prickled and sweat sprang out. He looked at the girl and she was pale but not tense, munching on her piece of fungus. She clicked her teeth faintly and he knew it was a signal. He ate.

The stomper lifted the man by his right shoulder. It was like two fingers in a mitten holding him three times his own height off the ground. He saw the beak and the eye and his sight dimmed in anguish

Then the right wing reached down and nipped the left shoulder of the rosy girl-body placidly crouching there. It swung her up to face the man momentarily under the great beak and the tricorn eye, and their own eyes met.

Very faintly she smiled and her eyes tried desperately to say, "I'm sorry" and "Goodbye, Flinter." His eyes cried in agony "No! No! I will not have it so!"

Then the two-fingered mitten became a nine-fingered mitten lapping him in darkness that bounced and swayed and he knew that the stomper was running into Lundy Forest. The wing was smooth and warm but not soft, and it smelled of cinnamon and sandalwood. The odor overpowered him and the man lapsed into stupor.

The man woke up into a fantastic dream. Luminous surfaces stretched up to be lost in gloom, with columns of darkness between. The spongy ground on which he lay shone with faint blue light. Luminous, slanting walls crisscrossed in front of him. Close at hand, behind and to the right, enormous bracket fungi ascended into darkness in ten-foot steps that supported a profusion of higher order fungi in many bizarre shapes.

He stood up and he was alone.

He climbed over a slanting root-buttress and saw her lying there. He called her name and she rose lightly and came to him. Radiant face, dimpled arms, round breasts, cradling hips: *his woman.* They embraced without shame and she cried thanks to Morwenna.

He said, "People have come out of the forest. What are the rules?"

"We must eat only the seeds of the pure white fungus—that's the least dangerous. We must walk and walk to keep our bodies so tired and hungry that they use it all. We must keep to a straight line."

"We'll live," he said. "Outside among our people, with our minds whole. We'll alternate left and right each time we round a tree, to hold our straight line. We'll come out somewhere."

"I will follow. May Morwenna go with us."

The fantastic journey wound over great gnarled roots and buttresses fusing and intermingling until it seemed that the root-complex was one unthinkably vast organism with many trunks soaring half-seen into endless darkness. Time had no feeling there. Space was a bubble of ghostly light a man could leap across.

Could leap and did, over and over, the woman following. The man climbed a curiously regular whitish root higher than his head and it writhed. Then, swaying back along its length, came a great serpent head with luminous ovoid eyes. While the man crouched in horror, waving the woman back, the monstrous jaws gaped and the teeth were blunt choppers and grinders, weirdly human looking. They bit hugely into a bracket fungus and worried at it. Man and woman hurried on.

Strength waned. The woman fell behind. The man turned back to her and the light was failing. The blue mold was black, the luminous panels more ghostly.

"It's night. Shall we sleep?" he asked.

"It's just come day," the woman said, pointing upward.

He looked up. Far above, where had been gloom, hung a pinkish-green, opalescent haze of light. Parallel lines of tree trunks converged through it to be lost in nebulosity.

"Daylight overpowers the luminous fungi," she said.

"We sleep, then walk again. Shall we find food?"

"No. We must always go to sleep hungry so we will wake again."

They looked, until tired out, for a place of shelter.

They slept, locked together in the cranny of a massive buttress. The man dreamed of his tame home-world.

He woke again into nightmare. In a twenty-foot fangrove of the white fungus they combed handfuls of black spores out of gill slots. The birdshot-sized spores had a pleasant, nutty flavor.

With the strength more walking. *Use it, use it, burn the poison.* Day faded above, and luminous night below came back to light the way. A rocky ledge and another, and then a shallow ravine with a black stream cascading. They drank and the man said, "We'll follow it, find an upland clearing."

They heard rapid motion and crouched unbreathing while a stomper minced by up ahead. It had a white crest.

On and on, fatigue the whip for greater fatigue and salvation at the end of endurance. They passed wild humans. A statuesque woman with dull eyes and yellow hair to her ankles, placidly feeding. Babies big as four-year-old normals, by themselves, grazing on finger-shaped fungi. An enormous human, fourteen feet tall, fat-enfolded, too ponderous to stand even in low gravity, crawling through fungus beds. The man could not tell its sex.

On and on, sleep and eat and travel and sleep, darkness above or darkness below, outside of time. The stream lost, found again, sourcing out finally under a great rock. And there, lodged in a black sandbank, the man found a man thigh bone half his own height. He scoured off the water mold with sand. He was armed.

The man walked ahead clutching his thigh bone, and the woman followed. They slept clasped together naked all three, man woman and thigh bone.

Stompers passed them and they crouched in sham feeding. The man prayed without words, *both or neither*. And hatred grew in him.

Snakes and giant slugs and the beautiful, gigantic, mindless wild humans, again and again, a familiar part of nightmare. The fat and truly enormous humans; and the man learned they had been male once. He remembered from far away where time was linear the voice of Grandfather Man: *Some are beyond saving, and those they kill.*

And a stomper passed, white crested, and far ahead a human voice cried out in wordless pain and protest. The man was minded to deviate from his line for fear of what they might see, but he did not. When they came on the boy, larger than the man but beardless and without formed muscles, the man looked at the tears dropping from the dull eyes and the blood dropping from the mutilation and killed him with the thigh bone. *Some are beyond saving.* And the hatred in him flamed to whiteness.

On and on, day above and day below in recurrent clash of lights. A white crested stomper paused and looked at them, crouched apart and trembling. The man felt the deepest, most anguished fear of all and beneath it, hatred surged until his teeth ached.

On and on. The man's stubble softened into beard, his hair touched his ears. On and on.

The land sloped upward and became rocky. The trees became smaller and wider spaced so that whole trunks were visible and the light of upper day descended. A patch of blue sky, then more as they ran shouting with gladness, and a bare mountain crest reared in the distance.

They embraced in wild joy and the woman cried, "Thank you, oh *loveliest* Morwenna!"

"Pia, we're human again," Cole said. "We're back in the world. And I love you."

Fearful of stompers, they moved rapidly away from the forest over steadily rising ground. The growth became more sparse, the ground more rocky, and near evening they crossed a wide moorland covered with coarse grass and scattered blocks of stone. Ahead a long, low fault scarp bounded it and there they found a cave tunneled into the rock, too narrow for a stomper. At last they felt safe. Morwenna rode silvery above the distant forest.

Water trickled from the cave which widened into a squared-off chamber in which the water spilled over the rim of a basin that looked cut with hands. Underfoot were small stone cylinders of various lengths and as his eyes adjusted Cole saw that they were drill cores.

"Prospectors made this," he told Pia, "in the old, innocent days when they still hoped to find heavy metals." Then he saw the graven initials, T.C.B., and the date, 157 A.S.

They ate red berries growing in their dooryard, gathered grass for a bed and slept in a great weariness.

Next day and the next they ate red berries and fleshy, purple ground fruits and slept, gaining strength. Secure in their cave mouth they watched stompers cross the moorland. When night fell they gazed at the bunched moons, but the three Maidens did not quite form a house and Hoggy Darn was still pursuing them.

"A few days," Pia said.

"If this isn't Emrys Upland, Arscoate will kill us with fire mist."

She nodded.

More stompers crossed the moorland, some white crested. They moved there randomly at night and from the forest came a far-off sound of stompers singing. The Maidens formed a house and Hoggy Darn grazed the side of it before they fled. To south and west faint rose glowed in the night sky.

"Fire mist," Pia said. "The nights of harrying have begun. Oh, Flinter, if this is really Emrys Upland it will be perfect."

"What will?"

"You—us—oh, I can't say yet."

"Secrets, Pia? Still secrets? Between *us*?"

"You'll know soon, Flinter. I mustn't spoil it."

The love in her eyes was tinged with a strangeness. She sought his arms and hid her face in his shoulder.

Stompers on the moorland all day so they dared not leave the cave. Flyers streaking high overhead, scouting.

"Pia, I believe this *is* Emrys Upland. I'll help after all with the great killing."

"You will help, Flinter."

"Afterward I'll take you to Belconti."

"We will never see Belconti, Flinter."

The strangeness in her eyes troubled him. He could not kiss it away.

Stompers crowding the moorland all night with their dancing, their vast singing coming to the cave from all round the compass. Rose banks distant in the night sky and Hoggy Darn crossing the House of the Maidens. Red Hoggy Darn, still lagging, still not catching it perfectly upright. The strangeness of Pia. The waiting, clutching a polished thigh bone.

At last the night when the mighty war song of the stompers went up unbearably, as the man had heard it that once before, and fire mist boiled along the distant mountains. Flyers shuttled across the sky, dropped, rose again. Blasters ripped the night with ion-pencils. Hoggy Darn gleamed redly on the threshold of the House of the Maidens that stood almost upright and perfect with silvery Morwenna at the vertex. Flyers blasted clearings in the throng of stompers, and grounded. Men boiled out of them, setting up Corbin powercasters here, there, another place, fighting as soon as their feet hit ground.

The man stood up and brandished the thigh bone.

"I must go down and fight. Wait here."

"I must go too," the girl said calmly.

"Yes, you must," he agreed. "Come along."

Stompers rushed by them and bounded over their heads and did not harm them. Blaster-torn stompers fell heavily beside them, threshing and snapping, and they were not touched. Men lowered weapons to point at the man and girl, shouting to one another out of mazed faces silently in the whelming music of the stomper chorus. Man and girl walked on.

Unharmed through the forest of singing, leaping shapes, hand in hand through a screen of fighting men that parted to admit them, they walked into the light of a glowing Corbin where a tall, gaunt old man stood watching their approach. The feeling of exalted unreality began to lift from Cole.

"Grandfather, give us blasters," he shouted. "We want to fight."

"The power is on you, lad, and you only half know it," the old man shouted back. "Stand here by the Corbin. Your fight is not yet." Tears stood in the fierce old eyes.

Across the moorland the fighting raged. Islands of men and women grouped round their Corbins held back the booming, chaotic sea of stompers that surged against them from all sides. Dikes of dead and dying grew up, men and stompers mingled. The flyers shuttled down and up again and more islands of men took shape. Hoggy Darn crossed the threshold and the savage war song of the stompers shook the night sky.

In a lull Morgan came in to the Corbin to change the wave track on his blaster. His face was a mask of iron joy and his eyes blazed.

"Morgan, if we are both alive after, I will kill you!" Cole shouted.

"No," Morgan rumbled. "You have been into the forest and come out again. It took you three weeks. It took me three hundred years. Clasp hands, my brother in hatred."

"Yes, brother in hatred." The exalted unreality began coming back strongly. "I want a blaster!" he howled at Morgan.

"No, brother in hatred, your fight is not yet," Morgan rejoined the battle, the ring of men standing braced in blaster harness fifty yards away, ripping down with interweaving ion-pencils the great forms leaping inward. Man and girl held hands and watched.

To the left trouble came to a nearby island. Stompers converged from all sides, abandoning the other attacks, impossibly many. They overran the defenders, attacking not them but the powercaster behind them, and piled up until the Corbin's blue-violet glare was hidden. A great blossoming of flame tore the pile of stompers apart, but the Corbin was dark.

"They blew out the power banks," Pia said. "They've never known to do that before. Now the men still living have only pack charges."

It was a new tactic, a death-hour flash of insight for Grandfather Stomper. Across the moor, island after island went dark and the war song grew in savage exultation, but the man thought it dwindled in total volume. Then it was their own turn.

Cole and Pia crouched away from the Corbin in the lee of a stone block and two still-twitching stompers. Beside them Morgan and Bidgrass fired steadily at the shapes hurtling above. When the Corbin blew, a wave of stinking heat rolled over them. All around, survivors struggled to their feet, using flame pistols to head-shoot wounded stompers, digging out and connecting emergency pack charges to their blasters. They were pitifully few and their new, dark island was thirty feet across.

The moor seemed dark with only the red of flame pistols and the violet flickering of power pack blasters. It seemed to heave randomly like a sluggish sea with the seen struggles of dying stompers and the felt struggles of lesser human bodies. Thinned now, stompers attacked singly or in small groups. Blasters flickered and ripped and went darkly silent as power packs discharged. The red of short-range flame pistols replaced them. But across the fault scarp ridge the tumult swelled to new heights and Corbin after Corbin there flamed out of existence in a bloom of rose-purple against the skyline.

In a lull Bidgrass shouted to Morgan. "That's costing them more than they have to give, over there. Listen. Can you hear it?"

"Yes, Father in Hatred," Morgan said. "They will break soon."

"Yes, when Arscoate lays the fire mist. They will come through here. I have one charge left."

"I have two, Father in Hatred. Change packs with me."
Cole found his voice and his senses once more.

"I must find a weapon! Grandfather, give me your flame
pistol!"

"Soon, lad. Soon now. Let the power take you," the old
man soothed.

Stompers streamed over the moor again and the fighting
flared up. The war song beat against the man's ears so that
he drew the girl nearer and shook the thigh bone. Blaster
fire flickered out altogether and the red blooming of flame
pistols weakened. But more and more stompers streamed
past without attacking. Then the man saw fire mist plume
lazily in the east, point after point coalescing all along the
forest edge.

"Now!" shouted a great voice beside him. "Now, lad!"

It was old Bidgrass, striding out like a giant, blaster
leveled in its carrying harness.

The shout released Cole and he saw it far off, coming
down the scrap rubble to the moor. Huger than any, white
crest thirty feet above the ground, Grandfather Stomper.
The war song roared insanely over the moor. Hoggy Darn
gleamed heart-midst of the three lady moons.

The grim old man aimed and fired. The great bird-shape
staggered and came on, left wing trailing. The old man
waited until it was nearly on top of him and fired again.
The stomper jerked its head and the bolt shattered the
great tri-part beak but did not kill it. With the right mitten-
wing it reached down and swung its adversary twenty feet
up, held him and haggled at him with its stumps of beak.

The old man's free right arm flailed wildly. Cole beat
the stomper's leg with the thigh bone and howled in
hatred. Then he saw the flame pistol lying where it had
fallen from the holster. He picked it up, but the power
was on him again and he did not use it. He hurled the
thigh bone at the stomper's head, diverting it for a second,
and tossed the pistol to old Bidgrass. He knew they could
not fail.

The old man caught the pistol. When the great head
swung back he held the muzzle against the tricorn eye and
fired. Red plasma-jet burned into the brain behind it. The
stomper bounded once in the air, dropped its slayer, ran
three steps and collapsed.

The stomper song changed suddenly. It became a mournful lament, a dying into grieving subsonics. Cole knew that note. He had heard it from the stompers in the stone-floored pen when the butchers were hacking off their heads. He knew that Grandfather Stomper was dead forever, after seven hundred years of war.

Flyers crossed above, blasters were still at work across the ridge, but the war was ended. The power, whatever that sense of exalted unreality might be, left Cole; and he felt naked and ridiculous and wondered what he was doing there. Then he saw the girl bending above Garth Bidgrass and regained control of himself.

The strong old man was smiling wearily.

"We've won the war, lad," he said. "The next task is yours."

"I'll help you," Cole said.

"You'll lead. Oh, I'll live, but not for long. Centuries ago, lad, there was a prophecy, and until tonight people like myself and Arscoate thought it was only poetry, however literally Morgan and the other ex-wilds took it."

"What was it?"

"It foretells that on the night Grandfather Stomper shall die the new Grandfather Man will come naked out of the forest with his beautiful wife and armed with a thigh bone, and that he will lead us in the even greater task of reclamation that comes after. *Your* ritual title of address is 'Father in Love,' lad, and I'm just a broken old man now. Take up the burden."

Cole's throat swelled, choking speech for a moment.

"I can start," he said.

Introduction

One of the major benefits I gained from this volume was the opportunity, on a conference call set up by Jim Baen, to speak with Robert Heinlein. In our discussion, Mr. Heinlein noted that the three writers who had the most influence on him were H.G. Wells, Mark Twain, (regarding whom, see later in this volume), and Rudyard Kipling. It was actually Ginny Heinlein who suggested, from an extension phone, that "The Long Watch" was a particularly suitable story for the present use.

As I said above, I was thrilled at the opportunity to speak with Mr. Heinlein—certainly one of the writers with the greatest influence on the SF field in general and on me in particular. I didn't realize when we talked that it really was about the last chance I ever could have had to do so.

—David Drake

The Long Watch

ROBERT A. HEINLEIN

"Nine ships blasted off from Moon Base. Once in space, eight of them formed a globe around the smallest. They held this formation all the way to Earth.

"The small ship displayed the insignia of an admiral—yet there was no living thing of any sort in her. She was not even a passenger ship, but a drone, a robot ship intended for radioactive cargo. This trip she carried nothing but a lead coffin—and a Geiger counter that was never quiet."

—from the editorial *After Ten Years*, film 38, 17 June 2009, Archives of the *N. Y. Times*

Johnny Dahlquist blew smoke at the Geiger counter. He grinned wryly and tried it again. His whole body was radioactive by now. Even his breath, the smoke from his cigarette, could make the Geiger counter scream.

How long had he been here? Time doesn't mean much on the Moon. Two days? Three? A week? He let his mind run back: the last clearly marked time in his mind was when the Executive Officer had sent for him, right after breakfast—

"Lieutenant Dahlquist, reporting to the Executive Officer."

Colonel Towers looked up. "Ah, John Ezra. Sit down, Johnny. Cigarette?"

Johnny sat down, mystified but flattered. He admired Colonel Towers, for his brilliance, his ability to dominate, and for his battle record. Johnny had no battle record; he had been commissioned on completing his doctor's degree in nuclear physics and was now junior bomb officer of Moon Base.

The Colonel wanted to talk politics; Johnny was puzzled. Finally Towers had come to the point; it was not safe (so he said) to leave control of the world in political hands; power must be held by a scientifically selected group. In short—the Patrol.

Johnny was startled rather than shocked. As an abstract idea, Towers' notion sounded plausible. The League of Nations had folded up; what would keep the United Nations from breaking up, too, and thus lead to another World War. "And you know how bad such a war would be, Johnny."

Johnny agreed. Towers said he was glad that Johnny got the point. The senior bomb officer could handle the work, but it was better to have both specialists

Johnny sat up with a jerk. "You are going to *do* something about it?" He had thought the Exec was just talking.

Towers smiled. "We're not politicians; we don't just talk. We act."

Johnny whistled. "When does this start?"

Towers flipped a switch. Johnny was startled to hear his own voice, then identified the recorded conversation as having taken place in the junior officers' messroom. A political argument, he remembered, which he had walked out on . . . a good thing, too! But being spied on annoyed him.

Towers switched it off. "We *have* acted," he said. "We know who is safe and who isn't. Take Kelly—" He waved at the loudspeaker. "Kelly is politically unreliable. You noticed he wasn't at breakfast?"

"Huh? I thought he was on watch."

"Kelly's watch-standing days are over. Oh, relax; he isn't hurt."

Johnny thought this over. "Which list am I on?" he asked. "Safe or unsafe?"

"Your name has a question mark after it. But I have said all along that you could be depended on." He grinned engagingly. "You won't make a liar of me, Johnny?"

Dahlquist didn't answer; Towers said sharply, "Come now—what do you think of it? Speak up."

"Well, if you ask me, you've bitten off more than you can chew. While it's true that Moon Base controls the Earth, Moon Base itself is a sitting duck for a ship. One bomb—*blooie!*"

Towers picked up a message form and handed it over, it read: I HAVE YOUR CLEAN LAUNDRY—ZACK. "That means every bomb in the *Trygve Lie* has been put out of commission. I have reports from every ship we need worry about." He stood up. "Think it over and see me after lunch. Major Morgan needs your help right away to change control frequencies on the bombs."

"The control frequencies?"

"Naturally. We don't want the bombs jammed before they reach their targets."

"What? You said the idea was to *prevent* war."

Towers brushed it aside. "There won't be a war—just a psychological demonstration, an unimportant town or two. A little bloodletting to save an all-out war. Simple arithmetic."

He put a hand on Johnny's shoulder. "You aren't squeamish, or you wouldn't be a bomb officer. Think of it as a surgical operation. And think of your family."

Johnny Dahlquist had been thinking of his family. "Please, sir, I want to see the Commanding Officer."

Towers frowned. "The Commodore is not available. As you know, I speak for him. See me again—after lunch."

The Commodore was decidedly not available; the Commodore was dead. But Johnny did not know that.

Dahlquist walked back to the messroom, bought cigarettes, sat down and had a smoke. He got up, crushed out the butt, and headed for the Base's west airlock. There he got into his space suit and went to the lockmaster. "Open her up, Smitty."

The marine looked surprised. "Can't let anyone out on the surface without word from Colonel Towers, sir. Hadn't you heard?"

"Oh, yes! Give me your order book." Dahlquist took it, wrote a pass for himself, and signed it "by direction of Colonel Towers." He added, "Better call the Executive Officer and check it."

The lockmaster read it and stuck the book in his pocket. "Oh, no, Lieutenant. Your word's good."

"Hate to disturb the Executive Officer, eh? Don't blame you." He stepped in, closed the inner door, and waited for the air to be sucked out.

Out on the Moon's surface he blinked at the light and hurried to the track-rocket terminus; a car was waiting. He squeezed in, pulled down the hood, and punched the starting button. The rocket car flung itself at the hills, dived through and came out on a plain studded with projectile rockets, like candles on a cake. Quickly it dived into a second tunnel through more hills. There was a stomach-wrenching deceleration and the car stopped at the underground atom-bomb armory.

As Dahlquist climbed out he switched on his walkie-talkie. The space-suited guard at the entrance came to port-arms. Dahlquist said, "Morning, Lopez," and walked by him to the airlock. He pulled it open.

The guard motioned him back. "Hey! Nobody goes in without the Executive Officer's say-so." He shifted his gun, fumbled in his pouch and got out a paper. "Read it, Lieutenant."

Dahlquist waved it away. "I drafted that order myself. *You* read it; you've misinterpreted it."

"I don't see how, Lieutenant."

Dahlquist snatched the paper, glanced at it, then pointed to a line, "See? '—except person specifically designated by the Executive Officer.' That's the bombs officers, Major Morgan and me."

The guard looked worried. Dahlquist said, "Damn it, look up 'specifically designated'—it's under '*Bomb Room, Security, Procedure for*,' in your standing orders. Don't tell me you left them in the barracks!"

"Oh, no, sir! I've got 'em." The guard reached into his pouch. Dahlquist gave him back the sheet; the guard took it, hesitated, then leaned his weapon against his hip, shifted the paper to his left hand, and dug into his pouch with his right.

Dahlquist grabbed the gun, shoved it between the guard's legs, and jerked. He threw the weapon away and ducked into the airlock. As he slammed the door he saw the guard struggling to his feet and reaching for his side arm. He dogged the outer door shut and felt a tingle in his fingers as a slug struck the door.

He flung himself at the inner door, jerked the spill lever, rushed back to the outer door and hung his weight on the handle. At once he could feel it stir. The guard was lifting up; the lieutenant was pulling down, with only his low Moon weight to anchor him. Slowly the handle raised before his eyes.

Air from the bomb room rushed into the lock through the spill valve. Dahlquist felt his space suit settle on his body as the pressure in the lock began to equal the pressure in the suit. He quit straining and let the guard raise the handle. It did not matter; thirteen tons of air pressure now held the door closed.

He latched open the inner door to the bomb room, so that it could not swing shut. As long as it was open, the airlock could not operate; no one could enter.

Before him in the room, one for each projectile rocket, were the atom bombs, spaced in rows far enough apart to defeat any faint possibility of spontaneous chain reaction. They were the deadliest things in the known universe, but they were his babies. He had placed himself between them and anyone who would misuse them.

But, now that he was here, he had no plan to use his temporary advantage.

The speaker on the wall sputtered into life. "Hey! Lieutenant! What goes on here? You gone crazy?" Dahlquist did not answer. Let Lopez stay confused—it would take him that much longer to make up his mind what to do. And JohnnyDahlquist needed as many minutes as he could squeeze. Lopez went on protesting. Finally he shut up.

Johnny had followed a blind urge not to let the bombs— *his* bombs!—be used for "demonstrations on unimportant towns." But what to do next? Well, Towers couldn't get through the lock. Johnny would sit tight until hell froze over.

Don't kid yourself, John Ezra! Towers could get in. Some high explosive against the outer door—then the air would whoosh out, our boy Johnny would drown in blood from his burst lungs—and the bombs would be sitting there, unhurt. They were built to stand the jump from Moon to Earth; vacuum would not hurt them at all.

He decided to stay in his space suit; explosive decompression didn't appeal to him. Come to think about it, death from old age was his choice.

Or they could drill a hole, let out the air, and open the door without wrecking the lock. Or Towers might even have a new airlock built outside the old. Not likely, Johnny thought; a *coup d'etat* depended on speed. Towers was almost sure to take the quickest way—blasting. And Lopez was probably calling the Base right now. Fifteen minutes for Towers to suit up and get here, maybe a short dicker— then *whoosh!* the party is over.

Fifteen minutes—

In fifteen minutes the bombs might fall back into the hands of the conspirators; in fifteen minutes he must make the bombs unusable.

An atom bomb is just two or more pieces of fissionable metal, such as plutonium. Separated, they are no more explosive than a pound of butter; slapped together, they explode. The complications lie in the gadgets and circuits and gun used to slap them together in the exact way and at the exact time and place required.

These circuits, the bomb's "brain," are easily destroyed— but the bomb itself is hard to destroy because of its very simplicity. Johnny decided to smash the "brains"—and quickly!

The only tools at hand were simple ones used in handling the bombs. Aside from a Geiger counter, the speaker on the walkie-talkie circuit, a television rig to the base, and the bombs themselves, the room was bare. A bomb to be worked on was taken elsewhere—not through fear of explosion, but to reduce radiation exposure for personnel. The radioactive material in a bomb is buried in a "tamper"— in these bombs, gold. Gold stops alpha, beta, and much of the deadly gamma radiation—but not neutrons.

The slippery, poisonous neutrons which plutonium gives off had to escape, or a chain reaction—explosion!—would result. The room was bathed in an invisible, almost undetectable rain of neutrons. The place was unhealthy; regulations called for staying in it as short a time as possible.

The Geiger counter clicked off the "background" radiation, cosmic rays, the trace of radioactivity in the Moon's crust, and secondary radioactivity set up all through the room by neutrons. Free neutrons have the nasty trait of infecting what they strike, making it radioactive, whether it be concrete wall or human body. In time the room would have to be abandoned.

Dahlquist twisted a knob on the Geiger counter; the instrument stopped clicking. He had used a suppressor circuit to cut out noise of "background" radiation at the level then present. It reminded him uncomfortably of the danger of staying here. He took out the radiation exposure film all radiation personnel carry; it was a direct-response type and had been fresh when he arrived. The most sensitive end was faintly darkened already. Half way down the film a red line crossed it. Theoretically, if the wearer was exposed to enough radioactivity in a week to darken the film to that line, he was, as Johnny reminded himself, a "dead duck".

Off came the cumbersome space suit; what he needed was speed. Do the job and surrender—better to be a prisoner than to linger in a place as "hot" as this.

He grabbed a ball hammer from the tool rack and got busy, pausing only to switch off the television pick-up. The first bomb bothered him. He started to smash the cover plate of the "brain," then stopped, filled with reluctance. All his life he had prized fine apparatus.

He nerved himself and swung; glass tinkled, metal creaked. His mood changed; he began to feel a shameful pleasure in destruction. He pushed on with enthusiasm, swinging, smashing, destroying!

So intent was he that he did not at first hear his name called. "Dahlquist! Answer me! Are you there?"

He wiped sweat and looked at the TV screen. Towers' perturbed features stared out.

Johnny was shocked to find that he had wrecked only six bombs. Was he going to be caught before he could finish? Oh, no! He *had* to finish. Stall, son, stall! "Yes, Colonel? You call me?"

"I certainly did! What's the meaning of this?"

"I'm sorry, Colonel."

Towers' expression relaxed a little. "Turn on your pick-up, Johnny, I can't see you. What was that noise?"

"The pick-up is on," Johnny lied. "It must be out of order. That noise—uh, to tell the truth, Colonel, I was fixing things so that nobody could get in here."

Towers hesitated, then said firmly, "I'm going to assume that you are sick and send you to the Medical Officer. But I want you to come out of there, right away. That's an order, Johnny."

Johnny answered slowly. "I can't just yet, Colonel. I came here to make up my mind and I haven't quite made it up. You said to see you after lunch."

"I meant you to stay in your quarters."

"Yes, sir. But I thought I ought to stand watch on the bombs, in case I decided you were wrong."

"It's not for you to decide, Johnny. I'm your superior officer. You are sworn to obey me."

"Yes, sir." This was wasting time; the old fox might have a squad on the way now. "But I swore to keep the peace, too. Could you come out here and talk it over with me? I don't want to do the wrong thing."

Towers smiled. "A good idea, Johnny. You wait there. I'm sure you'll see the light." He switched off.

"There," said Johnny. "I hope you're convinced that I'm a half-wit—you slimy mistake!" He picked up the hammer, ready to use the minutes gained.

He stopped almost at once; it dawned on him that wrecking the "brains" was not enough. There were no spare "brains," but there was a well-stocked electronics shop. Morgan could jury-rig control circuits for bombs. Why, he could himself—not a neat job, but one that would work. Damnation! He would have to wreck the bombs themselves—and in the next ten minutes.

But a bomb was solid chunks of metal, encased in a heavy tamper, all tied in with a big steel gun. It couldn't be done—not in ten minutes.

Damn!

Of course, there was one way. He knew the control circuits; he also knew how to beat them. Take this bomb: if he took out the safety bar, unhooked the proximity circuit, shorted the delay circuit, and cut in the arming circuit by hand—then unscrewed *that* and reached in *there*, he could, with just a long, stiff wire, set the bomb off.

Blowing the other bombs and the valley itself to Kingdom Come.

Also Johnny Dahlquist. That was the rub.

All this time he was doing what he had thought out, up to the step of actually setting off the bomb. Ready to go, the bomb seemed to threaten, as if crouching to spring. He stood up, sweating.

He wondered if he had the courage. He did not want to funk—and hoped that he would. He dug into his jacket and took out a picture of Edith and the baby. "Honeychile," he said, "if I get out of this, I'll never even try to beat a red light." He kissed the picture and put it back. There was nothing to do but wait.

What was keeping Towers? Johnny wanted to make sure that Towers was in blast range. What a joke on the jerk! Me—sitting here, ready to throw the switch on him. The idea tickled him; it led to a better: why blow himself up—alive?

There was another way to rig it—a "dead man" control. Jigger up some way so that the last step, the one that set off the bomb, would not happen as long as he kept his hand on a switch or a lever or something. Then, if they blew open the door, or shot him, or anything—up goes the balloon!

Better still, if he could hold them off with the threat of it, sooner or later help would come—Johnny was sure that most of the Patrol was not in this stinking conspiracy—and then: Johnny comes marching home! What a reunion! He'd resign and get a teaching job; he'd stood his watch.

All the while, he was working. Electrical? No, too little time. Make it a simple mechanical linkage. He had it doped out but had hardly begun to build it when the loudspeaker called him. "Johnny?"

"That you, Colonel?" His hands kept busy.

"Let me in."

"Well, now, Colonel, that wasn't in the agreement." Where in blue blazes was something to use as a long lever?

"I'll come in alone, Johnny, I give you my word. We'll talk face to face."

His word! "We can talk over the speaker, Colonel."
Hey, that was it—a yardstick, hanging on the tool rack.

"Johnny, I'm warning you. Let me in, or I'll blow the
door off."

A wire—he needed a wire, fairly long and stiff. He tore
the antenna from his suit. "You wouldn't do that, Colonel.
It would ruin the bombs."

"Vacuum won't hurt the bombs. Quit stalling."

"Better check with Major Morgan. Vacuum won't hurt
them; explosive decompression would wreck every circuit." The Colonel was not a bomb specialist; he shut up
for several minutes. Johnny went on working.

"Dahlquist," Towers resumed, "that was a clumsy lie. I
checked with Morgan. You have sixty seconds to get into
your suit, if you aren't already. I'm going to blast the
door."

"No, you won't," said Johnny. "Ever hear of a 'dead
man' switch?" Now for a counterweight—and a sling.

"Eh? What do you mean?"

"I've rigged number seventeen to set off by hand. But I
put in a gimmick. It won't blow while I hang on to a strap
I've got in my hand. But if anything happens to me—*up
she goes!* You are about fifty feet from the blast center.
Think it over."

There was a short silence. "I don't believe you."

"No? Ask Morgan. He'll believe me. He can inspect it,
over the TV pickup." Johnny lashed the belt of his space
suit to the end of the yardstick.

"You said the pick-up was out of order."

"So I lied. This time I'll prove it. Have Morgan call me."

Presently Major Morgan's face appeared. "Lieutenant
Dahlquist?"

"Hi, Stinky. Wait a sec." With great care Dahlquist
made one last connection while holding down the end of
the yardstick. Still careful, he shifted his grip to the belt,
sat down on the floor, stretched an arm and switched on
the TV pick-up. "Can you see me, Stinky?"

"I can see you," Morgan answered stiffly. "What is this
nonsense?"

"A little surprise I whipped up." He explained it—what
circuits he had cut out, what ones had been shorted, just
how the jury-rigged mechanical sequence fitted in.

Morgan nodded. "But you're bluffing, Dahlquist. I feel sure that you haven't disconnected the 'K' circuit. You don't have the guts to blow yourself up."

Johnny chuckled. "I sure haven't. But that's the beauty of it. It can't go off, *so long as I am alive*. If your greasy boss, ex-Colonel Towers, blasts the door, then I'm dead and the bomb goes off. It won't matter to me, but it will to him. Better tell him." He switched off.

Towers came on over the speaker shortly. "Dahlquist?"

"I hear you."

"There's no need to throw away your life. Come out and you will be retired on full pay. You can go home to your family. That's a promise."

Johnny got mad. "You keep my family out of this!"

"Think of them, man."

"Shut up. Get back to your hole. I feel a need to scratch and this whole shebang might just explode in your lap."

2

Johnny sat up with a start. He had dozed, his hand hadn't let go the sling, but he had the shakes when he thought about it.

Maybe he should disarm the bomb and depend on their not daring to dig him out? But Towers' neck was already in hock for treason; Towers might risk it. If he did and the bomb were disarmed, Johnny would be dead and Towers would have the bombs. No, he had gone this far; he wouldn't let his baby girl grow up in a dictatorship just to catch some sleep.

He heard the Geiger counter clicking and remembered having used the suppressor circuit. The radioactivity in the room must be increasing, perhaps from scattering the "brain" circuits—the circuits were sure to be infected; they had lived too long too close to plutonium. He dug out his film.

The dark area was spreading toward the red line.

He put it back and said, "Pal, better break this deadlock or you are going to shine like a watch dial." It was a figure of speech; infected animal tissue does not glow—it simply dies, slowly.

The TV screen lit up; Towers' face appeared. "Dahlquist? I want to talk to you."

"Go fly a kite."

"Let's admit you have us inconvenienced."

"Inconvenienced, hell—I've got you stopped."

"For the moment. I'm arranging to get more bombs—"

"Liar."

"—but you are slowing us up. I have a proposition."

"Not interested."

"Wait. When this is over I will be chief of the world government. If you cooperate, even now, I will make you my administrative head."

Johnny told him what to do with it. Towers said, "Don't be stupid. What do you gain by dying?"

Johnny grunted. "Towers, what a prime stinker you are. You spoke of my family. I'd rather see them dead than living under a two-bit Napoleon like you. Now go away— I've got some thinking to do."

Towers switched off.

Johnny got out his film again. It seemed no darker but it reminded him forcibly that time was running out. He was hungry and thirsty—and he could not stay awake forever. It took four days to get a ship up from Earth; he could not expect rescue any sooner. And he wouldn't last four days— once the darkening spread past the red line he was a goner.

His only chance was to wreck the bombs beyond repair, and get out—before that film got much darker.

He thought about ways, then got busy. He hung a weight on the sling, tied a line to it. If Towers blasted the door, he hoped to jerk the rig loose before he died.

There was a simple, though arduous, way to wreck the bombs beyond any capacity of Moon Base to repair them. The heart of each was two hemispheres of plutonium, their flat surfaces polished smooth to permit perfect contact when slapped together. Anything less would prevent the chain reaction on which atomic explosion depended.

Johnny started taking apart one of the bombs.

He had to bash off four lugs, then break the glass envelope around the inner assembly. Aside from that the bomb came apart easily. At last he had in front of him two gleaming, mirror-perfect half globes.

A blow with the hammer—and one was no longer perfect. Another blow and the second cracked like glass; he had tapped its crystalline structure just right.

Hours later, dead tired, he went back to the armed bomb. Forcing himself to steady down, with extreme care he disarmed it. Shortly its silvery hemispheres too were useless. There was no longer a usable bomb in the room— but huge fortunes in the most valuable, most poisonous, and most deadly metal in the known world were spread around the floor.

Johnny looked at the deadly stuff. "Into your suit and out of here, son," he said aloud. "I wonder what Towers will say?"

He walked toward the rack, intending to hang up the hammer. As he passed, the Geiger counter chattered wildly.

Plutonium hardly affects a Geiger counter; secondary infection from plutonium does. Johnny looked at the hammer, then held it closer to the Geiger counter. The counter screamed.

Johnny tossed it hastily away and started back toward his suit.

As he passed the counter it chattered again. He stopped short.

He pushed one hand close to the counter. Its clicking picked up to a steady roar. Without moving he reached into his pocket and took out his exposure film.

It was dead black from end to end.

3

Plutonium taken into the body moves quickly to bone marrow. Nothing can be done; the victim is finished. Neutrons from it smash through the body, ionizing tissue, transmuting atoms into radioactive isotopes, destroying and killing. The fatal dose is unbelievably small; a mass a tenth the size of a grain of table salt is more than enough—a dose small enough to enter through the tiniest scratch. During the historic "Manhattan Project" immediate high amputation was considered the only possible first-aid measure.

Johnny knew all this but it no longer disturbed him. He

sat on the floor, smoking a hoarded cigarette, and thinking. The events of his long watch were running through his mind.

He blew a puff of smoke at the Geiger counter and smiled without humor to hear it chatter more loudly. By now even his breath was "hot"—carbon-14, he supposed, exhaled from his blood stream as carbon dioxide. It did not matter.

There was no longer any point in surrendering, nor would he give Towers the satisfaction—he would finish out this watch right here. Besides, by keeping up the bluff that one bomb was ready to blow, he could stop them from capturing the raw material from which bombs were made. That might be important in the long run.

He accepted, without surprise, the fact that he was not unhappy. There was a sweetness about having no further worries of any sort. He did not hurt, he was not uncomfortable, he was no longer even hungry. Physically he still felt fine and his mind was at peace. He was dead—he knew that he was dead; yet for a time he was able to walk and breathe and see and feel.

He was not even lonesome. He was not alone; there were comrades with him—the boy with his finger in the dike, Colonel Bowie, too ill to move but insisting that he be carried across the line, the dying Captain of the *Chesapeake* still with deathless challenge on his lips, Rodger Young peering into the gloom. They gathered about him in the dusky bomb room.

And of course there was Edith. She was the only one he was aware of. Johnny wished that he could see her face more clearly. Was she angry? Or proud and happy?

Proud though unhappy—he could see her better now and even feel her hand. He held very still.

Presently his cigarette burned down to his fingers. He took a final puff, blew it at the Geiger counter, and put it out. It was his last. He gathered several butts and fashioned a roll-your-own with a bit of paper found in a pocket. He lit it carefully and settled back to wait for Edith to show up again. He was very happy.

He was still propped against the bomb case, the last of his salvaged cigarettes cold at his side, when the speaker

called out again. "Johnny? Hey, Johnny! Can you hear
me? This is Kelly. It's all over. The *Lafayette* landed and
Towers blew his brains out. Johnny? *Answer me.*"

When they opened the outer door, the first man in
carried a Geiger counter in front of him on the end of a
long pole. He stopped at the threshold and backed out
hastily. "Hey, chief!" he called. "Better get some handling
equipment—uh, and a lead coffin, too."

*"Four days it took the little ship and her escort to reach
Earth. Four days while all of Earth's people awaited her
arrival. For ninety-eight hours all commercial programs
were off television; instead there was an endless dirge—
the* Dead March *from* Saul, *the* Valhalla *theme,* Going
Home, *the* Patrol's own Landing Orbit.

*"The nine ships landed at Chicago Port. A drone tractor
removed the casket from the small ship; the ship was then
refueled and blasted off in an escape trajectory, thrown
away into outer space, never again to be used for a lesser
purpose.*

*"The tractor progressed to the Illinois town where Lieu-
tenant Dahlquist had been born, while the dirge continued. There it placed the casket on a pedestal, inside a
barrier marking the distance of safe approach. Space ma-
rines, arms reversed and heads bowed, stood guard around
it; the crowds stayed outside this circle. And still the dirge
continued.*

*"When enough time had passed, long, long after the
heaped flowers had withered, the lead casket was enclosed
in marble, just as you see it today."*

Introduction

Mr. Heinlein noted, during the conference call to which I referred earlier, that Twain—along with Kipling—was one of the writers who had most influenced him. That caused Jim Baen to mention the delightful essay Kipling did regarding his interview with Mark Twain . . . and Mr. Heinlein recalled that he'd used, as a brief scene in *To Sail Beyond the Sunset*, a little girl's meeting with Mark Twain.

He then volunteered that we could reprint the segment in this volume. We first intended to run it as the introduction to "The Long Watch"; but on reconsideration we decided to include the Kipling essay itself—with this scene from Mr. Heinlein's last book to introduce it.

—David Drake

Prologue

ROBERT A. HEINLEIN

"A democracy works well only when the common man is an aristocrat. But God must hate the common man; He has made him so dadblamed common! Does your common man understand chivalry? Noblesse oblige? Aristocratic rules of conduct? Personal responsibility for the welfare of the State? One may as well search for fur on a frog." Is that something I heard my father say? No. Well, not exactly. It is something I recall from about two o'clock in the morning in the Oyster Bar of the Benton House in Kansas City after Mr. Clemens's lecture in January 1898. Maybe my father said part of it; perhaps Mr. Clemens said all of it, or perhaps they shared it—my memory is not perfect after so many years.

Mr. Clemens and my father were indulging in raw oysters, philosophy, and brandy. I had a small glass of port. Both port and raw oysters were new to me; I disliked both . . . not helped by the odor of Mr. Clemens's cigar.

(I had assured Mr. Clemens that I enjoyed the aroma of a good cigar: please do smoke. A mistake.)

But I would have endured more than cigar smoke and raw oysters to be present that night. On the platform Mr. Clemens had looked just like his pictures: a jovial Satan with a halo of white hair, in a beautifully tailored white suit. In person he was a foot shorter, warmly charming, and he made of me an even more fervent admirer by treating me as a grown lady.

I was up hours past my bedtime and had to keep pinching myself not to fall asleep. What I remember best was Mr. Clemens's discourse on the subject of cats and redheads . . . composed on the spot for my benefit. I think—it does not appear anywhere in his published works, not even those released by the University of California fifty years after his death.

Did you know that Mr. Clemens was a redhead? But that must wait.

An Interview With Mark Twain

Rudyard Kipling

You are a contemptible lot, over yonder. Some of you are Commissioners, and some Lieutenant-Governors, and some have the V.C., and a few are privileged to walk about the Mall arm in arm with the Viceroy; but I have seen Mark Twain this golden morning, have shaken his hand, and smoked a cigar—no, two cigars—with him, and talked with him for more than two hours! Understand clearly that I do not despise you; indeed, I don't. I am only very sorry for you, from the Viceroy downward. To soothe your envy and to prove that I still regard you as my equals, I will tell you all about it.

They said in Buffalo that he was in Hartford, Conn.; and again they said "perchance he is gone upon a journey to Portland"; and a big, fat drummer vowed that he knew the great man intimately, and that Mark was spending the summer in Europe—which information so upset me that I embarked upon the wrong train, and was incontinently turned out by the conductor three-quarters of a mile from the station, amid the wilderness of railway tracks. Have you ever, encumbered with great-coat and valise, tried to dodge diversely-minded locomotives when the sun was shining in your eyes? But I forgot that you have not seen Mark Twain, you people of no account!

Saved from the jaws of the cowcatcher, me wandering devious a stranger met.

"Elmira is the place. Elmira in the State of New York—this State, not two hundred miles away"; and he added, perfectly unnecessarily, "Slide, Kelley, slide."

I slid on the West Shore line, I slid till midnight, and they dumped me down at the door of a frowzy hotel in Elmira. Yes, they knew all about "that man Clemens," but reckoned he was not in town; had gone East somewhere. I had better possess my soul in patience till the morrow, and then dig up the "man Clemens' " brother-in-law, who was interested in coal.

The idea of chasing half a dozen relatives in addition to Mark Twain up and down a city of thirty thousand inhabitants kept me awake. Morning revealed Elmira, whose streets were desolated by railway tracks, and whose suburbs were given up to the manufacture of door-sashes and window-frames. It was surrounded by pleasant, fat little hills, rimmed with timber and topped with cultivation. The Chemung River flowed generally up and down the town, and had just finished flooding a few of the main streets.

The hotel-man and the telephone-man assured me that the much-desired brother-in-law was out of town, and no one seemed to know where "the man Clemens" abode. Later on I discovered that he had not summered in that place for more than nineteen seasons, and so was comparatively a new arrival.

A friendly policeman volunteered the news that he had seen Twain or "some one very like him" driving a buggy the day before. This gave me a delightful sense of nearness. Fancy living in a town where you could see the author of "Tom Sawyer," or "some one very like him," jolting over the pavements in a buggy.

"He lives out yonder at East Hill," said the policeman; "three miles from here."

Then the chase began—in a hired hack, up an awful hill, where sunflowers blossomed by the roadside, and crops waved, and "Harper's Magazine" cows stood in eligible and commanding attitudes knee-deep in clover, all ready to be transferred to photogravure. The great man must have been persecuted by outsiders aforetime, and fled up the hill for refuge.

Presently the driver stopped at a miserable, little white wood shanty, and demanded "Mister Clemens."

"I know he's a big bug and all that," he explained, "but you can never tell what sort of notions those sort of men take into their heads to live in, anyways."

There rose up a young lady who was sketching thistletops and golden-rod, amid a plentiful supply of both, and set the pilgrimage on the right path.

"It's a pretty Gothic house on the left-hand side a little way further on."

"Gothic hell!" said the driver. "Very few of the city hacks take this drive, 'specially if they know they are coming out here," and he glared at me savagely.

It was a very pretty house, anything but Gothic, clothed with ivy, standing in a very big compound, and fronted by a verandah full of chairs and hammocks. The roof of the verandah was a trellis-work of creepers, and the sun peeping through moved on the shining boards below.

Decidedly this remote place was an ideal one for work, if a man could work among these soft airs and the murmur of the long-eared crops.

Appeared suddenly a lady used to dealing with rampageous outsiders. "Mr. Clemens has just walked downtown. He is at his brother-in-law's house."

Then he was within shouting distance, after all, and the chase had not been in vain. With speed I fled, and the driver, skidding the wheel and swearing audibly, arrived at the bottom of that hill without accidents. It was in the pause that followed between ringing the brother-in-law's bell and getting an answer that it occurred to me, for the first time, Mark Twain might possibly have other engagements than the entertainment of escaped lunatics from India, be they never so full of admiration. And in another man's house—anyhow, what had I come to do or say? Suppose the drawing-room should be full of people,— suppose a baby were sick, how was I to explain that I only wanted to shake hands with him?

Then things happened somewhat in this order. A big, darkened drawing room; a huge chair; a man with eyes, a mane of grizzled hair, a brown moustache covering a mouth as delicate as a woman's, a strong, square hand shaking mine, and the slowest, calmest, levellest voice in all the world saying:—

"Well, you think you owe me something, and you've come to tell me so. That's what I call squaring a debt handsomely."

"Piff!" from a cob-pipe (I always said that a Missouri

meerschaum was the best smoking in the world), and, behold! Mark Twain had curled himself up in the big armchair, and I was smoking reverently, as befits one in the presence of his superior.

The thing that struck me first was that he was an elderly man; yet, after a minute's thought, I perceived that it was otherwise, and in five minutes, the eyes looking at me, I saw that the grey hair was an accident of the most trivial. He was quite young. I was shaking his hand. I was smoking his cigar, and I was hearing him talk—this man I had learned to love and admire fourteen thousand miles away.

Reading his books, I had striven to get an idea of his personality, and all my preconceived notions were wrong and beneath the reality. Blessed is the man who finds no disillusion when he is brought face to face with a revered writer! That was a moment to be remembered; the landing of a twelve-pound salmon was nothing to it. I had hooked Mark Twain, and he was treating me as though under certain circumstances I might be an equal.

About this time I became aware that he was discussing the copyright question. Here, so far as I remember, is what he said. Attend to the words of the oracle through this unworthy medium transmitted. You will never be able to imagine the long, slow surge of the drawl, and the deadly gravity of the countenance, the quaint pucker of the body, one foot thrown over the arm of the chair, the yellow pipe clinched in one corner of the mouth, and the right hand casually caressing the square chin:—

"Copyright? Some men have morals, and some men have—other things. I presume a publisher is a man. He is not born. He is created—by circumstances. Some publishers have morals. Mine have. They pay me for the English productions of my books. When you hear men talking of Bret Harte's works and other works and my books being pirated, ask them to be sure of their facts. I think they'll find the books are paid for. It was ever thus.

"I remember an unprincipled and formidable publisher. Perhaps he's dead now. He used to take my short stories—I can't call it steal or pirate them. It was beyond these things altogether. He took my stories one at a time and made a book of it. If I wrote an essay on dentistry or theology or any little thing of that kind—just an essay that long (he indicated half an inch on his finger), any sort of essay—that publisher would amend and improve my essay.

"He would get another man to write some more to it, or cut it about exactly as his needs required. Then he would publish a book called 'Dentistry by Mark Twain,' that little essay and some other things not mine added. Theology would make another book, and so on. I do not consider that fair. It's an insult. But he's dead now, I think. I didn't kill him.

"There is a great deal of nonsense talked about international copyright. The proper way to treat a copyright is to make it exactly like real estate in every way.

"It will settle itself under these conditions. If Congress were to bring in a law that a man's life was not to extend over a hundred and sixty years, somebody would laugh. That law wouldn't concern anybody. The man would be out of the jurisdiction of the court. A term of years in copyright comes to exactly the same thing. No law can make a book live or cause it to die before the appointed time.

"Tottletown, Cal., was a new town, with a population of three thousand—banks, fire-brigade, brick buildings and all the modern improvements. It lived, it flourished, and it disappeared. To-day no man can put his foot on any remnant of Tottletown, Cal. It's dead. London continues to exist. Bill Smith, author of a book read for the next year or so, is real estate in Tottletown. William Shakespeare, whose works are extensively read, is real estate in London. Let Bill Smith, equally with Mr. Shakespeare now deceased, have as complete a control over his copyright as he would over his real estate. Let him gamble it away, drink it away, or—give it to the church. Let his heirs and assigns treat it in the same manner.

"Every now and again I go up to Washington, sitting on a board to drive that sort of view into Congress. Congress takes its arguments against international copyright delivered ready made, and—Congress isn't very strong. I put the real-estate view of the case before one of the Senators.

"He said: 'Suppose a man has written a book that will live for ever?'

"I said: 'Neither you nor I will ever live to see that man, but we'll assume it. What then?'

"He said: 'I want to protect the world against that man's heirs and assigns, working under your theory.'

"I said: 'You think that all the world has no commercial sense. The book that will live for ever can't be artificially kept up at inflated prices. There will always be very expensive editions of it and cheap ones issuing side by side.'

"Take the case of Sir Walter Scott's novels," Mark Twain continued, turning to me. "When the copyright notes protected them, I bought editions as expensive as I could afford, because I liked them. At the same time the same firm were selling editions that a cat might buy. They had their real estate, and not being fools, recognized that one portion of the plot could be worked as a gold mine, another as a vegetable garden, and another as a marble quarry. Do you see?"

What I saw with the greatest clearness was Mark Twain being forced to fight for the simple proposition that a man has as much right to the work of his brains (think of the heresy of it!) as to the labour of his hands. When the old lion roars, the young whelps growl. I growled assentingly, and the talk ran on from books in general to his own in particular.

Growing bold, and feeling that I had a few hundred thousand folk at my back, I demanded whether Tom Sawyer married Judge Thatcher's daughter and whether we were ever going to hear of Tom Sawyer as a man.

"I haven't decided," quoth Mark Twain, getting up, filling his pipe, and walking up and down the room in his slippers. "I have a notion of writing the sequel to 'Tom Sawyer' in two ways. In one I would make him rise to great honour and go to Congress, and in the other I should hang him. Then the friends and enemies of the book could take their choice."

Here I lost my reverence completely, and protested against any theory of the sort, because, to me at least, Tom Sawyer was real.

"Oh, he is real," said Mark Twain. "He's all the boys that I have known or recollect; but that would be a good way of ending the book;" then, turning round, "because, when you come to think of it, neither religion, training, nor education avails anything against the force of circumstances that drives a man. Suppose we took the next four-and-twenty years of Tom Sawyer's life, and gave a little joggle to the circumstances that controlled him. He would, logically and according to the joggle, turn out a rip or an angel."

"Do you believe that, then?"

"I think so. Isn't it what you call Kismet?"

"Yes, but don't give him two joggles and show the result, because he isn't your property any more. He belongs to us."

He laughed—a large, wholesome laugh—and this began a dissertation on the rights of a man to do what he liked with his own creations, which being a matter of purely professional interest, I will mercifully omit.

Returning to the big chair, he, speaking of truth and the like in literature, said that an autobiography was the one work in which a man, against his own will and in spite of his utmost striving to the contrary, revealed himself in his true light to the world.

"A good deal of your life on the Mississippi is autobiographical, isn't it?" I asked.

"As near as it can be—when a man is writing a book and about himself. But in genuine autobiography, I believe it is impossible for a man to tell the truth about himself or to avoid impressing the reader with the truth about himself.

"I made an experiment once. I got a friend of mine—a man painfully given to speak the truth on all occasions—a man who wouldn't dream of telling a lie—and I made him write his autobiography for his own amusement and mine. He did it. The manuscript would have made an octavo volume, but—good, honest man that he was—in every single detail of his life that I knew about he turned out, on paper, a formidable liar. He could not help himself.

"It is not in human nature to write the truth about itself. None the less the reader gets a general impression from an autobiography whether the man is a fraud or a good man. The reader can't give his reasons any more than a man can explain why a woman struck him as being lovely when he doesn't remember her hair, eyes, teeth, or figure. And the impression that the reader gets is a correct one."

"Do you ever intend to write an autobiography?"

"If I do, it will be as other men have done—with the

most earnest desire to make myself out to be the better man in every little business that has been to my discredit; and I shall fail, like the others, to make my readers believe anything except the truth."

This naturally led to a discussion on conscience. Then said Mark Twain, and his words are mighty and to be remembered:—

"Your conscience is a nuisance. A conscience is like a child. If you pet it and play with it and let it have everything that it wants, it becomes spoiled and intrudes on all your amusements and most of your griefs. Treat your conscience as you would treat anything else. When it is rebellious, spank it—be severe with it, argue with it, prevent it from coming to play with you at all hours, and you will secure a good conscience; that is to say, a properly trained one. A spoiled one simply destroys all the pleasure in life. I think I have reduced mine to order. At least, I haven't heard from it for some time. Perhaps I have killed it from over-severity. It's wrong to kill a child, but, in spite of all I have said, a conscience differs from a child in many ways. Perhaps it's best when it's dead."

Here he told me a little—such things as a man may tell a stranger—of his early life and upbringing, and in what manner he had been influenced for good by the example of his parents. He spoke always through his eyes, a light under the heavy eyebrows; anon crossing the room with a step as light as a girl's, to show me some book or other; then resuming his walk up and down the room, puffing at the cob pipe. I would have given much for nerve enough to demand the gift of that pipe—value, five cents when new. I understood why certain savage tribes ardently desired the liver of brave men slain in combat. That pipe would have given me, perhaps, a hint of his keen insight into the souls of men. But he never laid it aside within stealing reach.

Once, indeed, he put his hand on my shoulder. It was an investiture of the Star of India, blue silk, trumpets, and diamond-studded jewel, all complete. If hereafter, in the changes and chances of this mortal life, I fall to cureless ruin, I will tell the superintendent of the workhouse that Mark Twain once put his hand on my shoulder; and he shall give me a room to myself and a double allowance of paupers' tobacco.

"I never read novels myself," said he, "except when the popular persecution forces me to—when people plague me to know what I think of the last book that every one is reading."

"And how did the latest persecution affect you?"

"Robert?" said he, interrogatively.

I nodded.

"I read it, of course, for the workmanship. That made me think I had neglected novels too long—that there might be a good many books as graceful in style somewhere on the shelves; so I began a course of novel reading. I have dropped it now; it did not amuse me. But as regards Robert, the effect on me was exactly as though a singer of street ballads were to hear excellent music from a church organ. I didn't stop to ask whether the music was legitimate or necessary. I listened, and I liked what I heard. I am speaking of the grace and beauty of the style.

"You see," he went on, "every man has his private opinion about a book. But that is my private opinion. If I had lived in the beginning of things, I should have looked around the township to see what popular opinion thought of the murder of Abel before I openly condemned Cain. I should have had my private opinion, of course, but I shouldn't have expressed it until I had felt the way. You have my private opinion about that book. I don't know what my public ones are exactly. They won't upset the earth."

He recurled himself into the chair and talked of other things.

"I spend nine months of the year at Hartford. I have long ago satisfied myself that there is no hope of doing much work during those nine months. People come in and call. They call at all hours, about everything in the world. One day I thought I would keep a list of interruptions. It began this way:—

"A man came and would see no one but Mr. Clemens. He was an agent for photogravure reproductions of Salon pictures. I very seldom use Salon pictures in my books.

"After that man, another man, who refused to see any one but Mr. Clemens, came to make me write to Washington about something. I saw him. I saw a third man, then a fourth. By this time it was noon. I had grown tired of keeping the list. I wished to rest.

"But the fifth man was the only one of the crowd with a card of his own. He sent up his card. 'Ben Koontz, Hannibal, Mo.' I was raised in Hannibal. Ben was an old schoolmate of mine. Consequently I threw the house wide open and rushed with both hands out at a big, fat, heavy man, who was not the Ben I had ever known—nor anything like him.

" 'But is it you, Ben?' " I said. 'You've altered in the last thousand years.'

"The fat man said: 'Well, I'm not Koontz exactly, but I met him down in Missouri, and he told me to be sure and call on you, and he gave me his card, and'—here he acted the little scene for my benefit—'if you can wait a minute till I can get out the circulars—I'm not Koontz exactly, but I'm traveling with the fullest line of rods you ever saw.'

"And what happened?" I asked breathlessly.

"I shut the door. He was not Ben Koontz—exactly—not my old school-fellow, but I had shaken him by both hands in love, and . . . I had been boarded by a lightning-rod man in my own house.

"As I was saying, I do very little work in Hartford. I come here for three months every year, and I work four or five hours a day in a study down the garden of that little house on the hill. Of course, I do not object to two or three interruptions. When a man is in the full swing of his work these little things do not affect him. Eight or ten or twenty interruptions retard composition."

I was burning to ask him all manner of impertinent questions, as to which of his works he himself preferred, and so forth; but, standing in awe of his eyes, I dared not. He spoke on, and I listened, grovelling.

It was a question of mental equipment that was on the carpet, and I am still wondering whether he meant what he said.

"Personally I never care for fiction or story-books. What I like to read about are facts and statistics of any kind. If they are only facts about the raising of radishes, they interest me. Just now, for instance, before you came in"—he pointed to an encyclopædia on the shelves—"I was reading an article about 'Mathematics.' Perfectly pure mathemathics.

"My own knowledge of mathematics stops at 'twelve

times twelve,' but I enjoyed that article immensely. I didn't understand a word of it; but facts, or what a man believes to be facts, are always delightful. That mathematical fellow believed in his facts. So do I. Get your facts first, and"—the voice dies away to an almost inaudible drone—"then you can distort 'em as much as you please."

Bearing this precious advice in my bosom, I left, the great man assuring me with gentle kindness that I had not interrupted him in the least. Once outside the door, I yearned to go back and ask some questions—it was easy enough to think of them now—but his time was his own, though his books belonged to me.

I should have ample time to look back to that meeting across the graves of the days. But it was sad to think of the things he had not spoken about.

In San Francisco the men of "The Call" told me many legends of Mark's apprenticeship in their paper five-and-twenty years ago; how he was a reporter delightfully incapable of reporting according to the needs of the day. He preferred, so they said, to coil himself into a heap and meditate until the last minute. Then he would produce copy bearing no sort of relationship to his legitimate work—copy that made the editor swear horribly, and the readers of "The Call" ask for more.

I should like to have heard Mark's version of that, with some stories of his joyous and variegated past. He has been journeyman-printer (in those days he wandered from the banks of the Missouri even to Philadelphia), pilot-cub and full-blown pilot, soldier of the South (that was for three weeks only), private secretary to a Lieutenant-Governor of Nevada (that displeased him), miner, editor, special correspondent in the Sandwich Islands, and the Lord only knows what else. If so experienced a man could by any means be made drunk, it would be a glorious thing to fill him up with composite liquors, and, in the language of his own country, "let him retrospect." But these eyes will never see that orgy fit for the Gods!

With The Night Mail

A STORY OF 2000 A.D.

RUDYARD KIPLING

At nine o'clock of a gusty winter night I stood on the lower stages of one of the G. P. O. outward mail towers. My purpose was a run to Quebec in ""Postal Packet 162 or such other as may be appointed"; and the Postmaster-General himself countersigned the order. This talisman opened all doors, even those in the despatching-caisson at the foot of the tower, where they were delivering the sorted Continental mail. The bags lay packed close as herrings in the long grey underbodies which our G. P. O. still calls ""coaches."" Five such coaches were filled as I watched, and were shot up the guides to be locked on to their waiting packets three hundred feet nearer the stars.

From the despatching-caisson I was conducted by a courteous and wonderfully learned official—Mr. L. L. Geary, Second Despatcher of the Western Route—to the Captains" Room (this wakes an echo of old romance), where the mail captains come on for their turn of duty. He introduces me to the captain of ""162"—Captain Purnall, and his relief, Captain Hodgson. The one is small and dark; the other large and red; but each has the brooding sheathed glance characteristic of eagles and aeronauts. You can see it in the pictures of our racing professionals, from L. V. Rautsch to little Ada Warrleigh—that fathomless abstraction of eyes habitually turned through naked space.

On the notice-board in the Captains" Room, the pulsing arrows of some twenty indicators register, degree by geographical degree, the progress of as many homeward-bound packets. The word "Cape" rises across the face of a dial; a gong strikes: the South African mid-weekly mail is in at the Highgate Receiving Towers. That is all. It reminds one comically of the traitorous little bell which in pigeon-fanciers" lofts notifies the return of a homer.

"Time for us to be on the move," says Captain Purnall, and we are shot up by the passenger-lift to the top of the despatch-towers. "Our coach will lock on when it is filled and the clerks are aboard. . . ."

"No. 162" waits for us in Slip E of the topmost stage. The great curve of her back shines frostily under the lights, and some minute alteration of trim makes her rock a little in her holding-down slips.

Captain Purnall frowns and dives inside. Hissing softly, "162" comes to rest as level as a rule. From her North Atlantic Winter nose-cap (worn bright as diamond with boring through uncounted leagues of hail, snow, and ice) to the inset of her three built-out propeller-shafts is some two hundred and forty feet. Her extreme diameter, carried well forward, is thirty-seven. Contrast this with the nine hundred by ninety-five of any crack liner, and you will realize the power that must drive a hull through all weathers at more than the emergency speed of the *Cyclonic!*

The eye detects no joint in her skin plating save the sweeping hair-crack of the bow-rudder—Magniac's rudder that assured us the dominion of the unstable air and left its inventor penniless and half-blind. It is calculated to Castelli's "gullwing" curve. Raise a few feet of that all but invisible plate three-eighths of an inch and she will yaw five miles to port or starboard ere she is under control again. Give her full helm and she returns on her track like a whip-lash. Cant the whole forward—a touch on the wheel will suffice— and she sweeps at your good direction up or down. Open the complete circle and she presents to the air a mushroom-head that will bring her up all standing within a half mile.

"Yes," says Captain Hodgson, answering my thought, "Castelli thought he'd discovered the secret of controlling aeroplanes when he'd only found out how to steer dirigible balloons. Magniac invented his rudder to help war-boats ram each other; and war went out of fashion and Magniac he went out of his mind because he said he couldn't serve his country any more. I wonder if any of us ever know what we're really doing."

"If you want to see the coach locked you'd better go aboard. It's due now," says Mr. Geary. I enter through the door amidships. There is nothing here for display. The inner skin of the gas-tanks comes down to within a foot or two of my head and turns over just short of the turn of the bilges. Liners and yachts disguise their tanks with decoration, but the G. P. O. serves them raw under a lick of grey official paint. The inner skin shuts off fifty feet of the bow and as much of the stern, but the bow-bulkhead is recessed for the lift-shunting apparatus as the stern is pierced for the shaft-tunnels. The engine-room lies almost amidships. Forward of it, extending to the turn of the bow tanks, is an aperture—a bottomless hatch at present—into which our coach will be locked. One looks down over the comings three hundred feet to the despatching-caisson whence voices boom upward. The light below is obscured to a sound of thunder, as our coach rises on its guides. It enlarges rapidly from a postage-stamp to a playing-card; to a punt and last a pontoon. The two clerks, its crew, do not even look up as it comes into place. The Quebec letters fly under their fingers and leap into the docketed racks, while both captains and Mr. Geary satisfy themselves that the coach is locked home. A clerk passes the way-bill over the hatch-coaming. Captain Purnall thumb-marks and passes it to Mr. Geary. Receipt has been given and taken. "Pleasant run," says Mr. Geary, and disappears through the door which a foot-high pneumatic compressor locks after him.

"A-ah!" sighs the compressor released. Our holding-down clips part with a tang. We are clear.

Captain Hodgson opens the great colloid underbody porthole through which I watch over-lighted London slide eastward as the gale gets hold of us. The first of the low winter clouds cuts off the well-known view and darkens Middlesex. On the south edge of it I can see a postal packet's light ploughing through the white fleece. For an instant she gleams like a star ere she drops toward the Highgate Receiving Towers. "The Bombay Mail," says

Captain Hodgson, and looks at his watch. "She's forty minutes late."

"What's our level?" I ask.

"Four thousand. Aren't you coming up on the bridge?"

The bridge (let us ever praise the G. P. O. as a repository of ancientest tradition!) is represented by a view of Captain Hodgson's legs where he stands on the Control Platform that runs thwartships overhead. The bow colloid is unshuttered and Captain Purnall, one hand on the wheel, is feeling for a fair slant. The dial shows 4300 feet.

"It's steep to-night," he mutters, as tier on tier of cloud drops under. "We generally pick up an easterly draught below three thousand at this time o' the year. I hate slathering through fluff."

"So does Van Cutsem. Look at him huntin' for a slant!" says Captain Hodgson. A fog-light breaks cloud a hundred fathoms below. The Antwerp Night Mail makes her signal and rises between two racing clouds far to port, her flanks blood-red in the glare of Sheerness Double Light. The gale will have us over the North Sea in half-an-hour, but Captain Purnall lets her go composedly—nosing to every point of the compass as she rises.

"Five thousand—six, six thousand eight hundred"—the dip-dial reads ere we find the easterly drift, heralded by a flurry of snow at the thousand fathom level. Captain Purnall rings up the engines and keys down the governor on the switch before him. There is no sense in urging machinery when Aeolus himself gives you good knots for nothing. We are away in earnest now—our nose notched home on our chosen star. At this level the lower clouds are laid out, all neatly combed by the dry fingers of the East. Below that again is the strong westerly blow through which we rose. Overhead, a film of southerly drifting mist draws a theatrical gauze across the firmament. The moonlight turns the lower strata to silver without a strain except where our shadow underruns us. Bristol and Cardiff Double Lights (those stately inclined beams over Severnmouth) are dead ahead of us; for we keep the Southern Winter Route. Coventry Central, the pivot of the English system, stabs upward once in ten seconds its spear of diamond light to the north; and a point or two off our starboard bow The Leek, the great cloud-breaker of Saint David's Head, swings its unmistakable green beam twenty-five degrees each way. There must be half a mile of fluff over it in this weather, but it does not affect The Leek.

"Our planet's overlighted if anything," says Captain Purnall at the wheel, as Cardiff-Bristol slides under. "I remember the old days of common white vertical that 'ud show two or three hundred feet up in a mist, if you knew where to look for 'em. In really fluffy weather they might as well have been under your hat. One could get lost coming home then, an' have some fun. Now, it's like driving down Piccadilly."

He points to the pillars of light where the cloudbreakers bore through the cloud-floor. We see nothing of England's outlines: only a white pavement pierced in all directions by these manholes of variously coloured fire—Holy Island's white and red—St. Bee's interrupted white, and so on as far as the eyes can reach. Blessed be Sergeant Ahrens and the Dubois brothers, who invented the cloudbreakers of the world whereby we travel in security!

"Are you going to lift for The Shamrock?" asks Captain Hodgson. Cork Light (green, fixed) enlarges as we rush to it. Captain Purnall nods. There is heavy traffic hereabouts—the cloud-bank beneath us is streaked with running fissures of flame where the Atlantic boats are hurrying Londonward just clear of the fluff. Mail-packets are supposed, under the Conference rules, to have the five-thousand-foot lanes to themselves, but the foreigner in a hurry is apt to take liberties with English air. "No. 162" lifts to a long-drawn wail of the breeze in the fore-flange of the rudder and we make Valencia (white, green, white) at a safe 7000 feet, dipping our beam to an incoming Washington packet.

There is no cloud on the Atlantic, and faint streaks of cream round Dingle Bay show where the driven seas hammer the coast. A big S. A. T. A. liner (*Société Anonyme des Transports Aëriens*) is diving and lifting half a mile below us in search of some break in the solid west wind. Lower still lies a disabled Dane: she is telling the liner all about it in International. Our General Communication dial has caught her talk and begins to eavesdrop. Captain Hodgson makes a motion to shut it off but checks himself. "Perhaps you'd like to listen," he says.

"*Argol* of St. Thomas," the Dane whimpers. "Report owners three starboard shaft collar-bearings fused. Can make Flores as we are, but impossible further. Shall we buy spares at Fayal?"

The liner acknowledges and recommends inverting the bearings. The *Argol* answered that she has already done so without effect, and begins to relieve her mind about cheap German enamels for collar-bearings. The Frenchman assents cordially, cries "*Courage, mon ami,*" and switches off.

Their lights sink under the curve of the ocean.

"That's one of Lundt & Bleamers' boats," says Captain Hodgson. "Serves 'em right for putting German compos in their thrust-blocks. *She* won't be in Fayal to-night! By the way, wouldn't you like to look round the engine-room?"

I have been waiting eagerly for this invitation and I follow Captain Hodgson from the control-platform, stooping low to avoid the bulge of the tanks. We know that Fleury's gas can lift anything, as the world-famous trials of '89 showed, but its almost indefinite powers of expansion necessitate vast tank room. Even in this thin air the lift-shunts are busy taking out one-third of its normal lift, and still "162" must be checked by an occasional downdraw of the rubber or our flight would become a climb to the stars. Captain Purnall prefers an overlifted to an underlifted ship; but no two captains trim ship alike. "When *I* take the bridge," says Captain Hodgson, "you'll see me shunt forty percent of the lift out of the gas and run her on the upper rudder. With a swoop upward instead of a swoop downward, *as* you say. Either way will do. It's only habit. Watch our dip-dial! Tim fetches her down once every thirty knots as regularly as breathing."

So is it shown on the dip-dial. For five or six minutes the arrow creeps from 6700 to 7300. There is the faint "szgee" of the rubber, and back slides the arrow to 6000 on a falling slant of ten or fifteen knots.

"In heavy weather you jockey her with the screws as well," says Captain Hodgson, and, unslipping the jointed bar which divides the engine-room from the bare desk, he leads me on to the floor.

Here we find Fleury's Paradox of the Bulk-headed Vacuum—which we accept now without thought—literally in full blast. The three engines are H. T. & T. assisted-vacuo Fleury turbines running from 3000 to the Limit—that is to say, up to the point when the blades make the air "bell"—cut out a vacuum for themselves precisely as over-driven marine propellers used to do. "162's" Limit is low on account of the small size of her nine screws, which, though handier than the old colloid Thelussons, "bell" sooner. The midships engine, generally used as a rein-force, is not running; so the port and starboard turbine vacuum-chambers draw direct into the return-mains.

The turbines whistle reflectively. From the low-arched expansion-tanks on either side the valves descend pillarwise to the turbine-chests, and thence the obedient gas whirls through the spirals of blades with a force that would whip the teeth out of a power-saw. Behind, is its own pressure held in leash or spurred on by the lift-shunts; before it, the vacuum where Fleury's Ray dances in violet-green bands and whirled turbillons of flames. The jointed U-tubes of the vacuum-chamber are pressure-tempered colloid (no glass would endure the strain for an instant) and a junior engineer with tinted spectacles watches the Ray intently. It is the very heart of the machine—a mystery to this day. Even Fleury who begat it and, unlike Magniac, died a multi-millionaire, could not explain how the restless little imp shuddering in the U-tube can, in the fractional frac-tion of a second, strike the furious blast of gas into a chill greyish-green liquid that drains (you can hear it trickle) from the far end of the vacuum through the education-pipes and the mains back to the bilges. Here it returns to its gaseous, one had almost written sagacious, state and climbs to work afresh. Bilge-tank, upper tank, dorsal-tank, expansion-chamber, vacuum, main-return (as a liquid), and bilge-tank once more is the ordained cycle. Fleury's Ray sees to that; and the engineer with the tinted spectacles sees to Fleury's Ray. If a speck of oil, if even the natural grease of the human finger touch the hooded terminals, Fleury's Ray will wink and disappear and must be labori-ously built up again. This means half a day's work for all hands and an expense of one hundred and seventy-odd pounds to the G. P. O. for radium-salts and such trifles.

"Now look at our thrust-collars. You won't find much German compo there. Full-jewelled, you see," says Captain Hodgson as the engineer shunts open the top of a cap. Our shaft-bearings are C. M. C. (Commerical Minerals Company) stones, ground with as much care as the lens of a telescope. They cost £37 apiece. So far we have not arrived at their term of life. These bearings came from "No. 97," which took them over from the old *Dominion of Light* which had them out of the wreck of the *Perseus* aeroplane in the years when men still flew wooden kites over oil engines!

They are a shining reproof to all low-grade German "ruby" enamels, so-called "boort" facings, and the dangerous and unsatisfactory alumina compounds which please dividend-hunting owners and turn skippers crazy.

The rudder-gear and the gas lift-shunt, seated side by side under the engine-room dials, are the only machines in visible motion. The former sighs from time to time as the oil plunger rises and falls half an inch. The latter, cased and guarded like the U-tube aft, exhibits another Fleury Ray, but inverted and more green than violet. Its function is to shunt the lift out of the gas, and this it will do without watching. That is all! A tiny pumprod wheezing and whining to itself beside a sputtering green lamp. A hundred and fifty feet aft down the flat-topped tunnel of the tanks a violet light, restless and irresolute. Between the two, three white-painted turbine-trunks, like eel-baskets laid on their side, accentuate the empty perspectives. You can hear the trickle of the liquefied gas flowing from the vacuum into the bilge-tanks and the soft *gluck-glock* of gas-locks closing as Captain Purnall brings "162" down by the head. The hum of the turbines and the boom of the air on our skin is no more than a cotton-wool wrapping to the universal stillness. And we are running an eighteen-second mile.

I peer from the fore end of the engine-room over the hatch-coamings into the coach. The mail-clerks are sorting the Winnipeg, Calgary, and Medicine Hat bags; but there is a pack of cards ready on the table.

Suddenly a bell thrills; the engineers run to the turbine-valves and stand by; but the spectacled slave of the Ray in the U-tube never lifts his head. He must watch where he is. We are hard-braked and going astern; there is language from the Control Platform.

"Tim's sparking badly about something," says the unruffled Captain Hodgson. "Let's look."

Captain Purnall is not the suave man we left half an hour since, but the embodied authority of the G. P. O. Ahead of us floats an ancient, aluminum-patched, twin-screw tramp of the dingiest, with no more right to the 5000-foot lane than has a horse-cart to a modern road. She carries an obsolete "barbette" conning-tower—a six-foot affair with railed platform forward—and our warning beam plays on the top of it as a policeman's lantern flashes on the area sneak. Like a sneak-thief, too, emerges a shock-headed navigator in his shirt-sleeves. Captain Purnall wrenches open the colloid to talk with him man to man. There are times when Science does not satisfy.

"What under the stars are you doing here, you sky-scraping chimney-sweep?" he shouts as we two drift side by side. "Do you know this is a Maillane? You call yourself a sailor, sir? You ain't fit to peddle toy balloons to an Esquimaux. Your name and number! Report and get down, and be——!"

"I've been blown up once," the shock-headed man cries, hoarsely, as a dog barking. "I don't care two flips of a contact for anything *you* can do, Postey."

"Don't you, sir? But I'll make you care. I'll have you towed stern first to Disko and broke up. You can't recover insurance if you're broke for obstruction. Do you understand *that?*"

Then the stranger bellows: "Look at my propellers! There's been a wulli-wa down below that has knocked us into umbrella-frames! We've been blown up about forty thousand feet! We're all one conjuror's watch inside! My mate's arm's broke; my engineer's head's cut open; my Ray went out when the engines smashed; and . . . and . . . for pity's sake give me my height, Captain! We doubt we're dropping."

"Six thousand eight hundred. Can you hold it?" Captain Purnall overlooks all insults, and leans half out of the colloid, staring and snuffing. The stranger leaks pungently.

"We ought to blow into St. John's with luck. We're trying to plug the fore-tank now, but she's simply whistling it away," her captain wails.

"She's sinking like a log," says Captain Purnall in an

undertone. "Call up the Banks Mark Boat, George." Our dip-dial shows that we, keeping abreast the tramp, have dropped five hundred feet the last few minutes.

Captain Purnall presses a switch and our signal beam begins to swing through the night, twizzling spokes of light across infinity.

"That'll fetch something," he says, while Captain Hodgson watches the General Communicator. He has called up the North Banks Mark Boat, a few hundred miles west, and is reporting the case.

"I'll stand by you," Captain Purnall roars to the lone figure on the conning-tower.

"Is it as bad as that?" comes the answer. "She isn't insured. She's mine."

"Might have guessed as much," mutters Hodgson. "Owner's risk is the worst risk of all!"

"Can't I fetch St. John's—not even with this breeze?" the voice quavers.

"Stand by to abandon ship. Haven't you *any* lift in you, fore or aft?"

"Nothing but the midship tanks, and they're none too tight. You see, my Ray gave out and——" he coughs in the reek of the escaping gas.

"You poor devil!" This does not reach our friend. "What does the Mark Boat say, George?"

"Wants to know if there's any danger to traffic. Says she's in a bit of weather herself, and can't quit station. I've turned in a General Call, so even if they don't see our beam someone's bound to help—or else we must. Shall I clear our slings? Hold on! Here we are! A Planet liner, too! She'll be up in a tick!"

"Tell her to have her slings ready," cries his brother captain. "There won't be much time to spare . . . Tie up your mate," he roars to the tramp.

"My mate's all right. It's my engineer. He's gone crazy."

"Shunt the lift out of him with a spanner. Hurry!"

"But I can make St. John's if you'll stand by."

"You'll make the deep, wet Atlantic in twenty minutes. You're less than fifty-eight hundred now. Get your papers."

A Planet liner, east bound, heaves up in a superb spiral and takes the air of us humming. Her underbody colloid is open and her transporter-slings hang down like tentacles.

We shut off our beam as she adjusts herself—steering to a
hair—over the tramp's conning-tower. The mate comes
up, his arm strapped to his side, and stumbles into the
cradle. A man with a ghastly scarlet head follows, shouting
that he must go back and build up his Ray. The mate
assures him that he will find a nice new Ray all ready in
the liner's engine-room. The bandaged head goes up wag-
ging excitedly. A youth and a woman follow. The liner
cheers hollowly above us, and we see the passengers' faces
at the saloon colloid.

"That's a pretty girl. What's the fool waiting for now?"
says Captain Purnall.

The skipper comes up, still appealing to us to stand by
and see him fetch St. John's. He dives below and returns—at
which we little human beings in the void cheer louder
than ever—with the ship's kitten. Up fly the liner's hissing slings; her underbody crashes home and she hurtles
away again. The dial shows less than 3000 feet.

The Mark Boat signals we must attend to the derelict,
now whistling her death-song, as she falls beneath us in
long sick zigzags.

"Keep our beam on her and send out a General Warning," says Captain Purnall, following her down.

There is no need. Not a liner in air but knows the
meaning of that vertical beam and gives us and our quarry
a wide berth.

"But she'll drown in the water, won't she?" I ask.

"Not always," is his answer. "I've known a derelict
up-end and sift her engines out of herself and flicker round
the Lower Lanes for three weeks on her forward tanks
only. We'll run no risks. Pith her, George, and look sharp.
There's weather ahead."

Captain Hodgson opens the underbody colloid, swings
the heavy pithing-iron out of its rack which in liners is
generally cased as a smoking-room settee, and at two
hundred feet releases the catch. We hear the whir of the
crescent-shaped arms opening as they descend. The derelict's forehead is punched in, starred across, and rent
diagonally. She falls stern first, our beam upon her; slides
like a lost soul down that pitiless ladder of light, and the
Atlantic takes her.

"A filthy business," says Hodgson. "I wonder what it must have been like in the old days?"

The thought had crossed my mind, too. What if that wavering carcass had been filled with the men of the old days, each one of them taught (*that* is the horror of it!) that after death he would very possibly go for ever to unspeakable torment?

And scarcely a generation ago, we (one knows now that we are only our fathers re-enlarged upon the earth), *we*, I say, ripped and rammed and pithed to admiration.

Here Tim, from the Control Platform, shouts that we are to get into our inflators and to bring him his at once.

We hurry into the heavy rubber suits—the engineers are already dressed—and inflate at the airpump taps. G. P. O. inflators are thrice as thick as a racing man's "flickers," and chafe abominably under the armpits. George takes the wheel until Tim has blown himself up to the extreme of rotundity. If you kicked him off the c. p. to the deck he would bounce back. But it is "162" that will do the kicking.

"The Mark Boat's mad—stark ravin' crazy," he snorts, returning to command. "She says there's a bad blow-out ahead and wants me to pull over to Greenland. I'll see her pithed first! We wasted half an hour fussing over that dead deck down under, and now I'm expected to go rubbin' my back all round the Pole. What does she think a Postal packet's made of? Gummed silk? Tell her we're coming on straight, George."

George buckles him into the Frame and switches on the Direct Control. Now under Tim's left toe lies the port-engine Accelerator; under his left heel the Reverse, and so with the other foot. The lift-shunt stops stand out on the rim of the steering-wheel where the fingers of his left hand can play on them. At his right hand is the midships engine lever ready to be thrown into gear at a moment's notice. He leans forward in his belt, eyes glued to the colloid, and one ear cocked toward the General Communicator. Henceforth he is the strength and direction of "162," through whatever may befall.

The Banks Mark Boat is reeling out pages of A. B. C. Directions to the traffic at large. We are to secure all "loose objects"; hood up our Fleury Rays; and "on no account to attempt to clear snow from our conning-towers till the weather abates." Under-powered craft, we are told, can ascend to the limit of their lift, mail-packets to look out for them accordingly; the lower lanes westward are pitting very badly, "with frequent blow-outs, vortices, laterals, etc."

Still the clear dark holds up unblemished. The only warning is the electric skin-tension (I feel as though I were a lace-maker's pillow) and an irritability which the gibbering of the General Communicator increases almost to hysteria.

We have made eight thousand feet since we pithed the tramp and our turbines are giving us an honest two hundred and ten knots.

Very far to the west an elongated blur of red, low down, shows us the North Banks Mark Boat. There are specks of fire round her rising and falling—bewildered planets about an unstable sun—helpless shipping hanging on to her light for company's sake. No wonder she could not quit station.

She warns us to look out for the back-wash of the bad vortex in which (her beam shows it) she is even now reeling.

The pits of gloom about us begin to fill with very faintly luminous films—wreathing and uneasy shapes. One forms itself into a globe of pale flame that waits shivering with eagerness till we sweep by. It leaps monstrously across the blackness, alights on the precise tip of our nose, pirouettes there an instant, and swings off. Our roaring bow sinks as though that light were lead—sinks and recovers to lurch and stumble again beneath the next blow-out. Tim's fingers on the lift-shunt strike chords of numbers—1:4:7:—2:4:6:—7:5:3, and so on; for he is running by his tanks only, lifting or lowering her against the uneasy air. All three engines are at work, for the sooner we have skated over this thin ice the better. Higher we dare not go. The whole upper vault is charged with pale krypton vapours, which our skin-friction may excite to unholy manifestations. Between the upper and lower levels—5000 and 7000, hints the Marks Boat—we may perhaps bolt through if . . . Our bow clothes itself in blue flame and falls like a sword. No human skill can keep pace with the changing tensions. A vortex has us by the beak and we dive down a two-thousand foot slant at an angle (the dip-dial and my bouncing body record it) of thirty-five. Our turbines scream shrilly; the propellers cannot bite on the thin air; Tim shunts the lift out of five tanks at once and by sheer weight drives her bulletwise through the maelstrom till she cushions with a jar on an upgust, three thousand feet below.

"*Now* we've done it," says George in my ear. "Our skin-friction, that last slide, has played Old Harry with the tensions! Look out for laterals, Tim; she'll want some holding."

"I've got her," is the answer. "Come *up*, old woman."

She comes up nobly, but the laterals buffet her left and right like the pinions of angry angels. She is jolted off her course four ways at once, and cuffed into place again, only to be swung aside and dropped into a new chaos. We are never without a corposant grinning on our bows or rolling head over heels from nose to midships, and to the crackle of electricity around and within us is added once or twice the rattle of hail—hail that will never fall on any sea. Slow we must or we may break our back, pitch-poling.

"Air's a perfectly elastic fluid," roars George above the tumult. "About as elastic as a head sea off the Fastnet, ain't it?"

He is less than just to the good element. If one intrudes on the Heavens when they are balancing their volt-accounts; if one disturbs the High Gods' market-rates by hurling steel hulls at ninety knots across trembling adjusted electric tensions, one must not complain of any rudeness in the reception. Tim met it with an unmoved countenance, one corner of his under lip caught up on a tooth, his eyes fleeting into the blackness twenty miles ahead, and the fierce sparks flying from his knuckles at every turn of the hand. Now and again he shook his head to clear the sweat trickling from his eyebrows, and it was then that George, watching his chance, would slide down the life-rail and swab his face quickly with a big red handkerchief. I never imagined that a human being could so continuously labour and so collectedly think as did Tim through that Hell's half-hour when the flurry was at its worst. We were dragged hither and yon by warm or frozen suctions, belched up on the tops of wulli-was, spun down by vortices and clubbed aside by laterals under a dizzying rush of stars in the

company of a drunken moon. I heard the rushing click of
the midship-engine-lever sliding in and out, the low growl
of the lift-shunts, and, louder than the yelling winds without, the scream of the bow-rudder gouging into any lull
that promised hold for an instant. At last we began to claw
up on a cant, bow-rudder and port-propeller together;
only the nicest balancing of tanks saved us from spinning
like the rifle-bullet of the old days.

"We've got to hitch to windward of that Mark Boat
somehow," George cried.

"There's no windward," I protested feebly, where I
swung shackled to a stanchion. "How can there be?"

He laughed—as we pitched into a thousand foot blow-
out—that red man laughed beneath his inflated hood!

"Look!" he said. "We must clear those refugees with a
high lift."

The Mark Boat was below and a little to the sou'west of
us, fluctuating in the centre of her distraught galaxy. The
air was thick with moving lights at every level. I take it
most of them were trying to lie head to wind, but, not
being hydras, they failed. An under-tanked Moghrabi
boat had risen to the limit of her lift, and, finding no improve-
ment, had dropped a couple of thousand. There she met a
superb wulli-wa, and was blown up spinning like a dead
leaf. Instead of shutting off she went astern and, naturally,
rebounded as from a wall almost into the Mark Boat,
whose language (our G. C. took it in) was humanly simple.

"If they'd only ride it out quietly it 'ud be better," said
George in a calm, while we climbed like a bat above them
all. "But some skippers *will* navigate without enough lift.
What does that Tad-boat think she is doing, Tim?"

"Playin' kiss in the ring," was Tim's unmoved reply. A
Trans-Asiatic Direct liner had found a smooth and butted
into it full power. But there was a vortex at the tail of that
smooth, so the T. A. D. was flipped out like a pea from off
a finger-nail, braking madly as she fled down and all but
over-ending.

"Now I hope she's satisfied," said Tim. "I'm glad I'm
not a Mark Boat . . . Do I want help?" The General
Communicator dial had caught his ear. "George, you may
tell that gentleman with my love—love, remember,

George—that I do not want help. Who *is* the officious sardine-tin?"

"A Rimouski drogher on the look-out for a tow."

"Very kind of the Rimouski drogher. This postal packet isn't being towed at present."

"Those droghers will go anywhere on a chance of salvage," George explained. "We call 'em kitti-wakes."

A long-beaked, bright steel ninety-footer floated at ease for one instant within hail of us, her slings coiled ready for rescues, and a single hand in her open tower. He was smoking. Surrendered to the insurrection of the airs through which we tore our way, he lay in absolute peace. I saw the smoke of his pipe ascend untroubled ere his boat dropped, it seemed, like a stone in a well.

We had just cleared the Mark Boat and her disorderly neighbours when the storm ended as suddenly as it had begun. A shooting-star to northward filled the sky with the green blink of a meteorite dissipating itself in our atmosphere.

Said George: "That may iron out all the tensions." Even as he spoke, the conflicting winds came to rest; the levels filled; the laterals died out in long, easy swells, the airways were smoothed before us. In less than three minutes the covey round the Mark Boat had shipped their powerlights and whirred away upon their businesses.

"What's happened?" I gasped. The nerve-storm within and the volt-tingle without had passed: my inflators weighed like lead.

"God, He knows!" said Captain George soberly. "That old shooting-star's skin-friction has discharged the different levels. I've seen it happen before. Phew! What a relief!"

We dropped from ten to six thousand and got rid of our clammy suits. Tim shut off and stepped out of the Frame. The Mark Boat was coming up behind us. He opened the colloid in that heavenly stillness and mopped his face.

"Hello, Williams!" he cried. "A degree or two out o' station, ain't you?"

"May be," was the answer from the Mark Boat. "I've had some company this evening."

"So I noticed. Wasn't that quite a little draught?"

"I warned you. Why didn't you pull out north? The east-bound packets have."

"Me? Not till I'm running a Polar consumptives' sanatorium boat. I was squinting through a colloid before you were out of your cradle, my son."

"I'd be the last man to deny it," the captain of the Mark Boat replies softly. "The way you handled her just now—I'm a pretty fair judge of traffic in a volt-hurry—it was a thousand revolutions beyond anything even *I've* ever seen."

Tim's back supples visibly to this oiling. Captain George on the c. p. winks and points to the portrait of a singularly attractive maiden pinned up on Tim's telescope bracket above the steering-wheel.

I see. Wholly and entirely do I see!

There is some talk overhead of "coming round to tea on Friday," a brief report of the derelict's fate, and Tim volunteers as he descends: "For an A. B. C. man young Williams is less of a high-tension fool than some. . . . Were you thinking of taking her on, George? Then I'll just have look round that port-thrust—seems to me it's a trifle warm—and we'll jog along."

The Mark Boat hums off joyously and hangs herself up in her appointed eyrie. Here she will stay a shutterless observatory; a life-boat station; a salvage tug; a court of ultimate appeal-cum-meteorological bureau for three hundred miles in all directions, till Wednesday next when her relief slides across the stars to take her buffeted place. Her black hull, double conning-tower, and ever-ready slings represent all that remains to the planet of that odd old word authority. She is responsible only to the Aerial Board of Control—the A. B. C. of which Tim speaks so flippantly. But that semi-elected, semi-nominated body of a few score of persons of both sexes, controls this planet. "Transportaton is Civilization," our motto runs. Theoretically, we do what we please so long as we do not interfere with the traffic *and all it implies*. Practically, the A. B. C. confirms or annuls all international arrangements and, to judge from its last report, finds our tolerant, humorous, lazy little planet only too ready to shift the whole burden of public administration on its shoulders.

I discuss this with Tim, sipping maté on the c. p. while George fans her along over the white blur of the Banks in beautiful upward curves of fifty miles each. The dip-dial translates them on the tape in flowing freehand.

Tim gathers up a skein of it and surveys the last few feet, which record "162's" path through the volt-flurry.

"I haven't had a fever-chart like this to show up in five years," he says ruefully.

A postal packet's dip-dial records every yard of every run. The tapes then go to the A. B. C., which collates and makes composite photographs of them for the instruction of captains. Tim studies his irrevocable past, shaking his head.

"Hello! Here's a fifteen-hundred-foot drop at fifty-five degrees! We must have been standing on our heads then, George."

"You don't say so," George answers. "I fancied I noticed it at the time."

George may not have Captain Purnall's catlike swiftness, but he is all an artist to the tips of the broad fingers that play on the shunt-stops. The delicious flight-curves come away on the tape with never a waver. The Mark Boat's vertical spindle of light lies down to eastward, setting in the face of the following stars. Westward, where no planet should rise, the triple verticals of Trinity Bay (we keep still to the Southern route) make a low-lifting haze. We seem the only thing at rest under all the heavens; floating at ease till the earth's revolution shall turn up our landing-towers.

And minute by minute our silent clock gives us a sixteen-second mile.

"Some fine night," says Tim, "we'll be even with that clock's Master."

"He's coming now," says George, over his shoulder. "I'm chasing the night west."

The stars ahead dim no more than if a film of mist had been drawn under unobserved, but the deep air-boom on our skin changes to a joyful shout.

"The dawn-gust," says Tim. "It'll go on to meet the Sun. Look! Look! There's the dark being crammed back over our bows! Come to the after-colloid. I'll show you something."

The engine-room is hot and stuffy; the clerks in the coach are asleep, and the Slave of the Ray is ready to follow them. Tim slides open the aft colloid and reveals the curve of the world—the ocean's deepest purple—edged with fuming and intolerable gold. Then the Sun rises and through the colloid strikes out our lamps. Tim scowls in his face.

"Squirrels in a cage," he mutters. "That's all we are. Squirrels in a cage! He's going twice as fast as us. Just you wait a few years, my shining friend, and we'll take steps that will amaze you. *We*'ll Joshua you!"

Yes, that is our dream: to turn all earth into the Vale of Ajalon at our pleasure. So far, we can drag out the dawn to twice its normal length in these latitudes. But some day— even on the Equator—we shall hold the Sun level in his full stride.

Now we look down on a sea thronged with heavy traffic. A big submersible breaks water suddenly. Another and another follows with a swash and a suck and a savage bubbling of relieved pressures. The deep-sea freighters are rising to lung up after the long night, and the leisurely ocean is all patterned with peacock's eyes of foam.

"We'll lung up, too," says Tim, and when we return to the c. p. George shuts off, the colloids are opened, and the fresh air sweeps her out. There is no hurry. The old contracts (they will be revised at the end of the year) allow twelve hours for a run which any packet can put behind her in ten. So we breakfast in the arms of an easterly slant which pushes us along at a languid twenty.

To enjoy life, and tobacco, begin both on a sunny morning half a mile or so above the dappled Atlantic cloud-belts and after a volt-flurry which has cleared and tempered your nerves. While we discussed the thickening traffic with the superiority that comes of having a high level reserved to ourselves, we heard (and I for the first time) the morning hymn on a Hospital boat.

She was cloaked by a skein of ravelled fluff beneath us and we caught the chant before she rose into the sunlight. *"Oh, ye Winds of God,"* sang the unseen voices: *"bless ye the Lord! Praise Him and magnify Him for ever!"*

We slid off our caps and joined in. When our shadow fell across her great open platforms they looked up and stretched out their hands neighbourly while they sang. We could see the doctors and the nurses and the white-button-like faces of the cot-patients. She passed slowly beneath us, heading northward, her hull, wet with the dews of the night, all ablaze in the sunshine. So took she the shadow of a cloud and vanished, her song continuing. *"Oh, ye holy and humble men of heart, bless ye the Lord! Praise Him and magnify Him for ever."*

"She's a public lunger or she wouldn't have been singing the *Benedicite;* and she's a Greenlander or she wouldn't have snow-blinds over her colloids," said George at last. "She'll be bound for Frederikshavn or one of the Glacier sanatoriums for a month. If she was an accident ward she'd be hung up at the eight-thousand-foot level. Yes—consumptives."

"Funny how the new things are the old things. I've read in books," Tim answered, "that savages used to haul their sick and wounded up to the tops of hills because microbes were fewer there. We hoist 'em into sterilized air for a while. Same idea. How much do the doctors say we've added to the average life of a man?"

"Thirty years," says George with a twinkle in his eyes. "Are we going to spend 'em all up here, Tim?"

"Flap ahead, then. Flap ahead. Who's hindering?" the senior captain laughed, as we went in.

We held a good lift to clear the coastwise and Continental shipping; and we had need of it. Though our route is in no sense a populated one, there is a steady trickle of traffic this way along. We met Hudson Bay furriers out of the Great Preserve, hurrying to make their departure from Bonavista with sable and black fox for the insatiable markets. We overcrossed Keewatin liners, small and cramped; but their captains, who see no land between Trepassy and Blanco, know what gold they bring back from West Africa. Trans-Asiatic Directs we met, soberly ringing the world round the Fiftieth Meridian at an honest seventy knots; and white-painted Ackroyd & Hunt fruiters out of the south fled beneath us, their ventilated hulls whistling like Chinese kites. Their market is in the North among the northern sanatoria where you can smell their grape-fruit and bananas across the cold snows. Argentine beef boats we sighted too, of enormous capacity and unlovely outline. They, too, feed the northern health stations in icebound ports where submersibles dare not rise.

Yellow-bellied ore-flats and Ungava petrol-tanks punted

down leisurely out of the north, like strings of unfrightened wild duck. It does not pay to "fly" minerals and oil a mile farther than is necessary; but the risks of transhipping to submersibles in the ice-pack off Nain or Hebron are so great that these heavy freighters fly down to Halifax direct, and scent the air as they go. They are the biggest tramps aloft except the Athabasca grain-tubs. But these last, now that the wheat is moved, are busy, over the world's shoulder, timber-lifting in Siberia.

We held to the St. Lawrence (it is astonishing how the old water-ways still pull us children of the air), and followed his broad line of black between its drifting ice-blocks, all down the Park that the wisdom of our fathers—but every one knows that Quebec run.

We dropped to the Heights Receiving Towers twenty minutes ahead of time, and there hung at ease till the Yokohoma Intermediate Packet could pull out and give us our proper slip. It was curious to watch the action of the holding-down clips all along the frosty river front as the boats cleared or came to rest. A big Hamburger was leaving Pont Levis and her crew, unshipping the platform railings, began to sing "Elsinore"—the oldest of our chanteys. You know it of course:

> *Mother Rugen's tea-house on the Baltic—*
> > *Forty couples waltzing on the floor!*
> *And you can watch my Ray,*
> *For I must go away*
> > *And dance with Ella Sweyn at Elsinore!*

Then, while they sweated home the covering-plates:

> *Nor-Nor-Nor-Nor-*
> *West from Sourabaya to the Baltic—*
> > *Ninety knot an hour to the Skaw!*
> *Mother Rugen's tea-house on the Baltic*
> > *And a dance with Ella Sweyn at Elsinore!*

The clips parted with a gesture of indignant dismissal, as though Quebec, glittering under her snows, were casting out these light and unworthy lovers. Our signal came from the Heights. Tim turned and floated up, but surely then it was with passionate appeal that the great tower arms flung open—or did I think so because on the upper staging a little hooded figure also opened her arms wide toward her father?

In ten seconds the coach with its clerks clashed down to the receiving-caisson; the hostlers displaced the engineers at the idle turbines, and Tim, prouder of this than all, introduced me to the maiden of the photograph on the shelf. "And by the way," said he to her, stepping forth in sunshine under the hat of civil life, "I saw young Williams in the Mark Boat. I've asked him to tea on Friday."

As Easy as A.B.C.

RUDYARD KIPLING

*The A.B.C., that semi-elected, semi-nominated body of
a few score persons, controls the Planet. Transportation is
Civilization, our motto runs. Theoretically we do what we
please, so long as we do not interfere with the traffic and
all it implies. Practically, the A.B.C. confirms or annuls
all international arrangements, and, to judge from its last
report, finds our tolerant, humorous, lazy little Planet
only too ready to shift the whole burden of public administration on its shoulders.*

—With the Night Mail.

Isn't it almost time that our Planet took some interest in
the proceedings of the Aerial Board of Control? One knows
that easy communications nowadays, and lack of privacy in
the past, have killed all curiosity among mankind, but as
the Board's Official Reporter I am bound to tell my tale.

At 9.30 a.m. August 26, A.D. 2065, the Board, sitting in
London, was informed by De Forest that the District of
Northern Illinois had riotously cut itself out of all systems
and would remain disconnected till the Board should take
over and administer it direct.

Every Northern Illinois freight and passenger tower
way, he reported, out of action; all District main, local,
and guiding lights had been extinguished; all General Communications were dumb, and through traffic had been
diverted. No reason had been given, but he gathered
unofficially from the Mayor of Chicago that the District
complained of "crowd-making and invasion of privacy."

249

As a matter of fact, it is of no importance whether Northern Illinois stay in or out of planetary circuit; as a matter of policy, any complaint of invasion of privacy needs immediate investigation, lest worse follow.

By 9.45 a.m. De Forest, Dragomiroff (Russia), Takahira (Japan), and Pirolo (Italy) were empowered to visit Illinois and 'to take such steps as might be necessary for the resumption of traffic and *all that that implies*'. By 10 a.m. the Hall was empty, and the four Members and I were aboard what Pirolo insisted on calling "my leetle godchild" —that is to say, the new *Victor Pirolo*. Our Planet prefers to know Victor Pirolo as a gently, grey-haired enthusiast who spends his time near Foggia, inventing or creating new breeds of Spanish-Italian olive-trees; but there is another side to his nature—the manufacture of quaint inventions, of which the *Victor Pirolo* is, perhaps, not the least surprising. She and a few score sister-craft of the same type embody his latest ideas. But she is not comfortable. An A.B.C. boat does not take the air with the level-keeled lift of a liner, but shoots up rocket-fashion like the "aeroplane" of our ancestors, and makes her height at top-speed from the first. That is why I found myself sitting suddenly on the large lap of Eustace Arnott, who commands the A.B.C. Fleet. One knows vaguely that there is such a thing as a Fleet somewhere on the Planet, and that, theoretically, it exists for the purposes of what used to be known as "war." Only a week before, while visiting a glacier sanatorium behind Gothaven, I had seen some squadrons making false auroras far to the north while they manoeuvred round the Pole; but, naturally, it had never occurred to me that the things could be used in earnest.

Said Arnott to De Forest as I staggered to a seat on the chart-room divan: "We're tremendously grateful to 'em in Illinois. We've never had a chance of exercising all the Fleet together. I've turned in a General Call, and I expect we'll have at least two hundred keels aloft this evening."

"Well aloft?" De Forest asked.

"Of course, sir. Out of sight till they're called for."

Arnott laughed as he lolled over the transparent chart-table where the map of the summer-blue Atlantic slid along, degree by degree, in exact answer to our progress.

Our dial already showed 320 m.p.h. and we were two thousand feet above the uppermost traffic lines.

"Now, where is this Illinois District of yours?" said Dragomiroff. "One travels so much, one sees so little. Oh, I remember! It is in North America."

De Forest, whose business it is to know the out districts, told us that it lay at the foot of Lake Michigan, on a road to nowhere in particular, was about half an hour's run from end to end, and, except in one corner, as flat as the sea. Like most flat countries nowadays, it was heavily guarded against invasion of privacy by forced timber—fifty-foot spruce and tamarack, grown in five years. The population was close on two million, largely migratory between Florida and California, with a backbone of small farms (they call a thousand acres a farm in Illinois) whose owners come into Chicago for amusements and society during the winter. They were, he said, noticeably kind, quiet folk, but a little exacting, as all flat countries must be, in their notions of privacy. There had, for instance, been no printed news-sheet in Illinois for twenty-seven years. Chicago argued that engines for printed news sooner or later developed into engines for invasion of privacy, which in turn might bring the old terror of Crowds and blackmail back to the Planet. So news-sheets were not.

"And that's Illinois," De Forest concluded. "You see, in the Old Days, she was in the forefront of what they used to call 'progress,' and Chicago—"

"Chicago?" said Takahira. "That's the little place where there is Salati's Statue of the Nigger in Flames? A fine bit of old work."

"When did you see it?" asked De Forest quickly. "They only unveil it once a year."

"I know. At Thanksgiving. It was then," said Takahira, with a shudder. "And they sang MacDonough's Song, too."

"Whew!" De Forest whistled. "I did not know that! I wish you'd told me before. MacDonough's Song may have had its uses when it was composed, but it was an infernal legacy for any man to leave behind."

"It's protective instinct, my dear fellows," said Pirolo, rolling a cigarette. "The Planet, she has had her dose of popular government. She suffers from inherited agrophobia. She has no—ah—use for crowds."

Dragomiroff leaned forward to give him a light. "Certainly," said the white-bearded Russian, "the Planet has taken all precautions against crowds for the past hundred years. What is our total population today? Six hundred million, we hope; five hundred, we think; but—but if next year's census shows more than four hundred and fifty, I myself will eat all the extra little babies. We have cut the birth-rate out—right out! For a long time we have said to Almighty God, 'Thank You, Sir, but we do not much like Your game of life, so we will not play.' "

"Anyhow," said Arnott defiantly, "men live a century apiece on the average now."

"Oh, that is quite well! I am rich—you are rich—we are all rich and happy because we are so few and we live so long. Only *I* think Almighty God He will remember what the Planet was like in the time of Crowds and the Plague. Perhaps He will send us nerves. Eh, Pirolo?"

The Italian blinked into space. "Perhaps," he said, "He has sent them already. Anyhow, you cannot argue with the Planet. She does not forget the Old Days, and—what can you do?"

"For sure we can't remake the world." De Forest glanced at the map flowing smoothly across the table from west to east. "We ought to be over our ground by nine tonight. There won't be much sleep afterwards."

On which hint we dispersed, and I slept till Takahira waked me for dinner. Our ancestors thought nine hours' sleep ample for their little lives. We, living thirty years longer, feel ourselves defrauded with less than eleven out of the twenty-four.

By ten o'clock we were over Lake Michigan. The west shore was lightless, except for a dull ground-glare at Chicago, and a single traffic-directing light—its leading beam pointing north—at Waukegan on our starboard bow. None of the Lake villages gave any sign of life; and inland, westward, so far as we could see, blackness lay unbroken on the level earth. We swooped down and skimmed low across the dark, throwing calls country by country. Now and again we picked up the faint glimmer of a house-light, or heard the rap and rend of a cultivator being played across the fields, but Northern Illinois as a whole was one inky, apparently uninhabited, waste of high, forced woods.

Only our illuminated map, with its little pointer switching from country to country, as we wheeled and twisted, gave us any idea of our position. Our calls, urgent, pleading, coaxing or commanding, through the General Communicator brought no answer. Illinois strictly maintained her own privacy in the timber which she grew for that purpose.

"Oh, this is absurd!" said De Forest. "We're like an owl trying to work a wheat-field. Is this Bureau Creek? Let's land, Arnott, and get hold of someone."

We brushed over a belt of forced woodland—fifteen-year-old maple sixty feet high—grounded on a private meadow-dock, none too big, where we moored to our own grapnels, and hurried out through the warm dark night towards a light in a verandah. As we neared the garden gate I could have sworn we had stepped knee-deep in quicksand, for we could scarcely drag our feet against the prickling currents that clogged them. After five paces we stopped, wiping out foreheads, as hopelessly stuck on dry smooth turf as so many cows in a bog.

"Pest!" cried Pirolo angrily. "We are ground-circuited. And it is my own system of ground-circuits, too! I know the pull."

"Good evening," said a girl's voice from the verandah. "Oh, I'm sorry! We've locked up. Wait a minute."

We heard the click of a switch, and almost fell forward as the currents round our knees were withdrawn.

The girl laughed, and laid aside her knitting. An old-fashioned Controller stood at her elbow, which she reversed from time to time, and we could hear the snort and clank of the obedient cultivator half a mile away, behind the guardian woods.

"Come in and sit down," she said. "I'm only playing a plough. Dad's gone to Chicago to—Ah! Then it was *your* call I heard just now!"

She had caught sight of Arnott's Board uniform, leaped to the switch, and turned it full on.

We were checked, gasping, waist-deep in current this time, three yards from the verandah.

"We only want to know what's the matter with Illinois," said De Forest placidly.

"Then hadn't you better go to Chicago and find out?" she answered. "There's nothing wrong here. We own ourselves."

"How can we go anywhere if you won't loose us?" De Forest went on, while Arnott scowled. Admirals of Fleets are still quite human when their dignity is touched.

"Stop a minute—you don't know how funny you look!" She put her hands on her hips and laughed mercilessly.

"Don't worry about that," said Arnott, and whistled. A voice answered from the *Victor Pirolo* in the meadow.

"Only a single-fuse ground-circuit!" Arnott called. "Sort it out gently, please."

We heard the ping of a breaking lamp; a fuse blew out somewhere in the verandah roof, frightening a nest full of birds. The ground-circuit was open. We stooped and rubbed our tingling ankles.

"How rude—how very rude of you!" the Maiden cried.

"Sorry, but we haven't time to look funny," said Arnott. "We've got to go to Chicago; and if I were you, young lady, I'd go into the cellars for the next two hours, and take mother with me."

Off he strode, with us at his heels, muttering indignantly, till the humour of the thing struck and doubled him up with laughter at the foot of the gangway ladder.

"The Board hasn't shown what you might call a fat spark on this occasion," said De Forest, wiping his eyes. "I hope I didn't look as big a fool as you did, Arnott! Hullo! What on earth is that? Dad coming home from Chicago?"

There was a rattle and a rush, and a five-plough cultivator, blades in air like so many teeth, trundled itself at us round the edge of the timber, fuming and sparking furiously.

"Jump!" said Arnott, as we bundled ourselves through the none-too-wide door. "Never mind about shutting it. Up!"

The *Victor Pirolo* lifted like a bubble, and the vicious machine shot just underneath us, clawing high as it passed.

"There's a nice little spit-kitten for you!" said Arnott, dusting his knees. "We ask her a civil question. First she circuits us and then she plays a cultivator at us!"

"And then we fly," said Dragomiroff. "If I were forty years more young, I would go back and kiss her. Ho! Ho!"

"I," said Pirolo, "would smack her! My pet ship has been chased by a dirty plough; a—how do you say?—argicultural implement."

"Oh, that is Illinois all over," said De Forest. "They don't content themselves with talking abut privacy. They arrange to have it. And now, where's your alleged fleet, Arnott? We must assert ourselves against this wench."

Arnott pointed to the black heavens.

"Waiting on—up there," said he. "Shall I give them the whole installation, sir?"

"Oh, I don't think the young lady is quite worth that," said De Forest. "Get over Chicago, and perhaps we'll see something."

In a few minutes we were hanging at two thousand feet over an oblong block of incandescence in the centre of the little town.

"That looks like the old City Hall. Yes, there's Salati's Statue in front of it," said Takahira. "But what on earth are they doing to the place? I thought they used it for a market nowadays! Drop a little, please."

We could hear the sputter and crackle of road-surfacing machines—the cheap Western type which fuse stone and rubbish into lava-like ribbed glass for their rough country roads. Three or four surfacers worked on each side of a square of ruins. The brick and stone wreckage crumbled, slid forward, and presently spread out into white-hot pools of sticky slag, which the levelling-rods smoothed more or less flat. Already a third of the big block had been so treated, and was cooling to dull red before our astonished eyes.

"It is the Old Market," said De Forest. "Well, there's nothing to prevent Illinois from making a road through a market. It doesn't interfere with traffic, that I can see."

"Hsh!" said Arnott, gripping me by the shoulder. "Listen! They're singing. Why on the earth are they singing?"

We dropped again till we could see the black fringe of people at the edge of that glowing square.

At first they only roared against the roar of the surfacers and levellers. Then the words came up clearly—the words of the Forbidden Song that all men knew, and none let pass their lips—poor Pat MacDonough's Song, made in the days of the Crowds and the Plague—every silly word of it loaded to sparking-point with the Planet's inherited memories of horror, panic, fear, and cruelty. And Chicago—innocent, contented little Chicago—was singing it aloud to the infernal tune that carried riot, pestilence, and lunacy round our Planet a few generations ago!

"Once there was The People—Terror gave it birth;
  Once there was The People—it shall never be again!"

(Then the stamp and pause):

"Earth arose and crushed it. Listen, oh, ye slain!
  Once there was The People—it shall never be again!'"

The levellers thrust in savagely against the ruins as the song renewed itself again, again and again, louder than the crash of the melting walls.

De Forest frowned.

"I don't like that," he said. "They've broken back to the Old Days! They'll be killing somebody soon. I think we'd better divert 'em, Arnott."

"Ay, ay, sir," Arnott's hand went to his cap, and we heard the hull of the *Victor Pirolo* ring to the command: "Lamps! Both watches stand by! Lamps! Lamps! Lamps!"

"Keep still!" Takahira whispered to me. "Blinkers, please, quartermaster."

"It's all right—all right!" said Pirolo from behind, and to my horror slipped over my head some sort of rubber helmet that locked with a snap. I could feel thick colloid bosses before my eyes, but I stood in absolute darkness.

"To save the sight," he explained, and pushed me on to the chart-room divan. "You will see in a minute."

As he spoke I became aware of a thin thread of almost intolerable light, let down from heaven at an immense distance—one vertical hairsbreadth of frozen lightning.

"Those are our flanking ships," said Arnott at my elbow. "That one is over Galena. Look south—that other one's over Keithburg. Vincennes is behind us, and north yonder is Winthrop Woods. The Fleet's in position, sir"—this to De Forest. "As soon as you give the word."

"Ah no! No!" cried Dragomiroff at my side. I could feel the old man tremble. "I do not know all that you can do, but be kind! I ask you to be a little kind to them below! This is horrible—horrible!"

"When a Woman kills a Chicken,
  Dynasties and Empires sicken,"

Takahira quoted. "It is too late to be gentle now."

"Then take off my helmet! Take off my helmet!" Dragomiroff
began hysterically.

Pirolo must have put his arm round him.

"Hush," he said, "I am here. It is all right, Ivan, my dear
fellow."

"I'll just send our little girl in Bureau County a warning,"
said Arnott. "She doesn't deserve it, but we'll allow her a
minute to two to take mamma to the cellar."

In the utter hush that followed the growling spark after
Arnott had linked up his Service Communicator with the
invisible Fleet, we heard MacDonough's Song from the
city beneath us grow fainter as we rose to position. Then I
clapped my hand before my mask lenses, for it was as
though the floor of Heaven had been riddled and all the
inconceivable blaze of suns in the making was poured
through the manholes.

"You needn't count," said Arnott. I had had no thought
of such a thing. "There are two hundred and fifty keels up
there, five miles apart. Full power, please, for another
twelve seconds."

The firmament, as far as eye could reach, stood on
pillars of white fire. One fell on the glowing square at
Chicago, and turned it black.

"Oh! Oh! Oh! Can men be allowed to do such things?"
Dragomiroff cried, and fell across our knees.

"Glass of water, please," said Takahira to a helmeted
shape that leaped forward. "He is a little faint."

The lights switched off, and the darkness stunned like
an avalanche. We could hear Dragomiroff's teeth on the
glass edge.

Pirolo was comforting him.

"All right, all ra-ight," he repeated. "Come and lie down.
Come below and take off your mask. I give you my word,
old friend, it is all right. They are my siege-lights. Little
Victor Pirolo's leetle lights. You know me! I do not hurt
people."

"Pardon!" Dragomiroff moaned. "I have never seen Death.

I have never seen the Board take action. Shall we go down and burn them alive, or is that already done?"

"Oh, hush," said Pirolo, and I think he rocked him in his arms.

"Do we repeat, sir?" Arnott asked De Forest.

"Give 'em a minute's break," De Forest replied, "They may need it."

We waited a minute, and then MacDonough's Song, broken but defiant, rose from undefeated Chicago.

"They seem fond of that tune," said De Forest. "I should let 'em have it, Arnott."

"Very good, sir," said Arnott, and felt his way to the Communicator keys.

No lights broke forth, but the hollow of the skies made herself the mouth for one note that touched the raw fibre of the brain. Men hear such sounds in delirium, advancing like tides from horizons beyond the ruled foreshores of space.

"That's our pitch-pipe," said Arnott. "We may be a bit ragged. I've never conducted two hundred and fifty performers before." He pulled out the couplers, and struck a full chord on the Service Communicators.

The beams of light leaped down again, and danced, solemnly, and awfully, a stilt-dance, sweeping thirty or forty miles left and right at each stiff-legged kick, while the darkness delivered itself—there is no scale to measure against that utterance—of the tune to which they kept time. Certain notes—one learnt to expect them with terror—cut through one's marrow, but, after three minutes, thought and emotion passed in indescribable agony.

We saw, we heard, but I think we were in some sort swooning. The two hundred and fifty beams shifted, re-formed, straddled and split, narrowed, widened, rippled in ribbons, broke into a thousand white-hot parallel lines, melted and revolved in interwoven rings like old-fashioned engine-turning, flung up to the zenith, made as if to descend and renew the torment, halted at the last instant, twizzled insanely round the horizon, and vanished, to bring back for the hundredth time darkness more shattering than their instantly renewed light over all Illinois. Then the tune and lights ceased together, and we heard one single devastating wail that shook all the horizon as a rubbed wet finger shakes the rim of a bowl.

"Ah, that is my new siren," said Pirolo. "You can break an iceberg in half, if you find the proper pitch. They will whistle by squadrons now. It is the wind through pierced shutters in the bows."

I had collapsed beside Dragomiroff, broken and snivelling feebly, because I had been delivered before my time to all the terrors of Judgement Day, and the Archangels of the Resurrection were hailing me naked across the Universe to the sound of the music of the spheres.

Then I saw De Forest smacking Arnott's helmet with his open hand. The wailing died down in a long shriek as a black shadow swooped past us, and returned to her place above the lower clouds.

"I hate to interrupt a specialist when he's enjoying himself," said De Forest. "But, as a matter of fact, all Illinois has been asking us to stop for these last fifteen seconds."

"What a pity." Arnott slipped off his mask. "I wanted you to hear us really hum. Our lower C can lift street-paving."

"It is Hell—Hell!" cried Dragomiroff, and sobbed aloud.

Arnott looked away as he answered:

"It's a few thousand volts ahead of the old shoot-'em-and-sink-'em game, but I should scarcely call it *that*. What shall I tell the Fleet, sir?"

"Tell 'em we're very pleased and impressed. I don't think they need wait on any longer. There isn't a spark left down there." De Forest pointed. "They'll be deaf and blind."

"Oh, I think not, sir. The demonstration lasted less than ten minutes."

"Marvellous!" Takahira sighed. "I should have said it was half a night. Now, shall we go down and pick up the pieces?"

"But first a small drink," said Pirolo. "The Board must not arrive weeping at its own works."

"I am an old fool—an old fool!" Dragomiroff began piteously. "I did not know what would happen. It is all new to me. We reason with them in Little Russia."

Chicago North landing-tower was unlighted, and Arnott worked his ship into the clips by her own lights. As soon as these broke out we heard groanings of horror and appeal from many people below.

"All right," shouted Arnott into the darkness. "We aren't beginning again!" We descended by the stairs, to find ourselves knee-deep in a grovelling crowd, some crying that they were blind, others beseeching us not to make any more noises, but the greater part writhing face downwards, their hands on their caps before their eyes.

It was Pirolo who came to our rescue. He climbed the side of a surfacing-machine, and there, gesticulating as though they could see, made oration to those afflicted people of Illinois.

"You stchewpids!" he began. "There is nothing to fuss for. Of course, your eyes will smart and be red tomorrow. You will look as if you and your wives had drunk too much, but in a little while you will see again as well as before. I tell you this, and I—*I* am Pirolo. Victor Pirolo!"

The crowd with one accord shuddered, for many legends attach to Victor Pirolo of Foggia, deep in the secrets of God.

"Pirolo?" An unsteady voice lifted itself. "Then tell us was there anything except light in those lights of yours just now?"

The question was repeated from every corner of the darkness.

Pirolo laughed.

"No!" he thundered. (Why have small men such large voices?) "I give you my word and the Board's word that there was nothing except light—just light! You stchewpids! Your birthrate is too low already as it is. Some day I must invent something to send it up, but send it down—never!"

"Is that true?—We thought—somebody said—"

One could feel the tension relax all round.

"You *too* big fools," Pirolo cried. "You could have sent us a call and we would have told you."

"Send you a call!" a deep voice shouted. "I wish you had been at our end of the wire."

"I'm glad I wasn't," said De Forest. "It was bad enough from behind the lamps. Never mind! It's over now. Is there any one here I can talk business with? I'm De Forest—for the Board."

"You might begin with me, for one—I'm Mayor," the bass voice replied.

A big man rose unsteadily from the street, and staggered towards us where we sat on the board turf-edging, in front of the garden fences.

"I ought to be the first on my feet. Am I?" says he.

"Yes," said De Forest and steadied him as he dropped down beside us.

"Hello, Andy. Is that you?" a voice called.

"Excuse me," said the Mayor; "that sounds like my Chief of Police, Bluthner!"

"Bluthner it is; and here's Mulligan and Keefe—on their feet."

"Bring 'em up please, Blut. We're supposed to be the Four in charge of this hamlet. What we say, goes. And, De Forest, what do you say?"

"Nothing—yet," De Forest answered, as we made room for the panting, reeling men. "*You've* cut out of system. Well?"

"Tell the steward to send down drinks, please," Arnott whispered to an orderly at his side.

"Good!" said the Mayor, smacking his dry lips. "Now I suppose we can take it, De Forest, that henceforward the Board will administer us direct?"

"Not if the Board can avoid it," De Forest laughed. "The A.B.C. is responsible for the planetary traffic only."

"*And all that that implies.*" The big Four who ran Chicago chanted their Magna Charta like children at school.

"Well, get on," said De Forest wearily. "What is your silly trouble anyway?"

"Too much dam' Democracy," said the Mayor, laying his hand on De Forest's knee.

"So? I thought Illinois had had her dose of that."

"She has. That's why. Blut, what did you do with our prisoners last night?"

"Locked 'em in the water-tower to prevent the women killing 'em," the Chief of Police replied. "I'm too blind to move just yet, but—"

"Arnott, send some of your people, please, and fetch 'em along," said De Forest.

"They're triple-circuited," the Mayor called. "You'll have to blow out three fuses." He turned to De Forest, his large outline just visible in the paling darkness. "I hate to throw any more work on the Board. I'm an administrator myself but we've had a little fuss with our Serviles. What? In a big city there's bound to be a few men and women who can't live without listening to themselves, and who prefer drinking out of pipes they don't own both ends of. They inhabit flats and hotels all the year round. They say it saves 'em trouble. Anyway, it gives 'em more time to make trouble for their neighbours. We call 'em Serviles locally. And they are apt to be tuberculous."

"Just so!" said the man called Mulligan. "Transportation is Civilization. Democracy is Disease. I've proved it by the blood test, every time."

"Mulligan's our Health Officer, and a one-idea man," said the Mayor, laughing. "But it's true that most Serviles haven't much control. They *will* talk; and when people take to talking as a business, anything may arrive—mayn't it, De Forest?"

"Anything—except the facts of the case," said De Forest, laughing.

"I'll give you those in a minute," said the Mayor. "Our Serviles got to talking—first in their houses and then on the streets, telling men and women how to manage their own affairs. (You can't teach a Servile not to finger his neighbour's soul.) That's invasion of privacy, of course, but in Chicago we'll suffer anything sooner than make crowds. Nobody took much notice, and so I let 'em alone. My fault! I was warned there would be trouble, but there hasn't been a crowd or murder in Illinois for nineteen years."

"Twenty-two," said his Chief of Police.

"Likely. Anyway, we'd forgot such things. So, from talking in the houses and on the streets, our Serviles go to calling a meeting at the Old Market yonder." He nodded across the square where the wrecked buildings heaved up grey in the dawn-glimmer behind the square-cased statue of The Negro in Flames. "There's nothing to prevent any one calling meetings except that it's against human nature to stand in a crowd, besides being bad for the health. I ought to have known by the way our men and women attended that first meeting that trouble was brewing. There were as many as a thousand in the market-place, touching each other. Touching! Then the Serviles turned in all tongue-switches and talked, and we—"

"What did they talk about?" said Takahira.

"First, how badly things were managed in the city. That pleased us Four—we were on the platform—because we hoped to catch one or two good men for City work. You know how rare executive capacity is. Even if we didn't it's—it's refreshing to find any one interested enough in our job to damn our eyes. You don't know what it means to work, year in, year out, without a spark of difference with a living soul."

"Oh, don't we!" said De Forest. "There are times on the Board when we'd give our positions if any one would kick us out and take hold of things themselves."

"But they won't," said the Mayor ruefully. "I assure you, sir, we Four have done things in Chicago, in the hope of rousing people, that would have discredited Nero. But what do they say? 'Very good, Andy. Have it your own way. Anything's better than a crowd. I'll go back to my land.' You *can't* do anything with folk who can go where they please, and don't want anything on God's earth except their own way. There isn't a kick or a kicker left on the Planet."

"Then I suppose that little shed yonder fell down by itself?" said De Forest. We could see the bare and still smoking ruins, and hear the slagpools crackle as they hardened and set.

"Oh, that's only amusement. 'Tell you later. As I was saying, our Serviles held the meeting, and pretty soon we had to ground-circuit the platform to save 'em from being killed. And that didn't make our people any more pacific."

"How d'you mean?" I ventured to ask.

"If you've ever been ground-circuited," said the Mayor, "you'll know it don't improve any man's temper to be held up straining against nothing. No, sir! Eight or nine hundred folk kept pawing and buzzing like flies in treacle for two hours, while a pack of perfectly safe Serviles invades their mental and spiritual privacy, may be amusing to watch, but they are not pleasant to handle afterwards."

Pirolo chuckled.

"Our fold own themselves. They were of opinion things were going too far and too fiery. I warned the Serviles; but they're born house-dwellers. Unless a fact hits 'em on the head, they cannot see it. Would you believe me, they went on to talk of what they called 'popular government'? They did! They wanted us to go back to the old Voodoo-business of voting with papers and wooden boxes, and word-drunk people and printed formulas, and news-sheets! They said they practised it among themselves about what they'd have to eat in their flats and hotels. Yes, sir! They stood up behind Bluthner's doubled ground-circuits, and they said that, in this present year of grace, *to* self-owning men and women, *on* that very spot! Then they finished"—he lowered his voice cautiously—"by talking about 'The People'. And then Bluthner he had to sit up all night in charge of the circuits because he couldn't trust his men to keep 'em shut."

"It was trying 'em too high," the Chief of Police broke in. "But we couldn't hold the crowd ground-circuited for ever. I gathered in all the Serviles on charge of crowd-making, and put 'em in the water-tower, and then I let things cut loose. I had to! The District lit like a sparked gas-tank!"

"The news was out over seven degrees of country," the Mayor continued; "and when once it's a question of invasion of privacy, good-bye to right and reason of Illinois! They began turning out traffic-lights and locking up landing-towers on Thursday night. Friday, they stopped all traffic and asked for the Board to take over. Then they wanted to clean Chicago off the side of the Lake and rebuild elsewhere—just for a souvenir of 'The People' that the Serviles talked about. I suggested that they should slag the Old Market where the meeting was held, while I turned in a call to you all on the Board. That kept 'em quiet till you came along. And—and now *you* can take hold of the situation."

"Any chance of their quieting down?" De Forest asked.

"You can try," said the Mayor.

De Forest raised his voice in the face of the reviving crowd that had edged in towards us. Day was come.

"Don't you think this business can be arranged?" he began. But there was a roar of angry voices:

"We've finished with Crowds! We aren't going back to the Old Days! Take us over! Take the Serviles away! Administer direct or we'll kill 'em! Down with The People!"

An attempt was made to begin MacDonough's Song. It got no further than the first line, for the *Victor Pirolo* sent down a warning drone on one stopped horn. A wrecked sidewall of the Old Market tottered and fell inwards on the slag-pools. None spoke or moved till the last of the dust had settled down again, turning the steel case of Salati's Statue ashy grey.

"You see you'll just *have* to take us over," the Mayor whispered.

De Forest shrugged his shoulders.

"You talk as if executive capacity could be snatched out of the air like so much horse-powers. Can't you manage yourselves on any terms?" he said.

"We can, if you say so. It will only cost those few lives to begin with."

The Mayor pointed across the square, where Arnott's men guided a stumbling group of ten or twelve men and women to the lake front and halted then under the Statue.

"Now I think," said Takahira under his breath, "there will be trouble."

The mass in front of us growled like beasts.

At that moment the sun rose clear, and revealed the blinking assembly to itself. As soon as it realized that it was a crowd we saw the shiver of horror and mutual repulsion shoot across it precisely as the steely flaws shot across the lake outside. Nothing was said, and, being half blind, of course it moved slowly. Yet in less than fifteen minutes most of that vast multitude—three thousand at a lowest count—melted away like frost on south eaves. The remnant stretched themselves on the grass, where a crowd feels and looks less like a crowd.

"These mean business," the Mayor whispered to Takahira. "There are a goodish few women there who've borne children. I don't like it."

The morning draught off the lake stirred the trees round us with promise of a hot day; the sun reflected itself dazzlingly on the canister-shaped covering of Salati's Statue; cocks crew in the gardens, and we could hear gate-latches clicking in the distance as people stumblingly resought their homes.

"I'm afraid there won't be any morning deliveries," said

De Forest. "We rather upset things in the country last night."

"That makes no odds," the Mayor returned. "We're all provisioned for six months. *We* take no chances."

Nor, when you come to think of it, does any one else. It must be three-quarters to a generation since any house or city faced a food shortage. Yet is there house or city on the Planet today that has not half a year's provisions laid in? We are like the shipwrecked seamen in the old books, who, having once nearly starved to death, ever afterwards hide away bit of food and biscuit. Truly we trust no Crowds, nor system based on Crowds!

De Forest waited till the last footstep had died away. Meantime the prisoners at the base of the Statue shuffled, posed and fidgeted, with the shamelessness of quite little children. None of them were more than six feet high, and many of them were as grey-haired as the ravaged, harassed heads of old pictures. They huddled together in actual touch, while the crowd, spaced at large intervals, looked at them with congested eyes.

Suddenly a man among them began to talk. The Mayor had not in the least exaggerated. It appeared that our Planet lay sunk in slavery beneath the heel of the Aerial Board of Control. The orator urged us to arise in our might, burst our prison doors and break our fetters (all his metaphors, by the way, were of the most medieval). Next he demanded that every matter of daily life, including most of the physical functions, should be submitted for decision at any time of the week, month, or year to, I gathered, anybody who happened to be passing by or residing within a certain radius, and that everybody should forthwith abandon his concerns to settle the matter, first by crowd-making, next by talking to the crowds made, and lastly by describing crosses on pieces of paper, which rubbish should later be counted with certain mystic ceremonies and oaths. Out of this amazing play, he assured us, would automatically arise a higher, nobler, and kinder world, based—he demonstrated this with the awful lucidity of the insane—based on the sanctity of the Crowd and the villainy of the single person. In conclusion, he called loudly upon God to testify to his personal merits and integrity. When the flow ceased, I turned bewildered to Takahira, who was nodding solemnly.

"Quite correct," said he. "It is all in the old books. He has left nothing out, not even the war-talk."

"But I don't see how this stuff can upset a child, much less a district," I replied.

"Ah, you are too young," said Dragomiroff. "For another thing, you are not a mamma. Please look at the mammas."

Ten or fifteen women who remained had separated themselves from the silent men, and were drawing in towards the prisoners. It reminded one of the stealthy encircling, before the rush in at the quarry, of wolves round musk-oxen in the North. The prisoners saw, and drew together more closely. The Mayor covered his face with his hands for an instant. De Forest, bareheaded, stepped forward between the prisoners and the slowly, stiffly moving line.

"That's all very interesting," he said to the dry-lipped orator. "But the point seems that you've been making crowds and invading privacy."

A woman stepped forward, and would have spoken, but there was a quick assenting murmur from the men, who realized that De Forest was trying to pull the situation down to ground-line.

"Yes! Yes!" they cried. "We cut out because they made crowds and invaded privacy! Stick to that! Keep on that switch! Lift the Serviles out of this! The Board's in charge! Hsh!"

"Yes, the Board's in charge," said De Forest. "I'll take formal evidence of crowd-making if you like, but the Members of the Board can testify to it. Will that do?"

The women had closed in another pace, with hands that clenched and unclenched at their sides.

"Good! Good enough!" the men cried. "We're content. Only take them away quickly."

"Come along up!" said De Forest to the captives. "Breakfast is quite ready."

It appeared, however, that they did not wish to go. They intended to remain in Chicago and make crowds. They pointed out that De Forest's proposal was gross invasion of privacy.

"My dear fellow," said Pirolo to the most voluble of the

leaders, "you hurry, or your crowd that can't be wrong will kill you!"

"But that would be murder," answered the believer in crowds; and there was a roar of laughter from all sides that seemed to show the crisis had broken.

A woman stepped forward from the line of women, laughing, I protest, as merrily as any of the company. One hand, of course, shaded her eyes, the other was at her throat.

"Oh, they needn't be afraid of being killed!" she called.

"Not in the least," said De Forest. "But don't you think that, now the Board's in charge, you might go home while we get these people away?"

"I shall be home long before that. It—it has been rather a trying day."

She stood up to her full height, dwarfing even De Forest's six-foot-eight, and smiled, with eyes closed against the fierce light.

"Yes, rather," said De Forest, "I'm afraid you feel the glare a little. We'll have the ship down."

He motioned to the *Pirolo* to drop between us and the sun, and at the same time to loop-circuit the prisoners, who were a trifle unsteady. We saw them stiffen to the current where they stood. The woman's voice went on, sweet and deep and unshaken:

"I don't suppose you men realize how much this—this sort of thing means to a woman. I've borne three. We women don't want our children given to Crowds. It must be an inherited instinct. Crowds make trouble. They bring back the Old Days. Hate, fear, blackmail, publicity, 'The People'—*That! That! That!*" She pointed to the Statue, and the crowd growled once more.

"Yes, if they are allowed to go on," said De Forest. "But this little affair—"

"It means so much to us women that this—this little affair should never happen again. Of course, never's a big word, but one feels so strongly that it is important to stop crowds at the very beginning. Those creatures"—she pointed with her left hand at the prisoners swaying like seaweed in a tideway as the circuit pulled them—"these people have friends and wives and children in the city and elsewhere. One doesn't want anything done to *them*, you know. It's terrible to force a human being out of fifty or sixty years of good life. I'm only forty myself. I know. But, at the same time, one feels that an example should be made, because no price is too heavy to pay if—if these people and *all that they imply* can be put an end to. Do you quite understand, or would you be kind enough to tell your men to take the casing off the Statue? It's worth looking at."

"I understand perfectly. But I don't think anybody here wants to see the Statue on an empty stomach. Excuse me one moment." De Forest called up the ship, "A flying loop ready on the port side, if you please." Then to the woman he said with some crispness, "You might leave us a little creation in the matter."

"Oh of course. Thank you for being so patient. I know my arguments are silly, but—" She half turned away and went on in a changed voice, "Perhaps this will help you to decide."

She threw out her right arm with a knife in it. Before the blade could be returned to her throat or her bosom it was twitched from her grip, sparked as it flew out of the shadow of the ship above, and fell flashing in the sunshine at the foot of the Statue fifty yards away. The outflung arm was arrested, rigid as a bar for an instant, till the releasing circuit permitted her to bring it slowly to her side. The other women shrank back silent among the men.

Pirolo rubbed his hands, and Takahira nodded.

"That was clever of you, De Forest," said he.

"What a glorious pose!" Dragomiroff murmured, for the frightened woman was on the edge of tears.

"Why did you stop me? I would have done it!" she cried.

"I have no doubt you would," said De Forest. "But we can't waste a life like yours on these people. I hope that arrest didn't sprain your wrist; it's so hard to regulate a flying loop. But I think you are quite right about those persons" women and children. We'll take them all away with us if you promise not to do anything stupid to yourself."

"I promise—I promise." She controlled herself with an effort. "But it is so important to us women. We know what it means; and I thought if you saw I was in earnest—"

"I saw you were, and you've gained your point. I shall take all your Serviles away with me at once. The Mayor will make lists of their friends and families in the city and the district, and he'll ship them after us this afternoon."

"Sure," said the Mayor, rising to his feet. "Keefe, if you can see, hadn't you better finish levelling off the Old Market? It don't look slightly the way it is now, and we shan't use it for crowds any more."

"I think you had better wipe out that Statue as well, Mr Mayor," said De Forest. "I don't question its merits as a work of art, but I believe it's a shade morbid."

"Certainly, sir. Oh, Keefe! Slag the Nigger before you go on to fuse the Market. I'll get to the Communicators and tell the District that the Board is in charge. Are you making any special appointments, sir?"

"None. We haven't men to waste on these backwoods. Carry on as before, but under the Board. Arnott, run your Serviles aboard, please. Ground ship and pass them through the bilge-doors. We'll wait till we've finished with this work of art."

The prisoners trailed past him, talking fluently, but unable to gesticulate in the drag of the current. Then the surfacers rolled up, two on each side of the Statue. With one accord the spectators looked elsewhere, but there was no need. Keefe turned on full power, and the thing simply melted within its case. All I saw was a surge of white-hot metal pouring over the plinth, a glimpse of Salati's inscription, "To the Eternal Memory of the Justice of the People," ere the stone base itself cracked and powdered into finest lime. The crowd cheered.

"Thank you," said De Forest; "but we want our breakfasts, and I expect you do, too. Good-bye, Mr Mayor! Delighted to see you at any time, but I hope I shan't have to, officially, for the next thirty years. Good-bye, madam. Yes. We're all given to nerves nowadays. I suffer from them myself. Good-bye, gentlemen all! You're under the tyrannous heel of the Board from this moment, but if ever you feel like breaking your fetters you've only to let us know. This is no treat to us. Good luck!'"

We embarked amid shouts, and did not check our lift till they had dwindled into whispers. Then De Forest flung himself on the chartroom divan and mopped his forehead.

"I don't mind men," he panted, "but women are the devil!"

"Still the devil," said Pirolo cheerfully. "That one would have suicided."

"I know it. That was why I signalled for the flying loop to be clapped on her. I owe you an apology for that, Arnott. I hadn't time to catch your eye, and you were busy with our caitiffs. By the way, who actually answered my signal? It was a smart piece of work."

"Ilroy," said Arnott; "but he overloaded the wave. It may be pretty gallery-work to knock a knife out of a lady's hand, but didn't you notice how she rubbed 'em? He scorched her fingers. Slovenly, I call it."

"Far be it from me to interfere with Fleet discipline, but don't be too hard on the body. If that woman had killed herself they would have killed every Servile and everything related to a Servile throughout the district by nightfall."

"That was what she was playing for," Takahira said. "And with out Fleet gone we could have done nothing to hold them."

"I may be ass enough to walk into a ground-circuit," said Arnott, "but I don't dismiss my Fleet till I'm reasonably sure that trouble is over. They're in position still, and I intend to keep 'em there till the Serviles are shipped out of the district. That last little crowd meant murder, my friends."

"Nerves! All nerves!" said Pirolo. "You cannot argue with agoraphobia."

"And it is not as if they had seen much dead—or *is* it?" said Takahira.

"In all my ninety years I have never seen death." Dragomiroff spoke as one who would excuse himself. "Perhaps that was why—last night—"

Then it came out as we sat over breakfast, that, with the exception of Arnott and Pirolo, none of us had ever seen a corpse, or knew in what manner the spirit passes.

"We're a nice lot to flap about governing the Planet," De Forest laughed. "I confess, now it's all over, that my main fear was I mightn't be able to pull it off without losing a life."

"I thought of that, too," said, Arnott; "but there's no death reported, and I've inquired everywhere. What are we supposed to do with our passengers? I've fed 'em."

"We're between two switches," De Forest drawled. "If we drop them in any place that isn't under the Board, the natives will make their presence an excuse for cutting out, same as Illinois did, and forcing the Board to take over. If we drop them in any place under the Board's control they'll be killed as soon as our backs are turned."

"If you say so," said Pirolo thoughtfully. "I can guarantee that they will become extinct in process of time, quite happily. What is their birth-rate now?"

"Go down and ask 'em," said De Forest.

"I think they might become nervous and tear me to bits," the philosopher of Foggie replied.

"Not really? Well?"

"Open the bilge-doors," said Takahira with a downward jerk of the thumb.

"Scarcely—after all the trouble we've taken to save 'em," said De Forest.

"Try London," Arnott suggested. "You could turn Satan himself loose there, and they'd only ask him to dinner."

"Good man! You given me an idea. Vincent! Oh, Vincent!" He threw the General Communicator open so that we could all hear, and in a few minutes the chartroom filled with the rich, fruity voice of Leopold Vincent, who has purveyed all London her choicest amusements for the last thirty years. We answered with expectant grins, as though we were actually in the stalls of, say, the Combination on a first night.

"We've picked up something in your line," De Forest began.

"That's good, dear man. If it's old enough. There's nothing to beat the old things for business purposes. Have you seen *London, Chatham, and Dover* at Earl's Court. No? I thought I missed you there. Im-mense! I've had the real steam locomotive engines built from the old designs and the iron rails cast specially by hand. Cloth cushions in the carriages, too! Im-mense! And paper railway tickets. And Polly Milton."

"Polly Milton back again!" said Arnott rapturously. "Book me two stalls for tomorrow night. What's she singing now, bless her?"

"The old songs. Nothing comes up to the old touch. Listen to this, dear men." Vincent carolled with flourishes:

> *"Oh, cruel lamps of London,*
> *If tears your light could drown,*
> *Your victim's eyes would weep them,*
> *Oh, lights of London Town!"*

"Then they weep."

"You see?" Pirolo waved his hands at us. "The old world always weeped when it saw crowds together. It did not know why, but it weeped. We know why, but we do not weep, except when we pay to be made to by fat, wicked old Vincent."

"Old, yourself!" Vincent laughed. "I'm a public benefactor, I keep the world soft and united."

"And I'm De Forest of the Board," said De Forest acidly, "trying to get a little business done. As I was saying, I've picked up a few people in Chicago."

"I cut out. Chicago is—"

"Do listen! They're perfectly unique."

"Do they build houses of baked mudblocks while you wait—eh? That's an old contact."

"They're an untouched primitive community, with all the old ideas."

"Sewing-machines and maypole-dances? Cooking on coalgas stoves, lighting pipes with matches, and driving horses? Gerolstein tried that last year. An absolute blow-out!"

De Forest plugged him wrathfully, and poured out the story of our doings for the last twenty-four hours on the top-note.

"And they do it *all* in public," he concluded. "You can't stop 'em. The more public, the better they are pleased. They'll talk for hours—like you! Now you can come in again!"

"Do you really mean they know how to vote?" said Vincent. "Can they act it?"

"Act? It's their life to 'em! And you never saw such faces! Scarred like volcanoes. Envy, hatred, and malice in plain sight. Wonderfully flexible voices. They weep, too."

"Aloud? In public?"

"I guarantee. Not a spark of shame or reticence in the entire installation. It's the chance of your career."

"D'you say you've brought their voting props along—those papers and ballot-box things?"

"No, confound you! I'm not a luggage-lifter. Apply direct to the Mayor of Chicago. He'll forward you everything. Well?"

"Wait a minute. Did Chicago want to kill 'em? That 'ud look well on the Communicators."

"Yes! They were only rescued with difficulty from a howling mob—if you know what that is."

"But I don't," answered the Great Vincent simply.

"Well then, they'll tell you themselves. They can make speeches hours long."

"How many are there?"

"By the time we ship 'em all over they'll be perhaps a hundred, counting children. And old world in miniature. Can't you see it?"

"M-yes; but I've got to pay for it if it's a blow-out, dear man."

"They can sing the old war songs in the streets. They can get word-drunk, and make crowds, and invade privacy in the genuine old-fashioned way, and they'll do the voting trick as often as you ask 'em a question."

"Too good!" said Vincent.

"You unbelieving Jew! I've got a dozen head aboard here. I'll put you through direct. Sample 'em yourself."

He lifted the switch and we listened. Our passengers on the lower deck at once, but no less than five at a time, explained themselves to Vincent. They had been taken from the bosom of their families, stripped of their possessions, given food without finger-bowls, and cast into captivity in a noisome dungeon.

"But look here," said Arnott aghast; "they're saying what isn't true. My lower deck isn't noisome, and I saw to the finger-bowls myself."

"My people talk like that sometimes in Little Russia," said Dragomiroff. "We reason with them. We never kill. No!"

"But it's not true," Arnott insisted. "What can you do with people who don't tell facts? They're mad!"

"Hsh!" said Pirolo, his hand to his ear. "It is such a little time since all the Planet told lies."

We heard Vincent silkily sympathetic. Would they, he asked, repeat their assertions in public—before a vast public? Only let Vincent give them a chance, and the Planet, they vowed, should ring with their wrongs. Their aim in life—two women and a man explained it together—was to reform the world. Oddly enough, this also had been Vincent's life-dream. He offered them an arena in which to explain, and by their living example to raise the Planet to loftier levels. He was eloquent on the moral uplift of a simple, old-world life presented in its entirety to a deboshed civilization.

Could they—would they—for three months certain, devote themselves under his auspices, as missionaries, to the elevation of mankind at a place called Earl's Court, which he said, with some truth, was one of the intellectual centres of the Planet? They thanked him, and demanded (we could hear his chuckle of delight) time to discuss and to vote on the matter. The vote, solemnly managed by counting heads—one head, one vote—was favourable. His offer, therefore, was accepted, and they moved a vote of thanks to him in two speeches—one by what they called the "proposer" and the other by the "seconder".

Vincent threw over to us, his voice shaking with gratitude:

"I've got 'em! Did you hear those speeches? That's Nature, dear men. Art can't teach *that*. And they voted as easily as lying. I've never had a troupe of natural liars before. Bless you, dear men! Remember, you're on my free lists for ever, anywhere—all of you. Oh, Gerolstein will be sick—sick!"

"Then you think they'll do?" said De Forest.

"Do? The Little Village'll go crazy! I'll knock up a series of old-world plays for 'em. Their voices will make you laugh and cry. My God, dear men, where *do* you suppose they picked up all their misery from, on this sweet earth? I'll have a pageant of the world's beginnings, and Mosenthal shall do the music. I'll—"

"Go and knock up a village for 'em by tonight. We'll meet you at No. 15 West Landing Tower," said De Forest. "Remember the rest will be coming along tomorrow."

"Let 'em all come!" said Vincent. "You don't know how

hard it is nowaday even for me, to find something that really gets under the public's damned iridium-plated hide. But I've got it at last. Good-bye!"

"Well," said De Forest when we had finished laughing, "if any one understood corruption in London I might have played off Vincent against Gerolstein, and sold my captives at enormous prices. As it is, I shall have to be their legal advisor tonight when the contracts are signed. And they won't exactly press any commission on me, either."

"Meantime," said Takahira, "we cannot, of course, confine members of Leopold Vincent's last-engaged company. Chairs for the ladies; please, Arnott."

"Then I go to bed," said De Forest. "I can't face any more women!" And he vanished.

When our passengers were released and given another meal (finger-bowls came first this time) they told us what they thought of us and the Board; and, like Vincent, we all marvelled how they had contrived to extract and secrete so much bitter poison and unrest out of the good life God gives us. They raged, they stormed, they palpitated, flushed and exhausted their poor, torn nerves, panted themselves into silence, and renewed the senseless, shameless attacks.

"But can't you understand," said Pirolo, pathetically to a shrieking woman, "that if we'd left you in Chicago you'd have been killed?"

"No, we shouldn't. You were bound to save us from being murdered."

"Then we should have had to kill a lot of other people."

"That doesn't matter. We were preaching the Truth. You can't stop us. We shall go on preaching in London; and *then* you'll see!"

"You can see now," said Pirolo, and opened a lower shutter.

We were closing on the Little Village, with her three million people spread out at ease inside her ring of girdling Main-Traffic lights—those eight fixed beams at Chatham, Tonbridge, Redhill, Dorking. Woking, St Albans, Chipping Ongar, and Southend.

Leopold Vincent's new company looked, with small pale faces, at the silence, the size, and the separated houses.

Then some began to weep aloud, shamelessly—always without shame.

MacDonough's Song

RUDYARD KIPLING

Whether the State can loose and bind
  In Heaven as well as on Earth:
If it be wiser to kill mankind
  Before or after the birth—
These are matters of high concern
  Where State-kept schoolmen are;
But Holy State (we have lived to learn)
  Endeth in Holy War.

Whether The People be led by the Lord,
  Or lured by the loudest throat:
If it be quicker to die by the sword
  Or cheaper to die by vote—
These are the things we have dealt with once,
  (And they will not rise from their grave)
For Holy People, however it runs,
  Endeth in Wholly Slave.

Whatsoever, for any cause,
  Seeketh to take or give,
Power above or beyond the Laws,
  Suffer it not to live!
Holy State or Holy King—
  Or Holy People's Will—
Have no truck with the senseless thing.
  Order the guns and kill!
  Saying—after—me:

Once there was The People—Terror gave it birth;
Once there was The People and it made a Hell of Earth.
Earth arose and crushed it. Listen, O ye slain!
Once there was The People—it shall never be again!

The Songs of Rudyard Kipling

Rudyard Kipling wrote some of the most memorable tales in literature. He also wrote poetry—but not delicate sonnets or brittle verses. Kipling wrote **songs**—strong, lusty, full of life and filled with the vivid images and characters that make his stories so powerful.

Now you can enjoy Kipling's poems the way they were intended to be—as songs, set to music and performed by the inimitable Leslie Fish.

Cold Iron features Kipling's finest historical songs—ballads and tales of Roman legionnaires, Celtic warriors, knights, kings, and commoners. Sixteen songs, including "Cold Iron," "The Quest," "The Winners: A Death-Bed," "Tarrant Moss," "The Palace," "Heriot's Ford," "The Song of the Red War Boat," "The Pict Song," "The King," "Runes on Weland's Sword," "Goats, Pigs, and Buffaloes," "Puck's Song," "Very Many People," "Rimmon," "The Kingdom," and "Rimini."

The Undertaker's Horse contains the best of Kipling's poetry about his own day, including his life and times in India. Seventeen more songs, with "The Undertaker's Horse," "The Prodigal Son," "Boots," "The Old Issue," "The Hymn to Breaking Strain," "The Press," "The 'Birds of Prey' March," "Tubal and Jubal," "Hadramauti," "The Sergeant's Weddin'," "Bridge-Guard in the Karroo," "Dane-Geld," "Hyenas," "Natural Theology," "Danny Deever," "We and They," and "Tomlinson."

The Cold Iron Songbook is the companion songbook to *Cold Iron*. All 16 songs are here, complete with sheet music and guitar chords. Profusely illustrated and full 8½" x 11" size—perfect for anyone who wants to join in and sing!

You can order both cassette tapes and the songbook with this order form. Check your choices below and send the combined cover price/s, plus $1.75 for shipping for the first item and $.50 for each additional item, to: Baen Books, Dept. Firebird, 260 Fifth Avenue, New York, New York 10001.

☐ Cold Iron   OCP-14   60 minutes $11.00

☐ The Undertaker's Horse   OCP-48   60 minutes $11.00

☐ Cold Iron Songbook   OCP-14B   36 pages $7.00

757063

757062